U.S. Navy Dept. Bureau of Medicine and Surgery

Medical Essays

compiled from reports to the Bureau of Medicine and Surgery

U.S. Navy Dept. Bureau of Medicine and Surgery

Medical Essays

compiled from reports to the Bureau of Medicine and Surgery

ISBN/EAN: 9783337780296

Printed in Europe, USA, Canada, Australia, Japan

Cover: Foto ©Andreas Hilbeck / pixelio.de

More available books at **www.hansebooks.com**

MEDICAL ESSAYS:

COMPILED FROM REPORTS

BUREAU OF MEDICINE AND SURGERY,

BY

MEDICAL OFFICERS OF THE U. S. NAVY.

Published by order of the Navy Department.

WASHINGTON:
GOVERNMENT PRINTING OFFICE.
1872.

NAVY DEPARTMENT,
BUREAU OF MEDICINE AND SURGERY,
Washington, December 20, 1872.

The files of this Bureau having been found to contain numerous reports of cases interesting to the profession at large, and instructive to medical officers of the Navy in particular, Medical Inspector Albert L. Gihon has been detailed to select and collate them. As it is proposed to continue these publications, it is hoped that medical officers will be encouraged to report all cases of interest occurring to themselves, or observed at home or abroad.

JAMES C. PALMER,
Surgeon-General, U. S. Navy.

CONTENTS.

PRACTICAL SUGGESTIONS

IN

NAVAL HYGIENE.

BY

ALBERT LEARY GIHON, A. M., M. D.,

MEDICAL INSPECTOR, U. S. NAVY, MEMBER OF THE NAVAL MEDICAL BOARD.

James C. Palmer, Esq., M. D.,
  Surgeon-General United States Navy,
    Chief of Bureau of Medicine and Surgery,
      Navy Department:

SIR: I take occasion of the re-issue, under your instructions, of my Suggestions in Naval Hygiene, with the volume of Medical Essays about to be published by the Bureau, to express my thanks both to the members of the medical corps, who have received them so approvingly, and to the many officers of the line, who have given them a generous welcome, and in several instances have adopted the measures proposed.

Very respectfully, your obedient servant,

ALBERT LEARY GIHON, M. D.,
  Medical Inspector, U. S. Navy.

WASHINGTON, *December* 1, 1872.

CONTENTS.

THE PROVINCE OF NAVAL HYGIENE.

Notwithstanding the general knowledge of the fact that the better mode of relieving human flesh of the ills to which it is heir is to prevent them, very little is done toward lessening the amount of physical suffering among mankind. Not only are individuals improvident of health, but public communities neglect precautions that would avert many attacks of disease; and even governments, having control of armies and navies, are unmindful of preventive measures which would diminish the expense and promote the efficiency of these bodies.

It ought to be unnecessary to urge the importance of naval hygiene. If it be so requisite to study what to do and what to leave undone on shore, where everything demanded for the healthy maintenance of the body is in abundance, how much more strictly ought the laws of health to be observed on board ship, where human beings are crowded together in violation of all these laws, breathing a scanty supply of air vitiated by the retention of their own excretions, subsisting upon an unwholesome diet, their sleep always interrupted, and their minds continually disquieted by passions called into operation by the unnatural circumstances of their lives. Yet no sanitary code has ever been promulgated in our own service, nor, until recent years, has it been attempted elsewhere. The young medical officer is without a guide. As much confused by the manners of those around him as by the maze of rigging overhead, he credits whatever he is told and accepts, " it is the custom of the service," as palliating whatever appears barbarous and unnatural.

The same cause that has retarded the influence of civil hygiene has prevented the institution of sanitary regulations for the Navy. The real character and mission of the physician have not been recognized. He is regarded solely as a *medicine-man*, and there is a general rebellion against his authority when he prescribes to the well what they shall eat and drink, how they shall live, dress, and sleep, how their houses should be built, their lands tilled, and their food cooked. The public mind does not rise to the comprehension of the extent of province of our great profession. The scientific medical man is at most regarded as an "allopath," a sectarian amid globulistic and rational homœopaths, Thompsonians, and Swedish-movement curers.

The naval surgeon has had his domain still further retrenched. Despite the radical changes which time has effected in the service, there are still many who affect a deafness to his warnings through a fear lest the medical officer transcend his position. Traditional jealousies and want of confidence have been perpetuated. Some narrow-minded officers, cherishing this feeling of caste, use their power to resist what they pretend to consider encroachments upon their jurisdiction. Over the country are distributed the victims of this system, and many a grave has been untimely filled through inattention to sanitary recommendations. Every national vessel arriving at our naval sea-ports brings a number of invalid men and officers; the business of the naval hospitals is disproportionate to the size of the naval establishment; and this sacrifice of life and money will continue "until physicians have the place in the councils of military commanders that is due to science. The health history of the late wars in Europe is demonstrative in proof of the important fact that military life has been sacrificed in an enormous proportion to ignorance—that is, to the unwillingness of commanders to be advised on subjects which they could not themselves be supposed to know."—(Robert Jackson.) "From the neglect of the precautions specified, thousands of lives have been sacrificed which might otherwise have been preserved. The care of the health of the troops should certainly be one of the first duties of a military commander.

Unless his men are in good physical condition they can be of no service to him in carrying out the ends he may have in view, but are a hinderance to him and a burden to themselves. And yet how often it happens that those in command are heedless of the warnings and inattentive to the advice given by their medical officers."—(Hammond.) "It is urgently necessary that the influence of enlightened medical opinion be more and more felt in the administration of the Navy in all matters relating to health, for costly blunders still continue to be committed in the construction and arrangement of our ships of war, which seriously injure the efficiency of the crew, and which might be easily effected if every ship were thoroughly examined by a sanitary officer before she was commissioned. One of our iron-clads the Royal Oak, was found to be a most unhealthy vessel from first going to sea, and thrice had she to be inspected by a sanitary board before her high sick-rate was reduced. And this is but one of many similar instances that might be adduced."—(*Medico-Chirurgical Review.*)

The naval authorities of Great Britain and France have already acted toward the establishment of sanitary codes. The medical officers of our own service, therefore, would be delinquent in delaying longer to obtain the sanction of the Department to their recommendations, and that indorsement of authority which will secure their observance. In this let us disclaim any purpose of interference with any other corps. Cheerfully recognizing our obligations of obedience to the commanding officer and constituted authorities, we have no desire to do anything that is foreign to our calling as physicians. The sacred character of our profession bestows such honorable and enviable distinction and dignity upon its followers, that we need not seek to encroach upon the functions of others. We, therefore, demand that our motives in making these suggestions may be no longer impugned; but that our efforts to accomplish the legitimate objects of our vocation may be generously assisted by the other corps, that our common aim—the honor and efficiency of the service—may be attained.

THE EXAMINATION OF RECRUITS.

The province of naval hygiene begins at the recruiting-office. To banish disease from shipboard as effectually as possible, it is as necessary to guard against its admission within the bodies of the officers and men themselves as to prevent its development among them, just as the attempt to extirpate the syphilis of the public prostitutes of large cities is fruitless so long as men who are themselves affected are allowed access to them. Hence the importance of carefully guarding this avenue to disease. With the medical corps rests the entire responsibility of selecting the *personnel* of the Navy. The various grades of officers are examined prior to appointment by special medical boards, while the medical officer of the rendezvous is charged with the examination of all applicants for the subordinate positions of shipped and enlisted men in the Navy and Marine Corps, and with the rejection of all who are unfit for these branches of the service, whether on account of existing acute or chronic disease or deformity, or constitutional taint, infirmity, predisposition, or inheritance, physical or mental. Could this duty be always performed with rigid exactness, sick-lists would consist only of acute maladies and injuries; but, unfortunately, all the cachexiæ are represented on our medical returns. Many of these latent seeds of disease are hidden beyond the ken of the most acute observer; still there is reason to complain of the superficial manner in which these examinations are often conducted. It is not unusual for a man discharged with a certificate of ordinary disability from a naval hospital to re-appear at that hospital within a few weeks, either from the receiving-ship or from some vessel to which he had been transferred and found unfit for duty. A second discharge has been followed by reshipment at another station. Most of these cases wait until their arrival at a foreign port, and then present themselves with chronic and incurable maladies, for which they have to be invalided, and sent, at great expense, to a naval hospital in the United States, perhaps the very one they had left. Dr. Ruschenberger "sent a man home from on board of the United States ship Falmouth, at Rio de Janeiro, who twice imposed himself upon the recruiting officers with a fistula in perineo of several years' standing, for which he had been unsuccessfully treated at several civil hospitals." There are men who have passed years in the service in this way, without having ever completed a cruise. Hæmorrhois, prolapsus ani, fistulæ, reducible hernia, stricture of the urethra, functional cardiac diseases, syphilis, and chronic rheumatism are the complaints which are most frequently thus alternately concealed and reported. It is not presumed that all such cases can be exposed at the rendezvous, but greater care and minuteness of examination would reveal many of them, and the establishment of dynamometric tests would discover the · greater number, as well as convalescents from exhausting diseases. Thus, it would have prevented the shipment of a man with chronic luxation of the head of the humerus, whom I have encountered three or four times in the service, and who, while able to perform the usual movements of the shoulder-joint, could not accomplish violent circumduction without displacing the bone. Dr. Magruder, of the Iroquois, now fitting at the Philadelphia navy-yard for a cruise in the East Indies, informs me that he has had to transfer to the hospital, with phthisis pulmonalis, a recruit whom he found to have been surveyed and discharged from the service only eight months prior to his reshipment; and states that there are two other cases of incipient phthisis and one of the developed disease already on his list, although the ship has been but a few days in commission. A few years ago, a man who had recently shipped was discharged from the New York Naval Hospital with double inguinal hernia, which he confessed to have had five years; and among a list of forty-seven cases of pulmonary tubercle then in the hospital, (1860,) twenty-three had been in the service but a few weeks, and in most of these there was not a doubt that the early stages of the disease, or the tendency to its development, were positively indicated at the time ôf shipment by local physical signs or by evidences of constitutional impairment. Chronic rheumatism and subluxations are more difficult of detection, but even these can seldom perfectly dissemble all the abnormal actions of their articulations.

As a further check to the admission of disqualified men into the service, it is necessary to particularize descriptive lists, to specify and locate exactly every ineffaceable mark, scar, or peculiarity of the individual, and to describe more fully and accurately than is now done the general appearance and development of each person. This complete descriptive list should accompany the man throughout his connection with the service; when transferred from one vessel to another; when invalided and sent to a naval hospital; when discharged from that hospital, whether on certificate of ordinary disability or to duty; when discharged from the service, whether with ordinary or honorable discharge; and it should appear on all certificates of disability, death, or pension. In all cases of discharge for permanent disability from incurable affections or injuries, it should be filed at the Navy Department for reference when suspicion is entertained that such a man has reshipped, and as evidence against him, if this have been done, on his trial for the fraud he had perpetrated upon the Government. Men should also be instructed to preserve these lists carefully as conclusive and requisite for their identification. A recent instance within my own knowledge illustrates the necessity for minuteness and exactness in descriptive lists. Jeremiah Griffin presented himself at a rendezvous to ship as coal-heaver, and was refused by the recruiting-officer on the ground that he had already shipped and had failed to repair on board the receiving-ship. This he denied, and reference to the surgeon's register, although establishing the prior shipment of Jeremiah Griffin, coal-heaver, of the same height, age, and nationality as the applicant, exhibited in the column of remarks, "defective teeth," while the man then offering had a perfect set. Incompleteness of descriptive lists subjects the Government to fraudulent claims. John Smith, boatswain's mate, shipped and presented an honorable discharge on which he claimed three months' extra pay. He was well marked by the loss of a portion of a finger, but no mention was made upon the discharge which he presented, of the deformity, which had existed a long time. A seaman recently died, at the Naval Hospital at Philadelphia, with erosion of the entire penis, who had suffered amputation of a third of the organ, ten or twelve years before, at a civil hospital at Adelaide, Australia; yet, as Dr. Ruschenberger remarks in his report of the case, "there was no professional testimony as to the condition of the penil stump at the time of his last enlistment in the Navy." The sale and transfer of honorable discharges is readily carried on when descriptive lists are merely filled up with "eyes dark, hair dark, complexion dark, marks none," or "eyes light, hair light, complexion light, mark on arm;" and, furthermore, the interests of the man himself are often jeopardized by his name not being spelled in conformity with the original shipment, or by carelessness in transcribing the meager items of description. I have known Houghton, after only two years in the service, to return as Horton, Bacquiel as Boquil, Tuer as Ture, and Koulousi as Gulachi and afterward as Galusha; transformations which originated, perhaps, on board the receiving-ship, where some careless or uneducated clerk, in making out the roll of the crew to be transferred to a sea-going vessel, spelled by sound, or as well as he knew how, the names as they were read to him, and committed an error which may appear under a second mutation of form on the honorable discharge, filled up in a similar manner by another equally heedless clerk. Even should the man present himself for reshipment at the same rendezvous where he originally passed, the very medical officer who wrote the first descriptive list must perpetuate the error on the second to secure the sailor his three months' bounty, since its payment will be refused unless the reshipment agrees in name exactly with that on the face of the discharge. Instances of this are numerous. One related to me by Surgeon Kitchen occurred in January of this year, (1871.) A very worthy and intelligent petty-officer, named Charles L. Anthony, having refused to sign his name on reshipment Charles T. Anthony, as it had been erroneously entered on the books of the ship to which he had previously been attached and thus copied upon his honorable discharge, was, in consequence, refused the payment of the bounty to which his long and faithful service entitled him. In my own experience, Peter Woppel, as an honorable discharge styled him, though he protested that he was baptized Vaupel, and so wrote it in a legible hand, had to remain a Woppel until some other blunderer might convert him into a Wobble or something else; his claim for admission into the Naval Asylum, after twenty years' service, consequently being invalidated under the rule requiring that service to be under the same name, or great difficulty being occasioned in the adjustment of any pension claim in his favor. As it devolves upon the medical officer to fill up the blank descriptive list with the name, nationality, etc., of the recruit, it behooves him, for the sake of being exact, to cross-examine closely the answers that are made on these points. Many men, who profess to have been born in New York, Boston, or Philadelphia, will, when asked the precise place of birth, mention Cherry, North, or Penn streets, localities not remarkable for the fecundity of the females who dwell there. This is done through a fear lest only natives of the country will be accepted, or in the belief that it will insure them more favorable consideration; but when assured on these points, they frankly admit that they are of foreign birth. Confusion often arises from the number of identical names on board ship. I have seen a John Smith 12th. The most of these are simply "purser's names," and a little coaxing and argument will usually induce the man to acknowledge his proper name, and in other cases will reveal a middle name, which is seldom tendered unless asked for. Foreigners should be required to spell their names in their native languages, since it will often happen that a man may be designated Louis Blanc or Johann Schmidt, who would otherwise have become a numerical Lewis White or John Smith. Not unfrequently common English names are spelled incorrectly by the examiner himself. Since writing the above, I was in a rendezvous where I observed a young assistant surgeon enter the name of a recruit without asking the orthography, and to my inquiry how he knew that to be the proper spelling, he replied, "Oh! I judge so." Thus Thomson is given a p, Emory an e, and Fraley an i, merely as the indolent or indifferent examiner may judge proper. However acute he may be in other respects, no exercise of judgment will enlighten him whether Riley or Reilley, Dixon or Dickson, Wallis or Wallace, Fife or Fyffe, Sheppard or Shepherd, Diehl or Deal, Bailey, Bayley, or Baillie is correct. All this care on the part of the medical officer, however, will be thrown away unless the Government exacts a rigid adherence to the original returns of the rendezvous in spelling and every other particular, by every person whose duty it is to transcribe those returns. How readily could the applicant for re-enlistment, or the chronic invalid, who, as soon as sent on board ship and required to do duty, repairs to the sick-bay with a sprained back, a stricture of the urethra, or a rheumatic joint, be identified, if his descriptive list were filled up in some such manner as follows: John Henry Smith, seaman; native of Galway, Ireland; age, when shipped, $26\frac{5}{12}$ years; height, 5 feet $6\frac{1}{2}$ inches; figure, slender; hair, brown and curly; complexion, florid; face, square; forehead, low; nose, sharp; mouth, small; teeth, perfect; eyes, dark chestnut and sunken; broad cicatrix of scald on left shin; anchor on right hand; etc. All this involves a little more labor, but it is labor that the Government has a right to demand of its officers. The subject is so important that I have been induced to dwell upon it at some length. Every act of duty, however trivial, should be well done, and professional pride should deter every officer, whatever his rank, from affixing his signature to a subordinate's work until he has satisfied himself that it has been performed entirely free from mistake. The following series of errors in the descriptive list of the crew of a single

2 H

vessel, (the St. Louis,) effectually illustrates the magnitude of the evil sought to be corrected:

Isaac J. Borden, age 39; instead of Isaac *G.* Borden, age 31.

Petrie Martin, age 29; instead of *Pierre* Martin, age 40.

William *Evene*, native of *Hartford, Connecticut*; instead of William *Evans*, native of *Maryland.*

William J. *Herne*, native of *Maine*; instead of William J. *Hearne*, native of *Canada.*

Alfred McDonald; instead of *Alexander* McDonald.

Randall McVerrish; instead of *Ranald* McVerrish.

William *Sims ;* instead of William *Syms.*

Alexander *Gorman ;* instead of Alexander *O'Gorman.*

James *Nolen ;* instead of James *Noulean.*

George *McGoyn ;* instead of George *McGoyne.*

Christian Allvord ; instead of *Christop Allvorden.*

Frederick *Linderman ;* instead of Frederick *Lendman.*

William *Channer ;* instead of William *Charmerin.*

Daniel *Callihan*, native of *Rhode Island ;* instead of Daniel *Callaghan*, native of *New York.*

Cornelias Callighan ; instead of *Cornelius Callaghan.*

Peter *Durgan ;* instead of Peter *Dugan.*

Monroe *Durgan ;* instead of Monroe *Durgin.*

John *Custice ;* instead of John *Curtice.*

Charles J. *Conlogue ;* instead of Charles J. *Conologue.*

Andorous Dodge; instead of *Andorus* Dodge.

Agustus McEwen; instead of *Angus* McEwen.

•Benjamin A. *McClain ;* instead of Benjamin A. *McClane.*

Charles H. Smith, age 25, native of *Denmark ;* instead of Charles H. Smith, age 22, native of *Providence, Rhode Island.*

John Kelly, native of *Brooklyn ;* instead of John Kelly, native of *Philadelphia.*

John Brown, native of *Ireland ;* instead of John Brown, native of *Boston.*

Henry Johnson, native of *Russia ;* instead of Henry Johnson, native of *Prussia.*

George Brown, native of *Nova Scotia;* instead of George Brown, native of *New Hope, Pennsylvania.*

John Williams, native of *Sweden;* instead of John Williams, native of *Pennsylvania.*

Andrew Anderson, native of *Philadelphia;* instead of Andrew Anderson, native of *Norway.*

Patrick Fardy, native of *Maine;* instead of Patrick Fardy, native of *Ireland.*

George D. Vanness, native of *New York;* instead of George D. Vanness, native of *New Jersey.*

Samuel Wood, native of *Russia;* instead of Samuel Wood, native of *Maine.*

John Butler, native of *Boston*, Massachusetts; instead of John Butler, native of *Edgartown*, Massachusetts.

Jacob K. Woodbury, native of *Boston*, Massachusetts; instead of Jacob K. Woodbury, native of *Beverly*, Massachusetts.

George W. Martin, native of *Maine;* instead of George W. Martin, native of *Lynn, Massachusetts.*

John E. Woodbury, aged 35; instead of John E. Woodbury, aged 21.

No physical examination can be thoroughly and deliberately conducted in the five or ten minutes which, I have reason to believe, are the average time devoted to this purpose, particularly by young officers. More than thirty years ago, Surgeon Ruschenberger, prefacing the American edition of an essay by Deputy Inspector-General Marshall on the "Enlisting, Discharging, and Pensioning of Soldiers," declared that "the inspection of recruits, both for the Army and Navy, involving, as it does, the consideration of the interests of the Government and of individuals, which are often conflicting, is perhaps the most important and difficult duty which the surgeon is called upon to perform. Men who, through vice, dissipation, or misfortune, find it difficult to obtain a livelihood from private patronage, are very apt to seek employment in the Army or Navy, often with the sole view of obtaining medical attendance, and ultimately an asylum for pension; and even when the greatest caution and circumspection are observed, some unworthy and inefficient individuals gain admission into the service. Nor is this very surprising, when we consider that, prompted by their interests, recruits resort to every means within their knowledge to deceive the inspecting officer, whose examination is generally limited for each recruit to ten or fifteen minutes, a period much too short to ascertain the qualities of a horse, in which the most astute and wary jockey may be deceived."

Paragraph 166 of the Regulations for the Government of the Navy requires a muster of the officers and crew, at which the executive officer, surgeon, and paymaster shall be present, whenever a ship shall be put into commission, "for the purpose of verifying the descriptive lists, of ascertaining that the name of every man is correctly registered, and that every one has the exact uniform dress prescribed by regulations," at which muster any discrepancy in the descriptive lists, or error in the transfer roll, shall then be corrected. But if the objects of this regulation are not very generally ignored, except as regards the inspection of uniforms, the examination of the descriptive lists is certainly never conducted in the critical spirit intended, nor is such possible at a general muster; and even when errors are discovered paymasters very strenuously object to the alteration of the entries in their books. The three officers indicated should sit as a board and deliberately and carefully examine every individual of the crew singly with regard to the spelling of his name, his age, nativity, and correspondence with the other items of the descriptive lists.

The points to be particularly noted by the examining medical officer at the rendezvous, are—

1. *Name*—in full, middle, if any, and in his native language.
2. *Nativity*—specifying town or other locality.
3. *Age*—in years and months at time of shipment.
4. *Height*—in feet and fractions of inches.
5. *Circumference of thorax*—at the level of the nipples, after full inspiration and prolonged expiration.

6. *General development and figure*—slender, robust, corpulent, muscular, stooping, etc.

7. *Intelligence*—good, bright, ordinary, obtuse, etc.

8. *Face*—oval, square, high-cheeked, freckled, pock-marked, smooth, bearded, etc.

9. *Forehead*—high, low, receding, prominent, etc.

10. *Complexion*—pale, fair, florid, dusky, tawny, swarthy, quadroon, mulatto, negro, etc.

11. *Hair*—light or dark chestnut, brown, auburn, sandy, red, flaxen, gray, black, thin, bald, straight, curly, wool, etc.

12. *Nose*—large, small, aquiline, pug, flat, sharp, bent, etc.

13. *Mouth*—small, large, thick or thin lipped, etc.

14. *Teeth*—perfect, irregular, deficiencies, etc.

15. *Distinguishing marks*—smoothness or hirsuteness of surface, prominence of pomum adami, peculiarities of ensiform cartilage, hollowness of sternum, prominence, rotundity, or flatness of abdomen, unusual size or smallness of penis, scrotum, or testes, hollowness or prominence of anal region, bow-legs, knock-knees, splay-feet, largeness of hands, feet, or joints, besides every abnormal feature not inconsistent with perfect bodily vigor, such as nævi materni, discolorations, cicatrices, outgrowths, varicose veins, deficiencies, etc.

The certificate of the applicant that he is "not subject to fits," etc., (Form Q,) which precedes the physical examination, is usually signed without hesitancy and without regard to fact. Cases of epilepsy, stricture of the urethra, hæmorrhois, chronic rheumatism, old injuries, congenital and inherited affections, present themselves on the sick-list of every vessel in commission, encumber sick-bays, and materially interfere with the health and the comfort both of the well and of those who have become sick in the performance of duty. If the certificate of exemption from these complaints were required to be in the form of an oath, and its fraudulent signer were subjected to court-martial and punishment as a perjurer, these cases would soon become infrequent.

In this connection I desire to propose a system of physical examinations, which may assist the younger medical officers who have had little or no experience in such duty. It must be borne in mind, however, as Dr. Fallon, of the Belgian army, has well observed: "That rules and regulations on this subject, however carefully they may have been devised, and however minutely they may enter into detail, are but very imperfect guides. They furnish an outline, it is true, of the track which requires to be followed, but they do not enable us to escape many mistakes into which we may fall." The Prussian regulations for the medical examination of recruits, after reminding the surgeon that it is one of the most difficult and responsible of the duties he has to perform, add: "It is impossible to frame specific rules for the examination of recruits so as to obviate every difficulty. In a great variety of cases the decision must depend on the discretion and experience of the inspecting medical officer." Hence the impropriety of ordering newly-appointed officers to rendezvous, or of intrusting the physical examination of recruits and applicants for survey and pension to the assistant surgeons on board vessels to which their seniors are attached or in squadrons, since officers of experience are guided in a great degree by their knowledge of the duties and habits of sailors, the deceptions they are accustomed to practice, and the requirements of the service. The routine of examination, which I here propose, and no single detail of which should ever be omitted, will, I believe, indicate to the medical examiner every important point to which his attention should be directed.

1. The examiner must satisfy himself of the sobriety and cleanliness of the applicant. It is proper to require a bath before examination, for the better exposure of syphilides, etc.; and the least evidence of the narcotic effect of alcohol upon the eye, face, or heart should decide the medical officer to decline proceeding any further at that time.

2. The applicant having then made oath or affirmation of his freedom from any disability of which he is himself cognizant, let him stand erect before the examiner in a broad light, and perfectly

nude, with chin elevated, heels together, and arms hanging extended, and let him slowly turn so as to present his front, rear,
and sides in succession. This inspection will satisfy the examiner
of the unfitness of the applicant should he have an attenuated
or crooked form, cutaneous or other external disease, glandular
swellings and other evidences of the strumous cachexia, excessive
development of fat, softness of muscular tissue, œdema, deformi-
ties, tumors, extensive cicatrices, nodes, varicosities, etc. Evidences
of medical treatment, particularly when recent, in the shape of
leech-bites, discolorations from blisters, seton, issue, or scarifica-
tor marks, or cicatrices of operations, in connection with marked
diathesis, are valuable suggestions of liability to disease.

3. The general appearance being satisfactory, the next point
to be determined is the existence of venereal disease. I particularly advise a careful inspection of the internal epitrochlear spaces
and posterior cervical region for indurated lymphatic glandulæ,
as positively indicative of the existence of a syphilitic taint. The
penis should be scrutinized in its entire length, the prepuce re-
tracted, the glans and orifice carefully inspected, the urethra com-
pressed, and the man required to cough to eject purulent matter.
Most men affected with gonorrhœa or gleet wash out the urethra
by urinating immediately before entering the examining-room; so
that when there is any reason to suspect this disease, it is well to
look at the urethra again after all the other examination has been
completed. The flexion of the glans upon the dorsum, and firm
pressure near the bulb, generally occasion so much pain that the
man winces and exposes himself, even when there is no discharge
discernible. The scrotum should be carefully examined for vari-
cocele, cirsocele, orchitis, and the other diseases of these parts.
Any permanent abnormal condition, singularity of development,
retention of testis, induration of globus minor and vas deferens,
etc., should be noted on the descriptive list. Notwithstanding the
large proportion of sailors affected with stricture of the urethra, it
is scarcely possible to guard against their shipment except by
requiring them to certify on oath to its non-existence, and by

punishing them by sentence of court-martial on the subsequent exposure of the deception practiced. Few Americans could be persuaded, like the French, to submit to the introduction of a bougie; and it would be almost as repugnant to require them to urinate in the presence of the examiner.

4. Direct the applicant to stoop over, touching his toes with his fingers, the knees stiffened, and in a straight line with the legs, the feet apart, and the nates exposed to a strong light. Separate the latter widely, and inspect carefully to discover hæmorrhois, prolapsus, fistulæ of the anus and perinæum, etc. The latter diseases very often escape observation, and, when overlooked, constitute the grounds for so many applications for survey. I remember one man who had been operated upon for fistula ani at two hospitals, reported himself on my sick-list on board the Preble, was again the subject of operation, transferred to a third hospital, and discharged from the service. A few months later I again encountered him an inmate of that same hospital.

5. While the man is still stooping, make forcible pressure on each of the spinous processes of the vertebræ, to discover spinal affections, and over the renal regions for evidences of tenderness.

6. Cause him to rise and face the examiner; present both the dorsal and palmer surfaces of each hand; flex and extend every finger; grasp with the thumb and forefinger and with the whole hand; flex and extend the wrists and fore-arms; pronate and supinate the hand; perform all the motions of the shoulder-joints, especially violent circumduction; extend the arms at right angles from the body, and from that position touch the shoulders with the fingers; elevate the hands above the head, palm to palm, then back to back, and, while standing thus, examine the axillæ and groins for enlarged lymphatics, and the latter regions closely for fistulous openings, herniæ, and relaxation of the inguinal parietes predisposing to ruptures, compelling the recruit to bend forward, cough and strain repeatedly and violently. Inspect the abdomen for umbilical hernia, and for enlargement of the liver and spleen. Next cause him to evert and invert the feet; to stand on the

heels and then on tip-toe, coming down on the heel quickly and heavily, and lifting the toes from the floor; to bend each thigh alternately high up on the abdomen, and while standing on one leg to hop with each foot; to squat low down by bending both knees and thighs, and to rise quickly from this position; to perform all the motions of the hip-joint; to walk backward and forward slowly and at double-quick, and thus to exercise every articulation of the body in all its movements.

7. Examine the thorax by percussion and ausculation, especially in the infraclavicular and cardiac regions, at the same time observing the radial pulse; cross the arms upon the chest, placing each hand upon the opposite shoulder, and, inclining the body forward, examine the posterior regions of the thorax. Observe the movements of the chest during prolonged inspiration and expiration, recording its extreme dimensions by measurement with a tape in a horizontal direction immediately below the nipples. In this connection, the indications of the expiratory and inspiratory power afforded by the hæmadynamometer would be valuable. Observe the effects of violent exercise upon the pulse and respiration.

8. Examine the scalp for cicatrices, depressions, tinea, etc.; direct the head to be bent forward and backward, and to be rotated upon the neck; observe the motions of the lower jaw. Examine the ears for polypi, disease of the membrana tympani, etc. Test the hearing by asking questions in an undertone, at a distance, each ear being alternately closed by an assistant. Examine the eyelids and eyes, closing and opening them to observe the motions of the iris. Test the eye-sight by requiring the applicant to read test-types, or distinguish articles of various sizes and colors at proper distances, using each eye alternately. Note the absence of cilia, corneal opacities, redness of tarsal edges, obstruction of the puncta, etc. Throw back the head and inspect the nostrils for polypi, ozæna, etc. Examine the teeth, noting great defects. Absence of all the teeth of one jaw, or of all the molars, is sufficient reason for rejection, since imperfect mastica-

tion, especially when the man is restricted to the regular sea-ration, is very apt to cause dyspepsia and its consequences. Note if the cutting edges of the central incisors are excavated internally, believed, on good grounds, to be indicative of congenital syphilis. Depress the tongue and examine the fauces for hypertrophied tonsils, syphilitic ulceration, mucous patches, etc. Decided stammering or difficult enunciation are sufficient reasons for rejection.

9. Ascertain whether he has been vaccinated, or presents satisfactory evidence of having had variola.

10. Discover by adroit questioning with what diseases he has been affected, and of what his parents or near relatives have died. This part of the examination is important, as it enables the medical officer to discover the fatuity or imbecility of the applicant. Many officers probably remember a man named Benjamin Seaman, who has several times appeared in the service as an ordinary seaman. He was utterly inefficient on board ship, and was twice sent to naval hospitals. Any careful observer ought to have been satisfied, after a few minutes' conversation, that this man was of very feeble intellect. Unprincipled persons sometimes attempt to impose weak-minded boys upon the service to rid themselves of their care. I was witness to two such attempts, in the year 1860, at the naval rendezvous at New York, by ministers of religion, one of them an officer of a charitable orphan asylum.

At the risk of the accusation of imposing unnecessary labor upon the examiner, and of making the inspection needlessly tedious to the subject, I urgently advise the establishment of dynamometric tests for ascertaining the absolute and relative strength of the individuals presenting themselves for shipment, as furnishing important data for determining their ability to perform the labor and endure the fatigues of a nautical career. I do not recommended this, however, for the object proposed by the French hygienists—the stationing of the crew according to the indications of the dynamometer. Thus, Keraudren, writing on this subject, states, "Other things being equal, we consider those sailors who are endowed with great *manual strength* as the most proper to be stationed in the tops; we know what a prehensile power topmen require to gather up or reef a sail which is blown about or distended by the wind. Those men, on the contrary, who possess a considerable *renal* (lumbar) *strength* should be assigned to the battery, and particularly to the working of guns of heavy caliber." No complex apparatus will be required for the purpose I suggest. It is desirable to ascertain and record the hoisting, hauling, and lifting power of the individual. The number of pounds which he can lift a certain distance, or the height to which he can elevate a certain weight by pulling steadily on a rope led through a block overhead, will give the first; by hauling on a rope led horizontally through a block fastened at the level of the waist, the second will be ascertained; while the third may, of course, be obtained by attaching as many weights to a bar or ring as can be lifted the same distance in the ordinary way. These very simple contrivances may be extemporized on board any vessel, and may readily be introduced into the examining-room of the rendezvous. The numbers obtained are not to be entered on the descriptive list, but should be recorded on the medical officer's register for statistiscal purposes, along with those indicated by the hæmadynamometer, should its use also be authorized.

THE RECEIVING-SHIP.

The receiving-ship is the nursery of the man-of-war's man. First impressions are enduring, and the sailor will be permanently influenced by the examples he sees around him on entering the service. The receiving-ship should be a disciplined man-of-war. The recruit, with his civilian clothes, should cast off his civilian habits, and witness, at the very outset, the spectacle of order cleanliness, and discipline, to which he will be subjected during his whole naval career.

When the recruit leaves the rendezvous, he is furnished with a descriptive list and a due-bill for the authorized advance; but, instead of at once repairing on board, he returns to his boarding-house, indulges in a last debauch, and is finally carried off to the receiving-ship by his landlord. He is required to present himself clean, sober, and, until recently, outfitted. He is now allowed to obtain his clothing from the paymaster of the receiving-ship, but it is a matter of regret that this is not made compulsory. The furnishing of the outfit constitutes a large part of the business of boarding-house keepers, and of a class of persons who have shops attached to or adjoining the rendezvous, and who seize upon such of the recruits, usually boys, landsmen, and merchant-men, as they can persuade to patronize them.

The recruiting-office ought undoubtedly to be either on board the receiving-ship, or within the precincts of the navy-yard, and the agency of the landlord entirely ignored by the Government. The vast majority of men now received in the naval service are picked up by the "landshark" as soon as they are paid off from a cruise, supplied with rum, board, and money for prostitutes as long as he sees fit, and then carried by him to the rendezvous, where he receives their descriptive lists and the due-bills for their two or three months' advance, and whence he takes them back to his tavern, indulges them in a farewell spree, outfits them with worthless clothing, and then transfers them to the receiving-ship. If any of them have had honorable discharges, he increases his bill proportionally, and likewise receives the three months' extra pay to which that discharge entitles them. The descriptive list and due-bill ought in every instance to be delivered only to the recruit himself, who should be informed that he must obtain his outfit on board the receiving-ship, unless he is in possession of clothing from paymaster's stores. He ought to be required to proceed at once to the receiving-ship, and when this is not done, the medical officer of the rendezvous should inform him that he has to be re-examined, and that he must wash his body, dress cleanly, and have his hair cut short before reporting himself on board. After the second examination by the surgeon of the receiving-ship, which is preliminary and requisite to his acceptance, and which is absolutely necessary not only for detecting recent venereal affections, but for discovering anything that may have escaped the first examiner, he should be required to bathe thoroughly, using warm water and soap, under the supervision of the master-at-arms, in a part of the vessel especially assigned for that purpose, and be provided with the outfit of clothing indicated elsewhere. His former clothing should be returned to his family or disposed of for his benefit. From this time he should be regarded as the child of the Government, and should be cared for by the officers who represent that Government. He should be taught the necessity of obedience, the certainty of punishment for misdoing, and of reward for meritorious conduct, and he should be assured that the arm of authority by which he is chastised is also powerful to defend him from imposition and injustice. There is a class of persons who have filled certain petty-officers' positions on board receiving-ships for years, and who, like the sutlers at the various marine barracks, take advantage of their stations to extort money from new men on various pretenses, or make loans to them at exorbitant rates of interest. Some of these persons have acquired large fortunes by their nefarious trade, which they adroitly conceal from the officers of the vessel, who are continually changing and do not become familiar with or are indifferent to their extortions. Every transaction of this kind should be strictly prohibited by law, and every infraction of the law severely punished; a monthly allowance of pay, conditional upon good behavior, removing the excuse for obtaining money in this way. This is not ground foreign to hygiene. The moral health of a crew is as necessary to discipline and efficiency as the normal condition of their bodies. The superiority of the modern over the old-time sailor, as an intelligent, thinking man, is evident to the unprejudiced, and the late war demonstrated that he was no less zealous, brave, and competent than his ruder predecessors, who made a naval reputation for their country. It is the province of hygiene to correct all errors and abuses whatsoever which enfeeble the body, obtund the mind, or degrade the moral nature of the sailor. The purpose of its suggestions is to diminish sick-lists, empty brigs, and banish from the berth-deck the filth, obscenity, and profanity, of the existence of which only those are ignorant who never visit it except when it is prepared for inspection.

The sanitary regulations applicable to receiving-ships are the same as those I shall recommend to be adopted on board cruising vessels. They do not, therefore, need any special discussion in this place.

Before being drafted to a sea-going vessel, every man should be inspected by the executive officer as to the completeness of his outfit of clothing, and by the medical officer as to his health and cleanliness. The executive and medical officers of the sea-going vessel should also carefully inspect them as they come on board. Under the present system, men are sent away usually scantily clothed, sometimes in ill-health, and generally unclean in their bodies. I have known vessels to receive their crews in the winter season, a majority of the men being without mattresses, blankets, under-clothing, stockings, jackets, or overcoats, and many of them infested with vermin, with which they were compelled to suffer several weeks, the intensely cold weather rendering it impossible to cleanse their bodies. It is not uncommon to clear off the sick-list of the receiving-ship by sending its most troublesome *habitues* away with a draft, and when these men have to make a passage in a dispatch-boat or tug, to some distant navy-yard, they are frequently exposed for several days to the rigors of our coast, always insufficiently clad, and forced to sleep about the decks, without bedding, wherever they can find a place. Such men invariably report for treatm ent as soon as they get on board the vessel to which they. are ordered. Many others, who were well when they started, contract severe acute diseases, which disable them when their services are most required, and often entail permanent organic changes, for which they have to be invalided sooner or later during the cruise. The medical journal has usually to be opened as soon as the ensign is hoisted and the vessel put in commission, and the apothecary is at work compounding prescriptions before the cook has lighted his fire at the galley. The transfer of a case of parotitis from the sick-bay of the receiving-ship to that of the Tennessee, a transfer effected without the consent of the medical officers, resulted in the illness from that disease of more than seventy of the crew of the latter vessel. Every man-of-war should begin her cruise under the most favorable circumstances possible, and hygiene exacts nothing' so important as that every man shall be in good health and provided with all the clothing he may need. The necessity for the vessel remaining a few days at the navy-yard after going into commission is apparent, that omissions may be supplied and provision made for every possible contingency, but it is no less important for the Government to provide a proper transport, with adequate berthing accommodations, for drafts of men sent from one naval station to another.

There is a medical officer attached to every navy-yard, whose special and almost only recognized duty is to attend the sick among the officers and marine guard, and to examine applicants for enlistment in the Marine Corps. His more important functions should pertain to the sanitary considerations involved in the construction and proper preservation of the home of the sailor— questions similar to those within the province of civil health-officers. If it be important to require architects to consider hygienic principles in the construction of dwelling-houses, it is of no less consequence to insist that ship-builders shall have regard to the healthfulness and comfort of the structures in which so many thousand men have to pass so large a portion of their lives. In claiming for the medical corps this professional interest in the building of vessels, and the care of those in ordinary, no interference is sought with the customary routine of dock-yard duty. The recommendations of the medical officer are of general applicability, and would be better embodied in stringent regulations of the Department than left to the suggestion of individual officers. The medical officer of the navy-yard is, doubtless, the proper person to supervise the observance of these regulations, and call attention to their neglect by subordinates.

The objects it is urged upon the Department to enforce by regulation are—

1. To preserve vessels in ordinary and those building as dry as possible.

2. To keep them perfectly clean.

3. To provide the most perfect means for their ventilation.

4. To provide the most perfect means for the admission of light into their interior.

Dampness, dirt, foul air, and darkness are the direst enemies with which the sailor has to battle when afloat. They can never be wholly routed and conquered, but they may be subdued and rendered comparatively harmless. Leagued together, they slaughter more than all the adversary's powder and shot. The most accomplished ordnance officer has no more subtle and powerful ally, in the work of bringing death to his country's foes, than the poor hygiene of his opponents. Sir Gilbert Blane attributed the failure of the British arms during our war of Independence to the deficiency of numbers, and want of strength and energy of the men from excessive sickness and mortality, and declared that if the same death-rate in their navy had continued during the French revolutionary war seamen would no longer have been procurable, and their famous victories have never been achieved; so that, says Professor Guy, "it was not the seamanship and fighting qualities of our sailors alone that carried us triumphantly through that terrible contest, but a reduced mortality, due to the sanitary discoveries and reforms, which first recruited our population by saving lives in infancy and childhood, and then cut off from our forces, by sea and land, the destructive supplies of jail-fever, scurvy, dysentery, and small-pox." Therefore, while inventive talent is being strained to meet the exigencies of an exceptional state of war, let something be done to stay the murderers who are dealing out death as well in times of peace as in those of conflict.

It is not expected that ships can ever be made as comfortable and healthful as homes on land. The creatures that swim the sea and those that roam over the earth each have their habits. The carpeted and mirrored steamship, like the painted harridan, is pretty only in spots. Her foul and unclean parts are only masked by the local splendor. The attempt at reform need not, . however, be stopped because absolute perfection is impossible. Humanity demands that all should be done that may. The floating hells of the past century, and the rude, strange race who lived and died upon their ocean home, who spoke a language unintel-

3 H

ligible to shore folks, and were ignorant of the customs of the land world, have become historical. Sailors are men, and ships the habitations of men, but there is still filth and depravity and sickness where there might be cleanliness and decency and health. The medical corps is laboring to this end—not to overturn for the sake of overturning, as has been unkindly and maliciously insinuated.

The first great fact which should be impressed on all naval constructors, sailing officers, and dock-yard officials, is the necessity of keeping a vessel as *dry* as possible, not only when in commission and in ordinary, but even when on the stocks. The wood of which a vessel is composed is a dead organic substance, subject to molecular decay, which is accelerated by heat and moisture. The temperature is to a certain extent beyond our control, but it is not altogether out of our power to maintain a certain degree of dryness, which will not only retard this decomposition, but diminish one of the causes of that humidity on board ships which I shall presently show to be so prejudicial to the health of the crew. All vessels should be built under cover, in dry seasons of the year, of old and seasoned timber, and the operations of building should be conducted slowly, so that a circulation of air may take place between all parts of the frame. When timber has been allowed to soak in salt water for purposes of preservation, it should be thoroughly dried before being used in the construction of vessels. Green wood, from the amount of contained sap and the softness of its tissues, is more readily decomposed than old hard timber in which the wood cells are compact, and vessels constructed of it are notoriously unhealthy. Fonssagrives, whose excellent work on naval hygiene is the most complete that has ever been published, narrates two instances in point: "We are indebted to M. Delalun, *capitaine de vaisseau,* for the two following facts, demonstrating the influence of the mode of construction of vessels upon their salubrity. At Navarino the crews of our vessels were properly subsisted and were spared by the scurvy. The vessel of Admiral de Rigny alone, although it had fresh meat twice oftener than the others, was decimated by this affection. There were about eighty men constantly on the sick-list. The fact was explained by the humidity of the wood which was used in this vessel and by the rapidity of its construction. The improvised squadron of Antwerp (1812–'13) had been built of wood felled while in sap. At the end of eight years all these vessels were out of service, and there was not one of them that could be repaired. The ship L.'Hector, among others, was so rotten that she could not even be used as a hulk. She was constantly full of scorbutic cases." The histories of our own "ninety-day gun-boats" and "double-enders" illustrate the same fact.

Vessels in ordinary should be immediately housed over. When fitting out for sea, it should be the special duty of the watchman or ship-keeper to carefully close all hatches and ports in wet weather, and open them in dry. It is not unusual when a vessel is in the hands of the navy-yard *employees* to find her lower decks flooded with water or piled up with snow, even when her crew is hourly expected on board. Large painted awnings or tarpaulins should be provided and so arranged as to be quickly spread on the occurrence of rain or snow.

No vessel can be made absolutely impervious to water. It finds entrance by a thousand channels, by opening seams, by worm-holes, by leakage from tanks and casks, by the condensation of the aqueous vapor in the atmosphere. Great care should therefore, be taken in ship-building that it be allowed to run down freely into the limbers, and find access, without obstruction forward or aft, to the pump-well, whence it can be daily removed. Medical Inspector Joseph Wilson, in his work on naval hygiene, calls attention to a very common defect in pumps, which are too short to reach to the bottom of the well, and thus discharge all the accumulated water. I translate the following instance quoted by Fonssagrives from a thesis on dysentery by M. Collas, a surgeon in the French navy, illustrating the danger that may result from any obstruction to the discharge of this bilge-water: "The corvette La Triomphante was anchored at Nouka Hyva, at a point where there were no marshes. There was not a single case of dysentery on shore. Soon afterward this disease commenced to rage on board. The agitation of the vessel, first by a gale of wind and then by getting aground, soon caused new cases to appear. The hold was examined, and under the store-room a pool of stagnant water was found which could not run into the pump-well, the vessel being down by the head from the anchors on the bow. The place was carefully cleaned, and the epidemic disappeared."

It would be supposed to be impossible to make complaint of the uncleanliness of newly built vessels, but it is a fact that there are few which do not carry with them from the stocks as great a source of disease as the foulness accumulated by a whole ship's company during a cruise. There is a general neglect, inexcusable and criminal because it does not involve much trouble, to remove the chips and other remains of building-materials, which collect on the floor of the vessel and are planked up under the ceiling, where they remain year after year, decomposing under the influence of confined and heated air and the admixture of fresh and salt water constantly in the limbers. The report of the Portsmouth Relief Association upon the origin of the yellow fever which prevailed at Norfolk and Portsmouth, Virginia, in the year 1855, relates an instance of frightful extent of illness traceable to this cause; and an illustration quite as conclusive was furnished by the United States ship Macedonian during her cruise on the north coast of South America. The fact was communicated to me by her first lieutenant. Numerous cases of fever having occurred on board this vessel, it was remarked by her surgeon, now Medical Director Grier, that the men attacked were chiefly those who slept in the forward part of the vessel. A local cause was suggested and discovered by scuttling the fore peak. As soon as an opening was made, a noisome effluvium arose, and a candle introduced into the peak was instantly extinguished. Both sides were scuttled, wind-sails were let down, and, after the place was sufficiently ventilated to allow men to descend into it with safety, was cleaned out. More than fifty bucketfuls of putrescent vegetable matter and several hogsheads of foul discolored water were removed. From this time the disease disappeared. A letter in the London Times, September 18, 1861, from Halifax, where Her Britannic Majesty's ship Jason then was, states that "she is a new vessel, built of green wood; her bilges cannot be kept sweet; the officers have tried all means to do so without success. This is considered the principal cause of her being so unhealthy. The stench is abominable, particularly in the after part of the ship and in the officers' cabin, and the Jason is not the only sickly ship in which such a nuisance has existed."

Naval constructors will, doubtless, admit that when planning vessels the very last subject, if ever, in their thoughts is hygiene. They aim at buoyancy, speed, strength, lightness of draught, but never salubrity. The means of ventilating a ship in commission will be hereafter referred to, but the constructor has it in his power to make those means much more efficacious than they can be under the present system of internal arrangements. There should be no such thing as a solid bulkhead in the inhabited part of a vessel. Some of our finest ships have their berth-decks ruined by being divided into four or five close compartments by as many complete transverse bulk-heads. Every partition, those separating private apartments as well as those marking the larger subdivisions of ward-room, steerage, warrant officers' steerage, sickbay, etc., should be latticed or gratinged above and below. This can always be done without any sacrifice of strength. The cabin and ward-room bulk-heads and doors usually have Venetian blinds or perpendicular bars in their upper part, but the lower panels should also be permeable to air, and all other bulk-heads, whether of store-rooms, lockers, sail-room, shell-room, etc., should be arranged in the same way. Every place should be accessible to air, which should circulate freely forward and aft on every deck of the vessel. The furniture of officers' rooms is not only antiquated and inelegant, but such as unnecessarily diminishes the cubic air-space of the rooms. Cumbersome and unwieldy bureaus, bunks, and wash-stands are taken out and restored, cruise after cruise, without change or improvement. Instead of the huge box-like wash-stand, a neat iron upright, with rings for basin and pitcher, sockets for mug and soap-block, and hooks for towels, might be devised to occupy one-fourth the space. The bureau could be made of much lighter materials, and the bunk would be far more comfortable if constructed on the principle of the French swinging cradles. A neat style of clothes-locker might be contrived of wire, which would be cleaner, more commodious and more ornamental than the great wooden boxes and drawers that are now never opened nor closed without difficulty. These changes would furnish space for a much larger amount of respirable air, and if, in addition, all the bulk-heads were latticed, though only for a few inches at the top and bottom, the officers' room would not be such an inclosure of confined and heated air, from which the occupant escapes on deck in the morning with nausea, dyspnœa, and headache, and to which he returns with loathing at the dampness and foul smell he encounters.

The apertures for the admission of light are necessarily few. These are the gun-ports, air-ports, and hatchways. Sometimes deck-lights of very thick glass are introduced in the ward-room and cabins, and might, with great propriety and no risk, be distributed forward over the berth-deck.

These improvements are all feasible in old as in new vessels. Naval constructors would, undoubtedly, cheerfully exercise their skill in the furtherance of these hygienic objects if the matter were brought officially to their notice. Some of these gentlemen, with a laudable desire to contribute to the comfort of officers, have introduced the novelty of bathing-tubs, and I am, therefore, sure they would be no less disposed to devise improvements conducive to the health of those who have to inhabit the floating houses they put together.

HUMIDITY.

The great danger the sailor encounters is water. Not the mighty deep he traverses, on whose wide waste he is but an indistinguishable speck, and from whose depths he is only separated by a few inches of plank. It is not the water without his vessel that imperils his life so much as that within it—that which saturates his clothes and bedding, fills the air he breathes, and, creeping in wherever that air can enter, permeates the very tissue of the wood of which his ship is built. This is his enemy; terrible because unseen, powerful because denied, depreciated and therefore unresisted. Fewer lives are lost by shipwreck than by the operations of this subtle agent. Man's skill has mastered the fury of the ocean. He is able to oppose its storms and currents, and go upon its surface as he lists; but he makes no attempt to combat this insidious slayer.

The daily variations in the hygrometric constitution of the atmosphere do not amount to more than a few grains in weight per cubic foot. Air is saturated at 52° F. by 1.42 per cent. of its volume of aqueous vapor, in weight about four and a half grains to the cubic foot. As the temperature rises it becomes able to retain a larger quantity of vapor in solution, being saturated at 77° F. by three per cent. or 9.8 grains, while at the freezing-point it holds only a fraction over two grains, or less than one per cent. of its volume. Ordinarily, it seldom contains more than two or three grains, or from thirty to fifty per cent. of the quantity of water in the state of vapor required to completely saturate it. The fluctuations in humidity, which the rheumatic invalid appreciates so sensitively, sometimes correspond to a change of weight of less than a single grain. The marine atmosphere normally contains a larger amount of aqueous vapor than the terrestrial, and on board ship the proportion is further increased by the exhalation of fluid from the surface of the bodies of the men confined upon it, and very greatly by that from the lungs in the act of expiration, twenty-five to forty ounces of water being discharged daily by each individual in this way. The evaporation from a wet deck supplies water enough to the atmosphere to raise it to its point of saturation; and when this is repeated without regard to temperature and season, all those evils result which are attributed by the scientific to the prolonged influence of moisture and heat, and which have conferred upon the climate of the west coast of Africa its notorious unhealthfulness; and as far as my own observation has extended, it has generally escaped attention that these two morbific influences usually act in conjunction. According to Tyndall the aqueous vapor of the atmosphere absorbs solar heat radiations with rapidity, and the greater the amount of vapor and the more humid the atmosphere the greater will be the amount of heat absorbed, and consequently the smaller will be the excess of sun temperature over that of the shade. Hence, a ship, the atmosphere of which is always kept near the point of saturation by being frequently deluged with water, will have the temperature of its shaded parts raised almost to the height of those exposed to the unshielded sun. In temperate climates the usual average yearly excess of sun over shade is twenty degrees, and in the tropics it is three times as much. It is evident, therefore, that the beneficial effect of spreading awnings is very much diminished and the temperature of the lower decks greatly augmented, if the ship is kept damp; and this is not inconsistent with the fact that the occasional sprinkling of a dry heated uncovered spar-deck momentarily reduces the temperature through evaporation.

Since, then, such minute differences in the amount of aqueous vapor in the atmosphere disturb the harmonious action of the functions of the human body, how urgently necessary are those measures of precaution which are insisted on by medical men! There is but one opinion on this subject among naval surgeons all over the world. "Humidity," says Pringle, "is one of the most frequent causes of the derangement of health;" and Fonssagrives, the greatest authority on naval hygiene, uses this language: "The practice of medicine on board ship confirms the truth of this assertion: Whenever a vessel may be said to be very damp, it may be said to be an unhealthy vessel. All the authors who have written on the diseases of seamen, Rouppe, Lind, Poisonnier-Desperieres, Keraudren, Raoul, etc., are unanimous in attributing a very great importance to this etiological influence. The latter, after having, in his report on the cruise of the Caraibe, analyzed the causes of the production of scurvy on board different vessels, and discussed all other influences, as nourishment, sojourn in port or at sea, different stations, etc., finally attributed this formidable affection to the persistence of humidity. All are of one accord on the insalubrity of an atmosphere saturated with water, in which the cutaneous depuration greatly flags, and respiration is performed with difficulty."

English testimony is quite as decisive. Captain John McNeill Boyd, of the royal navy, candidly admits that "the objections to wet decks are supported by the medical officers, with such a weight of evidence that they cannot be gainsaid, and if the mate of a deck does not think the health of the crew a matter of indifference, he may so arrange the process of cleaning as to prove that dry decks are not incompatible with health;" and in the Life of Collingwood, it is stated that "his flag-ship, with a crew of eight hundred men, was on one occasion more than a year and a half without going into port, and never had more than six on her sick-list. This result was occasioned by his system of arrangement and his attention to *dryness*, ventilation, etc., but above all by the contented spirit of the sailors, who loved their commander as their protector and friend, well assured that at his hands they would receive justice and kindness, and that of their comforts he was more jealous than his own."

The unanimity of our own medical corps in this matter, instead of attracting that attention and respect it deserves from commanding and executive officers, is too often regarded as a simple perverse contrariety of opinion, having no other object than a mean and petty attempt to interfere with the routine of the ship; and this ungenerous belief will probably continue until the principles of hygiene are better understood by the officers of the other corps. The consequences of ignorance on this point were remarkably and conclusively demonstrated on board the Coast-Survey schooner Varina, during the autumn of 1860, while anchored off the navy-yard at Brooklyn. The officers of this little vessel, desirous of emulating the customs of their huger men-of-war neighbors, scrubbed their decks every day without regard to weather. Numbers of her crew soon became ill with bronchial, pulmonary, and rheumatic affections, and at one time nearly a third of them had been sent to the hospital. As soon as the fact was represented to Captain (afterward Admiral) Foote, then executive officer of the yard, he ordered the wetting of the decks to be discontinued, from which time her sick-list rapidly diminished.

A ship must be kept dry to be healthy; her crew must be healthful to be efficient. To promote this efficiency is alike the duty of medical officers as of commanders and lieutenants. But she must be kept clean, it is replied; cleanliness is likewise essential to health. The daily wetting of the decks, however, is not evidence of cleanliness, but of dirt. That is an ill-managed vessel which becomes so quickly foul. A well-arranged ship and well-conducted crew do not accumulate dirt. When the weather or sea necessitates the eating of meals below, not a crumb should be spilled from a mess-cloth. The cooks at the galley should be required to remove grease as they let it fall. Tarpaulins should be spread whenever the hold is broken out. The cleaning of mess-things, blacking of boots, brushing of clothes, and every other operation that can occasion dirt, should be done in the open air. The unclean berth-deck is so only because of the inattention or incapacity of the mate or other officer whose duty it is to take care of it.

Berth-decks and covered gun-decks do not require to be wetted oftener than once, or, at most, twice a month. They should then be cleaned thoroughly, and not upon any stated day, but when the weather is such as will justify it. A dry, clear, sunny day, after a prevalence of fine weather, is the most proper for the purpose. It should always be selected and indicated by the commander himself, who should solicit and be guided by the advice of the medical officer. On these days all other exercises should be suspended. Every man, except the cooks and such others as are engaged in the work, should be sent on deck with his bag and ditty-box, and should be compelled to remain there until the deck is thoroughly dried. Hot water should be supplied for the purpose from the galley, and the greatest care should be taken not to use it in such quantities as to overflow the coamings of the hatches into the hold. After scraping and scrubbing as much as is necessary, the greatest expedition should be made in removing the unclean water by squabs and squilgees, and then drying-stoves should be lighted and kept swinging until the decks are completely dried. The hatchways should, all the while, have been wholly uncovered, wind-sails let down to the deck, ventilators worked, and, when possible, air-ports opened. In this way a lower deck may be properly cleaned with the least detriment to the health of the ship's company.

When a prevalence of wet weather causes the decks to become damp, they should be scraped and drying-stoves should be frequently lighted. No other process of cleaning should ever be tolerated. A practice prevails on board some vessels, which cannot be too strongly reprobated, of going over the berth-deck every morning with a wet swab, for what purpose it is difficult to understand except it be to maintain an appearance of having observed the ancient custom of daily scrubbing, the decadence of which some officers class with the abolition of the cat, as among the causes of the degeneracy of the Navy.

The flying berth-decks of small vessels should be scrubbed and dried in the open air, as should also the hatch-covers, ladders, and gratings of all other vessels which are wetted on any other than the day for the general cleaning of the lower decks.

It is singular that while there is such difficulty in keeping water which finds an entrance from natural causes out of a vessel, there should be such a universal habit of deluging it above and below, and thus superadding an artificial and unnecessary cause of humidity. There is a general custom of wetting or "holy-stoning" the spar-deck every morning, which has been handed down from the past century, with other observances that are equally inconsistent with the intelligence of this age. It is very proper to do this when the crew have soiled the deck with soap-suds by washing clothes and scrubbing hammocks, and these occasions occur so frequently that there is no necessity for wetting it at other times, except after some special unclean work, as weighing anchor, coaling, provisioning, etc.

Small vessels are habitually wet when under way. This can be partially obviated by greater care in fitting bucklers to the hawse-holes, and by calking the bridle-ports.

In wet weather the officer of the deck should always promptly cause the boom-cover to be hauled out at sea, and the awnings to be spread and housed when in port, rather than cover the hatchways with tarpaulins.

In this connection I have to suggest a protection against getting wet, which, to the disgrace of the educated officers of the present day, has not been already generally instituted—a hood for the head. Men are compelled to visit this place and sit exposed to no matter how heavy a rain or intense a sun. This is one of the most potent sources of disease on board ship. A man gets out of his warm hammock at night, and returns to it with his clothes drenched with water. His blankets and mattress become wet, and in vessels where bedding is aired but once in two or three months, they remain damp and foul all that time. On board small vessels without sick-bays and water-closets for the sick, invalids often refuse to use the close-stool in the vicinity of their shipmates' messes, and watch an opportunity to elude the vigilance of the nurses and steal on deck. Very many cases of disease, mild in their incipiency, have been aggravated by this cruel exposure. Nothing can be easier than to provide a properly fitted tarpaulin or canvas cover for the head, which would not only defend from the rain, but from the spray continually breaking over the bows at sea. Even if unsightly, though it need not be so, a sacrifice of appearance is a small evil that will be productive of so much good. So many comforts have of late been instituted in cabins and ward-rooms that it were only generous to extend a semblance of them to the berth-deck and forecastle, where the customs of civilized life may be imitated without greater risk of effeminacy in the one case than in the other.

Another cause of humidity on board ship is provisioning, wooding, or coaling in bad weather. Unless absolutely necessary, these operations should be conducted only on dry days. No wet or green wood, wet or unclean casks, or wet coal should ever be allowed below the spar-deck. All coal and wood should have been kept under cover before being taken on board, and the latter should also have been deprived of its bark and baked. The hoops of all casks should also be barked, and the casks carefully swept prior to being sent below. It would be an additional safeguard to whitewash them, and this could be repeated whenever the hold was broken out. In this way the hold and spirit-room may be kept perfectly clean and dry.

It is a matter of controversy whether water should ever be purposely admitted into a vessel. It is manifestly improper when it is made a daily habit for the theoretical purpose of "keeping the vessel sweet," and the only occasion when it is allowable is when bilge-water has formed. In this case the latter should be pumped out, and fresh water admitted into the pump-well by a hose from the stop-cock in the ship's side, but not to exceed in amount the depth ascertained by the first sounding of the well. This should then be discharged, a second supply of water admitted and pumped out, and this operation should be repeated until the discharge from the pump-well is free from smell. On board some vessels a very reprehensible practice exists of opening the magazine-cock and flooding the spirit-room and hold. Such vessels will always be troubled with bilge-water, which forms the more rapidly as these wettings are frequent.

I would also urge the necessity of requiring hygrometric observations by the medical officers of every vessel in commission, with a careful particularization of the attendant circumstances, so as to establish on an indisputable basis of fact the propositions here advanced. These observations should be the duty of the assistant surgeon, and not be delegated to nurses or apothecaries, who would perform it in the same superficial manner as the quartermasters, who record the temperatures indicated by the dry and " wet-bob " thermometer. The points to be determined are the degree of relative humidity and the absolute weight of aqueous vapor in a cubic foot or litre of air. It is desirable that every medical officer, on duty on shore or afloat, should be required to make a detailed quarterly sanitary report, embracing not only a summary of these and other meteorological observations, but precise information on all the subjects that relate to the preservation of the health of the Navy, and which are certainly as important as the records of the failures to effect this object, as shown by the quarterly reports of sick and expenditure of medicines and medical stores necessary for their treatment.

VENTILATION.

It is scarcely possible on board ship to supply every man with the thousand cubic feet of space for air which physiologists declare to be the minimum that can be safely assigned, except when extraordinary provisions are in operation for its renewal. Probably no single-decked vessel in the service supplies one-third of that amount. The best authorities agree that a healthy man requires a supply of twenty cubic feet of fresh air every minute. Hammond states that thirty to forty are desirable, and Professor Donkin places the minimum at three thousand cubic feet per hour. According to Martin, "the constant movements going on in the atmosphere prove that the amount of change which nature has provided for healthy existence is unlimited. The test of ventilation in a sick-ward is the comparative freshness or purity of the air. The interesting experiment of Lariboisiere appears to prove that about four thousand cubic feet per hour are required to insure this." The amount of air which passes through the lungs is variously estimated at from three hundred to four hundred and eighty cubic feet, four per cent. of which, at the ordinary rate of respiration, is carbon di-oxide, (carbonic acid gas,) that is, one hundred times as much as normally exists in the atmosphere, while the proportion is largely increased when the latter is moist; consequently, were there no renewal of air by ventilation on board ship, one day would suffice to make its atmosphere irrespirable, since, according to Lankester, over six parts in ten thousand in a breathing atmosphere are adverse to comfort and obnoxious to health. The rapidity with which air is deteriorated by respiration may be understood by imagining a room seven feet in size in each of its dimensions, and having nearly the cubic capacity of three hundred and fifty feet, which, containing normally about one gallon of carbon di-oxide, will, at the end of two hours, all apertures being closed, have this amount raised to ninety-two and a half gallons by the respiration of a single adult man, showing that every particle of that air had passed through his lungs. This, however, is not the only noxious element acquired by air in apartments which are defectively ventilated. Every act of expiration discharges a large amount of aqueous vapor, raising its quantity, according to Dr. Craig, of the United States Army, from one to seventeen grains in a cubic foot; elevates the general temperature of the air, and thus increases its absorbent power for vapors; and further, adds a variable amount of organic matters, the presence of which is distinctly enough indicated, even to the unprofessional observer who leans over the fore or main hatch toward the end of the first watch, by the heavy mawkish odor, which appeals to the sense of taste as well as to that of smell. According to Gavarret, air thus vitiated is unfit for respiration, and may lead to serious accidents, not on account of the carbon di-oxide (carbonic acid gas) it contains, but from the mere presence of the putrid exhalations of the body, since organic matter in stagnant air, as that of berth-decks, putrifies as rapidly as that in stagnant water. Fonssagrives believes "that air may yet supply the chemical needs of respiration in a place crowded with men, when from the organic miasms which impregnate it, it has already become a deleterious agent," and thus quotes Piorry: "That which is the most dangerous in the vitiated air of confined habitations we do not know; chemistry does not inform us of it; but our senses, more delicate than chemistry, demonstrate to us, in an evident manner, the presence of deleterious putrid matters in the air in which man has long resided." Nor is respiration the only human process which empoisons the air. The whole cutaneous surface imperceptibly, but ceaselessly, contributes a determinate amount of aqueous vapor, carbon di-oxide, and organic emanations. Furthermore, to produce these nocuous elements, which are thus poured into the atmosphere, each adult on board ship, according to Dumas, completely disoxygenates twenty gallons of air every hour, requiring the hourly addition of more than a hundred gallons to simply restore its equilibrium, disturbed by this cause alone, without taking into account that necessary to wash away or dilute the morbific vapors and gases which have been added. Finally, the decomposition of provisions and ship's stores, especially coal, and that resulting from the admixture in the hold of fresh and salt water with the leakage of brine, molasses, vinegar, etc., all operate to deteriorate the atmosphere of the ship, not merely by the addition of the gaseous products of this decomposition, but, as in the case of the crew, by the direct removal of the oxygen, on which the fitness for respiration of the atmosphere depends. The problem of ventilation, therefore, is one of the most interesting and important that can occupy the naval hygienist.

The greater number of our national vessels are overcrowded with men. Few can berth their whole complement. With hammock-hooks only fourteen inches apart, less than the breadth of a man's shoulders, with numbers swinging under the top-gallant-forecastle, many of our single-decked vessels, when both watches are below, as in port, still have a dozen or more men who are compelled to billet themselves on deck, behind mess-chests, or wherever else they can stow themselves away. Frequently vessels are sent home from distant stations cumbered with men whose terms of service have expired, with prisoners, and, with manifest impropriety, the accumulated chronic invalids of the squadron. The ship-fever of emigrant packets, and the typhus, not uncommon on board men-of-war twenty years ago, and notably virulent among the transports employed during the Crimean war, were due to overcrowding. Fonssagrives narrates the case, among others, of the corvette La Fortune, which, having been employed in transporting Turkish troops, had two-thirds of her crew prostrated by this disease, of whom half were lost, and was obliged to land the rest at Messina. Even when the ill effects of overcrowding are not so disastrous and manifest, they are not compensated by any ad-

4 H

vantage whatsoever.   The effective number of the crew is reduced by a sick-list of from fifteen to twenty-five a day, and the invalids, who require to be returned to the United States, ultimately bring down the complement of men to the capacity of the vessel.   All this additional expense, as well as the discomfort which a large sick-list necessarily occasions to the well, might be obviated by a reduction of the ship's company at the outset.   As the small gunboats and iron-clads are the worst circumstanced in every sanitary respect, and besides being officered by young and inexperienced men are, in consequence of their lightness of draught, often required to cruise up narrow rivers and in unhealthy localities, they present, relatively, the largest number of disabled men, and thus have their effectiveness seriously impaired; hence, while especial care should be taken to provide for the proper ventilation, cleanliness, etc., of this class of vessels, it is desirable to limit their complements of men and officers to the smallest numbers absolutely necessary to work them, introducing every possible labor-saving appliance known to the nautical art, and dispensing with superfluous attendants by diminishing the number of officers' messes; and furthermore to change their crews annually by transferring them to the larger vessels of the squadron.

Very little attention is paid to the subject of ventilation by officers of the Navy.   I have heard them express incredulity when told there was danger from battening down hatches two or three days continuously, and I have seen a boy confined for some trifling offense six hours at a time for several successive days in a narrow " sweat-box," with only a few perforations at the top of the door, and none at the bottom or sides, and where, after sinking from fatigue below the level of the holes, he had to breathe an atmosphere as fraught with danger to his life as that of the most dreaded plague-ridden spot on earth.

The neglect to provide proper means of ventilation has been often attended with rapidly fatal consequences.   The case of the Black Hole of Calcutta, where one hundred and twenty-three persons out of one hundred and forty-six died after one night's

confinement in a room eighteen feet square, provided with only
two small windows, is familiar to every reader. Of three hundred Austrian prisoners confined in one room after the battle of
Austerlitz, two hundred and sixty died; and Carpenter narrates
an equally horrible catastrophe which occurred afloat : " On the
night of the 1st December, 1848, the deck passengers on board
the Irish steamer Londonderry were ordered below by the captain
on account of the stormy character of the weather, and although
they were crowded into a cabin far too small for their accommodation, the hatches were closed down upon them and the consequence was that out of one hundred and fifty individuals, no fewer
than seventy were suffocated before the morning." Instances of
less severity are of common occurrence on board men-of-war. On
one occasion, nine or ten prisoners were confined in the main hold
of a single-deck sloop-of-war and half of the hatch closed over
them. At the end of four hours one of the men was taken out
asphyxiated, and resuscitated with difficulty. The occupants of
" sweat-boxes " have often been found almost lifeless or have fallen
out insensible as the doors were opened. Dr. Billings, of the United
States Army, in his report on barracks and hospitals, published in
Circular No. 4, from the Surgeon General's Office, refers to instances of exhaustion and insensibility from confinement in
" sweat-boxes," as experimental evidence in determining the minimum amount of air on which life can be supported. In the same
able report, he fixes the proper allowance of fresh air for soldiers
in barracks at two thousand cubic feet per hour for each man.
It is useless to expect to violate with impunity the immutable laws
of our existence, and therefore, so long as the circumstances of
our nature require the inspiration of oxygen into the lungs and
the ingestion of food in the stomach, it will be just as impossible
to compel sailors to do without the one and be healthy, as to
abstain from the other and live. Statistical inquiries on mortality
prove beyond a doubt that of all the causes of death which
usually are in action, impurity of the air is the most important.
Guy states, in his recently published lectures on public health, as

the results of a laborious inquiry into the health of letter-press printers, and of others following in-door occupations, "that out of thirty-six thousand deaths a year in England and Wales, which I attributed to true pulmonary consumption, five thousand might be saved by increased space and improved ventilation in shops, work-shops, and factories; that among men doing the same work under the same roof, the liability to consumption was determined by the space; and that this might be narrowed to a point at which men would die as fast as by some contagious malady, so that here, as in Italy, consumption might seem to pass from one person to another." According to Dr. Parkes, the extraordinary amount of consumption which prevails among the men of the royal and merchant navies, and which in some men-of-war has amounted to a veritable epidemic, is in all probability attributable to faulty ventilation. I have remarked the same excess of tubercular disease of the lungs in our own naval service, and injustice has undoubtedly been done in many cases of phthisis pulmonalis which were certified "not to have occurred in the line of duty," but assumed to have had a remote inherited origin, when the disease was in fact directly attributable to the unwholesome and humid air they were compelled to respire, for the researches of Bowditch and Buchanan show that, independently of mere impurity of the atmosphere, there is a decided relation of cause and effect between dampness and consumption. The nosological heading "phthisis," on the quarterly report of sick, often represents only advanced cases of the disease, and not all of these, many being carelessly recorded as bronchitis chronica, while a very large proportion of incipient pulmonary tubercle is simply classed as bronchitis acuta or catarrhus. Constitutional predisposition assuredly existed in some of these, but the majority might have escaped the development of the disease had they lived under proper hygienic conditions, especially with regard to a sufficient supply of pure air.

Notwithstanding the importance of this matter of ventilation, few officers trouble themselves about it further than to order the wind-sails set when the weather is fine. These are certainly among the most important ventilating apparatus we possess, but they are seldom set in wet, cold, or very windy weather, although a larger proportion of the crew is below at these times, when the hatchways are also usually partly covered up. On many of these occasions they could be kept hoisted without inconvenience. They ought not to be lowered at every fresh breeze or rain-squall. A fire-tub placed under the foot of the wind-sail and watched would prevent the deck from becoming flooded with water, and in cold weather the men had better protect themselves by extra clothing than keep warm by confining and corrupting the atmosphere; for though the human odor is not perceptible when the temperature is low, the air is still loaded with organic matter, and disoxygenation and the exhalation of carbon di-oxide go on as at other times. Steamships are now generally heated by coils of steam-pipes, and if proper apertures are provided for the discharge of the heated and access of fresh air, they become excellent aids to ventilation. Wind-sails, of which there cannot be too many, require to be carefully watched while set. They should always be accurately trimmed to the wind, kept free from bends, and fastened down not more than a foot from the deck, never triced up by a lanyard to the beams. When the latter is done, those men who sleep exposed to the currents of air through them are apt to contract catarrhal affections. The bottom piece, sometimes added for ornament, should always be removed, a hoop taking its place, and large fenestrated openings being made in the sides of the wind-sail above the hoop. They should be hoisted however light the air, even in calms, when all the fore and aft sails should be set with their sheets hauled as flat as they can be got, not merely to assist in steadying the vessel, but to create a movement in the atmosphere through the rolling of the ship. In narrow rivers and inlets, ships at anchor should be sprung to the wind whenever feasible, the broadside of the vessel with its numerous apertures affording a very much greater surface for the admission of air than the bows, and the wind-sails not operating to becalm each other as when the wind is right ahead. On some stations, as Japan, this is a subject of stringent regulation on board the British men-of-war. A scuttle admitting a wind-sail or ventilator should always open into the sick-bay and yeoman's store-room, the latter the worst ventilated apartment in the vessel, its atmosphere being rendered still more impure by one or two lights kept constantly burning. When it is absolutely necessary to cover them, light iron gratings over all the hatchways are better than the ordinary heavy wooden covers or gratings, being more easily cleaned, and allowing larger apertures for the admission of air. When sailing-vessels are under way with courses and spencers set, powerful currents of air are directed downward through the open hatches. In steamers this is, in a measure, compensated for by the upward current induced by the elevation of the temperature of the engine-room atmosphere; but during the long anchorages in port, and especially during calm weather, when wind-sails are of little service, the galley-fire, should it be located on the berth-deck, is the only means for exciting motion in the stratum of air below the level of the lowest line of air-ports. Two or more large iron ventilating pipes or funnels, like those communicating with the fire-room on board passenger steamers and steam-vessels, in the Navy, should open on the berth-deck. In severe gales it is occasionally necessary to batten down all the hatches, closing every aperture by which air or water can enter, except a small scuttle in the main and steerage hatches, and at other times this has been done as a mere measure of precaution. In such cases the atmosphere soon becomes unfit for respiration, and much suffering is occasioned and danger incurred by the sick, and those whose duties confine them below. Much of this inconvenience, as well as that experienced from covering the hatches and skylights during the long rainy seasons of so many of the stations of our naval vessels would be obviated by ventilating-funnels, projecting six or eight feet above the spar-deck and fitted with movable cowls, carefully adjusted to the wind

When the hatches are battened down, both watches should be kept on deck, and the watch off duty allowed to sleep on the poop or other convenient dry place. The officers should also be required to remain in the open air, and the bed-ridden sick be removed to the spar-deck cabin, or to some equally sheltered and ventilated place when there is no such apartment.

Nor is this all that can be done toward ventilating a vessel. It is not merely sufficient to provide for the admission of fresh air, but that which is impure should be removed. It is discreditable to the mechanical ingenuity of our country that so few attempts have been made to devise machines which can effect this double purpose. On board steamers the problem would seem to be very easy of solution, air being propelled through a system of pipes traversing the vessel, and even kept in motion by punkahs or fans operated by the machinery when under way, or by a donkey-engine when at anchor. The officers of the French navy have taken the lead in this matter, commanding as well as medical officers having interested themselves in it. The apparatus of Captain Brindejonc and that of M. Peyre, though both of small size, are fully able to accomplish the objects proposed. The principle of the first is the same as that of the ordinary rotary fan ventilator, recently placed on board some of our vessels, a number of fans being made to revolve by means of a crank, in a cylinder, from which canvas tubes lead above and below for the admission and discharge of air. Though occupying but a small space and employing the labor of only one or two men a few hours every day, it is able to effectually supply every part of the vessel with fresh air. I have been attached to but one vessel in the Navy which has been provided with this apparatus, and even on board this ship, notwithstanding my repeated recommendations, it was only put in operation on two or three occasions, and then principally as a punishment for black-listers. Certainly, as a system of punishment, it is better to employ men at this work than, as may be daily seen, at polishing round-shot, scraping, painting, and rescraping iron stanchions, walking up and down the deck

carrying heavy loads, or sitting idly in the brig with their hands
and legs ironed, rejoicing in their exemption from labor. Simple
as is this apparatus in its construction, it is necessary to pay attention to the freedom of the tubes from bends and to the direction
in which they are led, while to produce a current of sufficient
velocity, that is, one moving at least two feet per minute, the
cranks should be turned with considerable rapidity. If two apparatus are put in operation at the same time, as is desirable, one
should be used forward and the other aft, the one discharging air
from below, while the other forces it from above, reversing the
direction of the currents every hour.

A captain in the French navy has devised a system of stowage
known as the "Arrimage Lugeol," by which the flour, salt, provisions, bean-lockers, rigging, and every other substance in the
hold subject to decomposition, are surrounded by aeriferous
canals. By wind-sails or ventilators introduced into these passages, currents of pure dry air may be distributed through every
part of the vessel, thus not only contributing to the health of the
crew, but also to the preservation of the provisions and other destructible stores. Such vessels are less apt to be overrun by
roaches and other vermin, which are active sources of offensive-
ness. As our own vessels are constructed, all that can be done is
to open the spirit-room, holds, sail-room, etc., every few days in
pleasant weather, lower wind-sails into them, and at other times
renew their atmosphere by the fan ventilators. The superior
means of cleansing and ventilating the decks, holds, bilges, in-
terspaces of the ribs, and those under the engine-rooms, which
have been introduced into the British service, are advanced improvements, from which Dr. Smart declares " high results may
be reckoned, and as these means are perfected, so we may calculate on a reduced rate of sickness and a diminished mortality
from yellow and remittent fevers, dysentery and broncho-pneu-
monia, to which may be assigned three-fourths of the present large
amount of phthisis."

The private mess-stores of officers contribute greatly to vitiate the air of the lower decks. The ward-room and other pantries, and the various store-rooms on the berth-deck and orlop contain eggs, fresh meats, and vegetables, which decompose rapidly and become very offensive. These rooms should all be accessible to air, through numerous openings in the bulk-heads, and they should also be opened and ventilated several times a week. I have already suggested the desirability of latticing all the bulk-heads on the berth and gun-decks to permit the free circulation of air forward and aft.

If proper attention is paid to these points, there will seldom be occasion for the employment of chemical disinfectants. Dryness, cleanliness, and ventilation are the most powerful disinfecting means. The holds, spirit-room, and store-rooms for provisions should be whitewashed every month, as well as all casks which are stowed below, and whenever these are broken out for the purpose of taking an inventory or for cleaning the hold, they should be swept and 're-whitewashed. Whitewash should also be used on the berth-deck beams and bulk-heads instead of paint. By absorbing carbon di-oxide, it assists in purifying the air. Lead nitrate, chlorinated lime and soda, carbolic acid, etc., are never more than aids to proper ventilation. They can never be carried in bulk sufficient to be serviceable alone, and, besides, their effects are only temporary.

LIGHT.

Light is a powerful vital stimulant. Removed from its influence, both plants and animals lose color, strength, and firmness of tissue. "Of all the elements which play a high part in the material universe, the light which emanates from the sun is certainly the most remarkable, whether we view it in its sanitary or scientific relations. It is, to speak metaphorically, the very life-blood of nature, without which everything material would fade and perish. Man in his most perfect type is doubtless to be found in the regions of the globe where the solar influences of light, heat, and chemical rays are so nicely balanced. Under the scorching heat of the tropics man cannot call into exercise his highest powers. The calorific rays are all-powerful there, and lassitude of body and immaturity of mind are its necessary results; while, in the darkness of the polar regions, the distinctive characters of our species almost disappear in the absence of those solar influences which are so powerful in the organic world."—(Sir J. Ranald Martin.) According to Dr. Edwards, the proper development of the body depends upon its free exposure to sunlight, absence of which he considers one of the external causes of those deficiencies of form seen in children affected with scrofula. The feeble, puny, and deformed offspring of those people who habitually live underground in cellars, caves, and mines, and in a less degree, of the dwellers in dark lanes and alleys, and of the inhabitants of the frigid zone, is due to the deprivation of light as well as to uncleanliness, starvation, and defective ventilation.

The greater part of the crew of a man-of-war has sufficient employment in the open air, but there are numerous individuals on board ship, whose special duties confine them below all day, who exhibit the pallid exsanguious appearance, the effect of habitually remaining in the dim twilight of the lower decks. All such persons should be permitted, or, if necessary, compelled, to go on deck and expose themselves to the sunlight every day. . Recovery from disease is accelerated by the beneficial influence of this agent. The occupant of a bright and consequently cheerful sick-chamber will leave it sooner and have less the aspect of an invalid than one who lies in continual shade behind heavy draperies in a gloomy apartment. So the sick and convalescent on board ship will improve more rapidly if kept on deck as much as possible, those unable to walk being placed in chairs or cots under the top-gallant forecastle, the break of the poop, or quarter-deck awning.

All the lower decks will be better illuminated by thick plates of glass set in the deck overhead. The only objection that can be opposed to them is that they are apt to leak, but this can easily be remedied by a renewal of the setting.

Artificial light is more injurious than beneficial. Every lamp and candle is an active consumer of oxygen, and therefore contributes to vitiate the air. Hammond's experiment shows that a single good sperm candle, burning at the rate of 135 grains an hour, will produce 9,504 grains (nearly 69 gallons or 11.6 cubic feet) of carbon di-oxide in twenty-four hours; and as many candles burn faster and produce more carbonic acid gas, it is within the bounds of fact to say that a candle, while burning, in the main causes as great a deterioration of the atmosphere as an adult person breathing in it during a similar length of time. Hence the minimum number of lights absolutely necessary should be placed on the berth-deck, and these always under open hatchways, that the upward current of the heated gaseous products of their combustion may assist the ventilation of the deck. Those officers who confine themselves to their rooms not only experience the pernicious effects of breathing an impure atmosphere, but have their sight impaired by the flickering blaze constantly near their eyes. Deck-lights of thick glass over their apartments would often enable them to dispense with the use of candles.

Another advantage attending the employment of whitewash on

the berth-deck, besides its effect in purifying the air, is that it multi-
plies the light admitted by the ports and hatchways.   All the furniture of officers' appartments and of the ward-room and steerages
should be painted white, the otherwise unpleasant uniformity being
relieved by a little gilded molding or ornamental decoration with
bright colors.   On the spar-deck an excess of white or metal
bright-work is objectionable, and should give place to light-blues,
greens, or yellows, or to the natural color of the wood.

CLOTHING.

Every man in the Navy should be required to possess the following articles of clothing:

One water-proof cap.
One water-proof pea-jacket.
One pair of blue cloth trousers.
Two pairs of blue satinet trousers.
Three blue flannel overshirts.
Four blue flannel undershirts.
Four blue flannel drawers.
Three white sheeting frocks.
Three pairs of white duck trousers.
One blue flannel jumper.
Four pairs of woolen socks.
One pair of boots.
One pair of shoes.
One straw hat.
One black silk neckerchief.
One mattress.
Two blankets.

Of which there should be supplied to the recruit, as an outfit, the pea-jacket, cap, neckerchief, shoes, mattress, and blankets, one pair of cloth and one of satinet trousers, a flannel overshirt, two undershirts, two pairs of drawers, and two of socks. Although only these things may be required at the outset, it is indispensable that the remainder be obtained as soon thereafter as possible, that the proper changes may be made in the event of getting wet. The British admiralty, with a view of lessening the indebtedness which men have to incur on entering the service.

has authorized the gratuitous presentation to certain recruits of a blue cloth jacket and pair of trousers, a blue serge frock, a white duck frock and trousers, a black silk neckerchief, and a pair of shoes.

Many sailors prefer to buy the materials from the paymaster and make their own clothing, being able to fit themselves better and to sew them together more neatly and enduringly. This affords occupation for the crew, and should, if only on that account, be encouraged. One of the most interesting spectacles presented on board a man-of-war is that of groups of men seated on their ditty-boxes between the guns busily sewing.

I have restricted the number of white clothes because they are seldom worn, on board some vessels never, and ought to be abolished. Their chief use is as a Sunday morning mustering-dress in the tropics, but in recent years the whim of the executive officer of the flag-ship, or in its absence, of the vessel, determines whether the dress shall be white shirts and pants, blue shirts and white pants, white shirts and blue pants, or blue shirts and pants, apparently more for the sake of variety than anything else, straw hats and blue caps, with or without white covers, extending the number of permutations. The absurdity of requiring a man to clothe his legs in flannel and his arms in white duck to-day, while to-morrow he is blue above and white below, ought to be evident to even the non-professional, as it is to the old quartermaster whose "rheumatiz" is made to shift from his shoulders to his loins and back again; but I have known ships on board which the daily dress-signal followed the card as regularly as the paymaster's stewards did in issuing the appropriate ration for the day. Whether white is or is not worn, under no circumstances, in no climate, ought the sailor to omit wearing flannel next the skin. This is a hygienic measure of the utmost importance, and should invariably be insisted upon. The flannel abdominal belt has been recommended as a substitute, but it is difficult to keep in position, and while doubtless of great benefit where dysentery is apt to occur, does not offer the same protection against pulmonary complaints and malarial diseases as the complete flannel suit. The single argument in favor of white is that it absorbs and transmits less solar heat, and is therefore cooler than blue; but if worn for this reason, the whole suit should be white and made of flannel, for the additional woolen under-clothing will more than counterbalance the advantage of the light-colored outside garment. The white dress as now worn is a useless expense and an unnecessary addition to the bag, and boys and landsmen will elude observation and wear no other clothing. In very hot weather both flannel under and overshirts may be left off, and a neat light flannel jumper substituted. If caps are worn in the tropics, they should be covered with white, but a light straw hat is the proper article of head-gear. The weight of the coarse sennit hat made on board ship is objectionable. If men are sent aloft or exposed to the sun on deck in the tropics, they should be advised to put wet handkerchiefs or cloths inside their hats, and allow a flap like an army havelock to fall over the neck.

Neatness and cleanliness of dress are always to be inculcated. Clothing should be kept in order. The custom of allowing men to have their bags on deck once a week, usually on Saturday, should be universal, and departed from only in emergencies. Clothes-lockers have been proposed as substitutes for bags, but the change is not desirable. The latter are more convenient, protect the clothes better from dampness, and can be taken on deck, and their contents exposed to the sun and air. They prevent the accumulation of dirt, unavoidable in lockers, and a not less important advantage is that they do not encroach so much on the air-space of the vessel. Their removal on deck, when the berth-deck is cleaned, allows the access of air to their racks. Ditty-boxes or bags are conveniences which every man should be permitted, preferably the former, since they can be arranged not only for sewing-articles, shaving-utensils, trinkets, and writing-materials, but may also serve as desks and stools. It would be well for the Government to supply them of uniform size, numbered with the bags. When not in use, they should be carefully stowed away in racks assigned for them.

The sailor can easily be taught habits of order and regularity. In a well-disciplined man-of-war the whole crew soon acquires them. If a berth-deck is always dry and clean, every bag and ditty-box in its place, the master-at-arms will have very little trouble with the men themselves. A few lazy, worthless fellows, however, if allowed to go unchecked, will inconvenience and confuse all the rest. The berth-deck is the man's home; his bag and ditty-box are to him what the privacy of the officer's room is to the latter, and it is, therefore, proper that he should enjoy as much comfort there as is possible under the peculiar circumstances of his life.

Under-clothing should be frequently changed. This does not require argument, yet it is a matter to which not the slightest attention is paid in the service. The officers' servants, landsmen, and many of the foreigners in the crew are habitually unclean, both in person and dress, and require careful supervision. Few of them provide themselves with proper outfits except by compulsion. They will keep a clean mustering suit, which they remove immediately after inspection, and a few clean articles in their bags to satisfy the quarterly examination of their contents, and will wear the same pair of drawers and socks for months. One of the most important duties of division officers is to attend to their men being properly provided with clothing, and it is equally important that, at every morning inspection at quarters, they should ascertain whether they are cleanly clad. It will soon be evident which men are habitually clean and neat, and which will require examination. Sufficiently frequent opportunities should be allowed for washing and drying clothes. At sea, unless the weather is very bad, this may be done daily; in port, twice a week. New navy-blue flannel requires frequent washing before the color ceases to come out, and men's skins and blankets are usually dyed an intense blue for several weeks when this is not done.

I have already insisted upon the necessity of keeping a vessel dry, and have indicated the means by which this object may be attained. I have omitted until this place to refer to the subject of damp clothing. Certain officers profess to believe it an attempt to make men delicate to insist that they shall remove their wet clothes, and point to the impunity with which some men continue in them for days. Where there is one such exception, there are many who succumb, sooner or later, and appear at the sick-bay. The French *Departement de la Marine* has not considered this matter unworthy of its interference. The *ordonnance* of August 15, 1851, prescribes that the watch officers shall see that the men do not keep on their wet clothes when their watch is over, and that they shall enter on the log all such accidental changes of dress. In bad weather, when the watch is piped down, and at all times when boats' crews return wet, let them be compelled to remove their wet clothes and deposit them in fire-tubs. The provision of outfit which I have recommended will allow three changes. Should the rain continue, and no occasion offer for drying the wet clothes, let each man remove his damp outershirt and trousers on turning in, and hang them on his hammock-hooks, to be resumed when he returns on deck. Men should not be allowed to expose themselves needlessly. Every one should be provided with a water-proof overcoat, and if the weather is not cold, be required to remove shoes and stockings. If too cold to go barefoot, boots should be worn. Similar precautions about wet feet should be exacted while washing decks. Few old sailors keep on their shoes when at this work, but landsmen and merchant sailors shipped for the first time, too lazy to take them off, will not do so unless compelled.

5 H

PERSONAL CLEANLINESS.

Occasionally a man notoriously filthy is ordered to be scrubbed in the head, or the negro servants are inspected during the morning watch by the master-at-arms; but beyond this, I have never witnessed nor heard of any inquiry by officers into the bodily condition of the crew. If a man's cutlass is bright and his overshirt clean, the inspecting officer is satisfied, although his axillæ, groins, and perinæum may be abominably dirty and verminous, his under-garments unclean and unchanged for weeks, and his bedding disgustingly foul and offensive. Even when some one with sensitive nostrils has obtained an order for the daily inspection of the ward-room boys, they are only compelled to strip to the waist, and if the collars of their shirts and wristbands are not very much soiled, they are pronounced clean, although their genitals, buttocks, and thighs have not been touched with water during the whole cruise. I have known officers' servants to come under treatment at the sick-bay, and to be discovered to have worn the same pair of drawers, night and day, for months.

It is not altogether the fault of the men that this is so. The human beast requires to be taught to be cleanly. Physicians know that sordid bodies, as well as sordid minds, are found even among the possessors of wealth and the occupants of prominent stations in society. Bring the rude, illiterate sailor, therefore, on board ship, still reeking with the foulness of the slums whence the land-shark has beguiled him, compel him to live, eat, and sleep uncleanly, deprive him of every semblance of personal comfort, never appeal to his reason or intelligence, but teach him that he is nothing but a slave or beast of burden—what result may be expected? Seamen are naturally careless. Left to themselves, they will neglect themselves. Some few men-of-war's men are exceptions, but the great majority of patients admitted into the naval hospitals from before the mast are shamefully unclean. Always the first, and sometimes the only, prescription they require is a warm bath and clean shift of clothing. What physician would ever think of attempting to accomplish a diaphoretic effect upon the begrimed, callous, hide-like cuticle of most sailors, until he has dissolved off as much as possible of it with warm water and soap, or borax? Yet I have heard officers frequently joke about the appearance of these dirt-encased fellows, and laughingly describe them as "veritable old shell-backs," or as "covered with barnacles."

Ninety per cent. of the men presenting themselves at the naval rendezvous are filthy in person, and every medical officer should refuse to examine them in such a condition ; and even after passing them he should direct them to bathe again before reporting on board the receiving-ship, otherwise they will remain dirty, will be transferred to some sea-going vessel in the same state. vermin on their bodies and in their hair, and they will continue so until they are discharged or become sick and are sent to a naval hospital and subjected to a compulsory bath.

When swimming is possible or allowed, usually about twenty or thirty of the crew avail themselves of it as a diversion, but months sometimes intervene between these opportunities. The customary usual time for washing is during the morning watch, after the decks are "holy-stoned." Some of the men strip to the waist and wash their necks, arms, breasts, axillæ, and feet, but the greater number do not. Scarcely any ever cleanse their thighs, groins, or buttocks. Officers of divisions are responsible for the unclean condition of their men. They should require them to present themselves at the morning inspection, not only with clean outer-apparel, but with clean under-clothing and clean skins. They can perform this duty without any abasement of dignity. It is less disagreeable for the division officer to make this inspection than for the medical officer to conduct an examination of a patient who has fistula ani, or to labor by the hour to dilate his strictured urethra. Many duties are unpleasant, but the object in view should reconcile us to their performance. Very properly, in ports where prostitutes are subject to examination, no man is allowed access to them until the medical officers are satisfied of his own exemption from venereal disease, and no greater outrage is committed upon the man's modesty when he is required to satisfy the officer of his division that he is clean in person. False modesty cloaks both vice and dirt, and the man who makes the loudest outcry about outraged sensibilities will be found to have the strongest reasons for avoiding exposure. Habitually clean men will very soon be discovered and relieved from examination; others will be shamed into an attention to their persons that they had never been taught at home nor seen practiced elsewhere; while the incorrigibly foul will be isolated and cleansed by force. It is not proposed that the men at quarters shall unbutton their pantaloons and submit to a close scrutiny of every square inch of their surfaces every day; but their spare underclothing should be frequently and carefully inspected. Provision should be made to allow general ablution by every man on board, and the divisional officer should satisfy himself in as private and delicate a manner as possible that this has actually and thoroughly been done. No man should be allowed to remain, as is often the case, for weeks with his skin of a deep-blue color from the dye-stuff of his rarely-washed new flannel shirt and drawers, and, in tropical climates, daily general ablution should be exacted of every member of the crew. If objection is made to the construction of a proper permanent bathing apparatus, a large firetub may be placed under the top-gallant forecastle, or in the manger, or in some other convenient situation, and surrounded by a screen, or the head-pump may be screened at certain times in the day and devoted to this purpose. In vessels where condensed water can be obtained in quantities, this should be used in preference to salt-water. Every man should be required to possess one or more towels, which should appear among the paymaster's stores, and facilities should be afforded every day for drying them. If a "sweat-rag," as the little piece of sheeting is termed, which some men use, is now seen flying anywhere to dry, it is immediately ordered down, even while the spans of the quarter-boats are fluttering with officers' towels. When the clothes-lines are not up, the men usually spread their "sweat-rags" upon their shoulders and back, and dry them there.

The hair, beard, and teeth are all neglected on board ship. It would be a difficult matter to compel old sailors to cleanse their teeth, but all the boys should be obliged to purchase tooth-brushes, and to use them regularly.

Firemen and coal-heavers should be compelled to bathe every day, when the vessel is steaming, but not immediately after quitting their stations. Cardiac diseases, pulmonary affections, acute inflammations, etc., are common among this class from their imprudent exposure to cool draughts, and from washing with cold water while their bodies are heated. The engineer on duty should attend personally to the disposition of men who come off watch, and not allow them to throw themselves under the ventilators, nor to bathe until a proper time has elapsed.

FOOD.

No objection can be urged against the quantity of food furnished by the Government, nor, if inspectors continue to do their duty as faithfully as at present, to its quality. That enough is supplied by the ration is evidenced by the amount thrown overboard by the cooks, and by the fact that there are few messes which do not commute one or more of their rations. The Government authorizes this to the extent of two rations for every ten men. It is idle to speculate upon the amount of carbon, oxygen, hydrogen, and nitrogen required to supply the waste of the body, and to endeavor to arrive, by chemical analysis, at the precise number of grains a man should be given to eat. The molecular waste of tissue depends upon climate, physical exertion, and health; but the naval ration undoubtedly supplies the maximum under any circumstances. The robust appearance of an American man-of-war's crew attests this fact, as do the zest and exclamations of surprise and delight with which foreign sailors partake of it when invited. In the French navy each man receives less than half a pound (214 grammes) of meat a day, and only 3.3 pounds (1,500 grammes) of animal food (beef, bacon, and cheese) and 16.5 pounds (7.5 kilogrammes) of vegetable substances (beans, peas, and rice) a week. In the American service each man gets every week from six and a half pounds of the former (beef, pork, and preserved meats) at sea, to eight and three-quarters pounds of fresh meat in port, and eleven of vegetables, (beans, rice, flour, dried fruit, desiccated potatoes, and mixed vegetables,) with a liberal allowance of sugar, molasses, vinegar, and pickles. This ration has been instituted sufficiently long for its effects upon the health on long cruises to be manifested.

That the former ration was not exactly what the human body required for its healthy maintenance was evident from the disturbances occasioned by its persistent use; but on two days on which salt beef and rice were then served out, preserved meats and vegetables are now substituted. The change leaves scarcely any other improvements to be suggested, except a more frequent issue of preserved beef or other meat in lieu of salt, an increase in the allowance of coffee and butter, and a further extension of variety in vegetables by the occasional substitution of peaches, sauer-kraut, and cranberries for dried apples. With these exceptions it is probably the best that can be devised, for temperate climates at least, to meet all the requirements of economy of space, capability of resisting decomposition, palatability and alimentariness, until experiments now being made with the object of preserving fresh meat by the abstraction of its moisture, allow the total abolition of salt meat as an article of diet. Dr. Alexander Rattray, surgeon Royal Navy, in an admirable report published by the admiralty, in their annual volume on the health of the British navy, has called attention to the injurious consequences of the use of salted meat, which he correctly styles an unnatural form of food, and which he recommends to be almost entirely displaced by preserved meat. Commanding officers should eagerly embrace every occasion of going into port or of speaking vessels at sea to obtain supplies of fresh meat and succulent vegetables. One pound and a quarter of fresh or three-quarters of a pound of preserved meat, which should not always be beef, may be substituted for a pound of salt; one pound of soft bread or of flour for the daily allowance of ship-biscuit; and fresh vegetables not to exceed in value the dried. When the stay in port is prolonged beyond a fortnight, salt food may be issued twice a week. Dr. Rattray has proposed a radical change in the British naval dietary, arranging it for temperate and tropical climates, for harbor and for sea. One prolific source of the disease in the Navy, on notoriously unhealthy tropical stations, is the neglect to adapt the diet, dress, and labor to the necessities of the climate.   Englishmen have been performing a great physiological experiment for many years in every quarter of the globe in their extensive colonial dependencies.   Carrying their national customs wherever they have intruded themselves, they have dressed, eaten, slept, and generally lived as they were accustomed in their own foggy island, with results that are now matters of scientific history.   The red-coated, leather neck-cased, over-laden soldier is not so often seen marching under a mid-day Indian sun; but despite all lessons, the wealthy Englishman, male and female, dines at seven off as many courses, drinks beer and brandy and soda, and goes home with "liver."   The Japan Weekly Mail, of Yokohama, for August 12, 1871, refers to a recent instance of culpable violation of sanitary laws by military authorities, for which the medical officers were in no way responsible, in the following terms:

The old story again!   The weary old story of life sacrificed, but sacrificed for nothing—to appease no gods ; to propitiate no demon; to gain no laurels; to chastise no enemy; to procure no benefit; to afford no example; to inspire no devotion.   Any moderately sensible judge of human affairs might have dreaded some such a catastrophe as has overtaken the Tenth Regiment and the newly-landed battalion of marines, which has arrived to relieve it.   The regiment is moved in marching order in the heavy clothes which a tropical climate converts into shirts of Nessus, with knapsacks, arms, and full paraphernalia.   They may have been moved on empty stomachs, but what with parade, the march to the quay, and the time required for getting on board, they are for three hours exposed to the sun before they get food or arrive under the shelter of an awning.   Meanwhile the plague has begun.   The full-blooded men are smitten with heat-apoplexy, and the wonder is that more do not succumb to the enemy.   Three good men fell victims to that march—men who had been long in the regiment, and who might have lived to feel the pride of belonging to it.   On the same day the marines, who have replaced them, come under the same fatal influences.   Three were struck down.   One is dead, others are in a dangerous state, and their recovery doubtful.   Now it is clear that coddling soldiers is absurd, but you cannot inure men to a hot sun by exposing them to its deadly rays.   You may gradually acclimatize them, and after all this you must handle them in the sun as in the presence of an enemy whom you may, with certain precautions, defy, but whom you cannot conquer. You must avoid him to the uttermost.   In war it may be necessary to face him ; in peace it can hardly be so.   The whole question is one of management and administration. The regiment was incontestably in good order; but why was it moved in August, with the thermometer at ninety, and the ominous typhoon-fly hovering about?

It is a physiological impossibility for the sailor at Singapore, Batavia, Hong-Kong, or Maranham to eat the same kind and quantity of food as at Kittery or Boston, where he shipped, and remain healthy and efficient. Messes in the tropics should, therefore, be allowed, advised, and encouraged to commute parts of the ration of meat for vegetables, especially rice, at sea, and for fruits and fresh vegetables when in port. Most messes stop one or more entire rations and draw their value in money, either to pay their several cooks, which should be prevented by not allowing "steady" cooks, or to create a fund for the purchase of potatoes, turnips, onions, or other vegetables as sea-stores, which should be encouraged, and conveniences afforded by the authorities of the ship for their storage in the boats, under the boom-cover, or elsewhere on the spar-deck. They enter into the composition of the morning "scouse," which is the favorite dish of the sailor, and they are better antiscorbutics than anything in the dispensary. When one has been a month at sea a roasted "spud" (potato) is relished with an avidity that only a man starved of his natural aliment can experience, and a plentiful supply of this vegetable will render unnecessary any large provision of lime or lemon-juice, or any other medicinal antidote to scurvy. It is commonly but erroneously believed that this disease has disappeared from the Navy. Medical Inspector Wilson, in his Naval Hygiene, relates two instances, during his experience, of the development of the scorbutic tendency on shipboard, the first occurring on the frigate Savannah, on her return from California during the Mexican war, and the second on board one of the vessels of the Japan expedition during her passage from New York to the Straits of Sunda. I have also had to treat the disease, the first time while attached to the sloop-of-war Levant, which, as in Dr. Wilson's second instance, was making a passage from New York to China via the Straits of Sunda, and again on board the Idaho in 1868, while *en route* for Japan by way of the Ombay passage. Short stoppages were made in both cases at Rio de Janeiro and at Cape Town, but the crews were not allowed liberty on shore, and consequently did not experience that indescribable but marked benefit which undoubtedly results from simple contact with the earth, the deprivation of which may be ranked with the want of fresh vegetable food as one of the efficient causes of the disease. The passage of the Levant was stormy, the men were exposed to continued rains and cold, their labor was arduous, and almost every article of the ration was badly spoiled. After a delay of only two days at Anjer, the ship resumed her course to Hong-Kong, where she arrived on the one hundred and eighty-third day from New York, a passage greatly exceeded by the Idaho, which did not anchor at Nagasaki until the two hundredth day. In neither of these cases did the disease manifest itself by those terrible symptoms formerly supposed to be essentially diagnostic. There were few individuals who sought to be excused from duty, but the general condition of the whole crew was below par; they performed their duties listlessly and slowly, and were cursed for being morose and lazy; they lost strength and appetite; their bodies were covered with mottled discolorations; their gums were tender and bled easily, causing those who chewed to attribute it to the tobacco, for which they lost taste; scratches, wounds, and bruises healed slowly or not at all; and men, often of the finest normal physique, succumbed readily to trifling causes of disease. Large numbers were subsequently invalided, whose disabilities really began at this time, and the actual money loss to the Government was far greater than would have been the expense caused by a few days' longer sojourn in port. Sporadic cases of scurvy appeared the current month, (November, 1871,) on board of several of the Russian escort squadron during their wet and stormy passage from Madeira to New York, though it was not protracted much beyond a month. A further delay at sea would have certainly been followed by serious consequences.

In foreign ports, bumboats attend all vessels whose crews are permitted to draw any portion of their pay. A small allowance of money, conditional upon good behavior, should always be made for this purpose, since the men have no other way of obtaining the fruits of the countries they may visit, and which in tropical climates ought to enter largely into their diet. Excessive indulgence, however, particularly on first joining a station, must be carefully guarded against. In some bumboats, which should always be inspected by the medical officer that no unripe fruit nor other improper articles may be offered for sale, boiled eggs, broiled chickens, fried fish, steaks, etc., are prepared, which the sailor, cloyed with the unvarying boil of the coppers, relishes exceedingly, and which it is highly proper he should be permitted to enjoy. A watchful and comprehensive hygiene neglects no occasion of catering to the native instincts of the body, in violation of which the seaman lives, and of recalling the customs of civilized life, from which he is unnaturally severed.

Besides vegetables, eggs, properly packed, might be allowed to be purchased by the several messes as sea-stores. They can easily be fried before the galley is given up to the officers' cooks, and they make a palatable morning meal. The practice of carrying live-stock to sea is of doubtful propriety. It encumbers the decks, diminishes the air-space, impoverishes the atmosphere, creates filth, and becomes diseased, while it benefits a very small proportion of the persons on board. Fowls are more easily kept clean and healthy than other live food, but their flesh is not superior in flavor or nutrient properties, nor better relished even by the sick, than that properly canned. This is especially true of the poor emaciated sheep and calves, which are sometimes killed for food after six or eight weeks' fright and torture on board a rolling ship. An exception may be made in the case of the large green turtle, which, whenever obtainable, should be taken to sea to be made into soup for the whole ship's company.

It seems to escape officers of the Navy that the *cooking* of the sailor's food has anything to do with its nutritive value or palatability. The ship's cook is appointed without any special questioning as to his ability to perform his duties, which, however, are of the simplest character. Everything given the sailor is boiled in the coppers, except in port, when some of the mess-cooks, by arrangement with the cabin or ward-room cooks, succeed in getting a piece of meat or a fowl roasted. The craving of the sailor for change is shown by the popularity of the scouses, which some commanding officers are thoughtful enough to encourage by allowing the range an extra supply of wood. Our galleys are not very commendable exhibitions of American inventive talent. It is certainly not impossible to contrive an apparatus possessing facilities for roasting meat and baking bread. In this matter, as in every other within the province of hygiene, the French are far in advance of all other nations. The *"cuisine distillatoire"* of Peyer and Rocher combines an oven for baking with an apparatus for distilling fresh water from salt, the coppers being at the same time heated by the steam, which is in process of condensation into fresh water. Freshly-baked bread, when properly made, ought to be substituted for biscuit whenever possible.

It is the duty of the officer of the deck to inspect the dinner prior to the serving out at seven bells' in the forenoon watch, As now conducted this inspection is a mere form. The ship's cook brings a mess-pan to the mast containing the choicest piece of meat from the coppers, which the officer of the watch inspects by cutting off a slice or two as a lunch. This duty should be performed by some other officer, preferably one of the medical corps, and the inspection should extend to all the messes and to all the food at every meal. The fresh soups are sometimes so badly made, the vegetables not being half cooked nor the meat properly boiled, that it is common for sailors to attribute to them all their digestive irregularities in port; yet some cooks are so expert in making these soups that officers find them very palatable as their own noonday meal. At sea the same complaint is general with regard to bean-soup. Sometimes this is due to the inferior quality of the beans, occasionally to the hardness of the water, but most frequently to the neglect to soak them properly (a whole day being sometimes necessary) in cold water and to boil them sufficiently long. Cooks often have the water in the coppers boiling before they add the meat for the soup, ignorant of the fact that the flavor and nutritious qualities of the latter depend upon the extraction of the soluble p rinciples of the meat, which only takes place when it is put in cold water and that slowly heated. On "duff" days, it is very proper to boil the water before the beef is added, since it is thereby prevented from yielding all its nutrient qualities to the water and is consequently more tender, juicy, and palatable. The "harness-cask," in which the meat is thrown after it has been issued by the pay-master's subordinates, and where it remains until ready to go into the coppers, is often imperfectly cleansed and allowed to become dirty from the accumulation of stale brine. It should be carefully and thoroughly washed after every using, and the master-at-arms should be required to inspect it daily with the coppers and all the cooking-utensils at the galley and the mess-things of the berth-deck cooks.

The tea and coffee especially require examination into the method of their preparation. Frequently they are such abominable mixtures that even the men refuse them, while there is no part of their ration of which they are more fond, none which is of greater importance to their well-being, nor any which is so easily prepared. Tea-water should be issued to the mess-cooks boiling, not more than ten minutes before the hour for the meal, and the mess-kettle should be kept tightly covered until the beverage is served out. Properly, coffee should be made by the ship's cook at the galley, and only issued a few minutes before breakfast is piped. As nutritive properties are of more importance to the sailor than delicacy of flavor and aroma, which he probably would not appreciate, it would be well to preserve a portion of the tea-leaves and coffee-grounds from each meal for addition to the ration of the following.

The usefulness of tea, coffee, and alcohol in the form of wine. beer, or whisky, as food-stimuli or accessory food, has been satisfactorily established by Anstie, Lankester, and others. An old writer, whose wisdom has never been questioned, epitomizes in Ecclesiasticus, chap. xxxix, v. 26, with a scientific precision to which the learning of nearly thirty centuries has but little to add: " The principal things for the whole use of man's life are water, fire, iron, and salt, flour of wheat, honey, milk, and *the blood of the grape*, and oil and clothing;" adding significantly in v. 27, "All these things are for good to the godly; so to the sinners they are turned into evil." The frightful consequences of intemperate indulgence in alcoholic liquors have resulted in the abolition of the spirit portion of the ration. If the substitution of a pint of beer or half a pint of wine for the gill of spirits, which the Department used to authorize, could have been effected, there is no doubt of the propriety and benefit of its issue. The objectionable feature of the old service of grog was that it was drank undiluted and upon an empty stomach. The moral argument that it engendered and fostered a fondness for intoxicating liquors applied only to boys and a few landsmen, most sailors, firemen, and marines having already acquired the taste and habit before entering the service. It is doubtful whether even three years of enforced total abstinence could destroy the appetite in the confirmed inebriate. In such cases the land-shark and prostitute can nullify in half an hour the resolutions of years. There are few medical officers in the Navy whose experience cannot furnish instances of officers of rank and education who have repeatedly violated the most solemn pledges and oaths to abstain from rum-drinking. Liberty on shore is so frequent, and the license allowed drunkenness on such occasions, through the neglect to punish its habitual occurrence, so general, that the mere abolition of the grog ration has, probably, accomplished little toward the checking of intemperance on board ship. Even under the old system, the opportunity to commute the grog for money to be spent in the bumboat or on shore was extensively embraced. On board a sloop-of-war having a complement of one hundred and sixty men, I have known only forty to drink

their grog.   Nevertheless, many excellent seamen have, undoubtedly, been deterred from shipping in the Navy, in consequence of
the commutation of the grog, and I am well satisfied that the majority of such men were not injured by the regular consumption
of the moderate quantity of spirits they received.   Fortunately,
tea, coffee, and tobacco, to a large extent, accomplish the same
results as alcohol.   Under their use the sailor better endures
fatigue and the vicissitudes of climate, is more cheerful in
mind, is better nourished, and in tropical regions experiences
less desire to eat an excess of meat.   Gasparin long ago called
attention to the fact that the Belgian miners performed their
arduous toil and maintained their robustness and health with a
diet notoriously scant, in consequence of the daily use of coffee;
and Anstie has adduced numerous instances "where the support
of the organism, in the absence of ordinary food, by stimulants,
(that is, agents which, by their direct action, tend to rectify some
deficient or too redundant material action or tendency,) is one of
the most .remarkable phenomena which can be offered to the
attention of the physiologist."   Von Tschudi relates that an
Indian, sixty-two years of age, worked for him (at excavation)
for five days and nights consecutively, without any ordinary food
at all, and with a very short allowance of sleep, and yet, at the
end of that time, was fresh enough to undergo a long journey,
simply because he was supported by the coca, which he chewed
from time to time.   He declares that the moderate eaters of coca
are long-lived men, and that they perform extremely hard labor,
upon a very little food, as miners, soldiers, etc., and he mentions
the fact that the custom of coca-chewing is of immemorial an-
tiquity in Peru; and Anstie adds: "Next, perhaps, to coca, in its
power of replacing ordinary food, we must reckon tobacco, and
next to tobacco in efficacy as a supplementary food, and far sur-
passing it in its effectiveness under certain circumstances, is
alcohol."   I do not desire to advocate the reissue of a daily
ration of grog.   Provision, however, should. be made for its
proper use in emergencies, as when the crew are exposed to a

long continuance of bad weather, and especially when the rolling
of the vessel prevents the lighting of the galley-fire and the
preparation of coffee or tea, when they have been more than thirty
days at sea and begin to manifest the consequent ill-effects of the
salt ration, or when they are subjected to intense mental or
physical effort, as in time of shipwreck, fire, or action. There is
no doubt that under such circumstances tobacco-chewers and
smokers find a mental and physical sustenance for which other
men instinctively and painfully crave; and we need not hesitate
to refuse to join the pseudo-moral crusade which would deprive
the sailor of the solace and support of his pipe and quid, when
so learned a therapeutist as Pereira declares, " I am not acquainted
with any well-ascertained ill-effects resulting from the habitual
practice of smoking." A similar observation is made by Dr.
Christison; and Hammond, whose carefully conducted experiments upon himself have conclusively established the physiological effects of these agents, states, " I have no hesitation in expressing my opinion that, in the great majority of cases, the moderate use of alcohol and tobacco is calculated to exert a beneficial effect upon the organism. This use, like that of every other
good thing which we have, must be guided by wisdom. To
transgress the laws of our being in the employment of these substances leads just as surely to punishment as the violation of any
other sanitary or physiological law. Like everything else capable of producing great good, alcohol can also cause great harm.
Our object should be to secure the one and provide against the
other. I am decidedly of the opinion that tobacco is beneficial
to those who, like soldiers, have a great deal of mental and bodily fatigue to undergo. But these remarks apply only to the moderate use. When employed to excess, there is no doubt that it
predisposes to neuralgia, vertigo, indigestion, and other affections
of the nervous, circulatory, and digestive organs." Dr. Gray,
writing on the medical aspect of the tobacco question, states that
" tobacco should be used as supplementary to food, not as a substitute for it. The season, therefore, for healthy smoking is after

a meal. Against moderate smoking, by a healthy person who enjoys it, not a single argument of any weight has yet been advanced." For those who are debarred from using tobacco and alcohol, an extra issue of coffee on turning out, and occasionally during .the night watches, will supply the demand of the system when it is improperly or insufficiently nourished.

Though comparatively little fault can be found with the component parts of the ration, the same is not true of the arrangement of meals. The usual hour for breakfast is 8 o'clock; for dinner, at noon; and for supper, 4 o'clock. By this system men eat three times within eight hours, and fast all the rest of the day. The objections to it are evident. Economy of fuel is no excuse for a practice that is so contrary to the simplest teachings of hygiene and common sense. It is far more easy to provide a larger quantity of wood and coal before setting out than to teach a man's stomach to regulate its functions according to the arbitrary dictum of his "superior officer." After the supper, the sailor gets nothing to eat for *sixteen* hours, although his most arduous duties frequently occur within that period, and although the craving for food is manifest even in officers, who eat their last meal so much later, and yet universally require the caterers of their messes to provide them a lunch before going on deck during the night and morning watches. At sea the labors of the night are probably more frequently laborious than those of the day; while in port the vessel may have been brought to anchor or gotten under way, and in the morning hammocks have to be scrubbed, clothes washed, and decks "holy-stoned;" and all this with an empty stomach. In hot climates, both men and officers always feel listless and indisposed for exertion in the morning, when a slight repast would give them the energy to perform their duties properly. Hammond advises that "soldiers should always be fed before they are sent to drills, parades, or other labor," and Macleod declares that he has little doubt that, if the precaution had been taken to supply the troops in the Crimea every morning with hot coffee, much of their mortality might have been avoided. I

6 II

therefore recommend that every man may be served a cup of coffee and piece of bread immediately after turning out, and that breakfast be eaten at 7 o'clock, dinner at noon, and supper at 6 o'clock, the dinner hour of many cabin and ward-room messes. In port all hands turn out at daylight, and should then have their bread and hot coffee; at sea, the morning watch comes on deck at 4 o'clock, and should be allowed coffee as soon as it can be made. The other watch is called with "all hands" at 7 o'clock, the hour I propose for breakfast. To give them time to lash and stow their hammocks, wash, and dress before breakfast, they should be called at ten or fifteen minutes before 7, in which quarter of an hour they will be able to do all they are required. The range should be given up to the berth-deck cooks to make scouses until fifteen minutes before 7 o'clock, which is early enough for the officers' cooks to begin their breakfast. In bad weather, unless the ship rolls too heavily for safety, or when the work is very arduous, fire should be kept in the galley and hot coffee served out to the middle and morning watches. It is getting to be a custom to light the galley-fire in the morningwatch, to make the officer of the deck his cup of coffee, when the ship's and officers' cooks take advantage of the opportunity to prepare coffee, which they retail to such men as are able or willing to pay their charges; but this is done surreptitiously, at an expense to the men which they cannot always afford, and in the cases of the officers' cooks at the cost of the officers, whose private stores supply the materials used. To prevent this fraud and to enable every one of the crew to be benefited by the procedure, the Government should make it a regular daily issue; or, if objection is urged to the increased cost of the ration, such a charge should be determined upon by the paymaster as will purchase the coffee required. I have known instances of ships' cooks who have amassed several thousand dollars during a cruise, by irregular sales, principally of coffee.

An improvement should be made in the furniture of the messes. Everything is repulsive about the sailor's mess-cloth, where each

man is using his fingers and the jack-knife with which he may
have been scraping masts or cleaning tar-buckets. A few
cheap, strong knives and forks, block-tin plates, cups, etc., might
be included among the paymaster's small stores. The British
sailor receives his mess-utensils from the government gratis. In
large ships, tables and camp-stools are provided for the men, and
might appropriately be made a part of the outfit of every vessel,
care being taken to stow them, when not in use, so as not to encroach on the air-space of the berth-deck.

The medical officers should frequently visit the messes and
inquire into everything relating to their subsistence. This duty
is especially enjoined upon the surgeon by paragraph 534 of the
Regulations for the Government of the United States Navy for
1870, and which, so far as the medical officer is concerned in his
character of physician, is the most important in the book. Hence
I quote it, and urge upon the young assistant surgeon the necessity of pondering seriously upon the grave responsibilities it devolves upon him:

He (the surgeon) shall inspect the provisions for the crew, and report to
the commanding officer when he may discover any that are unsound. He
will also cause the purity of the water to be tested before it is received into
the tanks, and he will make known to the commanding officer any want of
care or cleanliness in the preparation of food for the crew, or any instance of
personal neglect with regard to it, of which he may be cognizant. He will
also make known to the commanding officer everything which may come to
his knowledge as conducive to, or as militating against, the general health and
comfort of the ship's company.

Although these sanitary functions are manifestly among the
legitimate duties of the physician, the Navy Department, in these
instructions, very properly directs particular attention to them,
and every medical officer should be held strictly accountable for
the consequences of any violation of a proper hygiene which he
may have neglected to investigate and report.

POTABLE WATER.

Physiologists estimate that the daily loss of fluid by cutaneous and pulmonary exhalation is from one and three-quarters to five pounds; that of the thirty or forty ounces of urine excreted only two to seven per cent. are solid; and that seventy-five per cent. of the fæcal discharge of the twenty-four hours, which averages from four to six ounces, is water—a total loss of fluid every day of from three and a half to seven and a half pounds. The customary allowance of water on ship-board is one gallon a day for each person, of which half is given to the ship's cook for the coppers, and the balance put into the scuttle-butt for drinking. This allowance is sufficient under ordinary circumstances, but during hot weather the water is all drank up in the forenoon, and the landsmen and boys, who have been less employed than the rest of the crew, usually drink a disproportionate share. While, therefore, the issue of water should never be less than a gallon a day in temperate latitudes, this amount should be largely increased whenever the crew are exposed to unusual fatigue or to prolonged heat. The listless, careless way in which the men go through their exercises in tropical climates, is as much due to the stint of water as to the direct depressing effect of heat. According to Parkes, "the supply of water becomes a matter of the most urgent necessity when men are undergoing great muscular efforts, as it is absolutely impossible that these efforts can be continued without it. If we reflect on the immense loss of water by the skin and lungs which attends any great physical exertion, we shall see that to make up for this loss is imperative; and it is very important that this loss should be made up continually by small quantities of water being constantly taken, and not by any large amount at any one time."

An article which enters so intimately into the composition of the animal economy, which permeates every tissue, and forms the basis of the various circulating media, which has so much to do with the reparation of the body and the normal performance of its functions, should be as free as possible from nocuous qualities. The terrible mortality of the old-time vessels was due as much to the excess of saline and the presence of .putrescent matters in their water as to the neglect of any other of the measures which hygiene demonstrates to be indispensable to health. To this effect Pereira quotes a report of the British secretary of state for the home department: "The beneficial effects derived from care as to the qualities of water is now proved in the navy, where fatal dysentery formerly prevailed to an immense extent in consequence of the impure and putrid state of the supplies." Though a certain amount of saline constituents is essential to good potable water, a very slight excess of any one salt will occasion grave disturbance of health. Carpenter relates an instance where serious detriment to the health of a neighborhood was occasioned by using the water of a well containing only five grains of saline matters to the pint. According to Christison one two-thousandth of its weight of saline ingredients (thirty-five grains in the imperial gallon) renders water unfit for domestic purposes. French writers have incontestably shown that the intestinal disorders, which were common among the inmates of certain hospitals and prisons of Paris, were directly traceable to the use of well-waters containing calcium and magnesium sulphates. Parkes refers to the prevalence of diarrhœa on the Cape frontier stations, under his own observations, from the use of brackish water; the deleterious effects of our western river-waters on non-residents are widely known; and there is no doubt that malignant cholera is principally, if not exclusively, as Dr. Snow taught, transmitted through the medium of drinking-water.

So much, then, depending on the character of the water, it should never be received on board ship for drinking and culinary purposes until it has been submitted to the medical officers, faithfully and carefully examined by them, and pronounced potable. Notwithstanding the very serious interests involved, this subject has not received a tittle of the attention it deserves. Most medical officers, when notified that water is about to be taken on board, direct their apothecaries to add a piece of crystalized nitrate of silver to a tumblerful of the water, and if the precipitate produced is not a positive cloud filling the tumbler, and the taste not markedly brackish, consent to pass it. Frequently, this is the extent of the chemical means they have at hand, but the careless manner in which even this test is applied renders it practically useless. The taste of water, on which so much reliance is ordinarily placed, is a very unsafe guide, since, according to Parkes, " organic matter, when dissolved, is often quite tasteless; 55 grains of carbonate of soda and 70 of chloride of sodium per gallon are imperceptible; 10 grains of carbonate of lime give no taste; 25 grains of sulphate of lime very little; " yet, a potable water, according to the same authority, should never contain more than 20 grains of carbonate nor 10 of chloride of sodium, 16 of carbonate nor 3 of sulphate of lime, nor 3 of the carbonate and sulphate of magnesia.

Water, to be potable, does not require to be chemically pure. The stomach instinctively loathes water freshly distilled, rainwater recently fallen, and the water formed by the melting of ice and snow. The eminent hygienist Guerard describes good potable water as "limpid, temperate in winter, cool in summer, inodorous, of an agreeable taste. It should dissolve soap without forming clots; be fit for cooking dried beans; hold in solution a proper quantity of air, carbonic acid gas, and mineral substances; these last not exceeding 0.5 gramme to the litre, (35 grains per gallon.) Finally, it should be free from organic matters."

The river-waters, from which our principal naval stations are supplied, contain a far less proportion of saline constituents than this. According to Professor Barker, "the purest water supplied to any city in this country is that from Lake Cochituate, which supplies Boston, which contains but 3.11 grains (solid matter) in one gallon. The Schuylkill water (Philadelphia) contains 3.50 grains; Ridgewood, (Brooklyn,) 3.92; the Croton, (New York,) 4.78; Lake Michigan, (Chicago,) 6.68; the water which supplies Albany, 10.78." European rivers are seldom so pure. The Loire, Garonne, and Danube average about 10 grains; the Rhine 12; the Rhone 13; the Seine, Scheldt, and Thames range from 16 to 30. Fonssagrives restricts the proportion of salts which a potable water should contain to from 0.10 to 0.20 gramme per litre, (7 to 14 grains per gallon;) "beyond this the water is hard, indigestible, and unfit for cooking vegetables." Christison considers a water to be hard which contains one four-thousandth part, or 17½ grains of saline matter to the gallon, and says that that which contains not more than 14 grains will lather with soap, and may therefore be used for washing. The absolute amount of saline substances is, however, of less practical importance than the quantity of each particular salt, since a small amount of calcium sulphate will render a water harder than twice or thrice as much of alkaline carbonates, and if organic matters are also present, the reduction of the sulphate will render the water offensive from the disengagement of hydrogen sulphide.

The saline ingredients of ordinary river-water are principally the chlorides, sulphates, carbonates, and phosphates of sodium and calcium, the chloride, bromide, carbonate, and sulphate of magnesium, the chloride and sulphate of potassium, a little silica, oxide of iron, and occasionally other metallic salts. Of these, sodium chloride and calcium carbonate and sulphate form the largest proportion.

The medical officer of a man-of-war has no need to attempt a complete analysis of water, for which, indeed, he will have neither time, place, nor appliances, in conducting his examination as to its fitness for drinking and culinary purposes, but he should never give his consent to the reception on board ship of any water which does not possess the physical properties enumerated by Guerard, which curdles a standard solution of soap, which decolorizes a standard dilute solution of potassium permanganate, and which gives more than a faint white precipitate, insoluble in nitric acid, with silver nitrate, barium chloride, and ammonium oxalate. Most common waters have an alkaline reaction from calcium carbonate, held in solution by carbon di-oxide, but this gas is expelled by ebullition, the carbonate is precipitated, and forms the ordinary lining crust of tea-kettles. "Six grains per gallon of a lime-salt give a turbidity with oxalate of ammonia; sixteen grains a considerable precipitate; thirty grains a very large precipitate." "As only two grains per gallon of carbonate of lime can remain in solution after boiling, a large precipitate on the subsequent addition of another portion of the oxalate will show that the sulphate or chloride of lime is present." "Four grains per gallon of chloride of sodium give a turbidity with an acidulated solution of nitrate of silver; ten grains a slight precipitate; twenty grains a considerable precipitate." Sulphates to the amount of one or even one and a half grains per gallon give no precipitate with chloride of barium; at first, or on standing, three grains give a haze, and after a time a slight precipitate; above this amount the precipitate is pretty well marked."—(Parkes.)

Fortunately, there is now very little difficulty in obtaining a sufficient supply of excellent potable water at the principal resorts of our naval vessels, to obviate the necessity of watering ship with impure water—a necessity which, in the case of steamers, of course, never can exist. In some tropical sea-ports, as Anjer, where the water is necessarily largely impregnated with vegetable matter, filtered water may be obtained at a small charge, and I was once witness of the lamentable consequences of a commanding officer's refusal, through a mistaken spirit of economy, to incur this expense. Parkes quotes as a curious fact from Davis, in reference to the West Indies, that ships' crews, when ordered to Tortola, were "invariably seized with fluxes, which were caused by the water. But the inhabitants, who used tank (rain) water, were free; and so well known was this, that when any resident at Tortola was invited to dinner on board a man-of-war, it was no unusual thing for him to carry his drinking-water with him."

Should it become necessary to obtain water from unknown places, the medical officer should always examine its source, means of transit, preservation, etc. It is manifestly improper to fill up from stagnant pools, shaded and sluggish streams, marshes, mineral springs, etc., nor should any springs or wells ever be completely exhausted. During the late war I have known whole tanks rendered unfit for drinking by the final addition of a cask obtained by the exhaustion of a spring. Rain-water, though largely aerated, is insipid from deficiency of salts, while melted ice and snow lack both the necessary gaseous and mineral ingredients, and require the same treatment as distilled water to be potable. Captain Cook's attempt to water ship from an iceberg resulted disastrously to the health of his crew. Snow itself does not assuage thirst, and absorbs ammonia in such quantities that its ingestion is often attended with dangerous and, in several cases of children, fatal consequences.

Boat expeditions or exploring parties on land may sometimes be compelled to use only such water as they can get, when the preferable mode of purifying it will be by filtration through sand and charcoal. Water containing principally organic matters in solution is rapidly purified by means of potassium permanganate. Calcareous waters, containing the carbonate, may be improved by the addition of pure lime-water, which combines with the solvent, $(CO_2,)$ and precipitates it as carbonate, along with the rest of that salt which it had held in solution. Water containing calcium sulphate in excess is more objectionable than that holding an excess of carbonate, for though the addition of bicarbonate of sodium will likewise throw down the lime carbonate, the sodium sulphate left in solution gives the water a disagreeable taste and unpleasant laxative qualities. The objection to the popular French plan of purifying turbid water, entitled "*alunage de l'eau,*" which simply consisted in the addition of a small quantity of alum, was that, while clarifying the water, it merely converted the lime carbonate into sulphate, which remained in solution, and rendered the water worse than before. Youatt says that the horse, "through instinct or experience, will leave the most transparent and pure (?) water of the well for a river, although the water may be turbid, and even for the muddiest pool."

A common source of impurity in water brought on board ship is the leakage of the water-boat, casks, or tanks, in which it is conveyed from on shore. These are frequently old, are seldom or imperfectly cleansed, not properly calked and lined, or are open to salt spray or to the swashing of salt-water into the pump-well. A pint of sea-water contains from three hundred and six to three hundred and fifteen grains of saline substances, while less than two grains in that quantity are the most that can be drank any length of time with entire impunity; consequently a single gallon of sea-water will render unfit for drinking more than a hundred of otherwise pure water. Hence a sample of water should be examined out of every tank, and several, if it remains alongside of the ship any length of time. Where the young medical officer is in doubt whether the water examined falls far enough below the standard to be rejected, let him always decide against and decline to approve it.

The greater part of the water used on board steamers is distilled from the sea, and the attention of engineers and constructors has been directed to the production of an apparatus which shall accomplish this in the most satisfactory manner. The disagreeable empyreumatic odor and flavor usually attending water from this source, its chemical purity and consequent insipidity, are the principal faults which have to be remedied. The first depending on defective process of distillation, has been gotten rid of as this has improved. Perroy's apparatus, as modified by Bourel-Ronciere, in use in the French naval service, is probably the best yet devised; the steam generated by the boilers of the engine being condensed by the water of the sea surrounding the vessel, in the midst of a current of air, by which it is aerated, and deprived of empyreuma by filtration through granular animal charcoal. The filter consists of a tinned sheet-iron box, divided internally into four compartments, separated by vertical partitions pierced with alternate holes, so that the water produced traverses successively the entire mass of charcoal contained in the four compartments, and becomes immediately potable as it leaves the apparatus. The condenser is a simple tinned copper tube, placed on the outside of the keel, about a metre below the water-line, secured firmly to the vessel, and covered up so as to prevent its injury by the grounding of the vessel, but not to hinder her steerage-way. After running a certain distance outside, it enters the ship's side and discharges the fresh water obtained by the condensation of the steam under the cooling influence of the sea-water. Cocks at the two extremities regulate the admission of steam and the discharge of water. A minute analysis of the waters obtained on board La Circe, where Bourel-Ronciere performed his experiments with distillatory apparatus, was made at the naval medical school at Toulon, by M. Fontaine, *premier pharmacien en chef*, and demonstrated that at the first working of the apparatus they contained sodium chloride in sensible quantity, a few sulphates, and traces of organic matters; but Bourel-Ronciere claims that as the apparatus is worked the water becomes purer, and the quantity of saline matters is much diminished, and, after leaving Perroy's filter, it is sufficiently aerated to be healthy and salubrious. "The problem of the distillation of sea-water," adds A. Tardieu, from whom I have obtained these facts, "may thus be considered as practically settled." Fonssagrives proposes to supply the deficiency of saline matter in distilled water by the addition to every hundred gallons of a mixture containing about half a drachm of sodium chloride, a scruple of sodium sulphate, six drachms of calcium carbonate, a drachm and a half of sodium carbonate, and two scruples of magnesium carbonate, the aggregate amount of salification amounting to 5.4 grains per gallon. Besides the mechanical means for aerating the water, if the tank is only filled to the extent of two-thirds its capacity, the motion of the vessel will agitate it sufficiently to cause it to dissolve a larger proportion of the gaseous constituents of the atmosphere. A crystal of green ferrous sulphate will not produce the characteristic ocherish discoloration unless air is present.

Not infrequently water, unobjectionable when brought off or distilled on board, is seriously impaired after it has been placed in the tanks. This is the case when the latter have been white-washed inside, a practice that cannot be too severely condemned. I sailed from Boston, in the autumn of 1858, on board the Dol-phin, of which the tanks had been treated in this way, and, with every other officer and man, I was tormented with burning thirst, dryness of mouth and fauces, nauseous tastse, epigastric heat, etc., until we arrived at Buenos Ayres. The tea, coffee, and soups were also spoiled. Still another cause of the deterioration of water on board ship is overlooked. It is a very general custom to fill the tanks as soon as they have been emptied, with sea-water, either to preserve the trim of the vessel or to prevent cap-sizing, though on board steamers provided with distilling appara-tus there can be no possible pretext for using salt-water for this purpose. With the greatest care it is difficult to remove the ef-fects of this procedure, and the destruction of the brackishness of the water by the chemical action of the iron is inconsiderable; but usually, the only cleansing attempted is to pump out the salt-water, wash the tanks with a few gallons of fresh, and then re-plenish them. The tanks of some small vessels will not admit a boy, and frequently the beams of the berth-deck partly cover the man-hole openings, so that it is not possible to reach but a small portion of their surface. The substitution of iron tanks for casks is one of the greatest improvements hygiene has effected in mod-ern naval establishments, and its satisfactory results should secure attention to other suggestions emanating from this department of the medical profession. Tanks, however, require considerable care. They should always be thoroughly cleansed when emptied, scraped, well rinsed with fresh, preferably distilled water, and waxed before they are refilled. Galvanizing the inside of the tanks is open to the objection that it will add another foreign substance to the water in the shape of a salt of zinc. The scuttle-butt ought also to be of iron; it should be cleansed and waxed every month, and provided with a filtering diaphragm of sand

and charcoal, which must be occasionally removed and renewed. I have known vessels on which the scuttle-butt was not disturbed during the whole cruise.

Instead of the ordinary mess-pot holding nearly a quart, such as is used for tea and coffee, which is filled and emptied at a draught, and oftenest by the landsmen, writers, boys, etc., who require it least, a small tin drinking-cup, of the capacity of a gill, should be attached by a chain to the faucet of the scuttle-butt, and allowed to be filled but once at each drinking. This quantity is as much as should be swallowed at any one time, and will enable the man to get from ten to fifteen full draughts a day. The sentry on post should be instructed to prevent any particular set of men from using an undue share. The whole daily allowance should not be pumped into the scuttle-butt at one time, but at intervals, during the day; thus, if the entire daily amount is one hundred gallons, let fifty be introduced at 9 a. m., thirty at 2 p. m., and the balance at 8 p. m. The tea and coffee will supply its place at intermediate times. The addition of oat-meal to water is customary with engineers and firemen, a smaller quantity thus more effectually relieving thirst. At general quarters, not only the scuttle-butt should be filled, but the mess-kettles of the berth-deck cooks, which should be convenient to be passed on deck by the powder division. Similar provision for an extra supply of water should be made whenever any other protracted or exhausting labor is undertaken.

SLEEP.

The graphic descriptions by reporters of the filth of some of the unclean and degraded poor of our great cities would find a parallel on the berth-decks of many of our men-of-war at night. It is a place that few officers but those of the medical corps ever visit at that time; and the close bulkheads of the comparatively well-ventilated ward-room exclude the foul and stifling odors of the adjoining apartment. It is impossible to remain many minutes among the hammocks without experiencing a sensation of suffocation and nausea; indeed it is only necessary to lean over the main-hatch, toward the close of the first watch, to recognize the heavy mawkish odor that aris_s and betokens the over-crowding of human beings. That these beings are injuriously affected by what appeals so forcibly to our senses and excites disgust, does not admit of question. I have referred incidentally to this subject of overcrowding when speaking of ventilation, and have shown the evil of the system wh ch fills vessels with more men than they can berth, even with hammocks swinging so closely together that the movement of one man disturbs all those among whom he is wedged. The berthing capacity of every vessel should be determined by a commission of officers, wholly or in part of the medical corps, and should be the guide to the regulation of the armament, rather than that a certain number of guns should be put on board and a certain allowance of human muscle, like that of tackle and breechings, be subordinate thereto. The ship carrying a small battery, manned by a hundred athletic, healthy men, will be far more efficient than one bristling with cannon and encumbered with twenty or thirty daily sick, and twice as many more enfeebled convalescents.

At sea only one watch sleep below; but all the advantages

derived from the increased breathing-space thus affored are coun-
terbalanced by a horribly disgusting and abominable practice
which is enforced on board many—probably a majority of vessels
—of compelling the watch that come from deck to turn into the
hammocks of the men who relieve them. Perhaps an officer,
who never visits the berth-deck at night, and whose own bunk is
clean and dry, can complacently issue such an order and reply to
any remonstrance made that "men must not expect to get all the
comforts of life with eighteen dollars a month;" but the medical
officer, who is ever mindful of the solemn responsibilities of his
profession, will denounce this practice with every expression of
abhorrence. Fancy the loathing with which a clean man must
regard the compulsion to sleep in the bed of a fellow of unclean
habits, diseased with venereal, affected with cutaneous eruptions
or vermin, whose skin is naturally offensive, or whose blankets
are always wet from incontinence of urine or spermatorrhœa, or
the equal repugnance he must experience at having his own clean
bedding soiled by such a beast. There is never the shadow of
necessity to excuse this detestable custom. In pleasant weather
each watch should be compelled to "lash and carry." The unoccupied hammocks should not be left below, except when they
would get wet by being stowed in the nettings, and then they
should be allowed to remain on their appropriate hooks or be
piled up in some convenient place.

I have already insisted that the watch coming below should
remove their wet clothes before turning in, and that if they have
exhausted the three changes which a proper outfit would allow,
that they should remove their outer shirts and pantaloons, and
hang them on their hammock-hooks. In this way the contents
of the hammock may be kept dry and clean. No wet articles
should ever be stowed either in the hammocks or hammock-nettings.

All bedding should be exposed in the rigging to the air and
sun at least once a week, if the weather will permit. The blankets and mattress should be well shaken, and the latter should

be repicked once or twice during the cruise. Hennen, writing
on military hygiene, advises the daily exposure of soldiers' bedding to the sun. I have known vessels in which bedding had not
been opened for this purpose for several months, where there was
no care taken to prevent men turning in wet, and where the gon-
orrhœal, the syphilitic, the eczematous, those incontinent of urine,
and those affected with diarrhœa, slept alternately with the clean
in each other's bedding. Opportunities should be improved or
compelling the men to wash their blankets, one or both at a time,
and their mattress-covers, in fresh water. These articles become
quickly soiled with blue dye-stuff during the first weeks that new
flannel is worn. Although we have often imitated or adhered to
the customs of the British service with questionable profit, I cannot refrain from expressing a hope that our Government will
adopt the course of the lords commissioners of the British admiralty, who, " being desirous that the seaman, on entering, as far
as practicable, may be freed from the necessity of incurring debt,
are pleased to direct that all men and boys, on first joining one
of Her Majesty's ships, shall be supplied with a bed, blanket, and
bed-cover free of charge." As they are the property of the Crown,
and have to be returned, paymasters are interested in having them
kept in good order ; and the care taken to this end thus indirectly assists to a result which, with only hygiene recommending
it, would never have been attained.

The greasy black hammock-lashing is a relic of old-time customs, which should go the way of others of its kind. The neat
white " tie-tie," or stop, does not soil the hammock, lessens the
task of cleaning, and does not break the mattress. Hammocks
are adapted for it with very little trouble, and the bedding may
be more expeditiously tied up and taken on deck than when a
lashing has to be adjusted.

In pleasant weather the greater part of the watch on deck
sleep on the spar-deck, wherever they can find places. Unless
the decks are perfectly dry, this should be interdicted. Care
should also be taken that the men never lie down where they will

be exposed to dew or to currents of air through air-ports and scupper-holes. A large proportion of the aural diseases which appear on the medical returns of the service is occasioned in this way.

The necessary interruptions of the sleep of the sailor affect his health, but many of the needless discomforts and sources of disease may be abolished with great benefit to the service, as when " all hands" are called during the night in consequence of clumsily executed maneuvers or to punish a few lazy and inefficient men.

7 H

EXERCISE.

Among other " non-naturals " which require attention from the naval hygienist is want of exercise. The sailor's occupation furnishes occasion enough for physical development, but there is a numerous class of persons on board vessels of war, intrusted with special duties, who do not share the open-air labors of the mariner. These are the apothecaries, nurses, yeomen, schoolmasters, writers, masters-at-arms, ship's corporals, captains of the hold, permanent berth-deck cooks, officers' stewards, cooks, and servants, musicians, printers, painters, tailors, etc. They are recognizable at the weekly muster on Sunday by their pallid countenances, faltering gait, and untidy, slovenly dress. They are unclean and indolent as a class, are scantily provided with clothing, and form a large proportion of the sick. The dark and lonely corners where they abide are the favorite haunts of those guilty of those secret practices that are so rife on board some men-of-war. Many yeomen pass the entire day in the store-room, which sometimes is without a scuttle overhead, or even an auger-hole in the door, where they breathe a confined and stagnant atmosphere, still further impoverished and heated by two or three constantly burning oil-lamps or candles. The captain of the hold whiles away his leisure hours in the main hold, where he keeps his ditty-box, and the regular cooks seldom quit the vicinity of the galley before night, when the fires are extinguished. The system of steady berth-deck cooks reduces eight, ten, or more of the crew, according to the number of messes, to this etiolated condition, and it ought, therefore, to be discountenanced. Every man, except the higher petty-officers, should be required to perform the duty of mess-cook or caterer (for the former term is a misnomer) in rotation, changes being made at least monthly, and while attending to this duty he should not be excused from the regular exercises of his division or station, an alternate performing his mess-work. All others whose special duties confine them below should be compelled to pass a certain portion of each day, during the hours of daylight, in the open air. They should either be attached as supernumeraries to the regular divisions, or be exercised together at the great guns, at small-arms, single-sticks, rowing, or going aloft. No conflict of departments need occur in this if officers of the various corps are actuated by proper feelings toward each other and toward the service. It is not presumed that the surgeon will be deprived of the services of the apothecary or nurses whenever these may be required; nor that the paymaster will have to subordinate the business of his department to his writer's exercise; nor that the captain of the hold will have to neglect his work to play at top-man or loader and sponger; nor that the cabin and ward-room dinners shall become cold or go uncooked, and Mr. ———'s boy lay down his razor and leave the lathered chin unshaven when-ever small-arm men are called away. The special duties for which these individuals are respectively employed must be at-tended to in preference to everything else; but then the officer who directs or controls this special duty should not throw obsta-cles in the way of exercise, however distasteful it may be to the subordinate, by requiring untimely and unnecessary services, but, prompted by a desire to promote the general interests, should cheerfully co-operate to this end.

The multiplicity of officers' messes crowds our naval vessels with a superfluous number of ineffective, worthless, and trouble-some individuals, who eminently deserve the designation "idlers." A flag-ship may have a separate mess for the admiral or commo-dore, one for the commanding officer, (and I have heard another advocated for the fleet-captain,) one for the ward-room, (and for a while there were two of these,) one for the starboard and an-other for the port steerage, and one for the warrant-officers; each with its own steward, cook, and servants; each occupying the galley, which consequently becomes a theater of confusion and contention; each encroaching on the air-space of the ship by its independent store-rooms and pantries, and deteriorating its atmosphere by its accumulation of destructible stores, often in widely apart localities. I have known a brig-of-war so small that officers and men elbowed each other on deck, on board which the show of class distinctions was still kept up by four officers' messes. I am aware that the time has not yet arrived for expecting any reform in this matter, though more than one commanding officer has agreed with me that there is no good reason why a general officers' mess, presided over by the captain, should not be established, as in the Army, where the colonel sits at the head of the regimental mess-table. The ship is the analogue of the regiment or battalion, and experience has demonstrated that where military officers dine *en masse* their demeanor is no less gentlemanly and dignified, and their polite and friendly intercourse no more subversive of discipline than in the Navy, where inferiority of position is unremittingly indicated by the relative coarseness of the table-cloth, the number of the viands, the impudence of the steward, and the behavior of the mess-mates. On the contrary, many arguments may be adduced in favor of the former practice. The expense of entertaining foreign officials is wholly defrayed from our own officers' personal means; and when this is on a large scale, falls chiefly upon those of the ward-room. Many of our commanders have dined with foreign regimental messes, in company with cornets as well as colonels, without abasement of their own dignity, and visiting admirals and generals would doubtless feed with equal complacency in the presence of midshipmen, masters, and assistant surgeons. The objection of the inability of the junior officers to bear an equal share of such expenses could be overcome, first, by the Government providing an outfit of table and kitchen furniture for every ship, and, secondly, by its assuming, as in other services, all extra expenditures certified by the commander to have been incurred in the legitimate entertainment of foreign officials and the necessary re-

turn of civilities received from them : an outlay more than coun-
terbalanced by the saving in wages, subsistence, and sick-care of
the attendants no longer required. The monthly cost to each
individual of maintaining a general officers' mess in superior
style would be actually less than that now expended and wasted
by the inexperienced caterers of many midshipmen's messes.
Furthermore, the younger officers of the Navy would, from the
commencement of their career, be beneficially influenced by
the courteous and gentlemanly association and the exemplary
conduct of their seniors. Most steerage-messes, and lately
not only these, are often scenes of unbecoming turmoil and
indecorum. The absence of restraint, which induces even the
younger officers themselves to object to a common mess, is
merely a license for conduct which their parents would not tol-
erate at their own tables, and which would not be permitted in
any gentlemen's club on shore. The general mess, therefore,
would advance the *morale* of the service, while the hygiene of
the ship would be benefited by the consequent diminution of
the servant-class. It is not, of course, proposed to deprive the
commander of his private quarters and officer, where he can regulate discipline and discuss the weighty affairs of state with foreign dignitaries, nor any other officer of the seclusion of his own
apartment; but the common mess-room would be found an agreeable place for friendly and unofficial commingling, which would
lead to the re-establishment of those intimacies, once the bond
and pride of the Navy. The absorption of the steerage-messes
would, moreover, allow clerks, commanders, and paymasters to
be dispensed with. The duties of the former could appropriately
be performed by the midshipmen or ensigns in rotation, whom it
is desirable to have acquire a knowledge of the methods of official
correspondence and who ought to be as trusty repositors of State
secrets as the irresponsible parties now appointed. An assistant
paymaster should be attached to every vessel for clerical duty
and instruction, and the pharmaceutic work of the apothecary.
whom I have elsewhere, assuming the permanence of existing

conditions, advised to be made a steerage officer, would naturally and properly devolve upon an assistant surgeon.   Nor need the warrant officers stand in the way of this scheme.   They are few in number, inconsistent with the size of the naval establishment, and in a majority of the vessels of the Navy their duties are actually and efficiently performed by their mates, who could supply their places in all, except in the case of the gunner, whose more important responsibilities ought to pertain to commissioned officers especially educated and skilled in ordnance.   These mates would partake in that improvement of dress and privilege which I have asked for the petty [preferably, non-commissioned] officers, and thus be assim'lated to the corresponding grades in the army; while sufficient employment on shore could be found for the present holders of warrants, many of whom are estimable gentlemen, far superior to their enforced humble surroundings on board ship, as was done with the former master's corps, until their extinction by death or resignation.

CLIMATIC INFLUENCES.

The exposures incident to the sailor's life are supposed to fit him to endure with impunity extremes of temperature or any inclemency of season. It is a popular belief that no amount of soaking in salt water will give one cold, though an old salt who is not also a chronic rheumatic is a rarity. The carelessness consequent upon these ideas has its result, as shown by statistics, in shortening the seaman's life. However slow to contract disease or to be affected by ordinary vicissitudes, the unnatural circumstances under which he lives give an unfavorable character to all his complaints, and maladies of equal severity in their incipiency are, therefore, more fatal at sea than on shore. The most potent causes of disease in the seaman are not accidental exposure to cold, occasional getting wet, gluttonous eating of unripe fruit, nor indulgence in unrestrained debauch; but they are those which gradually undermine his constitution, and result from the neglect to adapt his diet, dress, and duty to the hygienic requirements of the climate in which he lives. Sailors are made up of the same tissues as princes and gentle folk, and though habit may modify the effects of natural causes, it cannot altogether nullify them. Darwin declares that "it is certain that with sailors their manner of life delays growth," as shown by the great difference between the statures of soldiers and sailors. It is now very generally believed that certain races were created for certain localities, if not created in or by them. Acclimation is no longer regarded as a fact, for such excellent authorities as Johnson and Martin assert that "residence confers only certain immunities and privileges, and that so far only is there truth in the doctrine of acclimation." Even this tolerance, created by a residence of a year or two in a foreign climate, is at the expense of constitutional vigor.   Dr. Bloodgood writes with respect to Panama what is equally true of many other inter-tropic pest-holes entered by our national vessels :   " Acclimation is impossible; no one of whatever race or country, who becomes a resident of the Isthmus escapes disease; not even beasts are exempt, and nothing but change of climate can eradicate the effects of the poisoning from that malaria."   The Government has, therefore, acted wisely in abandoning the practice of long cruises.   Three years are the most that can be safely passed on any one station notably unlike the native climate, since, with every attention to hygienic precautions, there will be such a general loss of constitutional strength among the crew that they will become ill from slight causes, and such permanent organic injury will be received by many officers as well as men as to unfit them for future energetic duty.   A British steam sloop-of-war, cruising on the Caribbean coast of Central America, in 1859, had had nearly three complete crews during the five years she had been in commission, and her commander told me that those officers and men who had remained from the beginning were becoming stultified in mind.   A liberal government like our own has no excuse in the saving of expense, if there really be any such, to commit the inhumanity of compelling its men and officers to remain so long from their families and country.   The best American merchant sailors will not enter the service while they are kept away beyond two years, and officers are not made better citizens and members of society if they are exiled until the recollection of home becomes almost a dream of the past.

Of extreme climates, the cold are more readily borne by our crews than the hot, being more like the rigorous winters to which they have been accustomed.   The effects of cold, moreover, can be better guarded against, not only by proper clothing but by the observance of a strict hygiene, especially in the matter of diet and ventilation.   Raw fat meat seems to be the appropriate food, though the scurvy of the frigid zone is not merely the result of improper alimentation, but of neglect of all the laws of health.

Instinct and appetite guide to what should be eaten, but foul air and filth are submitted to despite the frightful havoc they assist in causing. What an intelligent observance of sanitary laws will accomplish under the most unfavorable circumstances was markedly demonstrated in the Arctic expedition commanded and directed by Dr. Hayes.

The combined influences of protracted exposure to thee levated temperature, moisture, and organic growth and decay, which characterize tropical climates, and of an almost universally neglected hygiene, occasion serious functional disturbances, which lay the foundation of irreparable structural lesions, the peculiarities of which are, of course, familiar to the educated physician. The lungs and kidneys are brought into fuller activity under a low temperature, while the liver and skin are excited to greater functional effort under a high one. Zymotic fevers, diarrhœa, and dysentery are the most intractable of the complaints of the torrid zone, but they are so fully described in the current medical literature as to render unnecessary any special reference to their technical history. When the interests of the service require the visit to or prolonged sojourn in any unhealthy place, the advice and judgment of the medical officer must be relied on to provide for the special necessities of the time. The prophylactic administration of the salts of quinine, the diminution of the ration of meat and increase of the proportion of vegetables, the purchase of fruits, and the issue of spirits or its substitution by wine, are among those measures that should be left to his individual discretion. I have only to indicate a few precautions of universal applicability.

Although the permanent squadron on the west coast of Africa has been discontinued, vessels of the European fleet occasionally resort there, and the sanitary regulations of Secretary Preston, issued January 23, 1850, are still in operation, (*vide* paragraph 832, Regulations for the Navy, 1870,) and should be enforced on all other stations where similar climatic conditions prevail, as in the East and West Indies, and on the coast of Central America.

1. No officer or man will be permitted to be on shore before sunrise or after sunset, or to sleep there at night; this rule to apply not only to the continental coast but to the Cape de Verde Islands.

2. No United States vessel will ascend or anchor in any of the African rivers, except upon imperative public service.

3. Boat excursions up rivers, or hunting parties on shore, are forbidden.

4. Vessels, when possible, will anchor at a reasonable distance from shore; far enough not to be influenced by the malaria floated off by the land-breeze.

5. Convalescents from fever and other diseases, when condemned by medical survey, are to be sent to the United States with the least possible delay.

6. When the general health of a ship's company shall be reported as impaired by cruising upon the southern or equatorial portion of the coast, the earliest possible opportunity will be given them to recruit by transferring the ship for a time to the Canaries or other windward islands of the station.

7. Boat and shore duty, involving exposure to sun and rain, is to be performed, so far as the exigencies of the service will permit, by the Kroomen employed for that purpose.

8. All possible protection from like exposure is to be afforded to the ship's company on board; and *the proper clothing and diet of the crew, as well as the ventilation and care of the decks, will be made a frequent subject for the inspection and advice of the medical officers.*

9. These regulations are to be considered as permanent, and each commanding officer of the squadron, on retiring from the station, will transfer them to his successor.

The danger of sleeping or remaining on shore after dark in malarial climates, on account of the greater activity of the morbific cause or the greater susceptibility of its deleterious effects at that time, is generally understood; while the universally admitted atmospheric contamination implied in the use of the word *malaria*, though its particular character is not known, points to the prime necessity of keeping as far away from its influence as possible by avoiding anchorages in narrow streams and inlets and to leeward of prevailing winds, and by intervening such a surface of water as has been practically found to confer immunity, through the surmised absorption of the aerial poison. Hammond quotes the following paragraph in point, from Sir Gilbert Blane: "I have known a hundred yards in a road make a difference in the health of a ship at anchor, by her being under the lee of marshes in one situation and not in another." This has often been remarked in the bay of Rio de Janeiro, and Surgeon Bloodgood, United States Navy, has shown that it was the case in the harbor of Panama, when the Jamestown was so terribly scourged by yellow fever. In the British admiralty health reports it is stated that "the Hibernia, at Malta, during the cholera, was moored within one hundred yards of the infected districts, and the ship remained throughout the whole pestilence free from any fatal attack."

The fifth, sixth, and seventh of Secretary Preston's regulations are so exceedingly important that every infraction of them should be visited with the severest censure of the Department. Invalids should be sent home without delay; vessels should temporarily change their cruising grounds; and crews should be relieved as much as possible from duty, especially menial drudgery, involving exposure to sun and rain. Moseley and other writers on tropical climates advise that all merely laborious work should be performed by negroes, lascars, coolies, and others inured to the climate. As the Government authorizes the employment of Kroomen on the coast of Africa for boat and shore duty, many vessels of the Asiatic fleet have been provided with Chinese "fast-boats," manned by natives; but some commanding officers, either with a desire to save expense, or because they consider that "men are shipped for any work, and if they die their places can be supplied by others," compel their crews to do this duty, at all hours of the day, in any weather, and at any season. The cost of the fast-boat, however, will be many times defrayed by the saving of health. Admit that only ten men become ill from exposure to the heat of a single tropical summer, would it not have been more profitable to have had those men well and in efficient condition, than encumbering the deck with their cots, incommoding their shipmates, and interrupting the ordinary routine of exercise? Probably half of them will require to be invalided and returned to the United States, and the cost of passage home, the payment of wages for services never performed, and those of the green recruits, who supply the invalids' places, the subsistence of the latter for months at a naval hospital, and their subsequent pensioning for the balance of their lives, would have employed a score of native boats with crews unaffected by the climate, and given to the Government the strength and spirit of these five men to fight its battles. The other reason adduced for not employing Chinamen, which is no fiction, since it was advanced to me, is disgraceful to the character of an American officer. That it is not the theory of the Government is evident from the general order of January 23, 1850. The seaman is hired for other purposes than those of pulling pleasure parties of officers to and from the shore when the thermome ter stands above 100° F. He has devoted his life to the service of his country, and stands ready to shed his blood in its cause. The ship's batteries are that country's defenses, and he should be kept in a condition to man them. Without his strength and bravery, what will avail all the skill of the navigator, all the science of the ordnance officer, or all the planning and maneuvering of the commander ?

Besides avoiding the exposure of men by not sending them out of the vessel at improper hours, they should be protected on board ship from intense tropical heat both at sea and in port. Awnings ought always to be kept spread, fore and aft, when the temperature exceeds 80° F. They should protect not only the poop and quarter-deck, but the main-deck, forecastle, and head. As the awnings in port are usually very high from the deck, the protection they afford will be insufficient unless curtains are attached. They should be set before the spar-deck is perfectly dry, if it has been washed, that the slow evaporation may assist in keeping down the temperature; and if the deck becomes dry and hot during the day, it should be occasionally irrigated. Painting the hull of a vessel of a light color very materially affects the temperature of the covered decks. The tops should be provided with awnings, that those men on duty aloft may find a shelter when not on the yards nor in the rigging. The lookout on the topsail-yard should also be screened and relieved every half-hour, or, in calm weather, at shorter intervals, and, if this is impossible, should be dispensed with, except when imperatively necessary for the safety of the ship. Many men are victims to the routine of keeping lookouts aloft, when it would be sufficient to have them in the tops or even on deck. The sentries on post in the gangways should be protected by small awnings or flies, and they should be frequently relieved. Numerous cases of *coup-de-soleil* occur among this class, who are made to parade a gang-plank two hours at a time, dressed in a closely-buttoned uniform, and carrying a heavy musket and accouterments, without any more attempt at shelter than would be afforded in their own temperate climate. A pensioner on the navy list, some time since residing in New York, who is affected with hemiplegia, consequent upon insolation, was disabled under precisely such circumstances; and several others cases which resulted less seriously, occurred on board the same vessel in the East Indies. When boats are required to be sent away in the hot part of the day, their awnings should be spread, and this manifestly applies to the very largest launch and smallest dinguy, as to those ordinarily used.

In very hot weather (above 85° F.) no work nor exercise of any kind should be performed after 9 a. m. nor before 5 p. m., unless absolutely indispensable at that time, and then only under shelter, and the reasons for such unavoidable work or exercise should be entered on the log. Tarring rigging, scraping spars, scrubbing copper, painting ship, divisional exercises, small-arm drill, etc., at such a time, are barbarous because inexcusable. The dangers that are sought to be avoided are neither imaginary nor exaggerated. I have seen a new fore-topsail bent at 11 o'clock on a calm morning, the thermometer indicating 126° F. in the sun, and followed by the fatal sickness of the captain of the top, and the serious illness, within forty-eight hours, of seven of the men who had been at work upon the yard. The weather was pleasant all day long, and others concurred with me that the work could have been as well done early in the morning or late in the evening. Dr. Maclean, in Reynolds' " System of Medicine," relates several historical instances of insolation occurring in the field or barracks, among the most striking being the following: "The two wings of Her Majesty's thirteenth regiment marched, after some very ill-judged exposure and drilling in the sun, from Nuddea to Berampore, in the midst of the hot weather, and, as the result of one march, the day closed with a sick-list of sixty-three, and eighteen deaths in all." "The sixty-eighth regiment, quartered in Fort St. George, Madras, which attended the funeral of a general officer, and paraded in full-dress at an early hour in the afternoon, in one of the hottest months in the year, their tight-fitting coats buttoned up, their leather stocks as stiff and unyielding as horse-collars. round their necks, heavy cross-belts, so contrived as to interfere with every movement of the chest, heavy shakoes on their heads, made of black felt, mounted with brass ornaments, with wide, flat, circular tops, ingeniously contrived to concentrate the sun's rays on the crown of the head, and without protection in the way of a depending flap for the neck; so dressed, the men marched several miles. Before the funeral parade was over the soldiers began to fall senseless; one died on the spot—two more in less than two hours. Men suffering from insolation in various degrees were brought into hospital all that night and part of next day." "The ninety-eighth came from England in the Bellcisle, an old 74-gun ship, and suffered from overcrowding. On the 21st of July they took part in the attack on Chin-Kiang-Foo. The men were dressed precisely as those of the sixty-eighth. In this condition they had to take possession of a steep hill exposed to the fiercest rays of the sun shining out of an unclouded sky. A great many were struck down by the heat, of whom fifteen died." The most recent instance of criminal disregard of sanitary teachings has occurred since I began writing. The first battalion of the tenth regiment of British infantry was marched from its camp at Yokohama after parade on the morning of August 8, 1871, to the French Hatoba, where it embarked. The men were heavily armed and accoutered, and though exposed to the sun less than three hours, the thermometer at 92° F., shade temperature, six cases of sun-stroke occurred, of which three, two sergeants and a private, died. Three of the marines who relieved them, and who were landed immediately afterward and marched to the camp they had vacated, also succumbed to the heat.

The symptoms of insolation often occur among men not exposed to the direct rays of the sun—in the fire-room of steamers, on board the monitor class of armored vessels, in small, ill-ventilated cells. Dr. Kitchen informed me that while surgeon of the monitor Dictator it was common for men to be brought to him for treatment with coma, stertorous respiration, great heat of skin, full quick pulse, and often convulsions. The cause was manifestly enough the exhausting labors of a watch in the fire-room, where the temperature averaged 145° F., and where the ventilation was exceedingly defective, air that had been already respired being repeatedly returned. Maclean states that "insolation has frequently been observed on board ship, but almost always under conditions similar to those in barracks—that is, where overcrowding and impure air are added to the influence of excessive heat. Insolation is not uncommon on board the mail-steamers in the Red Sea in the hot months of August and September; it has been observed that most of the cases occurred while the sufferers were in the horizontal position in their ill-ventilated cabins," and he quotes the following: "Assuredly," says Dr. Butler, surgeon of the third cavalry, "those barracks most crowded, least ventilated, and worst provided with punkahs and other appliances to moderate excessive heat, furnished the greatest number of fatal cases." Surgeon Longmore, of the nineteenth regiment, notes that one-third of his cases and nearly half the deaths occurred in one company of the regiment quartered in the barrack, which was manifestly the worst conditioned as to ventilation, and, indeed, in every sanitary requirement. M. Bassier, a surgeon in the French navy, reports that the man-of-war brig Le Lynx, cruising off Cadiz, in the month of August, had eighteen cases of insolation out of a crew of seventy-eight men. The heat was excessive (91–95° F.) and much aggravated by calms. The ship was overcrowded, offering little space for the berthing of the crew. M. Boudin quotes the case of the French man-of-war Duquesne, which, while at Rio de Janeiro, had a hundred cases of insolation out of a crew of six hundred men. Most of the men were attacked, not when exposed to the direct heat of the sun, but at night when in the recumbent position—that is, when breathing not only a hot and suffocating, but also an impure air. Other morbid conditions often attend or follow heat-exhaustion. I have had two marines on my sick-list with abscesses developed during confinement in "sweat-boxes," in the months of June and August, in the tropics. In one the collection of pus was located in front of the neck; the man was comatose, and, on recovering consciousness, complained of no pain. In the other it was developed on the upper arm, and was attended with throbbing pain and greatly increased heat of surface. In both the pulse was full, hard, and strong, the respiration labored, and the body drenched with sweat, showing that the heat was as active a cause of disease as the impoverished air.

After a long and stormy passage through the Indian Ocean, the Levant arrived at Anjer Roads, in Java, on the 25th of March, 1856, when the heat was intense. Her crew were enfeebled and many of them exhibited evidences of the scorbutic cachexia, in consequence of the deteriorated and unsuitable character of their food, which the insufficient daily issue of wood did not allow to be properly cooked; of their short allowance of water, which was impure; of their confinement on board ship since the previous October, when she went into commission; and of their unusually arduous labors in the high southern latitudes, where they were exposed for several weeks to a continuance of cold, damp, and rainy weather. Notwithstanding their condition they were laboriously employed, working from daylight until dark for two days, getting on board wood which was wet and green, and water, white from organic impurities, and which had run through a series of dirty, wooden troughs into an equally dirty reservoir. The vessel sailed on the evening of the third day, and within a few hours that night twenty-four cases of cholera communis were reported, two of the lieutenants among the number. Few of these men were ever able afterward to do their duty properly. As events proved, this was their preparation for a tedious passage of forty-six days across the China Sea to Hong-Kong, a distance of only twelve hundred miles, but entirely within the tropics, (latitude 8° south to 20° north,) at the season of the change of monsoons, when the high temperature is not moderated by any breeze nor the scorching heat of the tropical sun scarcely ever shielded by a clouded sky, and when the glassy surface of the sea reflects and concentrates the heat upon the ship, whose black sides greedily absorb it. The deck-load of freshly cut green wood added an unwholesome moisture to the atmosphere, and the unfiltered water, with which the tanks had been filled, preferred for cheapness, soon decomposed and became offensive and unpalatable. The men had gorged themselves with oranges, mangosteens, and other fruit during their short stay at Anjer; but the supply of chickens, vegetables, and fruit which they brought away with them was soon exhausted, and they were again fed with the mahogany-like "salt horse," green fat pork, worm-eaten bread, weeviled beans, and musty rice, which they had had to eat in the chilly regions of the Southern Ocean. The paltry interval of three days in ninety-seven had brought no relief to their jaded and debilitated bodies; but they were occupied with the still severer labor of working ship for every "cat's-paw" under the additional morbific influence of a vertical tropical sun. Most of the intractable cases of diarrhœa and dysentery, and the large majority of deaths during the cruise, can be directly traced to this period. The asthenic habit of constitution, which rendered these complaints fatal, was evidently fixed upon them by the various concurrent circumstances in operation thus early in the cruise. After her arrival on the station, this vessel did not, like the rest of the squadron, employ a Chinese fast-boat, and the results of this and other violations of hygienic mandates were plainly shown in a sick-list of *thirteen hundred and forty-five* cases

8 H

during the thirty months of her commission. Nor were the sickness and inefficiency of the crew the only consequences of this utter disregard of sanitary laws. One of the officers, who inspected her at the end of her cruise, told me that she was the most unclean and ill-conditioned vessel he had ever seen.

Much of the sickness which is attributed to visiting infectious ports arises from the foul condition of the holds and limbers of the vessels themselves. Although the fever might not have appeared but for the visit to the port, it is equally true that it would not have been developed but for the uncleanness of the ship itself. The decay of the wood of the vessel and of the chips under the ceiling, the leakage of brine from provision casks and of molasses and vinegar from the spirit-room, the drippings of oil from the machinery of steamers, the sifting of coal-dust from the bunkers and of ashes from the fire-room, the influx of salt water, its admixture with fresh spilled from the tanks and the consequent death of the microscopic organisms which inhabit it, together form a putrescible mass, the malarious emanations from which pervade the vessel and occasion a general predisposition to zymotic and paroxysmal febrile affections; therefore, while so much attention is being given to the avoidance of unhealthy localities, let some little be paid to the smoldering pestilential fire —the artificial marsh over which so many human beings are living in fancied security. On this point very valuable testimony is borne by the annual report of the Health of the Navy, issued by the British admiralty, for the years 1865–'66: "The Madagascar was long infected with yellow fever at Rio de Janeiro, and when inspected it was discovered that the sides of the ship and the lining were in many places decayed, damp, and rotten, and on lifting the limber boards a quantity of black, offensive mud was discovered, the smell of which caused nausea, vomiting, and diarrhœa in several persons present." It is also stated in the case of the Isis, at Sierra Leone, that " there can be no question that the existence of the fever poison in that vessel did not depend on the locality, but on the vessel itself;" the latter even becoming a focus from which infection spread to other vessels, since "within six or seven weeks no fewer than twenty-eight deaths among the crews of two ships-of-war, from this malignant fever, were clearly due to communication with the Isis; all these deaths occurring exclusively among men who had gone on board that vessel." It is a point of great practical interest in respect to severe outbreaks of yellow fever on board ship, that "nearly all the vessels which have been most scourged in late years were unmistakably unhealthy ships, as evidenced by their larger number of cases of general sickness, not only during the yellow fever years, but also in those which preceded or followed them. This was the case with the Aube, Icarus, L'Eclair, and the same holds true of other vessels which have sustained fatal attacks of fever." The reputation of the L'Eclair was such that to efface the remembrance of the terrible disease the admiralty changed her name to Rosamond. Undoubtedly, the ultimate universal substitution of iron for wood in ship-building will be productive of immense sanitary advantages, on account of the freedom from the nocuous products of the decomposition of the material of the vessel and of the *debris* of its construction, and the greater facilities for keeping it clean and admitting air to the interior of its framework.

There is no question of the propriety of preventing access to a vessel of which the crew is affected with malignant, communicable diseases; neither is there any doubt of the urgent necessity of removing every individual of that crew without delay to some healthy and isolated place on shore. The system of quarantine, however, which proposes to imprison both sick and well upon the infected vessel until the endemic exhausts itself for lack of new victims, is a barbarous relic of popular ignorance and superstition. The sanitary regulations of the United States and Great Britain are sufficiently liberal, and at the large sea-ports are generally judiciously interpreted by the health officers; but in Portuguese, and especially in Spanish ports, the most annoying, frivolous quarantines are still exacted. I have known a man-of-war to sail from Philadelphia in midwinter, arrive at Cadiz after a passage of forty days, and be quarantined for having no bill of health; another, provided with the proper document, to be placed under observation because it did not bear the *vise* of the Spanish consul; and a third, coming from a port where there was no such official, to have the same fortune because the law did not provide for such a contingency. On another occasion I protested, ineffectually, to the health authorities of Fayal against the placing in quarantine of a detachment of officers and men who had gone to rescue a sinking merchantman, one hundred and fifty days out of port. Occasionally similar annoyances are experienced in our own country. During the period of my official connection with the United States navy-yard near Portsmouth, New·Hampshire, I had serious trouble with the local health officers, who refused to consent to the immediate debarkation of the crews of vessels sent north from the Gulf of Mexico, often with only mild pseudo-yellow fever, though abundant opportunities existed for isolating not only the invalids and convalescents, but the unaffected crew and the abandoned vessel. The various health authorities of New York and the other municipalities fronting on the bay have been but lately engaged in disgraceful squabbles over their several rights to grant *pratique* to vessels from suspected ports. Hence, it would be in the interests of commerce and humanity if the whole subject of quarantine were placed under the control of sanitary officers appointed by the General Government. Michel Levy and Fonssagrives, in their respective works on hygiene, have protested energetically against the useless and ridiculous impositions of the system of quarantine in vogue, and the medical officers of every navy are agreed that, no matter what the disease, both sick and well should be immediately removed from the vessel, which should be thoroughly cleansed and renovated. The health reports of the British admiralty state: "Within the last ten or twelve years cases of yellow fever have, on more than one occasion, been landed from ships of war in Plymouth and Hasler hospitals without any but good results. The results in Jamaica, in 1860, were eminently satisfactory. The same seems to have been the case in 1856, the most sickly year, when fever was prevalent on shore at Port Royal and Kingston." In the numerous instances of late years where crews, sick and well, have been landed at the island of Ascension, the disease seems to have speedily much abated, and in no instance to have extended to the garrison and other residents, always provided that direct communication with the infected ship was prevented; and Deputy Inspector General Smart, Royal Navy, relates striking proofs of the utility of landing the sick in suitable hospitals at Bermuda.

MORAL INFLUENCES.

The sailor of to-day is not the brute of fifty years ago. The barefooted, abject, illiterate being whose back bore the scars of the cat is not recognizable in the well-dressed, tidy, manly-looking seaman who receives his letters and papers regularly from home, and signs his name legibly to the shipping articles. The many foreign officers and civilians who witnessed the memorable inquiry into the circumstances attending the loss of the Oneida, at the British consulate at Yokohama, were impressed with the intelligent, fearless, and manifestly truthful manner in which the surviving lookout and helmsman gave their evidence, and particularly with the graceful style in which they affixed their names to the record. While it was once almost unnecessary to inquire whether a man could write his name, it is now the exception that "his + mark" appears on the rendezvous returns. The well-filled condition of the various ship letter-bags, and the general allotment of half-pay, attest the commendable home interest of the modern sailor. The quiet, dignified old quartermaster, who off duty sits conning his Bible; the young quarter-gunner reading stories and travels to a crowd of listeners; the ambitious ordinary seaman working out problems from the Bowditch borrowed from the navigator, are now to be seen on board every vessel of war. . There are some naval officers, generally themselves antiquated, who insist that the social improvement of the sailor has been at the expense of discipline and nautical knowledge; but there are others of equal experience and brighter minds who candidly acknowledge the contrary. The abolition of the cat was a natural consequence of this moral advancement; therefore the advocates for its restoration are only attempting to re-inoculate a convalescent body with the virus of the disease from which it has recovered. The necessity of former times, if there ever was such, has ceased, as witness the testimony of Fonssagrives, whose exhaustive work on naval hygiene establishes his authority : " We do not believe that the sailor of to-day is that of 1790; he has changed with the public character, and to desire to treat him in the same manner is to commit a flagrant anachronism. Physical suffering is, moreover, a bad appeal to make among men who are neither degraded nor vicious. This punishment excites hate more often than repentance, and has never reformed any one. The abolition of flogging, therefore, is a judicious measure. Besides, this punishment, like that of ' keel-hauling,' may be followed by grave accidents—sometimes mortal; and that alone should suffice, without any motive of moral propriety, to justify its abandonment." What is true of the soldier is also true of the sister profession of arms. " The day when soldiers were regarded as mere machines has passed away. An intelligent man, who knows what he is fighting for, and who is capable of appreciating the responsibility that rests upon him, is incomparably a better soldier than one who is incapable of such intelligent action."— (Hammond.) It is not claimed that all sailors are so exemplary ; nor is it expected that all the profane, licentious, and drunken will ever be transformed into upright, intelligent, well-conducted individuals. Although the general character has improved, great numbers are as depraved as they can become by unrestrained indulgence of their passions. The low haunts of maritime cities are still crowded, and the man-of-war's man, though distinguishable by dress and bearing, often lends himself to the general debauchery, and becomes as helpless a victim of the land-shark.

What can be done to correct these evils? Though it be no more possible to confer on every one the boon of moral health than to bring their bodies all into a condition of physical eucrasy, enough good may be achieved to reward all our efforts bountifully. Teach the sailor that he is a man, with a man's duties and capacities. Treat him as such, and require him to act as such. Develop his mind, which has been subordinate to his physical instincts, and that mind will do for him what legislative action or individual beneficence cannot. Ethical hygiene is a field in which every naval officer, and those of the medical corps particularly, should not be ashamed to labor.

I would first suggest, for the moral improvement of the sailor, that every vessel should be furnished with a library—not such as is now found in the cabin, behind a glass case, but a library to which every man on board can have access. Exclude sensational novels, and let it consist of works on natural history, general history, historical romance, travel, geography, popular science, biography and navigation; of encyclopediæ, magazines, and schoolbooks—some rudimentary, and others for advanced students. If these are not supplied by the Government, as is desirable, they can always be obtained, without much trouble, by subscription. They should be placed under the charge of the schoolmaster, or some other intelligent petty-officer, as the apothecary or pay-master's writer. Arrangements may readily be made with publishers to have files of newspapers mailed to vessels on foreign stations. Many officers considerately send their papers out on the berth-deck after having perused them. Religious associations, interested in the moral amelioration of the seaman, occasionally make donations of packages or boxes of books to sea-going vessels; but these are always so unattractively pious and devotional that the sailor, with evident disappointment, lays them aside, after endeavoring to read a page or two, and returns to his dominoes or checkers, when an interesting tale of travel or adventure pleasantly told, or an intelligible account of natural phenomena or scientific facts would have secured his attention, and contributed as well to his moral as to his mental culture. Men should be encouraged to write home, and I have, therefore, advised that ditty-boxes should be allowed in preference to bags, since not only can writing materials be better preserved in them, but they also serve as writing-desks. Some competent person should be appointed schoolmaster, to instruct not only the boys, but such others as desire to learn in reading, writing, arithmetic, and geography, and should never be diverted from his legitimate duties to act as "executive officer's clerk."

It is not enough, however, to increase the comfort of the sea-man on board ship, to supply him with reading matter, and to provide for his instruction. He will not be well if he never leaves the ship. Hygiene demands nothing more important, not merely for their physical well-being, but for their mental and moral healthfulness, than that the men should be allowed frequent liberty on shore. I have known a whole ship's company, except the boats' crews, servants, and a few privileged petty-officers, to be confined eight months on shipboard, without, in all that time, having once touched foot on land. Is it a matter of wonder, then, that when liberty was granted for forty-eight hours, at such long intervals, when old and young, adults and boys, were hurried on shore together, and told if they returned before the expiration of that time they would forfeit the remainder of their liberty, that in the delirium of finding themselves outside their prison-walls they abandoned themselves to unrestrained debauchery? Was the spectacle of bruised and bloated countenances, of which the ship was full for a fortnight after this season, calculated to improve the younger portion of the crew, or, as often happened when these youngsters were themselves the most riotous offenders, did their display, ironed, gagged, and bucked upon the poop, in the full view of the harbor, convince them of their folly and sinfulness? Dr. Wilson relates an instance which exemplifies the utter thoughtlessness with which some officers deal with these matters: " After a ship had been at anchor for several months in a foreign port, without any of the crew having been permitted to visit the shore, in a summary court trying a culprit I heard one of the members express his views by suggesting that the prisoner be sentenced to the seventh punishment, ' deprived of liberty on shore in a foreign station.'" The mysterious laws of health, psychical and physical, require that a man should visit the land, walk upon the earth, breathe its atmosphere, and inhale the odor of its trees and flowers. Let him see something more of the place to which he sails than the glimpse he catches through the bridle-port or over the rail, (for strict discipline does not permit a head to show above it,) that he may not have to make the mortifying admission when he returns home that he has never been on shore. Let him have an incentive to read, study, and inquire about the countries he visits, and with what interest will he visit them. Make the visits to the shore no longer a novelty and a recognized occasion for plunging into orgies and dissipation, but an opportunity for rational enjoyment, instruction, and exercise. That this is not a visionary's scheme was demonstrated by Commander, afterwards Admiral, Foote, on board the sloop-of-war Portsmouth, during her cruise in the China and East India seas in 1856–'57 and '58, when this system was pursued. Was this a well-disciplined ship? On none in the squadron were there so little need, and so small a record of punishment. Was she clean and well-conditioned? Her executive officer, Lieutenant, now Commodore, Macomb, to whom I refer for confirmation of my statements, well deserved the flattering report of the board of inspection. Was she efficient as a man-of-war? The conduct of her officers and men at the attack and capture of the Barrier Forts, near Canton, is a matter of official record, and certainly bore comparison with that of a sister-ship on which a different practice prevailed. Did she maneuver well? There are many still in the service who were then on board other vessels, and who remember the pride they experienced whenever she entered the crowded harbor of Hong-Kong, threaded her course through the many sail of every nation there congregated, and anchored, without mishap, wherever her commander desired. Was she a happy ship? Those who were fortunate enough to be attached to her agree that that cruise will be memorable, not only for its general interest, but for the harmony that pervaded the ship forward and aft, from the time of going into commission until the flag was hauled down. I do not desire it understood that this is an isolated case in the practice of our Navy. The book of Regulations for the Government of the Navy, issued in 1870, directs

in paragraph 1429 that "petty-officers and men will be permitted
to visit the shore on suitable occasions when it can be done without injury to the public service;" but the interpretation of the
terms "suitable occasions" and "injury to the public service"
depends entirely on the will or caprice of the commanding officer. I believe that those commanders who are pre-eminent for
professional skill and broad and liberal views of their duties and
obligations to those under their command, without exception,
authorize the granting of frequent leaves of absence to their crews,
though I have had but two opportunities of personally witnessing
the effects of this system on board the men-of-war to which I
have been attached during the seventeen years of my service in
the Navy. These were the brig Dolphin, commanded by the
present Admiral Steedman ; and the sloop-of-war St. Louis, when
under the command of Captain George Henry Preble. Men
seldom look back with any great satisfaction upon the months
they have passed away from home and country on a foreign
cruise; but I think few who were attached to these vessels,
whether as men or officers, do not often recall the happy associations connected with them. Throughout the many months the
latter ship was anchored in the harbor of Lisbon there was seldom a day that some of the crew were not on shore, and I remember not only the encomiums their conduct elicited, but on one
occasion, when a disturbance at the circus was attributed to some
of her men, with what promptness the journals of the city con-
tradicted the charge, indicated the young gentlemen who had
actually caused the difficulty, and intimated that these sons of
wealthy and influential citizens might profitably imitate the beha-
voir of the St. Louis sailors, who, of all the crews of the thirty
men-of-war of various nationalities then in port, were welcomed
on shore by the people.

Liberty should not be granted to too many men at one time,
else the half-dozen incorrigibles who are found in every crew will
make it an occasion for revenging private injuries or instigating
disorderly conduct. Let it be understood that every day in port

a single mess will be allowed to go on shore, and that whoever returns drunk, dirty, disfigured, or with clothes torn or missing, shall forfeit his right to go when it next comes his turn. Let such offender, after one deprivation, be again allowed liberty when his turn arrives a third time, and if again offending be permanently deprived the privilege. Let it also be understood that whoever overstays his leave compels the whole of the next mess to remain on board until he returns, and there will be few who will care to encounter the ill-will of their shipmates by so doing, and whose punishment will not be gladly witnessed by them. Opportunities for visiting the shore might also be multiplied by changing boats' crews weekly or semi-monthly, the coxswains only remaining the same. All hands would thus be able to partake of advantages now enjoyed only by a few. The institution of the system of frequent liberty, besides the sanitary good it accomplishes, serves to reward the meritorious and punish the worthless, and operates as a more powerful check to intoxication than pledges, lectures, or enforced abstinence.

As in many foreign ports efforts are being made to eradicate venereal disease by subjecting the public women to sanitary examinations, it is important that similar inspections be required of men going on shore. Unless very frequent leaves of absence are granted, men invariably indulge in sexual intercourse, whether diseased or not, and those affected with chronic gonorrhœa deliberately do so with the object of transferring the disease from themselves to the woman, a therapeutic effect which Jack has undoubtedly often observed, though he mistakes the rationale of the cure effected. Similarly well-founded is his horror of the doctor's attempt to prevent the suppuration of his "blue ball;" for though ignorant of the distinction between chancre and chancroid, he knows that a bubo that does not "break" will be followed by the horrible train of constitutional symptoms. As long as the sexual impulse exists it will be gratified, and, if not naturally, by such expedients as can be adopted, and the ingenuity will be exercised to devise novel modes of excitation. I have never

been attached to a ship in the service on board which manustu-
pration and pæderasty were not practiced, the latter, of course,
more rarely than the former. Other officers may deny that they
have heard of them, but I know these vices to be common, and
generally unknown only because uninvestigated or undiscovered.
"It is not to be denied that, however purified and fortified, the
sex-passion, in a healthy, continent adult, is very powerful; very
different from the sickly craving of the voluptuary, or the mad,
half-poetical desires of a boy." "How much severer occasional
incontinence makes the necessary struggle to remain continent at
all appears from the sexual distress which widowers or those married men to whom access to their wives is forbidden suffer."—
(Acton.) It can, therefore, scarcely be expected that the humble
wearer of blue flannel will excel him in blue broadcloth in that
mastery of his desires which theologians enjoin as necessary to
that purity of heart which is among the promised beatitudes, and
hence the naval hygienist has no other alternative than to recommend frequent liberty on shore as the only practicable means of
preventing the commission of secret sexual vices, though when
these habits are established even this will not serve to eradicate
them, as witness certain cases well known to medical officers in
our own and the British navy among officers of high rank.
Among the causes which formerly operated to enfeeble the sail-
or's constitution and shorten his life, I have no hesitancy in including celibacy. Reveille-Parise states that "amid the abundant statistics which have been collected lately, it has been demonstrated that bachelors live a shorter time than the Benedicts;"
and Dr. Stark, as quoted by Darwin, declares that "bachelorhood
is more destructive to life than the most unwholesome trades, or
than a residence in an unwholesome house, or district, where
there has never been the most distant attempt at sanitary improvement." In former days, in our own service, and even now, where
the systems of long enlistment and infrequent leaves of absence
prevail, the man-of-war's man was virtually a celibate. I have
known him return from an absence of three or four years, reship·

for another cruise, sometimes on the morrow, often the same week of his discharge, and thus pass years within the narrow compass of a ship's hull. Marriage, under such circumstances, was only a form, and even with officers was little better. A friend now high on the list, out of the first eleven years of his married life had not passed a sum-total of eleven months at home; and another, a British naval officer of rank, told me that though he had been married twenty-two years, he had lived less than an aggregate of one with his family. Instances like these will probably never again occur, at least in our own Navy, since every officer is by regulation entitled to a period of shore duty after each full cruise at sea, and sailors who obtain honorable discharges are also allowed three months' full pay on shore.

As an additional reward for good behavior, a liberal allowance of money should be made, and withheld from the undeserving, for the purchase of books, curiosities, or presents for friends at home. Most men have some dear relative or friend, for whom they desire to obtain some gift, and any expenditure for such an object should be sanctioned and encouraged.

There is so little to stimulate the ambition of the sailor on board a man-of-war that the superior class of native Americans are deterred from entering the Navy. In the merchant service the seaman aspires to become a mate or master, and, if industrious, temperate, and qualified, he succeeds; while in the Navy he may be twenty years a petty-officer without enjoying any increase of privilege over the ordinary seaman or landsman of as many days. His duties are more responsible, greater confidence is reposed in him, greater deference paid to his opinion; but he dresses as he has always done, he squats at the same mess-cloth, and is as much a prisoner on board ship. The Army offers opportunities of advancement through the non-commissioned grades to the line of promotion, and all such meritorious preferments are welcomed to their new station with the cordiality and public spirit characteristic of this arm of the national defense. It is a great defect in our naval organization that more distinction is not made between petty-officers and the rest of the crew. Their dress should be strikingly distinctive; they should constitute a totally separate mess; they should be granted greater indulgences, among them that of going on shore three or four at a time when their duties permit, without reference to the liberty allowed the other messes. They would then feel that the title officer was something more than a farce, and less deserving the adjunct "petty," and the silk-embroidered eagle on the arm would carry with it more respect than it does now under its familiar designation of "buzzard." The positions of mates and warrant-officers should be recruited from this class, and special effort should be made to ascertain and report all men qualified for and ambitious of obtaining such situations. The condition of the non-commissioned officers of the Marine Corps, who on shore are treated with the same consideration as the corresponding grades in the Army, is a peculiarly distressing one when they come on board ship and are subjected to the same restrictions and exactions as the petty-officers with whom they are there classed; and many very excellent sergeants have been .degraded and ultimately ruined by the humiliations which they have suffered in consequence of this system. The apothecary and yeoman, (the latter an unmeaning title, for which storekeeper should be substituted,) the one requiring a semi-professional education in pharmacy and the other intrusted with important pecuniary responsibilities, and probably also the schoolmaster, when one is allowed, properly belong to the class of appointed officers with the clerks of the commander and paymaster, and should mess with them in the steerage. Their duties require a far higher order of ability, for the clerks are only copyists, and their positions would become attractive to young men in the same genteel station in life were they removed from the coarse associations of the berth-deck. Much of the illicit treatment, especially of venereal complaints, by which the apothecary, unless closely watched by the medical officer, will attempt to eke out his inadequate salary, will be checked by giving this officer a status correspondent to the nature of his calling, as in the French, Brazilian, and other foreign navies. A still more important gain will be the getting rid of the class of imperfectly educated and broken-down drunkards, who now accept the position because their habits keep them from employment on shore, and of the still worse set of incompetents provisionally rated from the deck, who, however carefully the hospital liquors may be kept under lock by the medical officer, will steal part of those issued to the sick, or drink or sell the alcohol from the spirit-lamp or that from the percolator while making tinctures, or even the tinctures themselves, and who never compound a pill of calomel or quinine without running the risk of putting up corrosive sublimate or strychnine, or who add half an ounce of some potent liquid to a mixture when the prescription calls for half a drachm.

The act of Congress establishing honorable discharges and the institution of honorary badges indicative of every such discharge have accomplished excellent results. Care should be taken that every man entitled to the distinction receives it, and further that none is issued except in meritorious cases. I have seen an honorable discharge presented at a rendezvous by a man who desired to reship as a seaman, that being the rate he bore on the discharge, who, when examined, was found unable to send down a top-gallant-yard or reeve a top-sail buntline, and who finally admitted that he had not been in a top the whole cruise, but had been coxswain of the barge and arbitrarily rated seaman. The presentation of medals of honor, authorized by Congress, for conspicuous heroism during the rebellion, should be made a permanent institution. The pride with which Frenchmen display their little pieces of ribbon and the emulation excited among Englishmen by their Victoria cross and medal ought to have some parallel in the naval service of our own country.

Ennui and home-sickness affect the sailor less than the officer, but the monotony of his occupation and the protracted confinement on board ship ultimately cause him to become despondent and indifferent to his duties. Frequent occasions of visiting the shore and an abundance of reading-matter will do much to dissipate these enervating feelings; but I would suggest, without intending to interfere with the business of any other department, as a further means of occupying and interesting him, that more attention be paid on board ship to the minor works of nautical manufacture. Every one has observed the general interest excited by the occasional weaving of sword-mats and the crowds that cluster around the sailmaker's seat, the carpenter's bench, and the armorer's forge. Would it not be instructive as well as interesting to multiply these occupations, even though no immediate necessity existed for them? I do not suggest this, however, with the object of simply finding work for the crew. Spars, masts, and coamings have been scraped and painted, rescraped and repainted, and bright work, introduced wherever possible, blacked and polished, reblacked and repolished merely for the sake of keeping the men all the time occupied. Such unnecessary and distasteful work makes every one discontented and unhappy, particularly when accompanied with the announcement that " there will be no Sundays " on board the ship. The sailor has a considerable religious element in his character, and, though restive under long church services, he entertains a respect for everything sacred. In most vessels of the Navy the Sabbath is scrupulously observed. Saturdays also are very properly appropriated to the crew, that they may take their bags on deck, sew, arrange, and air their clothing, and examine their little possessions.

The depressing influences of sea life are to be further overcome by encouraging amusements and diversions. Music has its influence upon the sailor, as upon the dweller on shore. Witness how the fife causes him to redouble his exertions at the capstan when almost exhausted with fatigue. A ship with singers and instruments on board is always cheerful. The sounds of music, dancing, and laughter, which are heard toward sundown, indicate the contented crew, and wherever there are mirth and gayety there are not apt to be animosity and quarreling. Dominoes,

9 H

backgammon, and draughts are also sources of amusement. On
foreign stations many crews endeavor to enliven their time by
organizing theaters, glee-clubs, and negro-minstrel companies,
whose performances are often exceedingly creditable, while considerable ingenuity is displayed in getting up costumes and scenery. At other times they decorate their vessel for fancy balls, in
which they themselves assume the characters; and I have known
a dinner to be given by one ship's company to another, at which
speeches were made that could not have been excelled by the
officers. Often a little interest, encouragement, and pecuniary
assistance from the officers will lead to undertakings of this kind,
which might not otherwise have been originated. A magic lan-
tern, with a proper set of slides, would be invaluable for the occasional entertainment of the crew, particularly if its exhibitions
were accompanied with explanatory remarks by some of the officers.

Boat-racing, gymnastic feats in the rigging and on deck, swimming, fishing, hauling of the seine, and when the circumstances
of the place will permit, athletic games, as base ball, on shore,
washing clothes there, etc., will afford sport and diversion of in-
calculable benefit to the health of the crew, and contribute to the
diffusion of a spirit of happiness and contentment among them.
Target-firing, boat-racing, and sailing, and the landing of the
men for company, battalion, and howitzer drill are not only recrea-
tions but beneficial exercises. Some divisional officers infuse so
much interest in the ordinary exercises of the vessel by the enthu-
siastic, earnest and vivacious manner in which they impart their
instructions, and by the zeal with which they perform their duties, that their men always work with alacrity and pleasure.

While rewards, honors, and diversions are thus multiplied,
they must not be deprived of their value by inattention to the
necessity of punishing evil-doers. Discipline is the soul of a man-
of-war, and implicit obedience to the constituted authorities is
the prerequisite to discipline. It should be exacted of every man
and officer on board, and the example of submission to superior

authority should be set their crews by commanders and other officers themselves. Every regulation of the Navy Department, every order of the honorable Secretary of the Navy, and every act of Congress should be faithfully and fully obeyed, in the spirit and according to the letter, else the officer violating them cannot conscientiously punish those who infringe his rules.

There will be bad men on board all ships, who will interrupt order and harmony unless they are promptly and effectually punished. The act of Congress specifying the various allowable means of punishment was wisely and humanely framed. The penalties prescribed are efficacious, affecting the moral nature rather than causing physical suffering which may do permanent injury to the offender's health. The same spirit should actuate officers in imposing their lesser punishments. He who complains that he cannot manage a ship's company without his instruments of torture, only admits his unfitness for his position. A man of proper mental resources will find abundant means of bringing shame and mortification to the culprit by the withdrawal of privileges, the deprivation of spending-money, the restriction of liberty, the imposition of extra duties, particularly those of a disagreeable kind, etc. The bad are also indirectly but effectually punished whenever the good are conspicuously rewarded. Although forbidden by law, recent courts-martial have disclosed that confinement in "sweat-boxes," or, as they are euphemistically termed, "the cells," is still inflicted on board ships, at the risk of the life or jeopardy of the health of the man or boy who may have been guilty of some trivial offense. Besides its illegality, it is of a class with bucking and gagging, tricing up by the thumbs, the toes only touching the deck, or lashing on the inside of the rigging, the bare soles on the rattlins and rope yarns cutting into the wrists and ankles—barbarities unworthy the nineteenth century. As drunkenness is the source of most of the disturbances on board ship, if carefully guarded against there will never be occasion for gagging a man raving with alcoholic mania. When such cases do occur, rather than resort to means which aggravate the nervous symptoms and may occasion irreparable injury, let them be handed over to the medical officer, who by a little judicious treatment can soon quiet them. Punishment is thrown away on men whose brains cannot perform their functions. When reason and consciousness are restored, it will be appreciated and be of profit. No one thinks of gagging the noisy victim of delirium tremens, yet it would be as rational to do so as to try to smother the voice of the yelling inebriate.

THE SICK-BAY.

It is, of course, the paramount duty of the medical officer to
provide for the comfort of the sick.   In frigates the forward portion of the berth-deck is assigned to the sick-bay.   This apartment is always disproportionately small, usually badly ventilated,
imperfectly lighted, sometimes very wet, often foul and offensive
from leakage from the head-pipes, which lead through it, and
disturbed by the noise of the chain cables in coming to anchor
or getting under way.   The Guerriere and Tennessee are representatives of the finest and largest of the vessels of the modern
navy.   The former is a first-rate of about 2,500 tons, carrying
twenty-one guns; the latter a second-rate of 2,135 tons, with a
battery of twenty-three guns; and both are manned by crews
ranging from three hundred and fifty to five hundred men.   The
length of the berth-deck of the Guerriere is 310 feet, its average
breadth 28 feet, and its height between decks 6 feet 11 inches;
the corresponding measurements of the Tennessee's berth-deck
are 334 feet 4 inches length, 27 feet 9 inches average breadth,
and 7 feet 3 inches height; yet the sick-bay of the former has a
cubic capacity of only 2,275 feet, scarcely properly accommodat-
ing three patients; and that of the latter 4,867 feet, not more
than is required by five.   Important as is this portion of the vessel, its dimensions are rather a matter of accident or subordinate
to other considerations, than regulated by the numerical size of
the crew, the fitness of its location, the nature of the cruising
ground, and the probable amount of sickness.   Unless the sick-
bay can be removed to its proper site aft, it should be very much
enlarged and made as comfortable as possible.   Two or more
air-ports should open into it on either side, and a scuttle or hatch-
way should be cut through the decks overhead for the admission

of a wind-sail from either the spar-deck or, weather permitting, from the forward gun-deck ports. Several thick glass deck-lights should also admit light from the gun-deck. The entire bulkhead of the sick-bay should be made of light gratings, which should not be furnished with thick woolen curtains, as is commonly done. This apartment should be as impervious to water as it is possible to make it, and no pretext should ever sanction the discharge of the men's water-closets through its interior.

In sloops-of-war, brigs, and other single-deck vessels, the midship portion of the berth-deck is appropriated to the sick. Where there are midship lockers the mattresses are usually spread on top of them ; but this is inconvenient if the lockers require to be frequently opened, and as the hawsers, etc., which are usually stowed there, can be placed elsewhere, this space should be kept free from obstruction and devoted exclusively to the sick-bay.

To insist upon the cleanliness of this apartment would be to impugn the professional qualification of the medical officer, who, on board ship as in the bed-chamber on shore, regards this as a most important part of the treatment of every case. Everything should be scrupulously clean about the invalid. The canvas screen which isolates him, and the cot or hammock in which he lies, should be of natural whiteness, not soiled by grease and dirt; his head should rest upon a white-cased pillow, not be propped up by his boots or pea-jacket ; and a comfortable hospital mattress and clean sheets and counterpane should be substituted for his own rough, soiled blankets. The patent close-stool, now supplied all vessels from the Naval Laboratory, admirably answers its purpose of preserving the atmosphere of the sick-bay and berth-deck free from contamination. One or two cots should always be in readiness for the use of the sick. Even when ill but a few days it is a great relief for the sailor, who has been bent like a bow in his hammock, to lie in a horizontal position, and be able to stretch himself out at full length. The wooden cot-frame now in use is a clumsy affair that ought to give way to a light iron one easily gotten ready for service. The ambulance-cot devised by Surgeon Gorgas, United States Navy, for the especial purpose of transporting wounded men, ought to be supplied to every vessel. The cots containing fever invalids and other cases of serious illness should always be slung on the gun-deck of vessels with covered batteries, and when the weather will permit, such patients should be placed under the top-gallant forecastle of single-deck sloops.

The medical officer must decide how far the healthy members of the ship's company are to be inconvenienced by the sick. Usually the humanity of the sailor and officer prompts them to sacrifice every selfish interest in behalf of their invalid shipmates, but occasionally a churlish fellow is met who boasts that he has never been sick an hour in his life, and only grudgingly assents to or flatly refuses the requests of the medical officer. If the latter is known to be zealous, devoted, and self-sacrificing in the performance of his duties to the sick, he will seldom have any difficulty in having them properly cared for. I have had charge of cases of low fever and dangerous operations where the successful issue was largely, if not entirely, due to the assiduous and intelligent watching of the volunteer nurses. Occasionally an officer will insist on the blind adherence to routine duty, notwithstanding the urgent representations of the medical officer of the risk thereby occasioned to critical cases of sickness. Fortunate if no harm is done; but I was a witness some years ago of death under peculiarly distressing circumstances of this nature. A marine, exhausted by a severe pulmonary hæmorrhage on the previous evening, was lying in a cot on the berth-deck on a Saturday morning, the usual day for holy-stoning the deck. Although the danger of moving the man was fully represented, he was carried on deck and placed under the top-gallant forecastle, the removal being followed within less than ten minutes by a hæmorrhage, which quickly terminated fatally.

Other circumstances the same, food, air, light, and attendance, I am satisfied that invalids will recover more rapidly on shore than in the best possibly regulated hospital-ship. The most extensive experiment of this sort, which had then been made by our Government, was the Idaho, to the medical charge of which I was appointed in September, 1867. She was a steamship of the first rate, from which the machinery had been removed, and was stationed at Nagasaki, Japan, "to be used in part as a store and hospital-ship for the vessels of the Asiatic squadron." Although one of the largest vessels in the Navy, (2,638 tons,) she proved unfit for this double and incongruous purpose. It was originally contemplated to devote the whole main (berth) deck to hospital purposes, but the part actually under medical control for the use of the sick only extended forward from the main-hatch to the water-closets, an area containing twenty thousand one hundred and sixty cubic feet of air space, within which the plan provided for fifty iron bedsteads. I erected, however, only forty, of which thirty were usually occupied, each invalid even then having only six hundred and seventy-two cubic feet of space. This was subsequently further largely intrenched upon by the erection of prison-cells for the criminals of the squadron on the forward portion of the hospital-deck. Sir J. Ranald Martin states, in this connection, that "each man should have from fifteen hundred to two thousand cubic feet of air space; in very airy and exposed situations the smaller space will suffice." Among the most celebrated modern hospital establishments, the Lincoln Army General Hospital supplied fourteen hundred and forty-seven cubic feet of air space per man; the Herbert Military Hospital at Woolwich furnishes from twelve to fourteen hundred; the Blackburn Hospital at Manchester, seventeen hundred and ninety-four; the Lariboisiere, at Paris, from seventeen to nineteen hundred; the Boston Free Hospital, sixteen hundred, and the Episcopal Hospital at Philadelphia, two thousand. Furthermore, according to Hammond, a ward containing twelve hundred cubic feet should have its air completely renewed every hour, being at the rate of twenty cubic feet per minute, while a supply of thirty or forty is preferable. The ventilation of the Idaho was altogether insufficient, being effected solely through the ordinary

small round air-ports, high from the deck, and through the hatchways, wind-sails being usually conducted through the latter, but
very often led into the hold beneath the hospital, where an immense quantity of provisions and steamer-coal were stored, of
which the gaseous products of decomposition stained the paint-
work, created noisome bilge-water, and rendered the atmosphere
offensive. Large square ports through the ship's sides would
have supplied a greater abundance of fresh air and mitigated
these evils, but permission to have them cut could not be obtained.
The sick were further inconvenienced by the incessant noises
attending the daily evolutions of a man-of-war, which were regularly and completely carried on; by the working of the great
guns and howitzers; by the exercise of small-arm men and with
broad-swords and single-sticks; by the tumult and uproar of divisional and especially of general quarters; by the receiving and
discharging of coal and provisions for the squadron which had
no other outlet nor inlet than directly through the hospital; by
the trampling of men overhead; by the frequent drum-beats;
by the shrill whistling and loud bawling of the boatswain's mates;
by the trumpet-sounded orders of the officer of the deck; by the
piping of the side when officers came on board or left the ship;
and by the loud clanging of the bell striking half-hours in tones
heard at every bungalow on the neighboring hill-sides. For a
vessel to be as efficient as possible for hospital purposes it must
be absolutely disconnected from every other duty, and even then
it will lack the advantages of the hospital on shore—the quietude,
space, lightness, airiness, the shaded gardens for exercise, and
that indescribable influence of the land itself, to which I have
elsewhere referred.

When invalids must be treated on board ship, they should be
sent on shore for exercise, under proper surveillance, as soon as
convalescent. They who have this privilege will return to duty
much sooner than those restricted to the ship. I have seen men
slowly lingering weeks and months in a dark, stifling sick-bay in
the bows, hanging in a greasy hammock, wrapped in soiled

blankets, without sheets or other pillow than their boots or pantaloons, a dull-looking tin pint-pot of cold, nauseous tea or coffee and a piece of hard-tack, or a black tin pan containing a chunk of salt meat, stuck on a beam beside them, who were ultimately invalided and discharged from the service, who, comfortably circumstanced on a light airy deck, in a clean cot, between white sheets and properly bathed and fed, would soon have been able to have been carried on deck in a chair, for an hour's exposure to the sunshine, then taken on shore by a nurse for daily exercise, and finally discharged to duty. The medical officer should not detain a man on the sick-list a day longer than is necessary. His paramount duty is to maintain the *personnel* of the vessel in the most efficient condition, and when this is deranged to restore it without delay. No man, however, should be returned to duty until fully able to perform the work required of him, and any physician who could be guilty of such a violation of professional trust would justly deserve the contempt of his brethren and the scorn of all good men.

The practice of indiscriminate invaliding is exceedingly demoralizing. Men, in order to get away from ships which they dislike, feign sickness, or, when really ill, endeavor to retard their recovery; and, if discharged from the sick list, present themselves again and again at the dispensary, seeking to establish such a reputation for physical inability or worthlessness as will accomplish their object of getting surveyed and sent home. There are not a few officers in the Navy, professing valetudinarians, who offer themselves as candidates for survey whenever disagreeable, arduous, or dangerous duty is assigned them, and who, through the good nature, credulity, or negligence of the medical boards, generally gain their end. Not the least evil attending the invaliding of numbers of a crew is the necessity of shipping other men on a foreign station to supply their places, and experience has shown that a very large proportion of such recruits very soon themselves come under treatment for constitutional diseases which were undiscoverable, and which they swore did not exist, at the time of shipment. During the past summer I received a letter, dated at Callao, from Dr. John S. Kitchen, the surgeon of the United States steamship California, *en route* to join the Pacific fleet, stating: "We have on board six chronic diarrhœas and two epilepsies from the St. Mary's, all enlisted on this coast within six or eight months. Every one of them acknowledged that he had the disease before enlisting." Hence, a system of properly organized temporary hospitals on shore, at the headquarters of the several stations, will save the Government a large expenditure of money, and an enormous waste of excellent physical material. Men, however, who have actually succumbed to climatic influences, should be sent home, not by "the first public conveyance," which may necessitate months of waiting, but by the earliest opportunity, without regard to expense; since the sooner they are removed from the deleterious climate, the sooner they will be able to do duty elsewhere.

The proper treatment of malingering, which is especially common on board ships to which inexperienced medical officers are attached, should occur to every educated physician.

SANITARY REGULATIONS FOR THE NAVY.

I have epitomized the proposed set of sanitary regulations which follow from the suggestions briefly tendered in the foregoing pages, and submit them to my associates in the medical corps, and to such commanding officers as may be willing to apply to them the test of experiment, with a view to the ultimate institution by the Department, if not of these rules, of others which may better accomplish the hygienic objects desired.

Dryness, coolness, fresh air, sunshine, cleanliness of body, clothes and bedding, good food, pure water, temperance, refreshing sleep, occupation, exercise, cheerfulness, and contentment of mind are not only the best anti-scorbutics, but anti-dysenterics, anti-febrifics, and anti-morbifics in every sense. The hygienic precautions I have suggested receive an indorsement of unquestionable value from the following recommendations by Hennen, which, though intended for soldiers, are based upon those same general laws of health by which the human body is governed as well at sea as on land: " The true preventives to disease are shelter from the heat of the day, and from the dews and cold of night, avoiding the neighborhood of marshes, allowing men natural sleep, allowing vegetables in due proportion, a comfortable breakfast before duty in the morning, the daily exposure of bedding to the sun, the change of clothing after hot and rainy weather, flannel waistcoats or cotton shirts, frequent bathing, daily washing of the feet, and the serving out of spirits only in the evening." " If it be true, as it undoubtedly is," concludes Guy, in a review of the meliorating influences exerted by sanitary science upon the British navy, " that by improvements in diet, water supply and ventilation, in clothing and cleanliness, aided by superior medical treatment, and especially by vaccination, and by an improved discipline, tempered by mental culture and amusement; if it be that these improvements and reforms have saved life and prevented sickness to such an extent, that the effective force of our Navy has been more than doubled, that one ship, for every purpose of navigation and warfare, is at least equal to two of the same size and force, that a vessel can now keep the sea for twice or thrice the time that was possible less than a century ago; if it be true that, at the old rate of mortality, all Europe could not have furnished the seamen necessary for our defense and safety during the great revolutionary war, then it is a mere waste of words to argue that health, which is.the strength of all who work, is the great source of power to nations in their peaceful labors as in their warlike struggles." Blane early in the century attributed the improvement in the health of the British navy, which even then began to be notable, to the cessation of impressment, the issue of an anti-scorbutic ration, the increased encouragement to surgeons, and the better enforcement of medical regulations; and Inspector General Smart, one of the most distinguised of European sanitary authorities, further adds: " Since that era, the prevention of diseases among seamen has not been neglected; medical influence has continued its exercise with immense advantage to the sea-service. Peculiar hurts, wounds, and accidents, from which landsmen are exempt, must remain forever the special casualties of seamen; but even these may be deprived of much of their fatality. Scurvy and typhus have been banished from our Navy returns; but there still remain, with undue prominence, the reports of yellow fever, syphilis, rheumatism, and phthisis, which are, however, being reduced under hygienic measures more nearly to general ratios; and when that has been effected, the seaman's life, always hazardous, will be acceptable on account of its superior healthiness." If, therefore, commanding officers will listen to and be influenced by the advice of medical officers, berth-decks and gun-decks will not be incumbered with cots and hammocks, division officers will not have to complain that their guns' crews are incomplete, the efficiency of the vessel will be promoted, and when emergencies arise, as during the rebellion, when the national honor has to be vindicated, there will be a strong, stalwart set of zealous men to fight side by side with their officers, and repay tenfold those who have had such anxious regard for their health and comfort. " But an army in hospital," says Sir Ranald Martin, " as at Walcheren, at Rangoon, and in the Crimea—what availeth it to the statesman or the commander ?   It is an incumbrance—a waste—almost a nullity."

PROPOSED SANITARY REGULATIONS FOR THE NAVY.

I.

The greatest care must be exercised in keeping all parts of the vessel, especially those below the spar-deck, clean, dry, well lighted, and thoroughly ventilated.

II.

The berth-deck and covered gun-decks will never be wetted, except for thorough cleaning, and then only on very dry days, and not oftener than once a week; and the operations of cleaning and drying will always be conducted as expeditiously as possible.   Those men only engaged in the work will be allowed upon them, until they are perfectly dry.   Hot water will be used, wind-sails set, ventilators operated, air-ports and gun-ports opened, when not dangerous, and drying-stoves heated.   Mere wet-swabbing of the deck will be strictly forbidden at all times, and scraping resorted to instead.   When a continuance of bad weather keeps the berth-deck wet, drying-stoves will be frequently lighted, and it will be sanded, as will also be done when any unclean work is about being undertaken.

III.

Particular care will be exercised in keeping the hold and spirit-room dry.   They will be thoroughly whitewashed every month, and be frequently ventilated by the introduction of wind-sails and ventilators. Whitewash will be used on the beams, bulk-heads, and ship's sides of the berth-deck in place of paint.

IV.

No casks, boxes, or other articles will be stowed in the hold, unless clean and dry. No wet coal, nor wet or green wood will be ever sent below the spar-deck. Dry days will be selected for provisioning and coaling, unless the urgent necessities of the service positively forbid delay.

V.

All hatches, gratings, and ladders scrubbed or washed on other days than those for the general cleaning of the berth-deck, will be cleaned and dried in the open air.

VI.

Awnings and boom-covers will be promptly spread or housed on the occurrence of rain. The men will be required to protect themselves by water-proof clothing, and will not be permitted to sleep in wet clothes. The watches, when relieved at night, will be required to remove their wet clothes, and deposit them in tubs, provided for their reception, where they will remain until piped up to dry. Boats' crews, returning wet, will also be required to change their clothing.

VII.

Particular care will be exercised in sheltering " the head " by a hood in rainy weather, and by an awning when the heat is intense.

VIII.

All wet or damp clothing and sails will be exposed to be dried without delay.

IX.

When bilge-water has formed, it is to be entirely discharged, and fresh water allowed to flow into the vessel. After the lapse of an hour this is to be again discharged, and these operations will be repeated until the water is brought up free from odor, but the quantity of water introduced should never exceed the minimum indicated by the soundings of the well.

X.

Air-ports will be opened and wind-sails set whenever not attended with positive risk, and the latter will be kept carefully trimmed. All the lowermost parts of the vessel (including sail-room, yeoman's and officers' store-rooms, etc.) will be frequently opened for ventilation. Every effort will be made to maintain a free circulation of air forward and aft on each deck. All bulkheads separating apartments or marking subdivisions of the vessel will be latticed or grated, above and below, when not at the sacrifice of strength.

XI.

Ventilators will be placed on board every vessel in the Navy, and will be put in operation every night and morning; and in narrow tide-ways vessels will be kept sprung broadside to the prevailing wind.

XII.

Awnings will be kept spread while the temperature of the atmosphere exceeds 80° F., except after a continuance of rainy weather or during the operations of cleaning the lower decks.

XIII.

The exposure of the crew to the intense heat of the sun, especially in tropical climates, will be avoided by the performance of all labor or exercise not imperatively called for between these hours, before 9 a. m. or after 5 p. m.

XIV.

Every man will be required to possess sufficient clothing to change twice if exposed to wet.

XV.

Flannel or woolen garments must be worn next the skin at all seasons; and frequent changes of under-clothing and habitual neatness and cleanliness of dress must be insisted upon.

XVI.

When the weather will permit, at least two wash-days will be allowed every week.

XVII.

Cleanliness of person will be required of every man. Swimming will be allowed when practicable; if dangerous, a tub will be placed under the top-gallant forecastle, or the head-pump, or port-side of the manger, will be screened and used for general ablution. Any unclean man will be compelled to bathe under the supervision of the master-at-arms.

XVIII.

Firemen and coal-heavers will be afforded especial facilities for bathing, which, however, will be interdicted immediately after leaving the fire-room.

XIX.

Fresh food will be obtained every day, when possible, except the stay in port be prolonged, in which case it may be issued four or five times a week. Berth-deck messes will be allowed to carry potatoes, turnips, onions, &c., as sea-stores.

10

XX.

The crew will breakfast at 7 a. m., dine at noon, and have supper at 6 p. m. Hot coffee and biscuit will be issued immediately on turning out. All meals, including tea and coffee, will be carefully inspected as to character of preparation, and will be eaten on deck whenever the weather will permit.

XXI.

During a continuance of inclement weather the galley fire will be kept lighted all night, and hot coffee issued the watches.

XXII.

No water for drinking will ever be received on board, nor that distilled ever be issued, until it has been examined by a medical officer and pronounced potable, and no condensed water will ever be passed below into the tanks until properly cooled.

XXIII.

Every man will be required to sleep in his own hammock, each watch to "lash and carry." In bad weather the hammocks of the watch on deck will be kept down on the berth-deck on their appropriate hooks or in some dry place. No damp clothing will ever be stowed in the hammocks or hammock-nettings.

XXIV.

All bedding must be shaken and exposed in the rigging on dry, clear days once a week, if possible.

XXV.

The watch will not be allowed to sleep on deck in rainy weather, nor exposed to dew and currents of air through ports and scupper-holes.

XXVI.

The system of steady berth-deck cooks will be discountenanced. The yeoman, master-at-arms, ship's corporal, captain of the hold, writers, nurses, stewards, cooks, servants, and all others whose duties confine them below, will be required to pass a certain portion of each day in the open air during the hours of daylight. Special exercise at great guns, small-arms, single-sticks, rowing, and going aloft will be assigned to each of them.

XXVII.

Amusements, singing, dancing, gymnastic exercises in the rigging, sports on deck, boat-sailing and racing will be encouraged.

XXVIII.

Vessels will avoid notoriously unhealthy ports, rivers, or other localities, unless upon imperative public service, and in such places will anchor a sufficient distance from the shore to be protected from malarious influences; and all boat excursions, hunting-parties, or visits of men and officers on shore after sunset or before sunrise, or continuance there all night, will be strictly forbidden; and all boat and shore duty involving exposure to sun and rain will be performed, whenever possible, by the natives of the country.

XXIX.

When the general health of a ship's company shall be reported by the medical officers as impaired from anchoring or cruising in unhealthy localities, the earliest possible opportunity will be given to recruit, by transferring the vessel to some invigorating station, and invalids and convalescents from diseases induced by climatic influences will be sent to the United States without delay.

XXX.

Medical officers are strictly enjoined to exercise an unceasing vigilance over the sanitary condition of the vessels of the Navy and of the officers and men on board them, and to this end to inquire diligently and report to commanding officers, or to the Department, everything conducive to, or militating against, the health, comfort, and efficiency of each ship's company.

SANITARY REGULATIONS FOR TRANS-PORTS.

The causes that operate to make men-of-war unhealthy exist in greater force on board of vessels engaged in transporting troops. There is a greater accumulation of filth from the evacuation of the contents of the stomach by the sea-sick and of fæces and urine by those too lazy or unable to go to the water-closets; there is a more considerable impoverishment of air by the over-crowding of men; and the depressing influences of discontent, disappointment, and home-sickness, operate to a more powerful degree upon the soldier than the sailor. The steamers that carried three-months' volunteers to Annapolis in April, 1861, arrived, after only three days' passage from New York, in the most filthy condition imaginable, and, had the weather been hotter, or the passage a few hours longer, three-fourths of the troops would certainly have been disabled. As the military surgeons who accompany transports are frequently unused to the special exigencies of ship life, their labors will, probably, be somewhat facilitated by the following suggestions:

PROPOSED SANITARY REGULATIONS FOR TRANSPORTS.

I.

A spacious, convenient, light, well-ventilated part of the vessel should be selected for a sick-bay or hospital, which should be under the special care of the hospital steward and nurses, and whither all invalids, excepting trifling cases able to go on deck, should be tranferred as soon as reported ill.

II.

Besides the regular attendants upon the sick, two or three men, not subject to sea-sickness, should be detailed from each company to act as a *sanitary police*, who are to be under the immediate control of the medical officers. They should be divided into three watches and be kept alternately on duty, both night and day, in the ordinary succession of sea-watches. They should be required to patrol the sleeping quarters of the men, and be constantly on the alert to prevent any act of uncleanliness. Sea-sick men who vomit or discharge their urine and excrement on the deck or in their bunks, should be immediately removed to the spar-deck, and the excreted matters at once cleared away. The sea-sick should be compelled to remain on deck all the time and be placed on mattresses, if too ill to sit up. Compulsory exercise by being walked between two men and the compulsory ingestion of hot soup will hasten their recovery.

III.

All hands should be called at daylight, and be compelled to make up their beds neatly, rolling back the upper blanket to expose the interior, and then go on deck. The bunks should be carefully inspected every morning, and all wet blankets and clothing sent on deck to be dried on clothes-lines.

IV.

Clothing and accouterments should be kept in places assigned them, and not be allowed to encumber the bunks. A certain hour should be appointed for changing under-clothing, and access denied to it at all other times, except in special cases.

V.

The men should be kept on deck all day when possible, but never be allowed to lie down or sleep on a wet deck. Awnings should be spread forward and aft in hot or rainy weather, and the men should be further protected from rain by overcoats, which should never be placed in their bunks, but be hung up on their bunk-posts, or in a place appointed.

VI.

All air-ports should be kept open whenever possible, and wind-sails should be set all the time and pointed to every change of wind. In rainy weather tubs should be placed under them to collect the water. Every transport should be outfitted with ventilators, operated by hand or machinery.

VII.

If the troops remain more than a few days on board, their bedding should be exposed to the sun and air at least once a week.

VIII.

The men should be required to wash their bodies every morning, stripping perfectly nude when the weather will permit. If the transport cannot supply condensed steam for the purpose, salt-water soap should be provided for the ablution of the body and for washing clothes.

IX.

If the berth-decks are kept perfectly clean they will not require to be washed oftener than once a week, and this should be done only in dry weather and with hot water, which should be removed as rapidly as possible by swabs, squillgees, drying stoves, &c. The beams, bulk-heads, and bunk-posts should be whitewashed at the same time.

X.

Hot coffee and biscuit should be issued on turning out. Breakfast at 7 a. m.; dinner at noon, and supper at 6 p. m.; and all meals should be eaten on deck, except in very inclement weather.

XI.

The men should be occupied with their proper military exercises as much as possible, as well as be obliged to assist in working ship, hoisting ashes, getting up anchor, &c.

ERRATA AND ADDENDA.

Page 11, *line* 35: It cannot be too often repeated that the object of the physician on board ship is not to breed dissension, but to assist the executive authorities by maintaining the *personnel* of the Navy in its state of utmost physical efficiency; not to augment, but diminish sick-lists and empty sick-bays and hospitals. When a vessel with a complement of one hundred and fifty men has a daily sick-list of ten or fifteen, something is wrong. Both commanding and medical officers should be mutually interested in discovering and remedying that wrong, and it is often possible that the latter, through misjudged kindness, the imposition of malingerers, or an unpardonable feeling of spite, is as responsible as the former, whose unwise harshness, laxity of discipline, or neglected hygiene has disabled his vessel. "You, doctors, are so sensitive," remarked a commander to me a few days ago, "that we cannot suggest that a man is shamming without offending you." Let us hope that henceforth both commanding and medical officers, with a more perfect confidence in each other's professional integrity, will not hesitate to confer amicably on all questions concerning the hygiene of the ships and stations on which they serve.

Page 15, *line* 29. The records of the Bureau of Medicine and Surgery contain the following names, which are all intended to represent one individual: Charles Jacks, Charles Zerks, Clans Zeike, Clane Ezekiel, and Ezekiel Claue.

Page 19, *line* 21: Yet blunders gross as these are still committed. While preparing my monthly return of men examined for enlistment during July, 1872, at the Philadelphia rendezvous, with which I was then temporarily connected, I was induced to compare it with the recruiting officer's list, and was surprised to find that a man described as John J. Harrison on the surgeon's roll, was represented on the other simply as James Harrison. Referring to the original certificate of physical capacity, (Form Q,) it was evident that part only of the man's full name, John James, had been retained by the careless clerk, who prepared the records of the office. During the same month, Private Ketterer was recruited as Kettereer and described as Ketteerer, although he had legibly signed his name without any double e whatever. A still more flagrant case occurred a month later. I had sent in the descriptive list of Hermann Philipp Spengler, and in five minutes received an enlistment paper from the clerk for my indorsement filled up with the name of Hermann Phillip Spangler.

Page 21, *line* 9 : 11. *Eyes*—light or dark blue, gray, hazel, bicolored, prominent, sunken, etc.

12. *Hair*—light or dark chestnut, brown, auburn, sandy, red, flaxen, gray, black, thin, bald, straight, curly, wool, etc.

13. *Nose*—large, small, aquiline, pug, flat, sharp, bent, etc.

14. *Mouth*—small, large, thick or thin-lipped, etc.

15. *Teeth*—perfect, irregular, deficiences, etc.

16. *Distinguishing marks and peculiarities*—smoothness or hirsuteness of surface, etc., etc.

Page 34, *line* 1 : Read " shore-folk " for "folks."

Page 35, *line* 16 : Read "employés" for "employees."

Page 42, *line* 18 : Since the first issue of these suggestions, I have been favored by officers of experience, both line and medical, with numerous instances corroborating these views. A prominent case, related to me by Medical Director Maxwell, was that of the Powhattan, a vessel formerly remarkable healthy, which was anchored during the rainy season at Kow-luen, opposite Hong-Kong, and soon became totally ineffective from an enormous sick-list of pneumonia, dysentery, and fever. Agreeably to his recommendations, the ship went to sea with every furnace lighted and every port and hatch kept open until she was thoroughly dried, with the immediate abatement of the miasmatic affections which had decimated the crew. Admiral Boggs informs me that he, of all the naval officers commanding the mail-steamers to Aspinwall, escaped illness by having his cabin heated every evening; and he narrates a conclusive instance of the prophylactic influence of heat from his experience on the coast of Africa, when compelled to pass a couple of days on shore below Monrovia, he and all but two of his men remained with impunity by sheltering themselves at night in a hut in which a large fire was kept burning, while these two who slept outside, succumbed to the prevailing fever.

Page 43, *line* 17, *et seq.* : Read—by swabs and squilgees, and then drying-stoves should be lighted and kept swinging until the decks are completely dried, when they should be thoroughly coated with shellac. The common form of drying-stove is objectionable, because not provided with cover and pipe for discharging, through the ports or hatchways, the products of the combustion of the charcoal, an arrangement which should only be omitted when the vessel is rolling too much to allow its use.

Page 45, *line* 19 : After " has formed," read, and the bilges are so constructed that they cannot be cleaned in any other way.

Page 46, *line* 5 : Experiments are being made with an automatic bilge-pump, which proposes to prevent any accumulation of water in the bilges. It is also being attempted to provide for the ventilation of the vessel by a similar apparatus, a column of water acted upon by the rolling of the vessel being substituted for the mercurial column in the bilge-pump; and I learn from Rear-Admiral Boggs that he has introduced this ventilating-pump on board some of the light-ships, and that the escape-air issues in sufficient force to operate a fog-horn.

Page 48, *line* 3 : Read " ten " for "two."

Page 63, *line* 11 : The narrow leathern strap or belt, often worn around the waist, should be interdicted, on account of its interference with the circulation; the pantaloons and drawers being supported by buckles or lacings.

Page 63, *line* 18 : Surgeon E. D. Payne, United States Navy, has recently performed some interesting experiments testing the hygienic value of certain articles of sailor's clothing, and shown the very considerable elevation of temperature above that of the outside air, under the cap now worn. He has also called attention to the power of absorbing water from a damp deck possessed by the soles of the shoes with which men-of-war's men are now supplied.

Page 82, *line* 28 : The naval appropriation bill, approved May 23, 1872, provides, "That an additional ration of tea or coffee and sugar shall be hereafter allowed to each seaman, to be provided at his first 'turning out.'"

Page 91, *line* 35 : Condensed water should always be cooled before it is passed into the tanks. When this is neglected, the consequent elevation of temperature hastens the decomposition of the provisions usually stowed upon the tanks.

Page 101, *line* 20 : Read "offices" for "officer."

Page 101, *line* 27 : Read "clerks, commander's and paymaster's," for "clerks, commanders, and paymasters."

Page 107, *line* 3 : Read after "fever," and I learn from Medical-Director Beale that the Boxer lay twenty miles up the Cong, the most unhealthy of the African rivers, without detriment to the health of the crew, by merely anchoring three miles off shore.

Page 131, *line* 6 : Frederick James Brown, M. D., late of the royal navy, in a valuable little work entitled " Questions and Observations in Hygiene, recommended to the consideration of naval medical men," thus answers the question: "Is the general discipline of the ship strict or lax; and have you noticed, as a consequence of either system, distinctly referable to such, an increase of the real sickness of the ship, independently of the number merely on the list?"

"The answer to be returned to this question will be: I believe both health and comfort suffer under a lax state of discipline. And this is my reason for handling subjects which may be considered beyond my province by many who will read these pages.

"If the commanding officer should permit offenses, even the slightest, to be committed with impunity, and does not support the officers serving under him in the execution of their duty, both the officers and the petty-officers will become remiss and careless, and the men idle, dissipated, insolent, and refractory. Disease is the consequence of the indolence, filth, drunkenness, and badly-disposed mental condition of such a crew."

Page 144, *line* 1: When bilge-water has formed, it is to be entirely discharged, and if the bilges are not directly accessible for cleaning, but in this case only, fresh water may be allowed to flow into the vessel.

The accents have been inadvertently omitted by the printer in the following French words:

Page 26, *line* 34: Kéraudren.
Page 31, *line* 4: habitués.
Page 35, *line* 1: employés.
Page 41, *line* 8: Despérières, Kéraudren.
Page 47, *line* 15: Lariboisière.
Page 65, *line* 9: Département.

Page 90, *line* 28: Roncière.
Page 91, *lines* 13, 18: Roncière.
Page 115, *line* 20: débris.
Page 116, *line* 4: visé.
Page 116, *line* 26: Lévy.
Page 125, *line* 25: Reveillé.
Page 136, *line* 28: Lariboisière.

RESECTION

OF

HEAD OF FEMUR FOR GUNSHOT WOUND.

BY

W. E. TAYLOR, M. D.,
SURGEON UNITED STATES NAVY.

RESECTION OF HEAD OF FEMUR FOR GUNSHOT WOUND.

By W. E. Taylor, *Surgeon United States Navy.*

Naval Hospital, Mare Island, California,
July 12, 1870.

Name.—Charles B. Scott.
Grade.—Seaman.
Native of—Ireland; age, 34 years.
Shipped at—San Francisco, May 17, 1869.
Admitted from the United States Steamer Mohican, July 12, 1870.
Diagnosis by hospital ticket.—Gunshot wound.

FRED. E. POTTER,
Surgeon United States Navy.

Hospital ticket states: Time and place of occurrence, Teacapan River, west coast of Mexico, June 17, 1870. Origin: There is positive evidence that it was in the line of duty, the facts being as follows, viz:

Was wounded during an attack upon a piratical vessel, in Teacapan River, west coast of Mexico, June 17, 1870, the ball entering the left natis, midway between great trochanter of left femur and point of coccyx; have been unable to discover its exact locality; discharge, scanty; general health, fair; treatment, water-dressing, and anodynes when required.

On admission, general condition of the patient is decidedly below par; appetite is poor; does not sleep well, and complains of a great deal of pain in the left hip-joint, upon the least motion. In consequence of the long sea-voyage, (eleven days,) and his having been moved about so much, it is not considered advisable to make an examination of the injury until he shall have become somewhat rested. To have full diet and milk, and sulph. morphiæ at night.

13*th.*—Took gr.ss. sulph. morphiæ last night, but did not rest well.

14*th.*—Rested well last night without any morphia, and feels more refreshed to-day.   An examination of the wound was made, with the following results, viz : Patient is unable to lie upon his back, but lies upon his right side, with the injured limb semiflexed, and resting upon the right leg; the whole limb is inverted and rotated inward.   On account of this position it is difficult to get an accurate measurement of the injured limb, but, as far as can be ascertained, it seems to be about one inch shorter than its fellow.   The motion is very limited, but, with some pain and difficulty, the left leg and thigh can be moved a short distance outward.   The wound of entrance is small, and situated a little below the top of the great trochanter, and about two inches posterior to it.   The discharge from it is scanty, sanious, and fetid. Examination with a probe shows that the ball, after entering at the above-mentioned point, passed inward, forward, and a little upward.   The instrument readily passed for some distance in this direction, which led directly toward the neck and head of the bone.   After passing between two and three inches, the point of the probe was arrested against a rough solid body, and then seemed to pass on in a cavity lined with bone, for a short distance, when it became finally arrested.   From this it would seem that the neck of the femur had been pretty extensively fractured, and probably the head also.   Nothing was felt that was thought to be the ball.   The porcelain-pointed probe was also used, but failed to show any lead-marks.   Probe was much discolored. The ball is probably lodged in the head or cotyloid cavity.

From the length of time which has elapsed since the injury, it is likely that more or less callus has formed, and this, together with the awkward position of the limb, made the examination somewhat unsatisfactory.   The examination was made without using any anæsthetic.   The joint is not much swollen, but is very tender to the touch.   The patient is in a much better condition than could be expected after such a serious wound ; his appetite is improving; he has no hectic, and sleeps tolerably well; bowels regular.

R.—Quiniæ sulph., ʒi.
Ferri chlor. tinct., ʒi.
Glycerin., ʒiij.

Ft. sol.—S. Teaspoonful three times a day. To have full diet, milk and ale, and sulph. morphiæ at night, as required.

Wound to be dressed with oakum. Under the circumstances, some operation will doubtless be required, and it is desirable to get the patient in as good a condition as possible.

July 25th.—Patient has not improved as much as was anticipated, notwithstanding rest, nutritious diet, etc. He complains of constant pain in the limb, which he is unable to move or allow to be moved; and as he seems to be slowly failing, and there being evidently no prospect of recovery if treated on the expectant plan, the operation of excision of the injured parts was decided upon as giving him the best chance for life, especially as there was no injury to the large vessels and nerves, and very little damage to the soft parts. The nature of the case, the chances of life, and the risks of the operation having been fully explained to the patient, he cheerfully consented to submit to any operation that might be considered necessary. Accordingly it was determined to perform the operation to-day. The following-named medical gentlemen were present, viz: Surgeon John M. Browne, Assistant Surgeons J. A. Hawke and A. M Owen, United States Navy; and Drs. Weed and Vallijo, or Vallejo, California. At 11 o'clock a. m. the patient was placed thoroughly under the influence of chloroform by Assistant Surgeon A. M. Owen. The limb was brought to the straight position. This was easily accomplished, and during the movement well-marked crepitus was elicited. A straight incision was then made, commencing about two inches above the great trochanter, and carried downward over its center and along the outer side of the thigh for about eight inches. This incision was carried deeply, and the joint readily exposed and opened. The finger being then carried into the joint it was found that the neck of the femur was broken entirely across, and numerous fragments of bone could be felt in the cavity.   The thigh was then well adducted and pushed upward in order to render the trochanter prominent.   The muscular attachments were then carefully divided close to the bone, which, being well cleared, was pushed through the wound and sawn off just below the trochanter minor, with an ordinary amputating saw; after which the fragments of the neck and head were removed with the fingers and forceps.   The removal of these fragments, some twelve in number, was easily accomplished.   The ball, a conoidal one, weighing 240 grains, and very much battered, was also removed along with the fragments of the head, where it had lodged after causing the fracture.   The capsular ligament was pretty thoroughly removed.   No new bone had been formed. The wound of entrance was not interfered with, as it was so far removed from the line of incision.   Very little blood was lost— about four ounces.   Two small arteries required securing.   The entire wound was thoroughly syringed with a weak solution of permanganate of potassa in order to destroy fetor and remove clots of blood and osseous fragments.   After the bleeding had ceased the wound was partially approximated by four sutures, about two inches of the central portion being left open for drainage.   Patient was placed in bed, with the limb secured in the straight position in an ordinary fracture-box, and the wound dressed with oakum.   The patient bore the operation very well, and promptly rallied from the effects of the chloroform, soon after which he took gr. ss. sulph. morphæ in ℥ij of whisky, to be followed by beef essence, the morphia to be repeated at 3 o'clock p. m.

Upon examination of the injured bone, after its removal, it was found that the ball had struck the head of the bone at its junction with the neck, breaking the latter into three pieces, the line of fracture being oblique, and extending into and involving the head.   The head of the bone was also extensively comminuted, seven pieces being removed.   In all, eleven good-sized pieces were removed, exclusive of the upper portion of the shaft. The ball had lodged nearly in the center of the head. When mounted, the specimen showed quite a large opening at the point of entrance of the ball, for which no piece of bone could be found, this loss

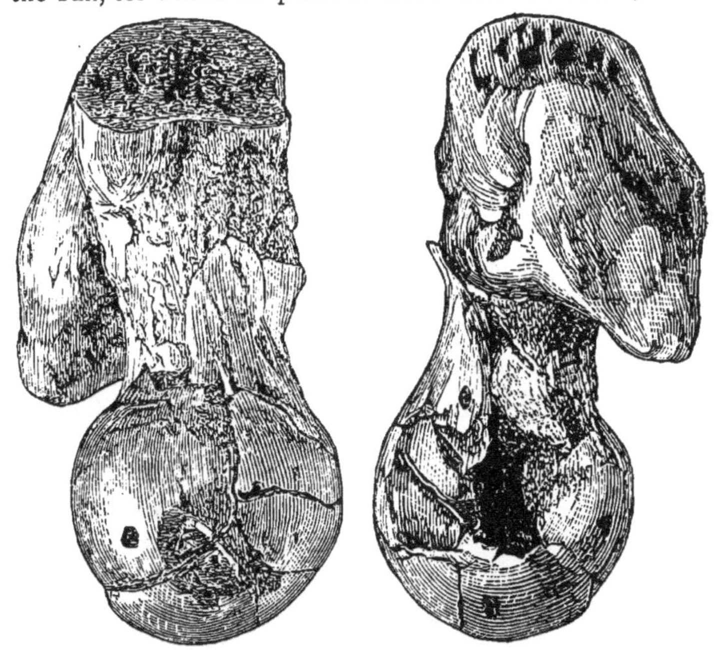

ANTERIOR AND POSTERIOR VIEWS OF THE FRAGMENTS OF THE HEAD OF THE FEMUR,
AS REPLACED AFTER OPERATION.

of substance being probably due to this portion being pulverized by the ball, and some having escaped with the discharge prior to the operation, and the remainder being washed out afterward. Almost all of the articular cartilage had been removed, and the remainder was much eroded by the action of the pus. The round ligament was uninjured, and was attached to one of the pieces of the head. According to the statement of the patient and others present at the time of the reception of the wound, the weapon was fired at a distance of about eighty yards, the patient being at the time in one of the cutters; and he was stooping when struck.

9 *o'clock p. m.*—Patient has no pain, but is very nervous and restless. Pulse 150 per minute. To have gr. ss. sulph. morphiæ, and repeat 12 o'clock. Beef essence, milk and whisky as required.

26th, 9 *o'clock a. m.*—Did not sleep well last night. Free from pain. Still quite nervous. Pulse 120. Tongue coated. Complains of want of sleep. Wound looks well, and is discharging bloody serum.

R.—Quiniæ sulphat., gr. ij.

S. Thrice daily. General diet to consist of beef essence and milk, with stimulants as required.

9 *o'clock p. m.*—Condition unchanged. Vomited freely during the afternoon. Attributed to too much milk.

27th, a. m.—Took gr. i morphiæ sulphat. during the night, and rested pretty well, and is more composed this morning. Had beef essence and one egg for breakfast. No pain. Pulse still frequent, 120, and irritable. Wound looks well, and is somewhat swollen and tender. Discharge more purulent and offensive. In consequence of the bedclothes becoming soiled and offensive the patient was carefully moved from his bed, and clean sheets, etc., substituted for those soiled, and when replaced in bed he was turned toward the right side in order to afford better access to the wound. Wound was dressed with oakum, moisted with sol. potassæ permanganat.

28th, a. m.—Patient was quite restless during yesterday afternoon. Took during the night gr. iss. morphiæ sulphat., and rested pretty well, and this morning is more comfortable, and not quite so nervous. For breakfast had beef essence and milk toast. Wound discharging moderately; discharge is more purulent, and not so offensive. He complains a good deal of excoriation of the skin about his hips and back, caused by contact with the discharge, together with free perspiration from the combined effects of debility and warm weather. There is also a small bed-sore on the right hip. The sores are dressed with ung. ox. zinc, and protected as well as possible with cotton batting, which is to be frequently changed. The wound is dressed twice daily, and at each dressing all the soiled articles are taken away and the pus removed by gentle pressure, the wound thoroughly sponged with sol. permang. potass. and dressed with oakum. To have Sherry wine instead of whisky, and grs. iij sulph. quiniæ thrice daily. General diet continued.

29th.—Patient was very nervous and restless all the afternoon of yesterday, and toward evening became delirious, which continued until 9 o'clock, pulse being 130, and irritable. As he suffered no pain, and insomnia seemed to be the principal trouble, it was determined to give hydrate of chloral instead of morphia. Accordingly, at 9 o'clock, grs. xxx of chloral were given in solution, with directions to repeat in one hour if necessary. In a few minutes he went to sleep, and when I visited him at 11 o'clock he was still sleeping quietly, and did not awake until 2 o'clock, after which he slept more or less until morning. Only one dose was given. This morning he feels much refreshed, looks more natural, and feels better than at any time since the accident. Pulse is 100, and pretty good. Wound looks well, and discharges laudable pus. Dress as usual. Treatment and diet continued. The good effect of the chloral was very marked; it seemed to fulfill the indication, and produced refreshing sleep.

30th.—Took grs. xxx of chloral at 9 o'clock last night, and grs. xx at 12 o'clock, and slept until 7 o'clock this morning, getting something like nine hours' refreshing sleep. Bowels not having been opened since 24th inst, ℥i. ol. ricini was given this morning, which operated quite freely. Appetite is good; pulse 96, and good, and he is not at all nervous. Wound is discharging pus quite freely. Removed him from bed to-day, and changed sheets, etc. Dress wound as usual, and repeat chloral at night.

31st.—At 10 o'clock last night took grs. xx of chloral, which was followed by vomiting; at 12 o'clock grs. x, after which he slept more or less until morning. He is quiet and cheerful, has no pain, pulse 96, and fair, tongue clean, and skin in a better condition, although he still perspires a good deal and complains of more or less discomfort from the excoriations on his back. Wound is discharging a moderate amount of laudable pus. All the nervous symptoms have gone, and altogether his general condition is very favorable. He spends a portion of his time in reading. Sutures were removed to-day, and there is partial union of the wound. Adhesive straps were applied, and the oakum dressing continued.

August 1st.—Patient became restless toward evening of yesterday. Took grs. xxx of chloral, but did not rest well.

2d.—Restless condition returned last night. Took grs. xx of chloral at 9 o'clock and grs. xx at 12 o'clock, after which he slept well, and this morning is more cheerful, and says he feels better than at any time since the operation. Appetite good, tongue clean, pulse 96. Removed from bed to-day and sheets changed. Wound discharging very freely. Continue, and to have 3ij cod-liver oil thrice daily.

3d.—Took grs. xi of chloral last night, and slept well. Condition about the same as yesterday. Increase quinine to grs. iv thrice daily, with gtts. xv acid. sulph. arom. To have beef-steak or mutton-chop for breakfast and dinner.

4th.—Took grs. xi of chloral last night in two doses, and slept several hours. Still improving. Dress wound as usual.

5th.—Took only grs. xxx chloral last night, and slept several hours. Bowels moved twice to-day naturally. Appetite good and tongue clean. Wound discharging very freely to-day. Patient complains of feeling very weak, but there is nothing to indicate any failing. Continue diet, and increase cod-liver oil to ʒss. twice a day.

6th.—Took grs. xxx of chloral, but did not rest well.

7th.—Patient was very nervous last night, and for a time partially delirious; he complained of feeling very drowsy, and was constantly yawning, but could not sleep. The chloral, in its usual dose, seems to have lost some of its effect, and, instead of increasing the dose, I determined to combine morphia with it, and at 9.30 p. m. gave him grs. xxx of chloral, and gr. ¼ morphia at

3 o'clock. He then slept very well, and is quite cheerful this morning. Wound dressed as usual. During the dressing, pus, mixed with florid blood, was quite freely discharged, the blood coming probably from the tender granulations. Continue all treatment.

8th.—Doing very well, and says he feels " first-rate." Took grs. xxx chloral and gr. ¼ morphia, and slept well. Wound dressed as usual, discharge moderate, and tinged with blood. He was removed from bed to-day, and the bedclothes changed. After being replaced in bed, some extension on the limb was made, but was not well borne. Is gaining in flesh, as indicated by his face.

9th.—Took chloral and morphia last night, and slept well. Appetite good, and bowels regular. Discharge from the wound is small in quantity and laudable.

10th.—Doing well in all respects. Took chloral and morphia as usual last night.

11th.—Slept well last night without any medicine, and feels very comfortable to-day. Appetite good. Pulse 90, and good. Wound all healed, except about one inch of the central portion, and a small opening at the lower end. Discharging a small quantity of laudable pus.

> R.—Quiniæ sulph., ℈ii.
> Acid. sulph. arom., ʒii.
> Aquæ, ʒiv.

Ft. sol.—S. Teaspoonful ter. die. Substitute ale for Sherry wine, and continue cod-liver oil and nutritious diet.

14th.—Since the 11th patient has done well. Sleeps some naturally, but takes regularly grs. xx chloral and gr. ¼ sulph. morphia at night, which always insures several hours of good sleep. Bowels regular. Pulse 90, and good. Wound healed, except the central portion. Discharge moderate and healthy. Appetite excellent; is gaining in flesh. Bedclothes changed to-day. Continued.

17th.—Doing well; had slight fever during afternoon of 15th instant, which lasted a short time, and passed off with moderate perspiration. This febrile movement seemed to have been caused by excitement on account of the death of one of the patients in the same ward. Skin is much more healthy in its action, and he does not perspire so much.

21st.—Improving. Wound discharges about ℥ii pus daily. Appetite excellent; takes soup, beaf-tea, steak, mutton-chop, and fruit, chloral and morphia at night. Increase cod-liver oil to ℥ss. thrice daily. He was removed from bed to-day, and the limb taken out of the fracture-box, and, all plaster and bandages being removed, the whole limb was thoroughly bathed with warm water and soap, and then well rubbed with soap liniment; adhesive strips were then re-applied, the limb replaced in the fracture-box, and counter-extension being made by means of the ordinary perineal band, extension was made by turning the screw. This is to be gradually increased, by means of the screw.

26th.—Appetite has failed somewhat during the past few days, tongue coated, bad taste in the mouth, and he complains of a sense of weight and discomfort in the epigastrium. Wound doing well, but the inguinal glands are enlarged and tender, and between them and the wound the skin is red and hot. Excoriations nearly healed. Discontinue extension and counter-extension, and patient is allowed to lie upon the right side for several hours, the limb remaining in the box, which is turned inwards. Omit cod-liver oil and quinine.

℞.—Mass. Hydray. grs. vi.

Ext. colo. comp., grs. iv.

Ft. pil. No. iij.—S. At 9 o'clock p. m., and ℥ss. ol. ricini in morning. Apply tinc. iodine to inflamed skin.

28th.—Bowels have been freely opened, and patient is much better in all respects. Appetite returning, tongue clean, and the inguinal trouble much improved. He is very cheerful. Bedclothes changed to-day. Hip is much more solid, and bears handling very well. He is able to move the foot and leg. The limb was taken out of the fracture-box to-day, and the adhesive plaster removed, and the leg allowed to rest easily on a pillow for several hours. After which it was lightly put up in the box, without adhesive plasters, as under the circumstances it is not considered advisable to make any further attempts at extension for the present.

> R.—Ferri et quiniæ cit., ʒiij.
> Glycerine.
> Aquæ āā, ℥ii.
> Ft. sol.—S. Teaspoonful ter. die, and ℥ss. cod-liver oil, once a day.

30th.—Discontinued chloral and morphia last night, as he now sleeps well without it. The chloral was first given on 29th July, and since then he has used about two ounces; it always suited his case admirably. Vomiting followed its use once, but this may have been accidental.

September 1st.—Improving; wound discharging moderately; inguinal trouble gone; bed-sores and excoriations all healed. Leg is removed from the box, and slight passive motion commenced, and then the limb is allowed to rest lightly on a pillow for several hours, and replaced in the box. Oil-silk removed from under the hip to-day, as it has a tendency to keep the parts moist.

4th.—Discharge diminished, and since the 1st instant has been thin and serous in its character. While changing his bedclothes to-day, he was raised to the erect position for a short time, but soon became faint. Takes ℥ss. cod-liver oil twice a day. Continue iron, quininé, and diet.

5th.—Some redness and swelling on the outer side of the thigh, just below the wound.

14th.—On the 7th instant was able for the first time, with assistance, to leave his bed, and sit for a short time on a chair, the limb being extended and well supported. Since then he sits up several hours daily. He is gaining in flesh, his face, chest, arms, and legs being much better filled out. Wound looks well; no purulent discharge at all; the serous discharge continues; its gross appearance closely resembles synovia, and it probably comes from remains of the joint tissues. There does not seem to be any disease of the bone.   Wound is sponged daily with tepid water, and dressed with lint.   Appetite good, bowels regular.

18*th.*—Wound all healed, save two small fistulous openings, about one inch apart, from which a small quantity of synovial-looking fluid can be pressed.   The whole limb, from the foot to the groin, was enveloped in a roller bandage, and a spica of the left groin being made, the foot was slung by a bandage carried around the neck, and thus supported, and with some assistance, he walked with crutches the length of the ward, about forty feet, sat down for a short time, and then returned.

22*d.*—With assistance he went down stairs to-day, and sat for a short time on the porch.   Out-door exercise to be continued as much as possible.   Discontinued cod-liver oil, iron, and quinine. General diet to consist of milk, beef-tea, beef-steak, mutton-chop, and fruit as needed.

26*th.*—Came down stairs to-day and walked with crutches for a short distance, outside of the building.

27*th.*—While walking yesterday he, by some means, used the limb injudiciously, and, to-day, complains of pain in the thigh upon attempting to walk, but has no pain when in bed.   To remain quiet for the present.

October 4*th.*—Still complains of pain in the hip when attempting to stand or walk.   The thigh and leg are œdematous and hard, having a brawny feel, particularly along the inner and outer sides of the thigh, at the knee, and along the anterior portion of the leg.   This condition has existed, however, for some time.   The foot is not swollen, nor has it been so at any time.   General treatment for the swelling to be daily sponging with tepid water and soap, friction with soap liniment, and occasional bandaging.

6*th.*—Complains of more or less pain in the hip when walking, evidently from the swinging about of the leg, for want of proper support.   The foot is somewhat inverted.   To-day a piece of stout iron wire was bent and carried like a stirrup, under the foot, up along the outer and inner side of the thigh, over the groin, and reaching almost to the left nipple.   This splint was then adapted to the various curves of the limb, and, when so fashioned, it was worn outside of the clothes, being held *in situ* by two or three strips of bandage. By this means the whole limb was kept quite steady, and he did not complain of any pain in walking.

10th.—Lower fistulous opening has healed. Takes a moderate amount of out-door exercise daily.

27th.—During the past ten days there has been some bloody discharge from the opening, and yesterday the lower fistula, which had been healed since the 10th instant, opened and discharged a small quantity of blood and pus. General condition excellent, and he gets along very well on his crutches, the limb being steadied by means of the wire splint.

November 10th.—Steadily improving. Since the 30th ultimo the fistulous openings have been occasionally injected with solutions of nitrate of silver, carbolic acid, acetate of lead, etc., of various strengths, in order to bring about healing from the bottom, but with, apparently, no good effect. The wound has been repeatedly examined with a probe; the instrument passes directly into the cotyloid cavity, but no diseased bone has been detected. The discharge doubtless comes from the remains of the old joint, and from the granulations.

December 4th.—Has walked regularly every day, and can now walk at least half a mile at a time. The wound is discharging more freely than usual, and in order to give a better exit to the pus and expose the parts well, the two openings were united by an incision of about one inch in length; the finger was then passed deeply into the wound, but did not detect any diseased bone; the upper end of the shaft of the femur seemed rounded off and well covered; the whole of the sinus had a velvet-like feel, and passed in the direction of the cotyloid cavity, but, owing to the small size of the sinus, the finger could not be passed quite that far, and the examination was completed with a probe; the instrument rested on the bone, which seemed well covered. The sinus is funnel-shaped, the neck being toward the acetabulum.

27th.—To-day patient went per steamer to San Francisco in

order to have a plaster cast taken of the pelvis, thigh, and leg with a view of having a suitable apparatus made for the purpose of strengthening and supporting the hip, and increasing the length of the limb.   He returned in the evening, having borne the trip, a distance of more than fifty miles, very well.

January 1, 1871.—Doing well; the œdematous condition of the thigh and leg has entirely disappeared, and the limb is quite natural in appearance, save, of course, the shortening and some atrophy of the muscles from long disuse.   Patient has discarded the wire splint, as the limb is now sufficiently firm to retain its position when he is walking on crutches.

20th.—The apparatus arrived to-day; it consists of Bouvier's splint, of sole-leather, as used for coxalgia, with the addition of one external lateral steel splint or brace, jointed at the knee and ankle, where it is attached to a shoe, with a thick cork sole, in order to increase the length of the limb, but leaving it one-half inch shorter than its fellow, this difference in length being considered necessary to avoid tripping in walking, which might otherwise happen, in consequence of impaired use of the knee and hip. The steel splint is so arranged that it can be entirely detached from the thigh-splint and shoe.   This was so arranged upon the supposition that in the course of time he could walk well enough without the splint, by using only the leather portion of the apparatus and the shoe.   The steel splint gives some increased support, but its main object is to correct and overcome the tendency to inversion of the limb.   It fitted very well, but at first felt very awkward.   The apparatus was substantially and elegantly made by Messrs. J. H. A. Folkers & Bro., instrument makers and dealers, San Francisco, and cost, complete, $148 currency.

21st.—For two or three days past there have been slight swelling and redness in the cicatrix, left by the bullet, and, to-day, this opened and discharged a small quantity of pus; it had been healed for about five months.   A probe being passed into this opening went as far as the acetabulum, and came in contact with one passed in the wound left by the operation.

30th.—To-day Scott went to Vallejo and was photographed, both with and without the apparatus.

February 1st.—Patient is this day transferred to the naval hospital at this station, in charge of Surgeon John M. Browne, United States Navy, the transfer being made on account of the new hospital being ready for the reception of patients. When transferred, his general condition is about as follows, viz: General health excellent, he being, perhaps, the healthiest-looking of all the patients; appetite good, sleeps well, and has not taken any medicine, save an occasional laxative, for four months. The left buttock is somewhat flattened; there is a small opening about the center of the line of incision, which discharges a small quantity of pus. The bullet-wound yet remains open, but shows a tendency to heal. The upper end of the shaft of the femur rests on the innominate bone, about on a level with the lower margin of the acetabulum, and the limb is about three and one-half inches shorter than its fellow. The hip is very firm and strong, and the whole weight of the body can be borne upon it. The knee is yet quite stiff, but is slowly improving; the foot is slightly inverted, but not so much so as prior to using the apparatus.

He has very good use of the limb, and can move it freely backward and forward and outward, and far enough inward to carry it across the other leg. He is becoming more accustomed to the apparatus, and there is no doubt but that in time he will be able to walk quite well with it without the aid of crutches. At no time have any abscesses formed in the limb. He has gained about thirty pounds since the operation of excision.

REMARKS.

This report terminates my official connection with the case; and inasmuch as the result cannot yet be positively known, it would, perhaps, be premature to make any comments or draw any conclusions. There is one point, however, worthy of mention, viz: That prior to the operation the patient complained of severe and constant pain, which ceased immediately upon the removal of the injured parts. This relief was so marked that even had the case terminated fatally, I think operative interference was warranted, with a view to euthanasia.

It will also be noticed that treatment by extension and counter-extension was abandoned after a trial of a few days, and I feel quite certain that this particular case did better without it.

The case was admirably suited for the operation of excision; a better one could not well have been selected.

There was no injury to the vessels or nerves, and none to the soft parts, save the small wound of entrance; the pelvic walls were not injured. There were no abcesses, and but little swelling about the joint. The neck and head of the femur alone bore the brunt of the injury.

____

AN ACCOUNT OF THE YELLOW FEVER

WHICH

APPEARED IN DECEMBER, 1866, AND PREVAILED ON BOARD
THE UNITED STATES SHIP JAMESTOWN, STORE
AND HOSPITAL-SHIP AT PANAMA.

BY

DELAVAN BLOODGOOD, A. M., M. D.,

SURGEON UNITED STATES NAVY.

____

AN ACCOUNT OF THE YELLOW FEVER WHICH AP-
PEARED IN DECEMBER, 1866, AND PREVAILED ON
BOARD THE UNITED STATES SHIP JAMESTOWN,
STORE AND HOSPITAL SHIP AT PANAMA.

By Delavan Bloodgood, A. M., M. D.,
Surgeon United States Navy.

On board the United States store and hospital ship Jamestown in Panama Bay, December 19th, 1866, at midnight, William McSoley, private marine, was suddenly seized with "pains in back," followed by "great thirst and oppression in chest." The 21st he was "very weak; unable to drill." The 22d he had "fever of an ugly character;" "says he feels as he did some years ago when he had severe typhoid fever;" "heat of skin very great;" "pulse rapid;" "tongue dry, and red at tip and edges." On the 24th he was "very much prostrated;" and the 25th his "prostration continued, with great pains in back." The 26th there was "great intestinal irritation;" "mind wandering;" "delirious at night, and attempted to leave his cot." From the last date McSoley slowly convalesced. This patient had been employed as sentry at the naval store-house in Panama from the 8th to the 19th of December inclusive. I subsequently learned that irritability of the stomach was a constant symptom during the first few days of his illness, and that he had numerous black liquid dejections.

Charles A. Gicquel, carpenter's mate, was seized during the night of December 30th with "slight chilliness, followed by fever, which has continued ever since;" "fullness of head;" "soreness of limbs." These symptoms were attributed to a debauch on shore. The 31st his symptoms were regarded as those of "inter. fever," and the next day, January 1st, 1867, as "remittent fever: fever recurs at irregular intervals, attended with a good deal of nausea; tongue loaded." January 2d, "Nausea was very distressing yesterday and last night, and continues to-day in a less degree." January 3d, "Tongue coated yellow; eyes jaundiced; stomach so irritable as to reject almost everything; great thirst, (the stomach symptoms the result of his debauch, no doubt.)" January 4th, "Stomach so irritable as to reject all nourishment; was delirious through the night." One o'clock p. m., "Gicquel seems to be sinking; pulse very weak; passing into insensibility; refuses obstinately to allow any medicine to be given him." He died at half past 9 o'clock that evening, the fifth day from attack.

Marcellus J. Maxwell, sergeant of marines, was admitted on the sick-list January 10th, having had "successive chills since last night; pain in the loins more than usually severe." The journal mentions for following three days, "continuous pain in back, and soreness of flesh very severe; thirst; tongue coated;" etc. Maxwell was discharged to duty February 2d. I was afterward informed by him that he suffered from nausea and vomiting during the first few days of his illness, and that in convalescence his arms and body became yellow.

January 12th.—Edward George Joyce, corporal of marines, was admitted on the sick-list with "fever of as yet no definite character." The 13th it was called "intermittent," and he was reported "convalescent" on the 14th; but 15th and 16th "not so well;" "fever at night." The 17th there was "return of fever; tongue very foul." The 19th "int. fever has become continued;" "tongue red at tip, and coated in middle;" "has diarrhœa." No further remarks of moment are recorded excepting that "diarrhœa was arrested," and "bronchial symptoms had developed," until the 23d, when his condition was accounted critical from an "unaccountable and exhaustive diarrhœa." Joyce died at midday on the 24th, and twelfth day from attack. During the last thirty-six hours of his life, as I learned, vomitings were frequent, and his corpse turned yellow.

On the 18th January, four men who had just been released

from " the cells "—dark and dank abysses of the orlop-deck— were admitted and continued on the sick-list five, twenty-three, twenty-six, and twenty-seven days, respectively. The records of their " chills," " pains," " great prostration," etc., in connection with the foregoing and following cases, are worthy of particular consideration.

January 21st, Bernard Hagan, boatswain's mate, was admitted with intermittent fever; the 22d he was charged with being drunk, and was disrated; on the 23d was noted, " has fever and diarrhœa;" the 24th, " diarrhœa and vomiting;" 25th, " violent retching yesterday, with hiccough," and at evening, " vomiting violent, throwing up mucus and blood." Hagan died at 10 o'clock that night, having been sick four days.

Edward Hanson, private marine, admitted at same time with Hagan, had "pains in back," "debility," "fever," "diarrhœa," "hemorrhage from nose and mouth;" but recovered, and was discharged from the sick-list the eighteenth day after seizure. This man was associated with McSoley (the case first cited) as sentry at the store-house on shore.

January 23d, Surgeon Marius Duvall, United States Navy, was attacked. Passed Assistant Surgeon F. L. DuBois found him (24th) with "high fever, intermittent type, result of climatic influences and exposure in walking a long distance over the reef in the midday heat of a tropical sun;" 25th, there was "persistent nausea and continued feeling of chilliness;" the 26th, "nausea continued—pain in scalp and ear;" 27th, the same; 28th, "passed a wretched night, retching and vomiting: very feeble and prostrate; has still eaten nothing; pulse 50;" 29th, "stomach still irritable, but passed a comfortable night by taking morphia; relished some champagne; 30th, "conjunctiva quite yellow— nausea and vomiting;" 31st, "has fever, and is flighty." February 1st, "depression of spirits;" "his urine has stained his clothes deep yellow." Dr. Duvall left, per steamer of 1st of February, for New York, according to recommendation of board of survey. "In order to prevent the spread of infection the articles used by Dr. Duvall were thrown overboard; the paint within a bath-tub in which he had urinated was turned completely black, so abnormal was the condition of his urine."

January 25th, two days after Dr. Duvall's seizure, James Burns, private marine, and Michael J. Sweeney, landsman, were attacked. Burns had a " hot but perspiring skin; pain in back; oppression in breathing; difficulty in swallowing;" 26th, "violent emesis;" 27th, "vomiting continued, with fullness in throat; eyeballs congested; 28th, the matters vomited were black, and he died the following day, the fifth of his illness. Sweeney started off with a " chill," followed by "emesis;" "pains in head, and conjunctiva congested;" the 26th, he had "vomiting and epistaxis;" 27th, "involuntary evacuations in cot; " vomitings of blood and black matter." Death resulted the next day, the fourth after seizure.

Appended to the closing accounts of these two cases is the following: "The congested conjunctiva, severe pains of back and head, choking sensation in throat, epigastric tenderness on pressure, with nausea, and finally the black-vomit, like coffee-grounds, render it *almost* certain that we have the yellow fever among us. It has lately been in Panama, but had disappeared. At present the city is very unhealthy."

Following Burns and Sweeney, Thomas J. Ward, ordinary seaman, was attacked the day afterward. He had fever, nausea, vomiting, prostration, yellowness of skin, etc., but convalesced, and was discharged February 21st.

The next day after Ward, William Devine, captain of the fore-top, was seized. Vomiting of bile occurred the second day, of black matter the third; suppression of urine, insensibility, hiccough, and yellowness of skin succeeded, and death on the fifth day.

John Dodd, private marine, who had been on the sick-list the preceding one hundred days with syphilis, chronic rheumatism, and calculus consecutively developed, on the 28th of January, well-marked symptoms of yellow fever—the chills, the fever, the nausea and vomiting, yellowness of skin, prostration, etc., but sustained it all and was discharged to duty March 25.

The next case in succession was that of Dennis Ryan, landsman.   He had a congestive chill on the evening of January 29th. The usual severe symptoms supervened—delirium, black vomit, and death on the 4th of February, having been ill six days.

February 2, John Hasson, captain of main-top, was admitted; and the pains, fever, chilliness, nausea, and congested eyes noted. February 3, there was continuance of fever and nausea, and epistaxis; "is well salivated."   February 4th, "yellow serum yielded from a blister over epigastrium;" " great nausea."   February 5th, he "had convulsions, suppression of urine, vomiting, depression of spirits."   February 6th, "hemorrhage from mouth."   February 7th, "hiccough, subsultus tendinum, strabismus," and death resulted the sixth day.

In the night of February 8th, Mr. John Adams, acting master, had a chill followed by fever and pains in the head, limbs, and back.   He took about fifteen grains of quinine each day until the 13th, when it was " suspended on account of headache and soreness of throat."   14th, his conjunctiva was very yellow. 15th, the case regarded as quite mild.   16th, " bronchitis supervened."   17th and 18th, "improving."   19th, he was "much troubled with cough and expectoration."   20th, "very severe bronchitis, with expectoration of greenish mucus and great difficulty in throwing it off his chest; pulse very feeble; eyes more yellow; copious watery discharges from bowels."   21st, "breathing very rapid, secretions all operating save biliary."   22d, "had five copious liquid stools; respiration loud and rapid; delirious; spat up blood."   He died at 4 o'clock p. m., the thirteenth day, and his corpse was yellow.

Frederick W. Stevens, private marine, was admitted February 10th, with "intermittent fever," and was given a calomel purgative, and during the three following days five-grain doses of quinine *ter in die.*   On the 14th, nausea and the more marked symptoms of yellow fever presented, and these were duly followed by epistaxis, hemorrhages, etc., and by death on the morning of February 21st, the eleventh day.

Thomas Smith, ordinary seaman, had a chill during the night of February 17th, which was followed by fever, and in the morning his eyes were much congested. February 19th, "fever, eyeballs painful, slept none, bowels and kidneys acting freely." The next day black-vomit set in, and he died that evening, the third day after seizure.

Isaiah Marjerison, private marine, was seized before daylight, February 27th, with the usual chill followed by fever. The second morning black vomit appeared, and next day there followed delirium, hiccough, and subsultus tendinum, all of which continued until suspended by death, March 2d.

The cases of Paymaster John A. Bates, jr., United States Navy, and John Braumer, private marine, which developed simultaneously with Marjerison's, will be reverted to after the following necessary explanations :

Under orders to the Jamestown, I sailed in the mail steamer from New York February 21st, 1867, reached Panama in the evening of March 1st, and went off to my duty soon after sunrise the next morning in the market-boat. I found fourteen cases, five of them very critical, on the sick-list, and that twelve deaths had already resulted from yellow fever. The same disease was prevailing on shore. Dr. DuBois, whom I superseded as successor to Dr. Duvall, had on three different occasions "fumigated" the ship, and had advised the commanding officer of the necessity for the removal of the vessel from that locality. I also proffered the unheeded advice that the ship should sail immediately for a cold climate, explaining that such a degree of local infection existed that there was no hope of the disappearance of the endemic fever while material remained for it to work upon. I recommended also that shore-visiting be stopped, that the prisoners be removed from the cells, and that no one be permitted to sleep on the orlop, or remain there longer than duty required. It is proper further to remark, in regarding the situation, that the Jamestown, newly commissioned, sailed from San Francisco in October, 1866, and reached her station in the middle of

November, anchoring in the bay about three miles S. S. E. from the city of Panama, and about half a mile E. by N. from Flamenco, the largest of three precipitous and contiguous islands. Flamenco is unused excepting as a burial-place, but the other two, Perico and Lleñas, are occupied by the Pacific Mail Steamship Company as depots for stores and coal, and for workshops and dwellings for the employés. Her arrival was just at the close of the rainy season, which commences in May, and during which the miasmatic exhalations are most manifest; when dampness and a greenish mold pervade everything; iron oxidizes with wonderful rapidity; furniture that is only fastened by glue falls to pieces; in short, the appearance and idea of disease are constantly impressed upon one. This period is usually inaugurated by showers which may last but an hour or two and not recur for three or four days; but as the season advances the rain-storms become intensified, till, deluge-like, they continue from day to day, accompanied by thunder and lightning such as can only be experienced in the tropics. The winds, which come mostly in squalls, are southerly, but they bring no cooling with them, only heaviness and oppression to the nervous system. Languor, lethargy, and loss of appetite are the immediate results, and fevers and diseases of the digestive apparatus the subsequent. This season had passed, for from the Jamestown's arrival, November 16th, until the end of the quarter and year of 1866, but seven rainy days were logged. Calms and light variable winds prevailed, and the average daily temperature was (Fahrenheit) 78°.2 at 6 o'clock a. m., 84°.1 at noon, 81°.2 at 6 p. m., and 78°.5 at midnight. The Jamestown had been in port about a month when the first cases of yellow fever appeared on board. She was roomy and tidy, and well ventilated excepting her orlop, where the pestilence first made its manifestation among the marines and prisoners, who were billeted and kept there, and where also were the bag-racks for the men; and as the clothing and bedding of the first three victims were sold by auction to the crew, some of the infected articles must have been festering

13 H.

in that locality ; which locality will again be called in question. The complement of officers and men numbered one hundred and eighteen, of whom four officers and three men had had yellow fever, and there were fourteen negroes—twenty-one persons in all who might be regarded as exempt from the danger. The report of sick for the fourth quarter, 1866, affords evidence of the general sanitary tone of the ship's company just previous to the outbreak of the fever. In those three months but thirty-six diseases had been treated, and of those were febris intermittens , one; febris remittens, three; febris continua, one; febris typhoides, one; diarrhœa, two; dysenteria, one; adynamia, one. The others were but trifling affections and injuries. McSoley's and Gicquel's diseases were included in the foregoing enumeration.

Passed Assistant Surgeon DuBois was detached ten days after I joined the Jamestown. Acting Assistant Surgeon E. T. T. Marsh, who preceded me aboard two days, remained a faithful and zealous coadjutor to the close of the scene.

To resume the cases of February 27th : Paymaster Bates at first complained only of a dull headache, and was taciturn and somnolent. He had no chill, but fever came on at evening and continued through the night. He took a blue-pill and had a hot foot-bath at the hour of retiring. During the two following days he vomited frequently and became greatly prostrated. When I first arrived on board, March 2d, his mind was clear, and he brightened up at seeing me, and was much interested in hearing of friends and in his letters just received, but in less than an hour he became bewildered, black-vomit was ejected, black liquid dejections were frequent, and prolonged sighing and hiccough set in. The surface of his body was cool. Surrounded him with bottles of hot water, applied sinapisms over abdomen and to extremities, and plied him with stimulants. Black-vomit recurred three times during the day ; after each act gave him, in mucilage, a few drops of chloroform in which an equal weight of camphor had been dissolved, and again small quantities of comp. spirits of ether with brandy ; ice *ad libitum.* Throughout the night he was very restless and partially delirious. Gave him milk-punch every hour, and the applications of warmth about the body were not relinquished. March 3d, his hiccough was very distressing, prolonged, and so loud as to be heard all over the ship. Remedies which the day before mitigated it then were unavailing. Black-vomit stools were frequent, and his pulse was scarcely perceptible at times, but would come up under extra stimulation. His stomach was quite tolerant to soup and brandy. Throughout the night delirium and jactitation were unintermitted. The applications of sinapisms and external heat were kept up, and stimulants given every twenty minutes. March 4th, observed about his mouth and alæ of nose and on forehead, a peculiar vesicular and pustular eruption; his body was yellow and sub-sultus tendinum constant, and he was also muttering in a tremu-lous manner. At half past 10 o'clock a. m. he became quiet for a few minutes, looked up consciously, said "Good-by," and died. He had been sick five days.

Braumer, attacked at the same time with Marjerison and Mr. Bates, was greatly terrified. The next day, February 28th, he "had spasms and vomiting," and March 1st was "very low." When I saw him (morning of March 2d) he was suffering severe pain in the back, and I ordered dry cups along the spinal column, milk-punch, and ice *ad libitum;* flying sinapisms and bottles of hot water to surround body. March 3d he was very restless and tremulous; the treatment was continued as on day before; 4th of March he vomited occasionally, and his mind was wandering. In the afternoon black-vomit appeared, he became delirious, and the secretion of urine was arrested. On 5th of March hemorrhage from mouth occurred, with soreness of throat; said that he "would die before sunset." Throughout the night he was wildly delirious, shouting, singing, and occa-sionally hiccoughing and ejecting black vomit; the external heat was kept applied, and stimulants given freely. March 6th he slept some; stomach was quite tolerant, and he voided a little bright-yellow urine. March 7th he had rested well during the night; his mind was clear; no nausea; eyes less congested; urine voided; pulse 48, and feeble; he continued doing well until the 12th, when, obtaining some salts and senna surreptitiously, he physicked himself prodigiously, but finally recovered and was discharged to duty.

March 1st Frederick Dallery, landsman, aged 19, had a chill, and there followed frontal headache, pain in back and limbs, suffused and pinkish eyes, which subsequently became yellow, as did his body; bowels were constipated, tongue pasty, and pulse irregular. Nausea and great prostration occurred the second day, and continued during the two or three following. His urine was voided involuntarily, staining the blankets yellow. Treatment: Perspiration induced by hot mustard baths, purgative of calomel followed by oil, hot soups, ice *ad libitum* (and this for all patients); also gave him fifteen grains of quinine after catharsis. He was discharged to duty the 17th of March.

While waiting on the beach the morning after my arrival I observed Mr. Charles A. Brown, mate, aged about 23, slowly advancing along the reef, frequently stopping to rest. He came up and went on board with me. He had passed the night at a hotel, where many deaths had but recently occurred, and where, upon his arrival from San Francisco, five days previously, he had remained two days before reporting on board the Jamestown. He had had a chill during the night, and the fever was then full upon him. As soon as we got on board he took fifteen grains of calomel, and was put into a hot-mustard-bath. But very slight diaphoresis followed. He was then given quinine fifteen grains, and the employment of stimulants commenced. He became greatly prostrated and agitated, firmly convinced that he must die. On the 3d of March he described a pain "like a cord was tied tightly around his back-bone." Nausea was constant, but he retained soup and stimulants. Sinapisms and bottles of hot water were employed, and he was given Hoffman's anodyne repeatedly. His neck first became yellow, and upon it and the face were a few vesicles, similar to those observed upon Mr. Bates. The secretion of urine was arrested, and black vomit set in at 1 o'clock p. m., thin and of the "bees-wing" variety, which ran from his mouth as if it was "pumped" out. The morning following, besides the black vomiting, black liquid stools were frequent; delirium and hiccough came on, and death succeeded at evening, on the third day. For thirty hours before death his stomach refused everything offered.

At eight o'clock in the evening of March 5th, Thomas Anderson, of the carpenter's gang, who had been working at the bench on the orlop, was seized with a chill. Fever, general pains, nausea, and the "white" vomiting regularly succeeded that night, and he slept none. He complained the next morning of a choking sensation, and the nausea lasted over the 6th. His eyes were quite yellow, and ptyalism resulted from a single purgative of calomel, followed by oil and quinine. He improved rapidly, and on the 18th, at his earnest solicitation, was discharged to duty, but the following evening had a relapse, with repetition of all original symptoms, from which, however, he safely recovered.

March 7th, the next case developed—that of Herman Zimmerman, boy, aged 16 years. He was one of the dingey's crew, and for falling asleep in his boat, and letting her get adrift when off for marketing on the morning of the 6th, was kept during the rest of the day pulling at his oars, in the sun, the boat being made fast to the boom. This did not come to my knowledge till sometime afterward. Distressing nausea and a sense of gastric distension were first complained of; gave him an emetic of ipecacuanha and mustard, and after its operation the nausea ceased. Hot mustard pediluvia and bottles of hot water were employed without exciting diaphoresis. He made loud and incessant complaints of the pains in his head and back, which were scarcely mitigated by large and repeated doses of compound spirits of ether and morphia. Bowels were purged by calomel followed by oil. The second day an abundant vesicular eruption appeared on the forehead and about the mouth. Stimulants were freely given. Restlessness, jactitation, and sleeplessness were unrelieved. On the 10th he became wildly delirious, lay upon his back, eyes staring, pupils dilated, head rolling from side to side, wailing incessantly, blood oozing from mouth, evacuations involuntary, and these conditions were unchanged until suddenly arrested by death, the 11th of March, the fourth day.

The next case was that of Henry Miller, seaman, a volunteer nurse, who had been in faithful attendance from the outbreak of the pestilence. He was seized in the night of the 15th of March with a chill, and immediately afterward most intense pains in head and back commenced. Several hot mustard-baths were required before the establishment of diaphoresis, after which we commenced giving twenty-grain doses of nitrate of potassa every third hour, and continued it for two days, with stimulants p. r. n.; also took several cut-cups from nucha and along spinal column. On the third day a vesicular and pustular eruption came out quite thickly on his face, neck, and arms. Nausea, vomiting, great prostration, and unfavorable symptoms generally continued until the 22d, when his convalescence began.

March 16th another case appeared. John Regan, gunner's mate, aged 35, had a chill at 11 o'clock a. m., and there was immediate and great prostration followed by "splitting headache," pains in back and limbs, and his eyes were suffused and pinkish. Ordered for him the hot mustard-bath and a mercurial purgative. After he had perspired freely for an hour, commenced giving him nitrate of potassa fifteen grains, repeated every two hours, and took a few cut-cups from nucha and back. Black vomit appeared on the 18th; the nitrate of potassa was continued with stimulants. On the 19th his ejections were white in the morning, but at evening again black; his conjunctiva yellow, and an abundant eruption resembling acne came out upon his arms and thighs. Treatment unchanged. On the 20th his stomach was too irritable to receive nourishment or medicines, and he again at evening ejected a large quantity of black-vomit. From the 21st he convalesced, and was discharged to duty April 1st with a pretty yellow body.

Mr. William T. Bull, aged about 25, paymaster's clerk at the naval store-house in Panama, died, March 23d, after five days' illness, having had black vomit profusely. He had been attended by a resident physician, an employé of the railroad company, and who denominated the disease "bilious intermittent fever," and denied that yellow fever existed on the isthmus. Mr. Bull was visited by Dr. Marsh during his illness, and seen by him just before death, and he recognized the malady as yellow fever, beyond any question.

At about midnight, March 21st, Harrold Nelson, aged 23 years, a sturdy seaman, was suddenly attacked. This man had but recently endured five days' confinement in the cells on the orlop-deck. He had no *black* vomit, but most of the other prevalent symptoms, and they were quite severe in degree. He was discharged to duty the twelfth day from seizure, and his treatment was very similar to Regan's; nitrate of potassa, after establishment of diaphoresis, being the principal remedy employed.

Charles Thompson, quartermaster, aged 28, and of full habit, came off watch at noon March 27th, and reported himself "sick." He seemed stupefied; skin was hot; pulse sluggish; eyes congested; and he " ached in every part of his body." Put him in the hot mustard-bath; gave a calomel purgative; took four cut-cups from nucha, and gave him fifteen grains of nitrate of potassa every two hours. March 28th; lay upon his back all day like a stunned animal; was aroused with difficulty, when he would complain of general pains. Put him again in the hot bath, repeated the cupping, and continued the administration of nitrate of potassa. 29th he voided six ounces of urine, the first since attacked; it yielded no albumen. His eyes were yellow; pains unchanged Continued the nitrate of potassa, with stimulants occasionally, and employed external warmth. On the 30th a pustular eruption appeared about his mouth, and on the 31st hemorrhage from mouth and nose; treatment continued as on the 29th. He slowly convalesced from April 1st, and was discharged to duty May 1st.

April 1st, the commanding officer received from the Secretary of the Navy an order "to proceed to sea with the Jamestown without delay, and to proceed as far northward as he might consider necessary for the re-establishment of the health of the ship's crew," and to bring up at San Francisco. We sailed, in compliance with that order, April 2d, at evening, the fever having then been endemic on board over three months. Never men more gleefully sprang aloft, never clank of windlass sounded more musically than on that occasion. To clear that hated bay, to shut out the sight of the head-boards which whitened the steep sides of Flamenco Island, seemed like escape from inevitable doom. In that reprieve further calamities were unexpected, inconsiderate of the "ferment" with which we were freighted.

The day before sailing, Charles Hawkins, steerage-steward, aged 30, and effeminate in appearance, was attacked; he was excessively prostrated, and there was great nervous oppression. Black-vomit appeared April 4th, recurred twice on the 6th, once on the 7th, and again on the 8th, and each ejection was profuse. He became delirious the 6th, and his mind remained unsettled until the 9th. A minute pustular eruption spread over his neck, and oozing of blood from the mouth and nose continued many days. The surface of his body turned bright yellow after the eighth day, and convalescence began on the 11th. The treatment was commenced by hot mustard-baths and a mercurial purgative, and during the first ten days gave nitrate of potassa in ten-grain doses, three or five times per day, as the condition of his stomach would allow. Milk-punch, egg-nog, brandy, ale, wine, were given as he fancied, and sinapisms and cups were frequently called into requisition.

Louis Ross, sail-maker's mate, was admitted April 11th, presenting the common symptoms and appearances. He stated that he had been feeling badly for two or three days, but kept at work on a sail that was needed. He experienced considerable difficulty in breathing, and a sense of thoracic distension; soreness of throat was also complained of, and he vomited frequently the ejections containing mucus and bile. He was treated with the hot mustard-bath, sinapisms, and external heat; the nitrate of potassa was regularly continued with stimulants. The case progressed favorably without any unusual developments, and was discharged the thirteenth day.

William Jared, yeoman, aged 21, the next subject, was attacked suddenly and severely in the evening of April 14th; he was put in the hot mustard-bath, given a mercurial purgative, and fifteen grains of nitrate of potassa every two hours. During the night of the 16th he became wildly delirious; surface of his body and the extremities were cold, and his face and ears leaden-hued. Took six ounces of blood by cups from nucha, shaved his head, repeated the bath, applied sinapisms to epigastrium, and continued the potas. nitr. His mind became clearer the 17th, but he was very nervous and restless. His eyes and skin were yellow, vomitings of white and bilious matter occasionally streaked with blood occurred, and the prostration was complete. He recovered, and was discharged the eighteenth day from seizure.

James McBeth, ordinary seaman, aged 19, and very robust, came down from his watch on deck at 1 o'clock in the morning of April 13th, having a light chill, which lasted but half an hour. Gave him two ounces of whisky, twenty grains of calomel, and turned him in under blankets. In the morning he made but slight complaint of dizziness and headache; there was no fever then nor during the following day; his eyes were clear, appetite good, and he slept well. ℞.—Potass. nitr., gr. x., t. d. The 16th and 17th nothing apparently was required; he wanted to go to duty, which was permitted on the 18th, but that evening he was seized with headache and shivering; his pulse was full, and eyes suffused and pinkish. He was put into the hot mustard-bath, and six ounces of blood taken by cups from the nucha. Fever came on, and continued all night with great thirst, and next day with nausea; he relished and retained, however, some mutton-soup and ale. Bowels were opened by calomel, followed by sodæ et potass. 13 tart., ʒss. On the 20th he was greatly prostrated; said that he " felt half dead and stunned." More blood was taken from nuchal region by cups. He vomited at noon and complained of soreness of throat; his tongue was tremulous, black in center, and yellow-edged. Gave him one dose of tinct. ferri chlorid., but it seemed to increase the nausea. Ordered milk-punch every hour, and flying sinapisms to be employed. On the 21st the headache was intense; skin hot like a "stove-pipe;" mind wandering. Again he was put into the hot mustard-bath, and two cups cut upon the temples. At midday black vomit appeared, and recurred at evening with hiccough. As his stomach would no longer retain milk-punch, its administration was continued by enema; external heat kept up. Delirium set in at night, and he remained unconscious, with short and labored breathing, until noon the next day, when he died. Black-vomit stools were frequent during his last day of life, and the eruption was abundant on neck and chest, and a few vesicles on the face; the body a dirty bronze color; no albumen in urine. Death resulted the fourth day from relapse, and ninth from first ailment.

Accompanying McBeth, when he returned in relapse, was Alonzo Horton, ship's cook, aged 36, shivering and complaining of headache and general pains. The surface of his body was cold, pulse sluggish, eyes brilliant. He was kept a long time in the hot bath, and afterward surrounded by bottles of hot water under his blankets, but without exciting diaphoresis. Several cut-cups were taken from his neck and back without relieving the pains, which were severest in the lumbar regions. April 19th bowels purged by calomel; his tongue had a seared appearance; gave nitrate of potassa, twenty grains, every two hours and a half. The pains in his back being intensified on the 20th, six more cut-cups were taken from the lumbar regions. White vomiting occurred at 9 o'clock a. m., black at 2, 4, and 9 p. m., with severe cramps, particularly in the legs. Suspended medicines on account of the nausea, though stimulants were well borne. Camphor and chloroform mixture were given after each act of vomiting. April 21st, no urine had been voided since 8 o'clock the previous morning; applied warm fomentations over the bladder, and resumed the administration of nitrate of potassa, and gave milk-punch every hour until midday, when black vomit recurred, precluding their continuance. Toward evening about an ounce of bright-yellow urine was drawn by the catheter, and later the same quantity was voided; no albumen contained. Between 7 and 11 o'clock that evening he had eight copious black-vomit stools. Milk-punch not being well borne, substituted undiluted brandy; soon that was ejected, after which it was given by enema every hour. The temperature of the body continued to diminish. At two o'clock in the morning of the 22d, hiccough, and delirium of a mirthful character, supervened; but soon stupor and mutterings succeeded, and continued until death, which followed before daylight, the fourth day. The corpse was completely bronzed in appearance.

These two cases were the first which had terminated fatally in forty-two days. We were then twenty days at sea, and in that time had progressed only seven hundred and fifty miles, and were still in a lower latitude than the place of departure. When the weather had been fair it was calm and stifling; when there was wind it came as a rain-squall, and ports were closed and hatches hooded, housing us in noisome vapor. Within a few degrees of the line, a blood-colored sun overhead, a hot and coppery sky surrounding,

> "Day after day, day after day,
> We stuck, nor breath nor motion;
> As idle as a painted ship
> Upon a painted ocean."

But moderately outfitted with luxuries for the sick, those few nearly exhausted—no ice nor chance for supplies—the prospect was dismal, and its disheartening effect clearly perceptible upon the ship's company.

Two days after the burials at sea, George Ellis, ordinary seaman, was attacked. The case was quite mild, but in its course the diagnosis was unequivocally substantiated. He became well enough for duty the ninth day.

Two weeks after my arrival on board the Jamestown I had a pretty sharp attack of fever, lasting three days, and which, though recorded as febris communis, I flattered myself might have been yellow fever in mild form. I also assumed security from the circumstance that after the arrival north of the Dacotah, in October, 1862, with yellow fever on board, which we contracted in the West Indies, I had a fever of considerable severity, with many symptoms common to the epidemic; but this 27th of April I was suddenly stricken down. A feeling of malaise had induced me to take a blue pill that morning, but at half past 10 o'clock a chill, preceded by a palpable *aura*, came upon me with great suddenness, and lasted three hours in spite of my being twice put into a hot mustard-bath, bottles of hot water surrounding, and blankets piled upon me. With sweating, high fever came on, frontal headache, almost insupportable pain in lumbar region, cramps in legs, and nausea was constant, with insatiable thirst. Dr. Marsh gave me, at 2 o'clock p. m., twenty grains of calomel, and took two cut-cups from nucha; also employed dry-cups along spinal column and flying sinapisms. Dr. Marsh recorded that my "eyes were suffused; tongue foul; pulse full and hard; great prostration. At 4 o'clock p. m. became delirious. R.—Potas. nitr., gr. xx, every three hours. Mind became clearer in evening." The pains were so intolerable down my back, thighs, and legs that the parts were painted over with tincture of iodine, and a full anodyne of comp. spirits of ether and morphia was administered. The prostration was so complete that I could neither rise up nor turn in my berth without assistance. Cathartic operated twice in the night; urine voided. April 28th Dr. Marsh's record is that I "passed a very restless night; eyes congested; tongue black through center and yellow at edges; thirst and nausea unmitigated; pulse slow and feeble; considerable fever and headache; all these symptoms accompanied by great prostration and disinclination for food; taking nitrate of potassa, ale, claret, or Sauterne, as before." My cognizance of occurrences that day was much confused. 29th, "fever continued through the day: passed a very uncomfortable night; expectorates dark matter, [which, flowing up in my throat without voluntary effort, had a saltish and oily taste;] treatment as yesterday. In p. m., on account of severity of pains, was given tinc. opii gtt. xl., by enema. Had eleven black-vomit dejectio ns during day." 30th, "the eruption, as mentioned in former cases, appeared about mouth and nose; eyes yellow and tongue foul; no inclination for food." In the evening was noticed "a great improvement as regards all important symptoms." The eighth day from attack I resumed my duties, though much debilitated and without appeti te. As sequelæ were oozing of blood from my gums, a continuous headache, and a protracted diarrhœa. During the first three or four days of my sickness, though realizing the impropriety and danger, I could not resist the impulse to throw off the clothing and attempt to get out of my berth, and I had recourse to various expedients to divert the attention or send away the attendants that I might accomplish it; although with the constant dread of exciting vomiting thereby, I could not restrain myself from large draughts if liquids were left within my reach; any, however, that were sweetish were particularly distasteful. Desirable as it is that the fullest and most minute observations be given by physicians of unusual diseases they may have survived, I regret, on that account, that during the progress of yellow fever in my instance the interest and attention, so far, as consciousness was complete, were most decidedly personal and very little professional. Dr. Marsh declared me to be a most troublesome patient.

Following is Dr. Marsh's record of the case of George Bradley, corporal of marines, aged 25, and very athletic, who, an hour and a half after my seizure, had a chill lasting over an hour, during which he was delirious. Copious perspiration followed after the hot mustard-bath, and his mind became clearer. Pains in head, back, and legs very severe, also in thorax. White vomiting soon occurred, afterward it was bilious, and at evening dark. Was given a mercurial purgative, had cut-cups to neck and back, and flying sinapisms were employed. Throughout the night he was very restless; voided his urine naturally. April 28th, eyes suffused; mind wandering. Repeated cut-cups to nucha, and gave hot soups and stimulants. No remission of fever, and he again vomited black matter. 29th, eyes yellow; eruption out on forehead and neck. Appetite good. Black-vomit, with hiccough, set in at half past 9 o'clock in the morning, and recurred six times during the day and evening. Was given ether one drachm, after each act, which afforded temporary assuagement. 30th, five ejections of black vomit occurred during the day; hiccough at intervals; mind clear; pulse quick and feeble. Milk-punch was given every hour by enema. Abdomen tympanitic; applied a poultice of mustard and vinegar, and gave forty drops of tincture of opium by enema. May 1st, black vomit and hiccough recurred at 10 o'clock a. m. with great thirst, and he became delirious at 2 o'clock; later he passed a perfectly white and clayey stool, and gulped up a large quantity of black-vomit; he continued unconscious, with short and labored respiration, until evening, when he died on the fourth day.

Two and a half hours after my attack, and one after Bradley's, Mr. Leakin Barnes, acting ensign, was similarly and as suddenly taken. His chill was prolonged, prostration and pains were excessive, and the matters vomited were white at first, and afterward streaked with blood. The eruption, which was quite extensive, appeared the third day. He convalesced favorably. Treatment, very nearly as described in preceding cases. This officer was an inveterate smoker, and also a chewer, but after recovering from this disease his taste for tobacco was entirely lost, nor had it returned when I last saw him, the following year.

April 29th, Charles Brown, ordinary seaman, was seized. He described his pains as "wicked." The disease progressed rather mildly; the diagnosis, however, was fully confirmed, and on the 7th of May he was convalescent.

William J. Rothman, carpenter's mate, aged 32, of saturnine habit, was the next attacked, on the 3d of May. The third day afterward the secretion of urine was arrested, and black-vomit set

in with delirium. He died May 9th, the sixth day. The eruption was present, and petechial on abdomen. No albumen in
urine. Treatment very similar to Bradley's.

Edward Slackford, ordinary seaman, was seized with a severe
chill followed by fever, pains, nausea, etc., at 1 o'clock p. m., and
George Thompson, private marine, at 4 o'clock the 5th of May.
The eyes of both were congested and pinkish; both vomited
white and bilious matter in the evening, and became delirious.
All of their symptoms were very similar, save that Slackford's prostration was the more excessive, and his delirium lasted the longer.
Their nausea and vomiting continued, and at the same instant,
in the evening of the 8th, each ejected about a quart of black
vomit. The eruption appeared on both, and their eyes and skins
were yellow. No albumen was detected in the urine of either.
On the fifth day a favorable change occurred with each, though
both were greatly prostrated, and Slackford wonderfully emaciated.
Thompson was discharged to duty May 22d, and Slackford 24th.
Treatment, as hereinbefore particularized—nitrate of potassa, after
diaphoresis was excited, and after purgation and stimulants
p. r. n.

Peter Sullivan, captain of the forecastle, in the evening of the
10th of May, experienced sudden prostration, with frontal headache and pain in back and legs; his eyes were dull, skin damp,
pulse sluggish, tongue pasty. Soon after he had a chill, succeeded by fever and vomiting of white and bilious matter, and
the pains in lumbar region became intensified. The eruption
appeared in due time, and the disease subsided as in regular
course. No trace of albumen in urine. He was discharged the
19th, but in four hours relapsed. By the 24th he was well enough
for duty. The treatment was employed which had almost become
" stock."

Edward Smith, apothecary, a youth of 19, accompanied me
from New York, accepting his appointment, knowing of the pestilence to be encountered and of the great danger to an unacclimated person suddenly migrating from a northern winter to an

infected ship in the tropics.   With a view to prophylaxis I gave him two grains of quinine, morning and evening, during the week after our arrival, and pil. hydrarg., gr. v, at intervals of ten or fourteen days; also five grains of nitrate of potassa with the quinine. This course was resumed for a few days at a time at irregular intervals for two months, and stimulants were occasionally given when his duties were more than usually fatiguing. Regular bathing was practiced.   But, in the evening of May 11th, he was seized with typhus icterodes.   We put him into the hot mustard-bath, and gave pil. hydr., after which high fever came on, and his mind wandered.   White vomiting occurred several times, his thirst was urgent, and he complained of a burning sensation in his throat. Flying sinapisms and bottles of hot water about his body excited but slight diaphoresis.   Took three cut-cups from nucha.   The pains were unrelieved, and he slept none; a burning fever continued all night.   Next morning warm saline enemata produced but one small stool; the mercurial was repeated, and three cut-cups were taken from his lumbar region; his head was hot, pulse 120, tongue seared.   In the afternoon the hot mustard-bath was repeated, inducing diaphoresis and moderating the fever and pains. Gave him claret and gum-water *ad libitum;* also ten grains of nitrate of potassa every two hours, which was retained, though food excited vomiting.   In the momentary absence of the nurse he got up, prepared and swallowed about two drachms of citric acid in six ounces of Tarragona wine.   May 13th, 2 o'clock a. m., fever and delirium increased; skin like a "stove-pipe;" bowels unmoved; repeated the saline enema without result.   At 4 o'clock he became quite unmanageable; two more cups were taken from nucha and three drachms of potassæ bitartras administered; after this he slept for a short time, the first since attacked, and his urine was voided involuntarily.   The nausea ceased so that he ate a little tapioca; he took also milk-punch every hour, and ten grains of nitrate of potassa every two hours. But soon the delirium increased, and his head rolled from side to side, with pupils widely dilated.   At half past 9 o'clock gave a turpentine enema without effect. Abdomen tympanitic; rubbed it over with croton-oil and applied a large blister. Three drops of croton-oil were placed upon his tongue; but no movement resulting, at 2 o'clock p. m. gave him another turpentine enema, when half an hour afterward there came away in his cot a large quantity of black offensive feces, and in the night he had two more involuntary evacuations, black and very offensive. His delirium became so violent that we were obliged to anæsthetize him, in which condition he rested an hour and a half. May 14th, not a favorable indication; five ounces of bright-yellow urine were drawn by catheter; none had been voided in twenty-four hours; it contained no albumen. At 5 o'clock p. m. black-vomit appeared, and recurred repeatedly and profusely in the night. He died early in the morning, May 15th, the fourth day.

Mr. Robert H. Carey, acting ensign, aged 36, was seized with chill and pain in head and back just before midnight, May 13th, and soon after vomited white and bilious matter, and the vomiting was repeated several times before morning. Copious diaphoresis was induced by covering him with blankets and giving hot drinks. ℞.—Pil. hydr., gr. xx. Statim.

14*th.*—He had high fever, frontal headache, pains down inside of thighs and legs, great thirst; his eyes were congested and pinkish, tongue white and flabby, pulse full, though not much accelerated. Four ounces of blood were taken by cups from his nucha, and he was given one drachm of nitrate of potassa during the day. At evening he had three black stools, and was stupid and somnolent.

15*th.*—He had slept all night, and was aroused with difficulty in the morning, when he complained as on the previous day. The general appearances were unchanged; skin and kidneys secreting; bowels free.

16*th.*—Still very somnolent. Eyes and skin yellow; eyeballs painful; no appetite; eruption out on neck and arms. Continued the nitrate of potassa, but no stimulants were given. He commenced convalescing the 17th, and the 22d was recovered.

14 H

Thomas Toner, landsman, aged 20, and slender in habit, was seized with a chill at half past 2 o'clock p. m., May 15th, and had the characteristic pains, with constant nausea. His left eye was merely suffused, while the right was entirely pink. The sight of the latter had been destroyed some years before, but in health the appearances of both eyes were similar. Ordered for him the hot bath, purgative, and nitrate of potassa.

16*th*.—He had considerable fever, but his pains had diminished to a sense of general " soreness of flesh." Pulse was feeble and quick; appearance of eyes unchanged; skin moist; urine voided naturally. Continued the nitrate of potassa, with stimulants.

On the 17th there commenced a general improvement, and from that date progressed favorably, and patient was discharged May 23d. The eruption appeared on neck and chin.

Peter Harmes, ordinary seaman, aged 24, and a stolid Teuton, was attacked suddenly, and at the same time with Toner. There were great prostration, prolonged chill, and intense pains. High fever followed after the bath. Nausea was constant, and fever with a " stove-pipe skin " continued throughout the night. Gave him twenty grains of nitrate of potassa every two hours, and took blood from nucha by cups.

16*th*.—Bowels purged by calomel given at the first; no mod_ eration of the fever; nausea distressing. Continued the nitrate of potassa.

17*th*.—Stupor and nervous depression; eyes yellow; tongue black; neuralgic pain in testes; nausea unrelieved. No urine had been voided in forty-eight hours. Drew off by catheter nearly a quart, which yielded an abundance of albumen. Continued the treatment.

19*th*.—A decided improvement commenced and continued. He was discharged May 27th. The eruption appeared on face and neck.

William Martin, steerage-cook, aged 22, was attacked before daylight, 17th of May, and all his symptoms were grave. Employed the hot mustard-bath, bottles of hot water, and gave purgative dose of calomel. High fever continued all day with great thirst, nausea, vomiting, and prostration. He took fifteen grains of nitrate of potassa every three hours. At evening white vomiting recurred, and the heat of skin and pain in head increased.

18th.—He passed the night very restlessly; stupor had advanced; skin yellow and dry, and emitted a musty and offensive odor; tongue dirty yellow, and denuded at edges; pulse excited and irregular. He was again put into the hot mustard-bath, the nitrate of potassa continued, with milk-punch *ad libitum.* He became delirious at evening, and his urine was albuminous.

19th.—No improvement; eruption thick on face and neck; medicine and stimulant continued as on preceding day.

20th.—Hemorrhage from mouth and nose occurred, and black vomit appeared at half past 10 o'clock a. m., and recurred several times during the day and evening. Delirium and hiccough also continued, and convulsions supervened before death, which resulted early in the morning of May 21st, the fourth day after his attack and our forty-ninth day at sea, in which time we had experienced twenty-six days of heavy rain, and the average daily temperature had been—maximum, 85°.7; minimum, 80°.3 F.

Henry Duell, ordinary seaman, was attacked May 19th, early in the morning, and pretty severely. Treatment was after the routine of cases, subsequent to leaving Panama. A decided and unusual improvement occurred during his second day of illness, though the distinctive features of yellow fever were observable. The favorable change I attributed, in a good measure, to a diminution of ten degrees in temperature.

The last case was developed May 23, in latitude 22° 35' north, longitude 126° west. Temperature, maximum, 72°; minimum, 68°. John Smith, quartermaster, was the subject. He was taken with a chill, followed by nausea, supraorbital headache, congested and pinkish eyes, incrusted tongue, severe pain in limbs and lumbar region, and fever of moderate character, which was maintained without any variation for two days. The fourth day his eyes and skin became yellow. He was discharged to duty May 28, our fifty-sixth day from Panama.   San Francisco was reached June 7, and our pilot's was the first sail to greet our eyes throughout that memorable passage of sixty-six days.

Thus succinctly are presented the inception, progress, and termination of as malignant an outbreak as our service has endured. Forty-eight cases and twenty-one deaths are enumerated, of which nineteen had developed before my arrival, and thirteen of them had fatally terminated; twenty-nine cases, with eight deaths, subsequently resulted, twenty of which, and six deaths, occurred at sea.   In regarding this summary, it is noticeable that three persons died without having had black-vomit or suppression of urine; one who died was ptyalised at an early stage of the disease; six recovered after having black-vomit; three survived in whom the secretion of urine was arrested; eight recovered having been delirious; after hemorrhage from mouth and nose five recovered; nine had black-vomit stools, of whom seven died; the urine of eleven patients was tested for albumen, and it was found but in two—one of those two patients died.   Possessing but a small quantity of nitric acid, and no test-tubes, we were unable to render fuller statistics in that particular.   Had the means for hypodermic medication been possessed, much more suffering could have been alleviated than our resources afforded.   Should duty again circumstance me as in the instance recounted, I would hardly employ a less effectual and prompt cathartic than croton oil.   Mercurials were not obviously beneficial.   I could not discern any utility from the administration of quinine, and early discontinued its employment, though on board the Dacotah, in 1862, its efficacy was very marked; but before the epidemic in that ship our crew had suffered severely from malaria, encountered during the summer up the James River, while co-operating with the Army in the first peninsular campaign.   But those manifestations were quite different from these of the Jamestown, and were much milder in type.   On the Dacotah we had twenty-five cases, and not one was lost; in two only did black vomit appear, and only in about half of them were displayed the characteristic discolorations. Beyond the modifications first before suggested, I would not depart from my line of treatment pursued. Especially efficacious seemed the agency of the nitrate of potassa as an eliminator of the specific poison by its diuretic and diaphoretic action, and not in a single instance did it seem to incite or increase visceral irritation. The moment for commencing stimulation, and the extent to which it may be carried, cannot be indicated by any general rule, and can only be judged by the particular conditions in each individual case.

Some further observations than the few hereinbefore given respecting topography and meteorology may be relevant and appropriately introduced here.

The walled city of Panama occupies a small peninsula about half a mile long by one-quarter in width, extending easterly from the bases of Mounts Ancon and Gabilan. The walls are crumbling in many places, and the western line and portion have been pulled down, and the wide and deep moat filled in for roadway-crossings in some places, but generally it is only piled and choked up with deposits of rubbish and filth. Within the city proper is a population of from three to four thousand, and nearly the same number inhabit the *arrabal,* or collection of miserable abodes, which extend like excrescences from the walls. Drainage is unknown. Even the water for drinking and culinary purposes is brought in on donkeys from a stream by no means taintless, outside the city limits. Water for the shipping, however, and with which we were supplied, is obtained from a stream on the island of Toboga, nine miles away to the southward, and, though reputatively very pure, is somewhat questionable to those who have observed the laundry and bathing operations along its coast, as, descending from the mountain, it lingers in shady and convenient pools. Scavengers are wanting, too, in Panama, save the buzzards; and the habits, persons, and dwellings of the lower orders (most interminably mixed as to blood), both without and within the walls, are repugnant and filthy. Disgusting odors assail the nostril at every turning, and the visage and demeanor of the denizens in general bear evidence of the perniciousness of their climate and its enervating effect. The tide rises fully twenty-two feet up to the city walls, but in receding leaves bare long edges of volcanic rock and coral with sand patches between, which afford lodging-places for offal and other refuse thrown out. Upon the ramparts, turning from the charming view of the islands which, under the enchantment of varied distances, adorn and diversify a bay next in celebrity after Naples and Rio, there is afforded a vista even more attractive—of mountains and gigantic forests, of valleys and jungles impenetrable, of lagoons within savannas on which half-wild herds are grazing; and where the foliage is rankest and flowers most gaudy are hidden the bayous with their slimy banks; and there, too, beneath the damp shade of the profuse vegetation which decomposes under the influences of moisture and a constant summer heat, is the lair of intensest miasm. The whole Isthmus is its habitat and has been for years, and undoubtedly will be to the end of time, and from no part or place has it been or can it be excluded. Acclimation is impossible; no one, of whatever race or country, who becomes a resident of the Isthmus escapes disease; not even are beasts exempt, and nothing but change of climate can eradicate the effects of the poisoning from that malaria. Intermittent, remittent, bilious, and congestive fevers and dysenteries are the usual results of the climatic influences, but under intenser excitation yellow fever appears. The belief is well grounded that yellow fever never leaves certain localities which it has once invaded and where the conditions for its existence are constantly maintained. It may seem dormant for a time, or only sporadically evincing its vitality before it rouses itself and appears epidemically. I know that it existed at Panama, at Toboga, and among the shipping of the bay while I was attached to the frigate Merrimack on the Pacific station in 1857–'59, and that it has played havoc in each of those designations several times since. At Aspinwall, when *en route* to the Jamestown, the late Dr. Klugé (victim at last to the Isthmus malaria) told me that he had recently treated ten employés of the railroad company who had yellow fever, and eight of them died. And at that time the numerous deaths along the line from Aspinwall to Panama were exciting special comment, though they were attributed to bilious, congestive, remittent, and intermittent fevers; or by two or three or more of such nosological combinations of terms a nomenclature was provided less oppugned to lucre than yellow fever, but none the less fatal to human existence. The evidence of the direct transportation of the yellow fever from Panama to the Jamestown is clear and indisputable, though for my temerity in maintaining that proposition, and for intimating that the Isthmus has not *par excellence* the most salubrious of climes, I drew upon myself the maledictions of the two Panamanian newspapers—the organs respectively of the two great commercial enterprises—in which leaders with emotional headings established, " The health of Panama," and vituperated, " The Jamestown's surgeon." Even a " member of the Royal College of Surgeons, England," in the employ of a third commercial organization, under his distinguished sign-manual published and proclaimed the sound sanitary condition of the Isthmus. The pestilence was conveyed, unquestionably, from the shore to the ship three miles out in the bay, first, by McSoley and Hanson, the marines who were on duty at the storehouse in one of the most unhealthy locations in Panama from December 8th to the 19th, at which last date they were returned on board with their bags, hammocks, and accouterments; and that night of the 19th McSoley was attacked with yellow fever, and Hanson on the following 21st of January: secondly, by Gicquel, who had been on shore for several days and nights doing some work for the commanding officer, and who, December 23d, was brought on board and confined under the sentry's charge; one week afterward he was attacked with yellow fever and died. The propagation of the pestilence was consummated on the orlop-deck, where McSoley and Hanson stowed their effects and slung their hammocks; where McSoley remained through his sickness; where Gicquel was confined, where he worked at the bench, where he was taken sick and remained until the day before his death, when he was removed to the gun-deck; where Sergeant Maxwell was sick, and where he and the other marines who had the fever slept; where the cells were from which the four patients were relieved January 18th; where some of the infected clothing of the first three victims probably was stowed after their deaths, and its distribution among the ship's company; where Anderson, attacked March 5th, worked at the bench; and where afterward worked Rothman, who died; and where Nelson had been confined for five days just before his seizure. In other localities the ferment seemed also to linger; for instance, I succeeded to Dr. Duvall's room and disease; after Mr. Bates' death Ensign Barnes occupied the paymaster's room, and had the fever; Mr. Carey was attacked in the room next to the one in which Mr. Adams died, and with which there was communication through the bulk-head; the officer who took Mr. Adams' room had had yellow fever, and hence escaped. The attendants upon the sick suffered to an extent that almost typified contagion. Dr. Duvall was among the early sufferers (Dr. Du Bois, having had the disease in the Gulf of Mexico, was an exempt almost to a certainty); Miller, the constant nurse up to March 13th, was then stricken down; my attack came next in order; then Edward Smith, the apothecary, sickened and died; and last Bradley, who was acting apothecary when I arrived with Smith, and who was retained as nurse and assistant in the dispensary until his fatal sickness.

It is pertinent, in considering the portableness of yellow fever, to cite the instance of the mail-steamer Golden City, which arrived at Panama March 4th, and the same day an officer of the Jamestown removed his wife from their lodgings on shore to the steamer for passage to San Francisco. Each day there was communication between our ship and the steamer, and a quantity of luggage was transferred from the former to the latter. The Golden City sailed on her return trip March 10th, but before reaching Acapulco the servant that attended the room occupied by the officer's wife (and by the officer also at Panama) died of yellow fever; and three other cases and two more deaths resulted before the cold latitudes were reached. It is possible that the "ferment" was received on board from the shore, but more probably it was carried from our ship—a question distressing to the parties who innocently but unwarily were thus concerned in it.

It is to be remembered that the rainy and *sickly* season ended before the pestilence broke out on the Jamestown, and that her stay at Panama was in the dry or *healthy* period, the climatology of which I daily observed and considered; and as evidences of its general phenomena, I noted that the average daily temperature during the first quarter of 1867 was (F.) 78°.2 at 6 o'clock a. m., 84°.2 at noon, 81°.9 at 6 p. m., and 79°.1 at midnight. There was an absence, for the greater part of the time, of northerly winds, which are commonly prevalent throughout the dry season, and rain-showers occurred quite frequently, so that the unpleasant dampness and moldiness penetrated everywhere—into books, bedding, clothing, and packages, no matter how secured. The atmosphere was sultry and stifling, and earthquakes, though slight, were not infrequent. In name only was the season either dry or healthy. At San Francisco I was permitted by the health-officer of the port to examine the sanitary reports furnished him by the surgeons of the Panama steamers on their arrival. I do not remember an exception but that, on every return voyage, for months from and after December, 1866, cases of yellow fever, or some exceedingly suspicious diseases, were returned; and the same held true at the port of New York. I have in preservation a formidable list of deaths which resulted from crossing the Isthmus in the ordinary line of travel during that year of 1867. An officer on board the United States steamer Resaca, at Panama, July 1st, 1867, wrote me that "the fever still continues here; deaths five per diem just now. One by one the strangers are picked off. The Panama Mail Steamship Company's steamer Montana had several cases, and lost two engineers just before leaving here last trip. The Bolivia (Columbian man-of-war) has it on board, and we have ceased all communication with the shore." Ten days afterward, the commanding officer of the Resaca reported that "the fever had appeared on the ship, and that, by advice of the medical officer, he should leave immediately for a cold climate; that it was very fatal among foreigners and the troops ashore; and that the surgeon of Her Britannic Majesty's steamer Scout had just died of it." (Nineteen others also died on board the Scout before she reached Esquimalt, Vancouver's Island, for which port she started at the instant of the appearance of the yellow fever among her people.) The Resaca drove northward under full steam, but before gaining the harbor of San Francisco, sixty-eight of her crew were stricken down and seventeen corpses hove overboard.

The Jamestown and Resaca were ordered to Sitka for disinfection by cold, and I rejoined my ship there in October, about a month after her arrival; and the following month I certified that, in my opinion, any cause sufficient to repropagate yellow fever within the Jamestown had ceased to exist; that frost or a low temperature, when continued a sufficient length of time, will effectually destroy the "ferment;" and that I considered that a sufficient length of time had elapsed. The Resaca returned south in January, and, though she has been employed in the tropics a good share of the time since, has not had another case of the fever. We, in the Jamestown, passed the winter in Alaska, and sailed from Sitka the last of May for Puget Sound, and thence to the Mare Island navy-yard, where our scarred veteran was dismantled.

The following winter, on returning to the island, I found the Jamestown refitting for sea; and though during her winter in the boreal regions she had been thoroughly broken out, cleansed, dried, and whitewashed three separate and several times, it was insisted upon as necessary that she should be "steamed," and accordingly was put through that process. She sailed finally on her cruise and into the tropics, where she has since been principally employed and now is, without having contracted any unusual sickness on board.

320 CLERMONT AVENUE, BROOKLYN, *May*, 1871.

AN ACCOUNT

OF

THE EPIDEMIC OF YELLOW FEVER WHICH APPEARED ON
BOARD THE UNITED STATES SHIP SARATOGA,
IN JUNE, 1869.

BY

LEWIS S. PILCHER, M. D.,

PASSED ASSISTANT SURGEON, U. S. N.

AN ACCOUNT OF THE EPIDEMIC OF YELLOW FEVER WHICH APPEARED ON BOARD THE UNITED STATES SHIP SARATOGA, IN JUNE, 1869.

By Lewis S. Pilcher, M. D., *Passed Assistant Surgeon, U. S. N.*

The United States ship Saratoga, third rate, came to anchor in the harbor of Havana, May 10, 1869, having left New York on the 21st of April previous. Her complement of officers and men comprised 17 officers, 105 men, 78 naval apprentices, and 24 marines; in all, 224 souls. She remained at Havana, not changing from her original anchorage, till the 7th of June following, when, cases of yellow fever having appeared on board with two deaths, she put to sea. Prior to leaving, a medical officer was transferred to her from the United States steamer Penobscot, on account of the death of her own surgeon. She arrived at Key West, Florida, June 10th, whence she set sail the following day, June 11th, under orders to proceed to Portsmouth, New Hampshire. Owing to the rapid extension of the disease, she put into New York, arriving there June 20th. During the passage from Key West to New York three deaths occurred. Immediately on arriving at the lower quarantine-station in New York Bay, the sick, sixteen in number, were transferred to the hospital-hulk Illinois. Seven new cases reported on the 21st, and one on the 23d; these, with one exception, were also transferred to the Illinois.

At noon of the 23d, the United States steamer Frolic was towed down from the navy-yard, and the entire remaining ship's company transferred to her. The crew received an entire change of clothing, but were obliged to take with them their old hammocks, blankets, and mattresses. The officers were allowed to take their bedding and only the clothes they had on at the time.

The Frolic was anchored near the Illinois, and the officers and crew of the Saratoga retained on board of her, in quarantine, until July 7th, but two more cases of fever appearing during that time, one on the 24th, and one on the 28th of June. They were relieved from quarantine July 7th, and transferred to the receiving-ship Vermont, at the navy-yard. During the course of the epidemic, thirty-seven cases occurred, with seventeen deaths.

In the harbor of Havana, during the spring and early summer of 1869, at the same time with the Saratoga, were the United States steamers Albany, Narragansett, and Penobscot. The first of these, with one or two short intervals, had been there since November 15, 1868; the two latter had been either in the harbor of Havana itself, or in neighboring ports of Cuba, since the beginning of March. The Albany and the Penobscot were in port at the time óf the outbreak of the epidemic on the Saratoga. Of these vessels the Saratoga alone, at this time, was visited by the disease, although later in the season, on both the Albany and the Narragansett, a few cases occurred, and on the Penobscot, which left for the north at the same time with the Saratoga, seven cases reported as remittent fever, none fatal, occurred before reaching Portsmouth, New Hampshire.

During the summer of 1869, yellow fever was prevalent throughout the West India Islands, but not to such an extent as to be considered in any place as epidemic. Out of the seven vessels constituting our squadron in those waters at the beginning of the summer, but one escaped its attacks.

During the year there occurred in all throughout the squadron thirty-one cases of yellow fever,* exclusive of those on the Saratoga, with seven deaths, being a percentage of deaths to cases of .22, or one death to every 4.43 cases.

The Saratoga, first visited, suffered the most, both in number of cases and in their malignancy, the percentage of deaths in the thirty-seven cases being .46, or 1 death in every 2.17 cases.

---

* La Roche, in his work on yellow fever, vol. i, p. 533, gives statistics of epidemics on twenty vessels, in tropical regions, gathered from published accounts, which give an average of 1 death to every 3.46 cases.

The following table shows the number of cases of yellow and remittent fever, respectively, that occurred on each of the vessels of the West India squadron during the year 1869, as reported:

Vessels.	REMITTENT FEVER.		YELLOW FEVER.	
	Cases.	Deaths.	Cases.	Deaths.
Albany	23	....	1	1
Yantic	9	....	8	3
Narragansett	....	....	14	1
Gettysburg	14	....	8	2
Penobscot	7	....	....	....
Saratoga	....	....	37	17
Total	53	....	68	24

There can be little doubt but that some cases, which were essentially identical with those reported as yellow fever, but which did not progress to a fatal termination, and did not manifest the worst phenomena of that disease, especially at the first appearance of the disease, before its true nature was recognized, were called and reported as cases of remittent fever. If so, and these cases could be placed in the proper column, the number of cases of yellow fever that really occurred in the squadron would be much increased, while the death rate, as compared with the cases in general, would be diminished. However, the figures as reported render sufficiently prominent the exceptional severity of the disease, as manifested on the Saratoga.

No reason why the disease should have appeared sooner, and in a more malignant form, on board the Saratoga than on board her consorts, can be found in the condition of the ship itself; which, on the contrary, was such as would tend to render it the least liable to become infected, and which afforded surroundings the best adapted to the care and favorable progress of such as should be attacked, should disease make its appearance. She was roomy and comfortable, well ventilated and lighted, and a model of neatness and cleanliness throughout. The *morale* of the ship's

company was excellent, and its general health unusually good.
For six weeks previous to the appearance of the first case of yellow fever, there had not been a single case of sickness on board,
even of the most trivial character. But though the ship itself
was in this excellent condition, the circumstances in which it was
placed were such as by their combination could not but be potent
agencies in the production of the results in questiou. These were
the season of the year and the non-acclimation of the ship's company, and the special evil influences pertaining to the harbor of
Havana, and particularly to that part of it in which the ship was
anchored.

In the latter part of May begins in Havana the so-called unhealthy season, which extends through the summer and into the
fall, to the last of November. At the very beginning of this season
the Saratoga arrived from the north with a crew entirely unacclimated, a time when the general climatic influences, at all times
unfavorable to the unacclimated, tended most to the production
of the special diseases incident to them. The harbor of Havana
is a land-locked bay, surrounded on all sides by hills, except at a
point on its northern aspect, where it communicates with the sea
by a narrow channel. Its northeastern boundary is a narrow peninsula, less elevated at its junction with the mainland than in the
rest of its course, permitting the prevailing easterly breezes to reach
the harbor. The usual rise and fall of the tide in the harbor is
very slight, while the only communication between the bay and
the sea is narrow and somewhat tortuous ; these conditions cause
the harbor to assimilate in character to a great stagnant pool. The
bay receives the water shed from the surrounding hills, the drain-
ings from the village of Regla, on its southern shore, and the
contents of most of the sewers of the city of Havana. From the
shipping with which it is crowded during the greater part of the
year, it receives additional filth. These causes render its water
very foul, and its stagnation favors the putrefaction of the filth
which it contains, which process is hastened and aggravated by
the uniformly high temperature at which the water is kept by the

conjoined influences of the Gulf Stream and the tropical sun. The effects of this are somewhat counteracted, during the so-called healthy or dry season, by the constant sea-breezes prevailing, and by the dryness of the atmosphere; but during the remainder of the year, when the sea-breezes fail, and at times are replaced by debilitating land-breezes, when the atmosphere is saturated with moisture, an opposite result obtains—the air becomes laden with the products of decomposition, and a high degree of virulency favored in their effects. The Saratoga, arriving at the beginning of this latter season, was anchored on the west side of the harbor, within a stone's throw of the quay lining the shore, and in close proximity to the track of a line of ferry-boats. The sea-breeze could reach her only after passing over the whole bay, becoming necessarily laden with its exhalations. The constant superficial agitation of the water in the immediate neighborhood of the ship by the ferry-boats favored, in an eminent degree, the rapid decomposition of the already putrescent matter contained in it, and the disengagement of the noxious effluvia resulting. In this position, without shifting her anchorage, the ship remained from May 10th to June 7th, when she put to sea, stricken with yellow fever. Three cases occurred nearly simultaneously: two on the 2d of June, those of Surgeon Quinn and Lieutenant Lamberton, and one on the 3d, that of Private Bowler. No further cases occurred till June 7th, when two more persons were attacked. Of these three cases, occurring nearly simultaneously, the habits, circumstances, and relations of each differed greatly, agreeing only in the one point, that they were all equally exposed to the general evil influences already named, pervading and surrounding the ship. Her two consorts, the Albany and the Penobscot, were anchored in another part of the harbor, and both escaped untouched by the disease at this time, unless the febrile cases, mentioned as having occurred on the Penobscot, be considered as essentially identical with those on the Saratoga, though milder in degree. All the cases that occurred on the Saratoga, thirty-seven in number, are exhibited in the following general tabulated statement:

15 H

General exhibit of cases.

Number.	Name.	Grade.	Age.	Nativity.	Date of seizure.	Date of transfer to hospital-ship.	Result.	Date and day of death.	Remarks.
1	J. P. Quinn	Surgeon	31	Vt	June 2		Death	June 6... 5th day	Partial suppression of urine; convulsions; coma; no black-vomit.
2	B. P. Lamberton	Lieutenant	23	Pa	June 2		Recovery		Urine for a time very scanty, albuminous, highly colored, containing bile pigment.
3	M. Bowler	Private	22	Ireland	June 3		Death	June 7... 5th day	Died comatose; black-vomit one hour before death.
4	J. Hudson	M. A	46	Va	Noon, June 7.?		Recovery		Convalesced from third day.
5	F. Harrison	Nav. appr.	16	N. Y	Ev'g, June 7		Recovery		Convales'd from fourth day.
6	C. Quick	Landsman	21	N. J	Ev'g, June 13		Recovery		Convalesced from third day.
7	B. Fitzgerald	Seaman	48	Ireland	Morn., June 14		Death	June 19.. 6th day	Black-vomit on last day.
8	J. Riley	Seaman	21	Ireland	Morn., June 14		Death	June 18.. 5th day	Epistaxis on third day; black-vomit on fourth day.
9	J. S. Giraud	Paym'r		N. Y	Morn., June 15	June 20	Recovery		Epistaxis; black-vomit; long and tedious convalescence.
10	R. Anderson	Q. M	43	Prussia	Morn., June 15	June 20	Recovery		Condition precarious for some time; convalescence tedious.

11	F. Robinson	Landsman	17	Va	Noon, June 15	June 20	Death	June 23.. 9th day	Mulatto. Epistaxis; black-vomit.
12	H. Diegel	Landsman	30	Prussia	Night, June 15		Recovery		Experienced pain only on left side of head and body.
13	A. Sweeney	Nav. appr	13	N. Y	Night, June 15		Recovery		Convalesced from third day.
14	G. N. Flagg	Lieutenant		Vt	Night, June 15		Death	June 20.. 6th day	Urine albuminous; black-vomit.
15	J. Anderson	Nav. appr	16	Cal	Night, June 16	June 20	Death	June 20.. 5th day	Deficient in intellec. Delirious from the first. Particulars of death not ascertained.
16	W. Carter	Gunner		Pa	Morn., June 17	June 20	Recovery		
17	S. S. Blodgett	Mate	21	N. Y	Morn., June 17	June 20	Death	June 20.. 4th day	Black-vomit shortly before death.
18	W. A. Failing	Mate	21	N J	Ev'g, June 17	June 20	Recovery		Convalesced from third day.
19	W. G. Tompkins	Boatswain		N. J	Ev'g, June 17	June 20	Recovery		Convalesced from third day.
20	W. H. Palmer	Corporal	29	D. C	Morn., June 18	June 20	Death	June 27..10th day	Very robust man. Had profuse black-vomit.
21	J. Henry	Private	33	N. Y	Noon, June 18	June 20	Death	June 21.. 4th day	Prematurely old. Great prostration from the first; tongue dry and black, with raw edges on the second day; black-vomit.
22	J. Reynolds	Private	25	Ireland	Noon, June 18	June 20	Death	June 23.. 6th day	Black-vomit before death.
23	M. Harford	Private	31	Ireland	Morn., June 19	June 20	Death	June 26:. 8th day	Excessive vomiting through out the attack; black-vomit before death.
24	S. Rothberg	Nav. appr	18	Poland	Eve'g, June 19	June 20	Recovery		
25	J. Henneberger	Private	21	N. J	Morn., June 20	June 20	Recovery		

General exhibit of cases—Continued.

Number.	Name.	Grade.	Age.	Nativity.	Date of seizure.	Date of transfer to hospital-ship.	Result.	Date of death.	Remarks.
26	H. C. Raebel....	Lieutenant	33	Germany	Morn., June 20.	June 20..	Death.....	June 25.. 6th day	Black-vomit; died in convulsions.
27	W. E. McMullen	Cap's clerk	22	Md	Morn., June 20.	June 20..	Death.....	June 22.. 3d day	Complicated by advanced phthisis pulmonalis; no black-vomit.
28	J. O. Corsa......	Nav. appr.	15	N. Y	Morn., June 21.	June 21..	Death.....	June 26.. 6th day	Particulars of death unascertained.
29	F. W. Crans	Nav. appr.	15	N. Y	Morn., June 21.	June 21..	Recovery .	....	
30	W. Watson	Q. M.......	23	Mass....	Morn., June 21.	June 21..	Recovery .	....	
31	L. S. Pilcher	Ass't surg.	24	Mich....	Noon, June 21	....	Recovery .	....	Transferred to Naval Hospital, Brooklyn, June 21.
32	W. W. Van Vleck	Lt. com'r .	25	N. Y	Morn., June 21.	June 23..	Death.....	June 29.. 7th day	Epistaxis; black-vomit.
33	A. L. Dixon.....	Carpenter .	....	Maine...	Eve'g, June 21.	June 23..	Death.....	June 26.. 3d day	Epistaxis; black-vomit.
34	J. C. Herbert....	Sailmaker .	....	N. Y	Eve'g, June 21.	June 23..	Recovery .	....	
35	J. McQuade.....	Seaman ...	24	Mass....	June 23.........	June 23..	Recovery .	....	
36	H. Brown........	Ord. sea'n.	24	England	June 24.........	June 24..	Recovery .	....	
37	F. E. Pratt.......	Nav. appr.	16	Mich....	Morn., June 28.	June 28..	Recovery .	....	

An examination of these cases gives the following :

Total number of—	Per cent. of cases.	Per cent. of deaths to cases.
Officers..	13	77	50
Men	105	9	33
Apprentices	78	9	29
Marines.	24	25	83
Souls on board	225	16	46

Earliest period of death, third day ; latest period of death, tenth day ; average period of death, fifth day.

Black-vomit occurred in 14 cases ; recovery after black-vomit in 1 case ; epistaxis noted in 5 cases ; recovery after epistaxis in 1 case ; particulars unascertained in 2 cases.

From the time that the ship left Havana until the evening of the 13th, a space of six days, no new cases occurred. During this time there was a succession of days of fine weather ; a gentle breeze from the northeast prevailed. All the hatches and air-ports were kept open. Those already ill progressed favorably, and the hope was entertained that the disease had been checked. A new case in the evening of the 13th, and two more the next morning, re-awakened apprehension. During the afternoon of the 14th the weather experienced a rapid change, becoming cold and stormy, with rain and wind. This continued through the night and the next day, necessitating the closing of the hatches, thus rendering the air of the vessel close and bad, while, at the same time, much necessary exposure to the inclemencies of the weather resulted to the officers and men. Although the ship made north of Cape Hatteras on the 15th, and the weather again became fine, with cool and refreshing breezes, the rapid extension of the disease dates from that day. Six cases on the 15th, one on the 16th, four on the 17th, three on the 18th, two on the 19th, and three on the 20th, successively appeared. Of these, two died before reaching New York, while a third, Lieutenant Flagg, expired just before the ship came to anchor. In many of these cases, in addition to the general influences, acting as predisposing and efficient causes, it was possible to trace special exciting causes which determined the attack. Thus, in one case, an officer, while perspiring freely, became chilled by sitting in a draught of air; four hours after the fever was fully developed. Another, returning from the deck with his clothing wet with rain, neglected to remove it at once, sitting down for some time in his damp garments; an attack of the disease followed almost immediately. Another, after the arrival of the ship at New York, indulged once in liquor to intoxication. His debauch left him laboring under the fever, which resulted in his death. In the last case that occurred, that of the boy Pratt, on the Frolic, five days after the transfer from the infected vessel, he had lain down to sleep in a gangway of the vessel, where he became chilled through during the night. As a result, there followed a typical case of yellow fever, the stages well defined, and the icterus attending convalescence very marked.

In most of the large number of cases which occurred on the 21st, seven in all, particular causes of similar nature to those already given can be traced to which they may be referred. The large number of cases occurring on that day, and their almost complete cessation from that time, is somewhat remarkable, and seems to indicate the utility of the measures for disinfection which were adopted, and especially to be due to the speedy removal of the men from the infected ship to one free from such taint. In the circumstances attending the cases of yellow fever on this vessel, there were none which indicated that the disease was in any way propagated by contact with the sick, or by exposure to the emanations or secretions from their bodies. On the contrary, those who were most about the persons of the sick escaped entirely.

The apothecary and four nurses, all unacclimated and unprotected by a previous attack of the disease, who were with the sick continually, night and day, and, in some cases, unavoidably received upon their persons matters vomited by the dying, were none of them attacked.

Commander Whiting, who filled his cabin with the sick officers, and who was constantly among all the sick, encouraging them by cheerful words and aiding them by his attentions, was one of the two commissioned officers on board the vessel who alone escaped the disease.

The medical officer received from the Penobscot was able to resist the disease till after the arrival of the vessel at New York, when, consequent upon exposure for some time to the hot sun in passing from the Saratoga to the Illinois, and upon unusual exertion in superintending the removal of certain of the sick, and upon reaction from the mental strain of the preceding two weeks by the transfer of all care to others, he was attacked, the circumstances giving no support to any theory of contagiousness in the disease.

This officer was succeeded by Surgeon H. M. Wells, temporarily detached from the New York Naval Hospital, who, transferred with the rest from the Saratoga to the Frolic, remained until their release from quarantine. During this time he spent much of each day on board the hospital-hulk with the sick, being assiduous in his attentions to them, without contracting the disease. Further, notwithstanding the number of the sick transferred to the Illinois, not one of the quarantine officials or attendants was attacked by the disease. In the transfer of the sick special care was taken to prevent as much as possible any articles from accompanying them which might act as fomites.

Upon the arrival of the ship at quarantine active measures were adopted for disinfection. Carbolic acid was poured down the pumps, and introduced into the bilge at other points. Carbolated lime was strewn about the decks, and chlorine gas was liberated by the common salt mixture throughout the ship, the hatches being closed. During the summer following the latter measure was repeated several times, and in the intervals the most thorough ventilation secured.

Throughout the course of the epidemic, in the cases that occurred, there was absent any sthenic action, no furious delirium, no raging heat of the skin, no strong, full arterial pulsations. In but few cases did any delirium occur, and then it was low and muttering in its character. The skin from the first, in the majority of cases, was warm and moist, and the pulse, though very frequent at the outset of the attack in most, yet was always weak and soft in character. Its variations and characteristics in the different cases were found to be valueless as an indication of the intensity or the tendency of the attack.

The following table exhibits its frequency from day to day in ten cases:

Names.	Pulsations per minute.					Result of case.
	1st day.	2d day.	3d day.	4th day.	5th day.	
Quick......................	112	98	66	60	72	Recovery.
Fitzgerald.................	90	76	76	68	76	Death on night of fifth day.
Riley......................	100	90	92	92	100	Do.
Giraud.....................	112	90	84	92	......	Recovery.
R. Anderson...............	96	72	60	68	76	Do.
Robinson..................	120	88	88	58	64	Death on ninth day.
Diegel....................	96	60	60	......	......	Recovery.
T. Anderson..............	120	92	88	......	......	Death on fifth day.
Carter....................	130	88	92	......	......	Recovery.
Blodgett..................	104	100	88	......	......	Death on fourth day.

Complete suppression of urine occurred in no case. In the majority of cases, even of those terminating fatally, its secretion remained free. The nearest approach to suppression was in the case of Surgeon Quinn, the symptoms attending whose death indicated uræmic poisoning. In other cases the urine, though free, was highly albuminous, a condition which supervened in such of those cases which were at all prolonged, whether eventuating in death or recovery, as were under the observation of the writer. In the cases which were treated wholly on board the quarantine hospital-hulk, no examinations of the urine, as to the presence of albumen, were made. The condition of the bowels presented no features worthy of note. More or less constipation was present at the outset of many of the cases, relieved by gentle cathartics in all cases. The tongue, at the outset, was covered with moist white fur, in some cases presented a punctated appearance, afterward changing in its appearance as the disease progressed, either gradually clearing off, or becoming dry, and brown or black, and in some cases clearing off rapidly, presenting then a raw appearance, as if entirely denuded of its epithelium. In the three cases which terminated fatally, during the passage from Key West to New York, death was heralded in each by this latter condition of the tongue, the denudation beginning first at the edges, on each side, and thence spreading over the whole tongue. In the last of these cases, in which life was prolonged to the sixth day, the dorsum of the tongue became dry, black, and scaly during the last day.

Apparent heat of the head, out of proportion to that of the body in general, was noticed in every case. This persisted for some time after all other symptoms ameliorated. Its subsidence was regarded as an unerring indication of the establishment of convalescence.

Intense frontal or orbital headache, described as passing from temple to temple through the eyes, with injection and suffusion of the conjunctiva, was a constant symptom attending the beginning of an attack. Pain in the back was also usually great. In one case pain in the calves of the legs was bitterly complained of. In one case pain was experienced in the left temple, and in the left side of the body only. Tenderness of the epigastrium and a peculiar sensation of fullness at that point, especially on deep inspiration, were usual.

The most prominent and distressing symptom was gastric irritability. In some cases, despite the careful avoidance of all irritation, uncontrollable vomitting persisted through the first stage of the disease. In these, after a short calm, in nearly every instance, the vomitting again recurred, soon presenting the peculiar appearance termed black vomit.

In the greater number of cases, however, after one or two paroxysms of vomiting when first seized, though the irritability of the stomach remained great, it was repressed by the measures adopted; the slightest indiscretion, however, again provoking vomiting. After the period of calm following the subsidence of the symptoms attending the febrile paroxysm—in many of these latter also—vomiting then appeared spontaneously, ending in black vomit and death. Much thirst was complained of in most of the cases.

The general measures of treatment adopted on board the Saratoga were directed toward supporting the system, and aiding it in its efforts to eliminate the poison with which it was saturated. Special symptoms it was endeavored to meet as occasion required.

The treatment as continued on board the hospital-hulk, after the transfer of the cases thither, was essentially the same. All internal remedies of a depressing character were avoided; indeed, the irritability of the stomach universally precluded the administration of any internal remedy, even had such been deemed advisable. The most accessible point was the skin, the action of which it was endeavored to sustain and promote by wrapping the patient in blankets wrung out in hot water—as a substitute for the hot bath, which the want of a bath-tub prevented from being adopted—and by sponging the skin, from time to time, with tepid water and vinegar. At the earliest possible moment, food and stimulants were methodically administered according to the condition of the patient.

In the whole course of the epidemic, the most prominent symptom which presented itself was the extreme irritability of the stomach; the local measures of treatment adopted were chiefly directed toward this, to prevent its occurrence if possible, and to lessen its severity when present. A careful avoidance of every source of irritation, whether medicinal or alimentary, was insisted upon; counter-irritation by sinapisms to the epigastrium was effected when occasion seemed to demand; pellets of ice were allowed to melt in the mouth, for the double purpose of controlling gastric irritability and of alleviating thirst; nothing but fluids, and those in very small quantities often repeated, were administered. These were the measures that were found to be most effectual in preventing and alleviating this symptom. In addition, various medicaments, as carbolic acid, turpentine, aromatic spirits of ammonia, the effervescing draught, and others, were used in most of those cases in which the measures first mentioned did not prove sufficient, but without decided benefit.

Frontal headache, invariably great, was alleviated by cold applications to the forehead and temples. Pain in the back, much complained of, by sinapisms and cuppings.

The importance of avoiding carefully any unusual exposure or fatigue, or irregularities of diet, or the giving way to excessive anxiety, and of preserving the general condition of the body in the most perfect health possible, as prophylactic measures, was plainly shown by the circumstances which seemed to determine the attack in many instances, some of which have been mentioned.

In a number of instances in which men presented themselves at once upon the first appearance of those symptoms which usually marked the onset of the disease, as chills, heat of head, intense frontal headache, and fever, with very frequent pulse and furred tongue, from fifteen to twenty grains of quinine were given immediately. In a short time complete relief was experienced, with no recurrence of the symptoms. Whether this result was a mere coincidence or an effect cannot be said, yet the impression grew continually stronger that it was the effect of the quinine administered, as although in all cases the result was not so favorable, yet, in no cases presenting the same symptoms, in which quinine was not administered at once, as stated, did the disease fail to continue and to pass through its usual course.

SANITARY CONDITION

OF THE

UNITED STATES ASIATIC SQUADRON DURING THE PERIOD
OF TWO YEARS, FROM APRIL 1, 1868, TO MARCH
31, 1870.

BY

ROBERT T. MACCOUN, M. D.,

MEDICAL INSPECTOR, UNITED STATES NAVY; FLEET SURGEON, ASIATIC
SQUADRON.

SANITARY CONDITION OF THE UNITED STATES ASIATIC SQUADRON DURING THE PERIOD OF TWO YEARS, FROM APRIL 1, 1868, TO MARCH 31, 1870.

By ROBERT T. MACCOUN, M. D.,

Medical Inspector, United States Navy; Fleet Surgeon, Asiatic Squadron.

The influence of climate on the health and mortality of man in different portions of the glode is becoming more and more a subject of interest to scientific as well as practical medicine, now that we can be whirled around the earth's surface, with comparative comfort, in the short period of ninety days.

Places hitherto remote are now of easy access. Japan was almost a *terra incognita* a few years since, and a voyage to China was thought to be a great undertaking. But now these countries seem to be brought to our very doors, by means of the Pacific Railway and the Pacific Mail Company's splendid steamers. This facility of transit swells the tide of travel, either for business or pleasure; hence the influence of this change of locality, upon those who wander from their homes, is a matter of peculiar interest at the present time.

The limits of the Asiatic squadron extend from the equator to about 42° of north latitude. Within these lines we have the whole of the northern tropical and a greater portion of the northern temperate zones. The first of these, styled by Alexander Keith Johnson the tropical disease realm, is characterized by great atmospheric heat and humidity; and the prevailing diseases are dysentery, diarrhœa, cholera, hepatic affections, and malarial fevers. .

That portion of the station north of this, included in the temperate zone, extending along the coast of China, is characterized by the same diseases during the summer and autumn months, while in winter, typhus fever, pulmonary affections, and rheumatism prevail. The islands forming the Japanese Empire, having an exceptional climate, will be considered further on.

The squadron for a greater part of the time was composed of ten ships, with an average force of fifteen hundred men; and the following table will show the classes of disease, sickness, and mortality during the period indicated:

Table showing the classes of disease and number of admissions and deaths in the Asiatic squadron for two years, from the 1st of April, 1868, to the 31st of March, 1870, in a force of fifteen hundred men.

Class.	Under treatment April 1, 1868.	Admitted.	Discharged.	Died.
Febrile or miasmatic..	24	374	395	3
Digestive...	6	820	824	2
Respiratory...	7	363	268	2
Circulatory...	......	19	17	2
Nervous..	1	132	131	2
Integumentary..	4	369	373	......
Fibrous and osseous	9	287	296	......
Exhalants and absorbents	......	3	3	......
Genito-urinary..	......	17	17	......
Enthetic*..	12	732	744	......
Cachexiæ...	1	45	46	......
Eye and ear	1	58	59	......
Injuries, accidents	8	474	476	6
Total....................................	73	3,693	3,749	17

* In addition to the above there were over six hundred persons treated for venereal diseases, who were not excused from duty.

From the above table the sickness is represented by three thousand six hundred and ninety-three admissions, and the mortality by seventeen deaths.* Of the latter, six were from accidents, one from typhoid fever, two from small-pox, two from dysentery, two from pulmonary diseases, two from cardiac affections, and two from diseases of the nervous system. This is a remarkably small mortality for this station; especially so as regards intestinal and malarial fevers. There were eight hundred and twenty admissions for dysentery and diarrhœa, with only two deaths; yet a few years ago these diseases were the scourge of the East, very few of our ships escaping a severe visitation from them during some period of the cruise.

It will naturally be asked, Why this great reduction of sickness and mortality in a region hitherto considered so unhealthy? The answer is, The adoption of a better system of hygiene, both afloat and on shore, an ample supply of pure drinking-water, a better diet for the men, a more enlightened method of medical treatment, and, finally, the opening of Japan offering facilities for a change of climate.

Until recently the supply of water on the China coast having been taken from rivers in the vicinity of filthy towns and cities, or from streams flowing through rice-fields,* was vitiated by decayed animal and vegetable matter, and hence the exciting cause of intestinal affections and malarial fevers. But there is a great improvement in this respect; at many points we find abundance of good water at present. This is especially the case at Hong-Kong, where immense stone reservoirs have been constructed, which are filled from pure mountain-streams, affording an ample supply for every demand.

At Shanghai, also, where the river-water is extremely unwholesome, excellent water is now brought from a lake, some miles above the native city, for the supply of the foreign settlement and shipping. At other points on the coast, where the water is im-

---

* Four deaths are reported among those who were invalided home during the two years.

† In both China and Japan human excrement is carefully preserved and returned to the soil.

pure, the distilling apparatus now attached to all steam-vessels is called into use; therefore this fruitful cause of disease is obviated.

The allowance of fresh meat and vegetables several times during the week, or even daily, if deemed necessary in the hottest weather, tends to maintain a better condition of the system, and render it less liable to disease.

Attention to drainage, and an improved method of constructing houses in the English towns and European settlements, have also greatly improved their sanitary condition; and our ships have been greatly benefited by the custom of covering the berth-deck with shellac, thereby avoiding dampness, as well as by a greater attention to the cleanliness of the hold and bilges.*

At Hong-Kong, where the range of the thermometer is from 45° to 90° of Fahrenheit, with heavy rain-falls from May to August, and subject to great changes of temperature during the winter months, the mortality from fever and dysentery was formerly excessive. The troops, especially, suffered severely, owing to their being quartered in poorly constructed frame barracks, and sleeping upon the ground floor. But since the erection of new buildings, which are of stone, well ventilated, well drained, with sleeping apartments raised one story from the ground, they enjoy a comparative immunity from disease. In this connection I must mention that venereal diseases are less virulent and much less prevalent at this place than formerly, owing to a strict system of registration and inspection of all public women. The average number of sick in the English barracks has been reduced one-third by this measure. We have also reaped the benefit of it ourselves, for after a liberty of forty-eight hours given to one of the ships of the squadron, with a crew of nearly five hundred men, only six cases of chancroid were returned.

The low-lying site of Shanghai, scarcely raised above the level

---

*An improved arrangement of the holds of our ships is greatly needed: (*vide* communication No. 6, series 1868, to the Chief of Bureau of Medicine and Surgery.)

of the Woosung River, and exposed to marshy exhalations, will always render it an unhealthy place of residence; yet even here there has been a great decrease in sickness and mortality, with improved drainage, and greater personal care as regards diet and exposure to the sun during the hot season. Ships obliged to remain here throughout the summer should take a short trip to sea every two or three weeks. This is the plan pursued by the English, who are very careful of the health of their men.

In regard to the treatment of tropical dysentery, once the most formidable disease in the East, a wonderful change has taken place. In our day, a disciple of Todd thrills with holy horror as he reads the general rules recommended by Sir James McGregor for adoption in the army, during the peninsular war, or those more recently advised by Sir Ranald Martin. These consist mainly in calomel and blood-letting, the latter, according to Sir James McGregor, to be repeated until the stools are free, or nearly free, from blood. Depletion, either general or local, and the mercurial treatment advised by Dr. Johnson, are now, happily, things of the past, at least among the most enlightened practitioners. The object now is to husband the strength of the patient, however acute may be the symptoms under this depressing disease. Since the adoption of a more conservative treatment, the mortality from dysentery in India has been reduced from 7.1 per cent. to 1.3 per cent., and the record of the squadron only shows two deaths from that disease in two years.

I come, now, to the islands of the Japanese* Empire. Lying between the thirtieth and fortieth parallels of north latitude, they possess one of the most salubrious climates in the world, and are properly styled the sanitarium of this portion of the East.

At Yokohama, latitude 35° 26' north, situated within eighteen miles of Yeddo, and the headquarters of all the foreign squadrons, the mean annual temperature is 59° Fahrenheit; minimum, 48°; maximum, 92°. The most disagreeable feature of the climate is the heavy rains from April to August. The average rain-fall is

---

* Ni-pon—*ni* sun, *pon* source.

about fifty inches, annually ; but during the year 1868–'69—rendered remarkable throughout the world for its meteorological phenomena—it rose to one hundred and twenty inches. Excellent water, from mountain-streams, can be procured at the principal ports of Japan, yet the necessity for a high standard is not so important as in China, owing to the frequency of intestinal affections.

Malarial fevers, as far as my observation goes, are rare, even among the rural population, who dwell amid their damp rice-fields. The most prevalent diseases are rheumatism, typhus fever, small-pox, syphilis, ophthalmia, and cutaneous affections.

Typhus fever and small-pox need be feared only during the cold, damp weather of winter and spring. The Japanese having no means of heating their houses shut them up closely in cold weather, to keep warm. They generally overcrowd them, and have no appliance for ventilation. This, together with bad drainage and defective sewerage, is no doubt the exciting cause of fever in their cities.

Cutaneous diseases are exceedingly common among them, and especially scabies, which is of the most inveterate kind, often lasting during a life-time. In cases of long standing it becomes pustular and scaly, and the sufferer presents a disgusting appearance, being sometimes literally covered with sores and scabs. This is among the poorer classes, however, who rarely, if ever, change their clothing. The Japanese are described as a cleanly people, and as far as the use of the bath is concerned this is true. Bathing-houses are seen all over their cities, filled with bathers of both sexes, who enjoy, promiscuously, their hot bath. But they do not change their garments. In fact, they think it very strange that foreigners find it so necessary. An American physician, who has resided for many years in the country, told me he was once traveling in company with a Japanese doctor who said to him, " It must be a great inconvenience to you foreigners to be always changing your clothes. I have worn these I have on for six months, and still they do not smell badly !"

The most formidable enemy we have to contend with in the shape of disease is syphilis. This prevails to a frightful extent, and in its most virulent form. The true chancre is vastly more common than it is either in Europe or America, and the secondary manifestations are usually very severe. Gonorrhœa is also very intractable, and notwithstanding every precaution, epididymitis is a frequent complication.

Even vice is systematized in Japan. The government not only sanctions, by license, houses of prostitution, but derives a direct revenue from this source. A quarter in every town and city of the empire is inclosed and set apart for purposes of debauchery, which is covered by no veil of mystery as in other lands.

In the city of Yeddo there is a large district devoted to the courtesans, called the Yoshi-wara. This is laid out in broad avenues, planted with pine shade-trees, ornamented with beautiful gardens, and contains some of the finest buildings in the capital, next to the daimios' palaces. This region is presided over by a chief, whose headquarters is the gankiro, a species of casino, fitted up in splendid style, for the amusement of the higher classes of the Yoshi-wara, and used for banquets, dancing, concerts, theatrical exhibitions, etc. The chief of the gankiro gathers recruits for his establishments by purchasing young girls from seven to eight years of age, of indigent parents, who are unable to maintain a large family. Their first years are spent in acquiring an education, the older girls instructing the younger in music, singing, dancing, embroidery, etc., and many of them become famed for their accomplishments. When a girl is grown up her master is ready to part with her if he receives a good offer; if not, she remains attached to one of the houses. It is said not to be an uncommon occurrence for a man to choose a wife* from among these courtesans. The fact of a girl having been brought up in that capacity does not operate unfavorably against her in a social point of view, the fault being charged to her parents, who sold her in childhood.

---

* This has been denied by Aimé Humbert. (*Vide* Japon Illustré, 1870.)

During the past year Admiral Sir Harry Keppel, then commanding the English fleet on this station, detailed a naval surgeon, with the consent of the Japanese government, to open a hospital at Yokohama, in the quarter set apart for courtesans, with the view of instructing native physicians in the use of the speculum. It is hardly time to witness any striking results from this humane endeavor to save thoughtless men from the consequences of their own folly, yet, from the aptitude of the Japanese in adopting everything novel and useful, I think we may safely look for a great abatement of the evils of syphilis.

In conclusion, I will add that, from the observations of physicians who have been long resident in Japan, it may now be safely stated that it possesses one of the most salubrious climates in the world; while, on the other hand, all experience proves that the coast of China is remarkable for its unhealthiness. Yet, even there, a better acquaintance with the nature of the climate, a greater personal care, as regards food, clothing, exposure to the sun, etc., enable foreigners, in a great measure, to combat its deleterious influences.

ON DIABETES.

BY

JAMES McCLELLAND, M. D.,

MEDICAL DIRECTOR, U. S. N.

ON DIABETES.

—

By James McClelland, M. D.,

Medical Director, U. S. N.

———

Notwithstanding the rapid progress of medical science, the pathology of diabetes is still involved in obscurity. Even the seat of the disorder is yet a point of controversy. It is true that physiology has shed much light upon the phenomena of glycogenesis, that chemistry has explained to us the peculiar nature of the discharge, and anatomy demonstrated a few morbid changes, but neither these, nor the labors of Prout, Pavy, Bernard, Schiff, and others, have thrown enough light upon the subject to lead to a satisfactory conclusion. Among ancient writers, *diabetes mellitus* was regarded as a urinary disorder, having its seat primarily and idiopathically in the kidneys. They likened it to *lientery*, from the excessive destruction of tissues, and the rapidity with which the solids and fluids of the body were hurried forward to the kidneys; and this view of Galen's* was adopted without much change by Aretæus and Trallian. The same doctrine was supported by Ruysch, Dupuytren, Thenard, Henry, and Satterley, but they associated with the renal mischief some secondary or sympathetic derangement of the chylifacient viscera. Willis, Sydendam, Place, Latham, and some others, regarded it as a "dyscrasy or intemperament of the blood produced by a morbid action of the assimilating powers." Nearly a century ago, Darwin,† in his ingenious essay, argued that "the disease is dependent upon a retrograde motion of the lacteals, and is consequently seated in the lacteal vessels." But this hypothesis, plausible as it

———

* Galen, De Crisibus, lib. I, cap. xii; De Loc. Affect., lib. vi, cap. iii.
† Darwin, Prize Essay, 1778.

was, found few supporters. Even Frank,* who at first accepted it, gave up the doctrine of a retrograde motion, but still believed that the disease had its seat in the lymphatic system. And so we find the stomach, or some of the chylifactive organs, the blood, the lacteals, and the kidneys, have each in turn been the field for speculation concerning the nature of this disorder. For years the weight of authority was in favor of some lesion of the digestive organs, and was doubtless strengthened by Rollo, who fixed the seat of the disease in the stomach, believing it to consist "in an increased action and secretion with a vitiation of the gastric fluid, and probably too active a state of the lacteal absorbents; while the kidneys and other parts of the system, as the head and skin, are only affected secondarily." This hypothesis, which supposes the blood to be formed imperfectly from the first, and the morbid change of animal salts for sugar to be the work of the stomach or its auxiliary organs, was combated by Latham, who believed the stomach, as well as the kidneys, to be perfectly sound. Some recent writers regard the liver as the *fons et origo mali*. Pavy inferred from experiments made in conjunction with Dr. Owen Rees, that the morbid condition in diabetes is not the want of decomposing power in the lungs, nor the overproduction of sugar in the liver, but in the formation in this organ of glucose, instead of true hepatic sugar. Andral supposes it is due to an abnormal activity in the sugar-forming function produced by hepatic congestion, and Roberts believes it " consists proximately in some disturbance of the destiny and functions of the amyloid substance of the liver." Dr. Bence Jones advances the theory that diabetes may arise from deficient oxidation of the non-nitrogenous compounds, and Dr. B. H. Coates, of Philadelphia, suggests that it may be caused by an original defective formation in the organs of digestion; analogous to dwarfishness, deficiency, or malformation of the limbs, excessive thinness or obesity. As early as 1692 Camerarius† conceived diabetes to be a *nervous* affection, and

---

* Frank, De Cur. Hom. Morb. Epit., tom. v, pp. 54-57.
† Diss. de Diabete Hypochondriacorum Periodico, 1696.

looked upon the pains in the loins, and the excessive discharge of limpid urine, as analogous to symptoms in hysteria. In 1785. Cullen adopted this view, and classed the disease among the *neuroses ;* but he does not seem to have been quite satisfied with his reasons for so doing, for in one of his aphorisms* he says : "In most cases, the proximate cause is some fault in the assimilatory powers, or those employed in converting alimentary matter into the proper animal fluids." Recent physiological investigations having somewhat confirmed the views of Camerarius, it is not unlikely that we shall find diabetes again regarded as a disease of the nervous system. It is well known that the inhalation of chloroform, ether, nitrous oxide, and other gases have been followed by the presence of sugar in the urine. Irritation of the cranial nerves has produced it, and pregnancy, diseases of the respiratory organs, intemperance in eating and drinking, have done the same. Reynosa states that he found the urine saccharine after the use of narcotics, quinia, mercury, and other drugs. But these are cases of *incidental glycosuria.* Many late writers seem disposed to regard the disorder as of nervous origin, and certainly as much can be said in favor of this hypothesis as of any other. Becquerel† noticed it as the result of cerebral and spinal lesions. Roberts traced it in several cases to mental emotions. Landouzy saw it brought on by violent grief; and Rayer mentions a case as coming on after a violent fit of anger. Various diseases and injuries of the brain and spinal cord are mentioned by Pavy, Fritz, Goolden, Fischer, and others, as exciting causes. Roberts, though he believes that the disease "consists proximately in some disturbance of the destiny and functions of the amyloid substance of the liver,"‡ acknowledges that "this disturbance may be due originally to disease far away from the liver itself, in some part of the sympathetic chain which controls

---

* Cullen, Pract. of Phys., Aph. MDXII.
† Brit. and For. Med. Chir. Rev., 1858, p. 199.
‡ Urinary and Renal Diseases, p. 192.

this function." Luys[*] and Monneret[†] found serious pathological changes in the fourth ventricle. Tardieu[‡] records a case in which the *medulla oblongata* was found congested; and Richardson one in which, after death, an ossific growth was found pressing upon the *pons varolii*, and an abscess in the posterior cerebral lobes. Schiff, Bernard, and Pavy produced diabetes artificially by puncturing various parts of the nerve centers and organic nerves, as the floor of the fourth ventricle, between the origin of the auditory nerves, at the point of origin of the brachial nerves and the spinal cord opposite the second dorsal vertebra. The latter experiment on rats produced permanent glycosuria. In a very able paper read before the New York Academy of Medicine, February 2, 1871, Dr. Gouverneur M. Smith, of that city, defined *diabetes mellitus* to be " a disease of the nervous system, depending either upon centric or upon eccentric disturbance; by centric, implying cerebral lesion; by eccentric, referring to peripheral irritation transmitted to the brain, and reflected either to the liver or other parts, inducing the formation of sugar, and likewise generally reflected to the kidneys, exciting excessive diureses."[§]

Of course this definition is not intended to include every form of glycosuria, but it may serve to explain the etiology of an important group of cases of which but little is known. I shall now pass to the dietetic treatment of this disease without pretending to discuss the various remedies which have been extolled as curatives; for, as might be expected from the diversity of opinion upon the pathology of diabetes, we find equal inconsistency and confusion in its therapeusia. Sydenham says : "*In hoc effectu, uti et in omni diabete ex quacunque* προφασει *originem ducat, curativæ indicationes ad sanguinem invigorandum corroborandumque, ac pariter ad fluxum urinæ præternaturalem restringendum :*"[‖]—that

---

[*] Bulletin de la Soc. de Bibliog., 1860.
[†] Gaz. d. Hôp., Jan. 11, 1862.
[‡] Ed. Times and Gaz., Feb., 1862.
[§] New York Med. Record, March, 1871, p. 26.
[‖] Opera Omnia, epist. 1, p. 289.

the curative indication must be completely directed toward invigorating and strengthening the blood, as well as restraining the preternatural flux of urine. And this is about all *we* can do; but to do it effectually, and to restrain and prevent the undue tendency to a production of sugar in the system, our dependence will have to be upon the *materia alimentaria* rather than on *materia medica*. The necessity for an animalized diet in the management of diabetes appears to have been early recognized. Willis confined his patients chiefly to milk or farinaceous substances, while Sydenham directed Spanish wine,* and a diet of beef, mutton, and the like, doubtless with the intention of supplying the deficiency of the animal salts and of counteracting the secretion of sugar. Not that an exclusive animal diet will entirely prevent the formation of saccharine matter. The experiments of McGregor and of Griesinger prove the contrary; but the sugar secreted under a strictly animal diet is so scanty that the worst effects of the disorder may be suspended, perhaps cured, if its use be persevered in. Unfortunately, however, many patients cannot long endure it. There seems to be such a natural craving for mixed food, that, vary it as we will, in time it will become irksome. To Surgeon-General Rollo we are indebted for reducing to a system the dietetic plan of Sydenham and of Home. He enforced upon his patients an entire abstinence from every species of vegetable matter, limiting them to flesh alone, and under this treatment the tendency to a secretion of saccharine matter is less than under any other regimen save that of skimmed milk. The latter has been recently proposed by Dr. Arthur Scott Donkin, of the University of Durham, though we find a milk diet recommended in this disease by Dr. Thomas Willis, of Oxford, nearly two centuries ago. From the earliest times milk has been used as a medicine, as well as an article of food. Hippocrates, Galen, Celsus, and Dioscorides agree in considering it wholesome and nutritious, and of great use in many diseases, though Celsus says it is apt to disorder the stomach and to produce headache, hypochondria, and

---

* Opera Omnia, epist. I.

flatulence. Its praise was not confined to medical men. Pliny[*]
mentions the cure of gout by it, in which disease modern authors,
Van Sweiten and others, fully confirm its efficacy. Marcus Teren-
tius Varro[†] says of it : " *Est omnium rerum quas cibi causa capimus
liquentium maxime alibile, et id ovillum,*[‡] *inde caprinum :*" it is the
most nourishing of all liquid articles which we take for food; and
this is the case first with that of sheep, and then of goats. Simeon
Seth, Ruffus, and Paul, of Ægina,[§] recommend it highly in dysentery and phthisis; and a host of physicians, from Stephens to
Karell, of St. Petersburg, laud its virtues as a therapeutic agent.
Bouchardat, however, (whose great experience in diabetes is unquestionable,) doubts its efficacy in this disease, and forbids its
use. Roberts also looks upon it as a doubtful article of food,
though he found one of his diabetic patients improve materially
under its use. One of the greatest advantages of milk is that it is
food not too highly concentrated. For perfect digestion it seems
necessary that the ingesta must be of a specific degree of density,
for if the food be too fluid or too gelatinous the stomach will be
equally impeded in its operations. The interference of a too
highly concentrated aliment with the digestive power may account
for beef extracts and other substances in the highest state of con-
centration proving useless, and in some cases even injurious ; and
may also be the reason why milk is so rapidly beneficial in the
enfeebled digestion of diabetes. In it we have a mixture of solid
and liquid aliment of proper density, which in its dietetic relations
may be considered as intermediate between animal and vegetable
food. It contains albuminous, saccharine, and oleaginous matters,
which, being readily assimilated, quickly supply nutriment to the
exhausted system, without exciting that degree of vascular action
which is produced by most animal substances. The constituents
of skimmed milk are, according to Berzelius :

---

[*] Hist. Nat., xxviii, p. 38.
[†] De Re Rusticâ, ii, p. 11.
[‡] Scaliger's edition De R. R., p. 7, has *ovinum.*
[§] Paulus Ægineta, tom. 1, p. 154,

Water	928. 75
Casein, with a trace of butter	28. 00
Sugar of milk	35. 00
Hydrochlorate and phosphate of potash	1. 95
Lactic acid, acetate of potash, and a trace of lactate of iron	6. 00
Earthy phosphates	. 30
	1, 000. 00

In asses' and mares' milk, the proportion of *casein* is much less, rarely exceeding one and a half per cent. Hence the value of cows' and of goats' milk in the treatment of diabetes would seem to depend upon their superior richness in *casein*, which is the most highly azotized of all the nutritive proximate principles. It is at the expense of this protein compound that the organized tissues of the body are built up, though we know that for the perfect formation of all the animal tissues albumen and fatty matter are essential. To its presence, in a soluble form, may be ascribed the rapid and great diminution in the quantity of the urine, in from twenty-four hours to three days, as noticed by Donkin. Physiological experiments prove that under albumen, (and it is said that all the proteinaceous compounds, albumen, casein, fibrin vitellin, legumen, and gluten, are probably identical in chemical constitution,*) the *whole quantity of urine* is lessened, the urine becomes more concentrated from the relative increase of solids and the amount of urea and uric acid is increased. It is a noticeable fact, however, that under an exclusively albuminous diet, too long continued, an injurious effect is produced upon the system. Hammond proved, by experiment upon himself, that, under its use, the weight of the body materially declined; that the " water, soluble and the whole quantity of inorganic salts of the serum were diminished, and the solids, albumen and extractive, increased in quantity. In the whole blood there was a dimi-

---

* Hammond, Physiolog. Mem., p. 85.

nution of the water, blood corpuscles, soluble and total amount of inorganic salts and fat, while there was an augmentation of the solids, fibrin, albumen, and extractive."* Long ago Magendie proved that it was impossible to sustain health on any single alimentary substance; but this does not apply to protein compounds, for Hammond thinks it "fully proven that before the general health becomes injured by a too long exclusive use of albumen, that enough of this substance can be assimilated to repair the waste of tissues and support the respiratory functions."† This may be so in the case of a robust experimentalist, and, in many instances, where the constitution is not shattered, and the digestive organs weakened, but in diabetes, where the vital powers are generally at their lowest ebb, *skimmed* milk—which does not contain all the substances which enter into the composition of the tissues . of the body—will hardly be found sufficient to sustain life. The fact is, we can lay down no special dietary for this disorder, as almost every case must be a law to itself. We know that there is a natural tendency to *asthenia*, which must be obviated by a judicious regimen, but of the necessities in each case the practitioner alone must be the judge. The rule laid down by Dr. Donkin is that the skimmed milk diet "*must be persevered in, methodically and exclusively, until convalescence is established.*" That *method*, in its administration, is absolutely necessary to success, appears to have been recognized by ancient authors, for Paulus Æginetæ,‡ (who copies from Ruffus and Oribasius,) says: "He who drinks milk ought to abstain from all other food until it be digested and pass downward. It is best, therefore, *to drink it in the morning*, newly milked, and to take no food after it, nor any hard exercise, because this would make it turn acid. But it is better to walk about gently and rest between, without sleeping." The italics are mine; and I would here remark that the *time* of its administration is of much consequence. The nutritive and

---

* Hammond, Physiolog. Mem., p. 103.
† Ibid., p. 104.
‡ Vol. 1, p. 154, sect. lxxxvii.

restorative influence of milk is greater when taken early in the morning, because the absorbent system at this period is in its most active state; besides, a quantity of the fluid can then be borne without inconvenience, which at any other time would be followed by the most painful oppression. I must take exception to that part of the rule which requires the milk to be used " exclusively until convalescence is established." Without a judicious employment of other dietetics, I fear that many cases (particularly those of a tuberculous nature) would sink under that general exhaustion of the vital powers which it is our object and duty to avert. Therefore, while acknowledging the remedial value of skimmed milk in the treatment of diabetes, I am forced to the conclusion that there are many cases like the following, which will show the necessity of not depending upon it as an *exclusive diet.*

Mrs. A. B., a native of Philadelphia, fifty years of age, of medium height, florid complexion, and nervo-sanguine temperament; has never been robust, having suffered from spinal irritation, and from repeated attacks of gout in the stomach. Ever since 1869 her health has been failing, owing to mental excitement and other causes; but it was not until the middle of December, 1870, that a marked change was noticed in her appearance. Most of her symptoms were then ascribed to change of life, and to a vegetable diet, to which she had exclusively confined herself for one or two years. About February, 1871, her emaciation became quite perceptible, her appetite and thirst were inordinately increased, and by the middle of March all the symptoms of diabetes were developed. She was considerably troubled with dyspepsia, headache, nervous tremors, palpitation of the heart, and dimness of sight. Her bowels were constipated or irregular, and the renal secretion excessive. Eight to ten pints of pale urine, possessing the characteristic apple odor, of a specific gravity not below 1040, were secreted daily. She complained of constant aching pains in her loins, and in anterior surface of thighs, and of a sense of sinking, or " falling to pieces," as she expressed it. Her appetite

17 H

now became voracious, and her thirst intense, her memory more impaired, and eyesight so defective that she frequently exclaimed, " I believe I am going blind ; I cannot see." These symptoms were accompanied by fits of despondency, a constant fear of impending evil, and extreme general debility. On testing her urine by Trommer's, Moore's, and Luton's tests, an abundance of sugar was discovered. Microscopic examination revealed the presence of innumerable crystals of oxalate of lime and of epithelium—rather a rare occurrence—which may account for the intense hypochondriasis, pain in the loins, and distressing sense of fatigue in this case. Having satisfied myself of the nature of her disease, I determined to try the effect of skimmed milk, so highly recommended by Dr. Arthur Scott Donkin, in an article " On a purely milk diet in *diabetes mellitus*," &c. (London Lancet, January, 1870.) Accordingly, on Monday, the 20th March, 1871, I directed six pints of milk (carefully skimmed and previously warmed) to be taken in divided doses every three hours, and prohibited all other food. The result was peculiarly gratifying, as her hunger and thirst were diminished during the day, and she felt more comfortable. From this date the accompanying table will show the daily amount of urine secreted, its specific gravity, and quantity of solids, so that I shall make but few remarks upon the progress of the case :

Date.	Quantity.		Specific gravity.	Solids.			Sugar.
	Pts.	*oz.*		*Oz.*	*dr.*	*gr.*	*Grains.*
March 20, 1871	6	3	1040	9	1	58	2638
March 21, 1871	4	13	1017	2	6	36	657
March 22, 1871	2	8	1018	1	4	26	96
March 23, 1871	2	14	1020	1	5	34	164
March 24, 1871	2	5	1030	2	2	24	404
March 25, 1871	1	12	1034	2	1	11	320
March 26, 1871	2	4	1025	2	1	20	340
March 27, 1871	2	3	1028	2	1	0	320
March 28, 1871	1	8	1030	1	4	35	105
March 29, 1871	1	14	1032	2	0	40	260

Date.	Quantity.		Specific gravity.	Solids.			Sugar.
	Pts.	*oz.*		*Oz.*	*dr.*	*gr.*	*Grains.*
March 30, 1871	1	12	1032	1	7	42	240
March 31, 1871	2	4	1026	2	0	18	278
April 1, 1871	1	8	1029	1	5	40	120
April 2, 1871	1	12	1028	1	5	45	135
April 3, 1871	1	14	1026	1	5	35	115
April 4, 1871	1	14	1032	2	0	40	200
April 5, 1871	1	15	1032	2	0	54	314
April 6, 1871	1	14	1032	2	0	24	294
April 7, 1871	2	5	1026	2	0	37	297
April 8, 1871	3	9	1022	2	5	41	601
April 9, 1871	2	3	1032	2	3	36	476
April 10, 1871	2	2	1032	2	3	10	450
April 11, 1871	2	0	1032	2	1	57	377
April 12, 1871	1	9	1032	1	6	00	340
April 13, 1871	1	14	1032	2	2	29	309
April 14, 1871	2	8	1028	2	3	33	473
April 15, 1871	2	8	1030	2	5	10	590
April 16, 1871	2	2	1032	2	3	4	444
April 17, 1871	2	9	1026	2	0	54	314
April 18, 1871	2	4	1026	2	0	19	279
April 19, 1871	3	1	1022	2	2	44	420
April 20, 1871	2	12	1022	2	0	48	328
April 21, 1871	2	10	1024	2	0	41	300
April 22, 1871	1	7	1032	1	4	44	64
April 23, 1871	2	4	1022	1	5	45	155
April 24, 1871	3	7	1018	2	1	6	316
April 25, 1871	2	3	1024	1	6	1	101
April 26, 1871	2	6	1026	2	1	12	332
April 27, 1871	3	0	1020	2	0	38	298
April 28, 1871	3	2	1014	1	4	3	23
April 29, 1871	2	4	1022	1	5	45	125
April 30, 1871	2	14	1016	1	4	42	60
May 1, 1871	2	12	1016	1	4	19	39
May 2, 1871	2	4	1024	1	6	25	165
May 3, 1871	2	8	1024	2	0	2	265
May 4, 1871	2	9	1022	1	7	21	220
May 5, 1871	2	15	1024	2	2	21	410
May 6, 1871	2	7	1026	2	1	40	400
May 7, 1871	3	9	1022	2	5	46	606
May 8, 1871	2	13	1020	1	7	25	220
May 9, 1871	3	3	1020	2	4	26	506

Date.	Quantity.		Specific gravity.	Solids.			Sugar.
	Pts.	oz.		Oz.	dr.	gr.	Grains.
May 10, 1871	3	8	1020	2	3	20	460
May 11, 1871	3	8	1020	2	3	20	460
May 12, 1871	3	3	1020	2	1	36	356
May 13, 1871	3	3	1020	2	1	36	556
May 14, 1871	2	7	1020	1	5	36	116
May 15, 1871*	3	7	1014	1	5	36	4 gr. per oz.
May 16, 1871	3	7	1016	1	7	44	5 gr. per oz.
May 17, 1871	2	15	1020	2	0	17	6 gr. per oz.
May 18, 1871	2	2	1020	1	4	46	4 gr. per oz.
May 19, 1871	2	15	1018	1	6	37	4 gr. per oz.
May 20, 1871	2	1	1022	1	4	38	6 gr. per oz.
May 21, 1871	3	0	1016	1	5	15	4 gr. per oz.
May 22, 1871	2	12	1018	1	5	41	4 gr. per oz.
May 23, 1871	2	5	1022	1	6	8	5 gr. per oz.
May 24, 1871	2	6	1026	2	1	53	5 gr. per oz.
May 25, 1871	3	6	1016	1	6	5	4 gr. per oz.
May 26, 1871	2	9	1026	2	0	0	5 gr. per oz.
May 27, 1871	1	15	1034	2	3	1	3 gr. per oz.
May 28, 1871	2	4	1032	2	4	11	4 gr. per oz.
May 29, 1871	2	4	1032	2	4	11	3 gr. per oz.
May 30, 1871	2	0	1032	2	1	57	3 gr. per oz.
May 31, 1871	2	0	1032	2	1	57	3 gr. per oz.

* From the 15th to the 31st of May the quantity of sugar was obtained by making use of fresh yeast to establish vinous fermentation.

On Tuesday, the 21st March, six pints of milk were administered, and the urine was reduced in quantity (in twenty-four hours) from six pints three ounces, specific gravity, 1040, containing over nine ounces of solids, to four pints thirteen ounces, specific gravity, 1017, containing two ounces six drachms and thirty-six grains. During the day she had a slight attack of diarrhœa, and expressed distaste for the milk.

March 22d.—Under the same diet the urine was reduced to two pints eight ounces; specific gravity, 1018; solids, one ounce four drachms twenty-six grains. Skin clammy, pulse 98. She complained of headache, nausea, and debility.

March 23d.—The improvement in the renal secretion continued, but her strength was rapidly failing. She complained of headache, inability to make the slightest exertion, intense pain in loins and thighs, nausea, and increased amblyopia.* Pulse 104. Both hunger and thirst had now completely abated, and the amount of urine passed in twenty-four hours amounted to but two pints fourteen ounces specific gravity, 1020; solids, one ounce five drachms thirty-four grains.

March 24th.—Urine secreted, two pints five ounces; specific gravity, 1030; solids, two ounces two drachms and twenty-four grains.

March 25th.—I found my patient so much exhausted that I scarcely felt justified in pursuing further the exclusively milk diet, and, after consultation with a medical friend, I decided to give but fifty ounces of skimmed milk per diem, and to supply additional nutriment by a suitable proportion of beef-tea. Under this treatment she became stronger, and expressed herself as "feeling much better." One pint twelve ounces of urine were secreted; specific gravity, 1034. Pulse 94.

From the 25th of March to 1st of April there was a steady improvement in her symptoms. The renal secretion ranged from one pint eight ounces to two pints four ounces; specific gravity, from 1026 to 1034. Her diet was varied occasionally with poached eggs, mutton, squab, spinach, and Camplin's biscuit. The oxalates disappeared from the urine under the use of nitro-hydrochloric acid in infusion of serpentaria, and with them went many of her distressing symptoms. On the whole, she appeared more cheerful and less weary ; her eyesight had improved, and she felt generally more comfortable. On the 29th March there was a copious deposit of uric acid. From the 1st to the 7th of April the urine varied in quantity from one pint eight ounces to two pints five ounces ; specific gravity, from 1026 to 1032.

---

* It will be seen that the amblyopia did not cease upon the administration of animal food, (as it did in one of Griesinger's patients,) neither did it follow the course observed by Lécorché, "*De L'amblyopie Diabétique*," Gaz. Hebdom., Nov., 1861.

April 8th.—Patient caught cold, and felt less well in consequence. She had a night-sweat, and complained of great debility. Urine, three pints nine ounces; specific gravity, 1022.

April 16th.—Her night-sweats returned, but were promptly checked by sulphate of quinia combined with oxide of zinc. From this time until the 8th of May she continued to improve. Specific gravity of urine varied from 1018 to 1026.

May 8th.—Not so well, and toward evening many of her old symptoms returned. The quantity of urine was much increased, though the specific gravity did not rise above 1024. This unfavorable change was probably brought about by the patient indulging in ice-cream containing corn-starch. As her strength had now improved sufficiently to justify a return to the exclusively skim-milk diet, I again placed her upon it, directing, as before, six pints daily, in divided doses; but on the 13th I was obliged to give her beef-tea, eggs, &c., as she complained of being unable to subsist upon the milk alone.

From this time until the conclusion of this report (June 1, 1871) there was a daily improvement in all her symptoms. Her appetite is now good, her rest sound and natural. She has gained in flesh, (seven pounds during the period of treatment,) and though the urine is still glycosuric, the improvement in her health is so great that she expresses herself as feeling " perfectly well."

CASE OF EROSION OF THE ENTIRE PENIS.

(Compiled from naval hospital records.)

BY

W. S. W. RUSCHENBERGER, M. D.,

UNITED STATES NAVY.

CASE OF EROSION OF THE ENTIRE PENIS.

(Compiled from naval hospital records.)

By W. S. W. RUSCHENBERGER, M. D.,

United States Navy.

W. T. Park, seaman, native of Boston, Massachusetts, aged sixty-three years, was admitted into the Naval Hospital, Philadelphia, April 22, 1870, from the United States steamer Iroquois, on account of "ulcer of the penis." Has been about twenty-five years in the naval service. His stature is about five feet ten inches, symmetrical, well developed; he has the aspect of muscular strength and general robust health. His penis is reduced to a stump of about a half inch long, which is ulcerating. The record of the case in the hospital shows only that the ulcer was dressed with an aqueous solution of carbolic acid, and that it seemed to be healing slowly.

May 20.—An unsuccessful attempt to pass a catheter was made and repeated June 13 and 27, under the influence of an anæsthetic.

June 30.—Condition of patient unchanged. Dr. P. J. Horwitz attempted to introduce a catheter this morning, but failed.

July 2.—Ulcer increasing slowly. Continue carbolic acid lotion.

July 10.—Last night the patient had a severe chill followed by fever.

> ℞. Hydrarg. pil.,
> Jalapæ pulv., āā gr. vi.
> Colocynth. ext. comp., gr. iij.
>
> M. S. a. fit. pil. iij. Stat. sumend.

The bowels were freely moved.   Pulse 100 : tongue clean ; condition of ulcer much the same.

R. Spts. ætheris nitros., ʒi.
    Ammoniæ liq. acetat., ʒiii.
M. A tablespoonful every half hour.

July 11.—Ulcer remains the same.   The surrounding tissues are considerably inflamed and indurated ; the inflammation has the appearance of erysipelas.   Has slight fever this morning ; bowels moved.   Continue the mixture, and apply lead and opium wash to inflamed parts.

July 12. Inflammation subsiding ; no fever : omit mixture.

R. Quiniæ sulph., gr. xxv.
    Ferri chlorid. tinct., ʒi.
    Aquæ, ʒvi.
M.   A tablespoonful thrice daily.   Port wine, ʒij. thrce times a day.

July 14.—Some discoloration about the hip-joint ; complains of great soreness on attempting to walk.

July 15.—Condition unchanged.   Complains of want of sleep.

R. Chloral hydrate, gr. xv.
    Aquæ cinnamomi, ʒiij.
M. ft. haust. s. s.   To be repeated in half an hour.

July 20.—Improving slowly ; less discoloration of tissues (?) : condition of ulcer remains the same ; complains of want of sleep. Chloral hydrate, gr. xx in solution at night ; it seems to affect him very pleasantly.

July 23. Condition unchanged ; rather more pain.   Chloral has delightful effect.

July 25.—Not so well ; condition of parts about the same. Complains of pain in the right side, which extends from about the third lumbar vertebra to ensiform cartilage.   Bowels regular ; tongue clean ; appetite very poor ; pulse 90.

R. Chloral hydrate, gr. xxx.
    Aquæ cinnamomi, fʒvi.
M. ft. sol.   One half at once, and the remainder in half an hour.

Evening.—Continues to have very severe pain in side, which is greatly aggravated on the slightest motion of the body; about 3 o'clock p. m. took chloral hydrate, gr. xxx. Slept about half an hour.

> R. Morphiæ sulph. sol., ʒij.
> Aq. camph., ʒij.
> M. S. a. One half at once, and in half an hour the remainder if necessary.

July 26.—Has less pain in the side; appetite improving; morphine at night.

July 27.—Condition of parts remains about the same; continue lotion.

August 2.—General condition improving; ulcer and surrounding parts unchanged; continue treatment.

August 12.—Ulcer in groin becoming larger; is about one and a half inches deep. [This is the first reference to the groin on the record.]

August 20.—Condition no better; ulcer in groin steadily increasing. Generous diet with wine, quinine, and iron. A twenty-grain solution of nitrate of silver applied to ulcer of groin this evening.

August 25.—Gradually becoming worse.

> R. Liq. sodæ chlorin., ʒij.
> Aquæ, ʒx.
> M. Apply with lint several times daily. Discontinue acid carbolic.

September 2.—Condition about the same. Ulcer in groin increasing in size. This morning Professor S. D. Gross made an unsuccessful attempt to pass a catheter. He looks upon the case as one of epithelioma, and recommends the same treatment to be continued. [The record does not state why efforts to pass a catheter were made. The flow of urine from the bladder was always free.]

September 20.—Slight hæmorrhage, which was probably venous, from the ulcer of groin last night. Continue treatment.

September 26.—Continues to have slight hæmorrhages from the groin; condition otherwise unchanged. Continue treatment.

[Surgeon Ruschenberger succeeded Surgeon Horwitz in charge of the hospital, October 1.]

October 6.—The patient declares that generally he feels pretty well, and that, until after the efforts to pass instruments into his bladder had been made, he never had trouble in micturition, and has very little, if any, now; the act is most easily accomplished by assuming an almost prone position, but as the parts in the vicinity of the outlet of the bladder are unavoidably bathed in urine at the time, it is always attended with discomfort. The patient lies upon his back, the right side rather lower than the left, with the knees wide apart and slightly flexed to accommodate the increased size of the scrotum, the two diameters of which are estimated at not less than four and six inches. Its tissues are thickened and dense, and its weight is a source of discomfort, for the relief of which the patient carefully adjusts a cushion or pad beneath it after every change of position. The surface is generally dark-colored, with here and there a slightly reddish blush. The raphe is prominent, reddish, smooth, and extends to the extremity of the spongy portion of the penis, now not more than an inch in length. The remnants of the corpora cavernosa are shorter, projecting above the skin of the pubis less than a half inch, so that the surface of the penil stump is irregularly beveled. This is caused by granulations of about an eighth of an inch in diameter, of a deep salmon-red color. The urethra, or rather the outlet from it, is an irregular opening of half an inch diameter, at the bottom of which may be seen a tiny pool of liquid, chiefly urine, rising and falling with the motions of the diaphragm.

Whenever any inspection of the parts is attempted the patient wears an aspect of dread of pain, holding his expanded right hand in a protecting way before them, often saying he cannot bear the least touch. The fold of the right groin is occupied by an ulcerated cavity of an inch and a half deep, and two and a half long; the edges of this opening are bounded by everted lips, about three-eighths of an inch wide, smooth on the side of the opening, but ragged on their outer edge. This lip might be compared to a flat pink braid-trimming around a button-hole. From this ulcer issues a bloody serum, and sometimes pure blood. The odor of the patient is that peculiarly disgusting cancerous stench which carbolic acid in this case does not entirely suppress. The thigh below the ulcer is swollen, red, and tender.

The patient states that ten or twelve years ago he sailed from London on a merchant-vessel, and after departure venereal sores appeared on his penis. On arriving at Adelaide, Australia, his condition required his admission into an English hospital. More than a third of the penis was amputated at the institution; and after some months he recovered. He shipped April 29, 1868, on board the United States steamer Unadilla at Hong-Kong, and was transferred to the United States steamer Iroquois October 17. About a year afterward a rope fell from aloft, the end of which did not quite reach the deck, so that it rebounded, from its elasticity, and struck the extremity of the stump of his penis; an ulcer followed, and he was admitted on the sick-list in November, 1869.

Ulcers dressed with iodoform; one grain of opium night and morning.

October 8.—Swelling of thigh increased; loss of appetite; tongue clean; pulse 100.

> ℞. Liq. ammoniæ acetat., ʒiij.
> Spts. æther. nitros., ʒi.
> M. Cap. ʒss. qq. 2nda. h.

October 9.—Swelling increased; erysipelatous in appearance; pulse 110.

> Ferri tinct. chlorid., gtt. xx. Ter die sumend.

October 10.—Pulse 90; condition of thigh unchanged; persist. Iodoform and glycerine to thigh and ulcers.

October 11.—Pulse 110; thigh very much swollen and inflamed; obscure fluctuation below Poupart's ligament; appetite good—persist.

R. Camphoræ pulv., Ʒss.
Hydrarg. ung., ℥ss.
Belladon. ext., gr. x.
Glycerine, Ʒi.
M. ft. ung. liq.   Smear over upper part of thigh.

October 12.—Patient was placed under influence of a mixture of ether and chloroform, and an incision made about two and a half inches below Poupart's ligament, and two inches on inner side of median line of thigh, giving exit to about eight ounces of very fœtid pus. Dressed with lead and opium wash on lint, covered with oiled silk. Reaction from anæsthetic excellent; pulse 70; tongue clean; appetite good.

October 13.—Rested well; pulse 70; tongue clean; abscess discharges freely; pus very fœtid; thigh is considerably swollen and red. Applied carbolic acid, Ʒi, aquæ, ℥viij, on lint, and dressed as before.

October 15.—Removed a quantity of broken-down tissue; discharge free; thigh less swollen; not so much inflamed; appe tite poor.

R. Potassii iodidi,
Ammoniæ muriat., āā Ʒi.
Cinchonæ tinct. comp., ℥iv.
M. Cap. ℥ss. q. q. 4 ta. h.   Omit iron.

October 17.—Appetite improved; no fever; tongue clean; in-flammation of thigh rapidly subsiding; small amount of slough removed. Ulceration on penis improved; persist.

October 19.—Thigh about its natural size; abscess free from slough; opening healing; persist.

October 26.—No marked change in aspect of ulcers. Faradized.

November 9.—Faradized daily for ten minutes since last note. Redness is abated during the application of the electric current. Groin about the same; edges of ulcer very thin and serrated; aspect changes daily.

November 12.—Opening in groin covered with a dark gray slough. Faradized on alternate days.

November 21.—Slight hæmorrhage from groin ; ulcer increasing : that of penis about the same.

December 1.—Considerable hæmorrhage last night from the groin ; opening steadily increasing in size. General treatment continued.

December 8.—Patient's general condition improving.

December 12.—Severe chill yesterday, followed by fever.

December 13.—No return of chill. Erythematous blush over hypogastric region, (perfectly defined by a tranverse straight line above,) thighs, and scrotum.

December 14.—Spirits better ; erythematous blush nearly dis-sipated.

December 15.—Edges of ulcer of groin bleeding, which dress-ing arrested.

December 16.—No hæmorrhage ; blush slight.

December 17.—Blush has disappeared.

December 18.—Considerable hæmorrhage from edge of ulcer ; arrested by dressing.

December 20.—Ulcer, illuminated by light reflected from a concave mirror, appears clean, except at bottom, where there is a dark, unhealthy slough about two inches in breadth, by one and a half deep.

December 21.—Slight hæmorrhage from edge of ulcer.

December 22.—General health much improved.

January 12, 1871.—There are two elevations about the size of a pea, about an inch below root of penis, and two papulæ in pubic region, bearing the appearance of fresh implantations.

January 17.—Ulcer not so clean.

January 18.—Pain in dressing ; ulcer looks badly.

January 19.—A thin, watery, offensive discharge, containing cheesy floculi, from a small opening about an inch below the ulcer, which is painful while dressing. Carbolic acid, ʒij, to a pint of water. This dressing smarted for a short time.

January 20.—Offensive odor of discharge corrected.

January 22.—Faradization, which has been continued every

two or three days, abandoned.   Galvanized with thirty of Smee's cells; no immediate effects observed.   An hour afterward complained of pain and stiffness in the surrounding parts.

January 28.—A large quantity of hæmato-purulent matter came away with the dressing.

January 29.—Solution of permanganate of potassa placed under the bed to correct odor in the ward.

February 20.—Papulæ, before mentioned, increasing in size; two on the scrotum about to coalesce ; several others observed on pubic region.

March 1.—Yesterday the scrotum became painful and tender. At 9 o'clock p. m., attacked with severe nervous rigor, which lasted an hour.   This was followed by swelling of the scrotum and a deep erythematous blush over it, the pubic region, and thigh.   The line of demarkation on the abdomen well defined. Constipated; bowels moved by Seidlitz powders.   There is a furfuraceous condition of the forehead, temples, and ears without itching.   Arseniate of soda.

March 2.—Erythema extending ; scrotal swelling increased.

> R.: Liq. plumb. subacetat., ℨi.
> Aquæ, ℥vi.
> M. Apply to erythematous parts.

March 7. Erythema has disappeared; scrotal swelling diminished.   Ulceration of groin extending slowly.   Several elevated ulcerations on the scrotum and hypogastric region; appetite fair; bowels regular; sleeps well.

March 15.—Surface of ulcer in groin foul and sloughy; discharge fœtid ; œdema of right foot.

March 17.—Œdema of foot increasing ; ulcers extending.

March 24.—Galvanization has been continued every second day.   Complains of burning pains during, and for an hour after, the application.   Hard, brawny swelling surrounds the ulcer in the groin; integument red ; more pain.

March 28.—Œdema of foot continues.   Except one on the scrotum, which looks more healthy, the ulcers are spreading.

April 5.—Ulceration at root of penis does not increase, but that in the groin is extending toward the crest of the ilium. A layer of gray pultaceous matter covers the bottom. Odor excessively fœtid; pain more severe; sleeps badly. Opii tinct., gtt. xx, h. s. s.

April 8.—Complains of great pain in groin and limb, which is much swollen. Thinks he passes less urine than formerly. No appetite; tongue coated.

℞. Liq. ammoniæ acetat., ℥iijss.
Spts. ætheris nitros., ℥ss.
M. Cap. ℥ss. qq. 3tia. h. At bedtime, opii tinct., gtt. xx.

April 9.—No appetite; did not sleep; irritable. Limb much swollen; edges of ulcer in groin excessively painful.

April 11.—Limb less swollen; cavity of ulcer filled with an excessively fœtid discharge. Slept well.

April 13.—Feels better. Slept all night and for three hours yesterday afternoon.

April 21.—Removed a large lump of offensive matter from ulcer.

April 25.—Leg and thigh diminished in size; parts appear to be cleaner.

May 1.—General condition better. Granulations are appearing in the large cavity; discharge less; appetite good.

May 12.—Granulations in large cavity increasing.

June 2.—Ulcer in groin seems to be gradually closing; slight hæmorrhage from it. Leg œdematous; scrotum large as ever. Ulcers on hypogastric region increasing; appetite good; sleeps well.

June 3.—Parts photographed. Galvanization, which has been used regularly on alternate days, suspended. Earth dressing applied morning and evening.

June 14.—Dressing affords much comfort; odor very much less.

June 8.—On removing the dressing this morning, a number of maggots were discovered in the ulcers of the groin and abdomen.

18 H

They were removed with forceps, and carbolic acid freely applied to the whole surface before re-applying the earth.

June 10.—No maggots; carbolic acid applied previous to each earth dressing.

June 12.—Ulcer in groin stationary; patient comfortable.

June 15.—Intense pain in leg and foot all night. Administered sol. morph. sulph., $\mathfrak{z}$ij, and opii ext., gr. ij. Not until after the limb was faradized this morning was the pain relieved.

June 16.—

R. Sodæ arseniatis sol., $\mathfrak{z}$ss.
Ferri vini amari, f$\mathfrak{z}$ss.

M. A teaspoonful ten minutes after each meal. Suspend liq. ammoniæ acetat.

June 18.—Appetite failing. Two ounces of port wine morning and evening, and a half-pint bottle of ale at dinner.

June 19.—Discharge from small ulcer on scrotum shows under the microscope only pus corpuscles, but no epithelial scales or cells.

June 20.—Much pain in leg and foot last night. Opii ext. gr. ss., at bedtime.

June 21.—Severe shooting pain in leg last night; sleepless; anorexia; bowels regular. Faradized.

June 22.—Slept well; less pain. Faradized.

June 23.—Slept well without anodyne.

June 25.—No change of condition. Found five maggots in ulcer. Carbolic acid applied prior to application of earth-dressing.

July 1.—About noon discovered arterial blood oozing from ulcer in groin, which was arrested by cold water, after a loss of about two ounces. In the evening feels more comfortable.

July 2.—Slight oozing of blood from floor of larger ulcer; granulations feeble; less pain this a. m. About noon lost not less than two pounds of arterial blood from the groin, at first in a jet; arrested by cold water; dressed with matico.

July 3.—Œdema less; has movement of ankle. Pulse 80, weak; anorexia; insomnia, but no restlessness. Face exsanguine.

July 5.—Insomnia; no pain; anorexia; pulse 72; skin moist; œdema less; face pallid.

> ℞. Carnis extracti, ʒi.
> Capsici tinct., ℳxx.
> Aq. fervent.,
> Vini portensis, āā℥iv.

M.   A wineglassful every four hours.

At 10 p. m. lost about two ounces of arterial blood from groin. Prostration great; pulse weak, 98; face pallid and pinched; lips blue.   Removed earth; checked hæmorrhage with cold water, and dressed with carbolic acid.   Frumenti spiritus, ℥ss.

July 6.—No return of hæmorrhage.   Isthmus between large and small ulcers in groin has sloughed away.   Patient complains of excessive prostration.   Packed the cavity with matico, and covered with earth dressing.

July 7.—Treatment continued.

July 8.—At 6 a. m. was discovered lying on his back, right leg flexed, with about four ounces of blood in the rubber sheet beneath him.   He had died without notice of his ward companions or attendants.

Autopsy.—By Surgeon A. C. Rhoades, assisted by Assistants Surgeons M. L. Ruth, and J. T. Wells, eight hours after death. Body not emaciated; rigor mortis marked.

	Measurement of—	
	Diseased limb.	Sound limb.
	Inches.	*Inches.*
Circumference five inches below anterior superior spine.........	23	18
Circumference eight inches below anterior superior spine........	21	16
Circumference five inches above condyle of femur.............	18	13

Head.—Not examined.

Chest.—Old pleuritic adhesions on right side.   Numerous small abscesses scattered through upper lobes of both lungs, which were of a dark color. At apex of right lung there were several small cretaceous bodies.

Heart empty ; muscular fiber pale; otherwise healthy.

Abdomen.—Liver weighed 50 troy ounces; light yellow color ; fatty ; tissue softened ; transverse diameter 12, and antero-posterior 7½ inches.

Gall-bladder contained 2 ounces bright yellow bile, and four gall-stones.

Right kidney, weight 4½ troy ounces, length 4¼, and breadth 2 inches; capsule healthy. In upper part of corticle portion was an abscess, the size of a hazel-nut, filled with pus. Several cysts in left kidney. Other viscera normal.

The right external iliac artery and vein, just above Poupart's ligament, surrounded by a heterologous indurated deposit.

Ulceration of groin 5 inches long, 2 inches wide, 1 inch deep at deepest part, with ragged excavated edges, extending in the direction of Poupart's ligament ; penis entirely eroded ; urethra 3 inches long, obstructed by a large suppurating ulcer. Its seeming external orifice was a sinus, extending some distance alongside of it, which probably explains why attempts to pass a catheter were unsuccessful.

Scrotum much enlarged and thickened. Under the microscope sections of the inguinal ulcer appeared to consist of grayish broken-down tissue and pus-cells ; no epithelial cells were observed.

Remarks.—The hospital record of this case is not as satisfactory as might have been had its commencement been more fully noted. It is regretted that there is no professional testimony as to the condition of the penil stump at the time of his last enlistment in the Navy. The officer whose duty it was to inspect the person of this man, when he shipped at Hong-Kong in 1868, does not remember whether he had lost any part of the penis, but presumes he would have recollected such deficiency in any recruit passed by him.

The date of first appearance of disease in the groin is not recorded.

The patient declared himself to be most comfortable when the atmospheric temperature of the ward was at from 55° to 65° F.; when it was above that he complained of heat.

While in the hospital no complaint attracted attention to the chest, nor was there any symptom suggesting that the condition of the respiratory apparatus was not perfect. This is worth notice, because *post-mortem* examination revealed " numerous small abscesses scattered through the upper lobes of both lungs."

The patient stated that his sense of erections was as perfect after the almost entire obliteration of the penis as ever, and that sometimes in dreams he had sexual intercourse, which was accompanied in fact by seminal emissions.

The administration of faradaic currents afforded comfort. The first applications were followed by marked decrease in the size of the scrotal swelling, and afforded relief by reducing its weight. They were made on alternate days during ten minutes, from the 26th of October, 1870, till January 22, 1871, almost three months. Kidder's apparatus, with two of Smee's cells, was used.

A galvanic current from thirty cells of Smee's battery, manufactured by Kidder, was substituted for faradization, and continued on alternate days during four months. At first but fifteen cells were used; afterward thirty were employed.

The earth dressing consisted of the clayey soil of the hospital grounds, (which was carefully dried, ground, and passed through a No. 20 sieve,) thickly dusted in and over the diseased parts. A paste of the same material and water was spread upon strips of blue paper, such as that used in preparing Seidlitz powders, with which the whole was covered. This is in accordance with the mode of earth-dressing followed by Dr. Addinell Hewson, of the Pennsylvania Hospital, who saw this case. The discharges being very free, and micturition being effected only in a prone posture, it was necessary to renew the dressings night and morning. Great abatement of stench and much comfort to the patient are clearly ascribable to this dressing. At the same time a very ill-conditioned stump of an amputated finger was treated in the manner above described, with entirely satisfactory result. About a half dozen dressings, at intervals of three or four days, completed the cure, although it was conjectured when the patient entered the hospital that a second amputation would be required.

Coarsely powdered matico leaves, moistened into a pasty consistence with water, lightly packed in the inguinal ulcer, was promptly followed by arrest of hæmorrhage. This paste always came away in a single mass, leaving the ulcerated cavity free from every particle of the matico. This quality or property renders the use of matico preferable to that of most hæmostatics.

The disease seemed to spread by new implantations on the apparently sound skin. There was first seen a tiny red spot upon which, in the course of a day, a minute vesicle, not more than a twentieth of an inch in diameter, formed. In the course of twenty-four hours this bursted, leaving an excavation. Around it other vesicles appeared and followed the same course. At the end of ten or twelve days there was a hemispherical mass a quarter of an inch in diameter with a strawberry-like surface, upon which vesiculization went on, but more and more slowly as the disease advanced. None healed.

REPORTS

UPON

CERTAIN ENGLISH HOSPITALS,

BY

EDWARD SHIPPEN, M. D.,

MEDICAL INSPECTOR, U. S. N., FLEET-SURGEON EUROPEAN STATION

Navy Department,
Office of Medical Inspector-General, U. S. N.,
Washington, July 31, 1872.

Sir: The accompanying reports of Fleet-Surgeon Edward Shippen, relative to European hospitals and military medical schools, made in compliance with official instructions, are respectfully referred to the Department.

Its attention is especially invited to the report upon the naval medical school at Netley. For over forty years the medical corps of the United States Navy has been making slow but sure advances toward the elevation of similar corps in the navies of Europe. The progress has been made in despite of great and unnatural obstacles. From the appointment (by warrant) of ignorant apothecaries, native or foreign, as surgeon's mates, or, the intrusion of the incompetent favorites of influential politicians, the Government, in 1828, protected itself by establishing boards of examination. These up to the present time, by their increasing experience and scrutiny of their examination, have largely advanced the character of the medical corps, and guarded the interests of the naval service and of humanity. It is, however, still a subject of regret that we are yet behind other nautical powers in exacting the sufficient evidence of capacity from those to whom are intrusted the lives of all who commit themselves to the hazards of naval service. The Department is aware that when I had the honor to administer the Bureau of Medicine and Surgery, the Bureau endeavored to continue the progress of the naval medical corps, and that both verbally and by official communication, it, with respectful urgency, recommended a higher curriculum, and that the facilities of our large naval hospitals should be used to train and discipline those young medical officers who had been found qualified for the service—not the objectionable measure of a Government education in the professional acquirements, fitting them for admission to the service, but securing to them, after they have established a claim of fitness, the higher training and the military discipline required to make them fully efficient in their new and special vocation. The report of Fleet-Surgeon Shippen˚ shows with what care, and how thoroughly, the British government secures the necessary special instruction for its naval medical officers, before assigning them to their complicate duties on board a man-of-war. It is certain that the interests of our naval service, as well as of science and humanity, will be promoted by following, even distantly, the distinguished model of naval medical teaching at Netley.

Very respectfully,

WM. M. WOOD,

Inspector-General Hospitals and Fleets, U. S. N.

Hon. GEO. M. ROBESON,

Secretary of the Navy,

Navy Department, Washington, D. C.

United States Flag-ship Wabash, (first rate,)
Southampton, England, July 8, 1872.

Sir: I have to report that circumstances prevented me from leaving the flag-ship, to carry out certain inspections I was ordered to make, until a comparatively recent period, when I started in compliance with an order from Admiral Alden, from which the following is an extract: "Referring to your letter to me of the 15th ultimo, in regard to carrying out the plan of inspection of hospitals, etc., (referred to in the instructions from the Inspector-General of Hospitals, of 2d November, 1871, and in the order of the Hon. Secretary of the Navy, of 13th November, 1871,) you are directed to proceed, whenever your are ready, to Switzerland, to inspect the military medical establishment, particularly at Berne; thence to Paris, remaining a sufficient time to obtain the information you are directed to procure. Thence you will proceed to England. As your instructions from the Hon. Secretary of the Navy refer more particularly to the English establishment in comparison with our own, it is presumed that most of your time will be passed there, visiting London, Chatham, Greenwich, Great Yarmouth, and any other places which, from information received, you may consider important."

In consequence of these orders I proceeded to England, via Switzerland and France, and have now the honor of inclosing herewith some of the results of my observations, embodied in a report.

I am, very respectfully, your obedient servant,

Edward Shippen,
Medical Inspector, U. S. N.

Wm. Maxwell Wood, M. D.,
Medical Inspector-General of Hospitals and Fleets,

Navy Department, Washington, D. C.

REPORTS

UPON

CERTAIN ENGLISH HOSPITALS.

By EDWARD SHIPPEN, M. D.,
MEDICAL INSPECTOR, U. S. N., FLEET-SURGEON EUROPEAN STATION.

Upon reaching Lyons, on my way to Switzerland, I found it necessary to delay there, to obtain a consular certificate, to enable me to leave France. This was replaced by a regular passport from our minister in Berne, to enable me to re-enter France. In the latter case it was indispensable.

During my detention of a day I inquired as to the condition of the Hôtel Dieu, at Lyons, which is one of the oldest and largest of the civil hospitals of France. It was crowded during the Franco-German war, and I was informed by our consul (General Osterhaus) that the mortality within its gloomy, massive old walls, among both French and Germans, was something perfectly frightful; and that the death-rate, at any time, is very large. The French medical authorities resisted every application to get the wounded put under canvas or in pavilions. General Osterhaus could give me no more than the result of his own observation, and he said it was extremely doubtful if any could be had at the hospital, even had my time permitted a delay for the purpose. But the general had an extended experience in our own recent war, and he assured me he had never dreamed of anything like such mortality. At last he interfered, with such success as to have been instrumental in the parole, or exchange, of a number of German prisoners. These were sent home in winter weather their chances being considered so much better than if they had remained in hospital at Lyons, with almost a certainty of being carried off by typhus, pyæmia, or hospital gangrene.

The French pretend to recognize the merits of the American ambulance ·system, and field treatment generally; but it is, after all, in a patronizing, partial way, as, indeed, they are apt to regard anything which has not its origin in a French brain.

On arriving at Berne, I found that, although Switzerland has no standing army, every able-bodied young man is liable for military service at twenty years of age, and is put in the *landwehr* at about thirty-five. They are called out for a certain number of days, in each year, for drill and exercise. There is, however, a full and complete military staff maintained by the federation, and a surgeon-general is a member of this staff. He has offices in the Federal Palace, at Berne, and is allowed a secretary. The heads of each department are similarly accommodated.

There are several hospitals in Berne, but none devoted exclusively to military purposes. One or two are quite large, but very antiquated in build, etc. They have the small windows and double sashes for winter, which are in general use, and are perhaps below criticism, as compared with some modern hospitals. The splendid natural drainage and airy situation, however, counteract many of the defects in the buildings themselves, and I was told that very general success attended surgical operations within their walls.

On proceeding to Paris, considerable time was occupied in the formalities necessary to obtain a general permission from the minister of marine and colonies (through the kind assistance of Mr. Washburne) to visit the naval hospitals and naval medical schools of France. There are three of the latter; one at Rochefort, one at Toulon, and one at Brest.

This permission was finally obtained, in the form of a card with printed permission, signed by the minister's chief of staff, (a rear-admiral,) and with a place for the autograph of the bearer, who is identified by this means upon presenting himself. This permission it is absolutely necessary to have, and I can now avail myself of it at any time that I may find myself in any of the ports named above.

Passing over to England, at the termination of these formalities, I spent most of my time there, as my instructions demanded.

General Schenck was kind enough to get permission from the admiralty (which permission was promptly given) for me to see everything I pleased.

The kindness and politeness of Sir Alexander Armstrong, the medical director-general of the navy, and of Sir Galbraith Logan, the director-general, army medical department, were most gratifying. Both these gentlemen were very prompt in writing to direct that I should be shown everything at the places under their control which I might have occasion to visit.

ST. THOMAS HOSPITAL.

While waiting in London for the permission alluded to, I visited St. Thomas Hospital. This is the newest in London, has an immense endowment, and was opened last year by the Queen, with great ceremony. Situated upon the Thames embankment, at Westminster bridge, just opposite the Houses of Parliament, and having thus the river on one side, with the splendid causeway of the enbankment and, not far off, on the other side, the extensive gardens of Lambeth Palace, it occupies an exceptionally fine position for the heart of London. This hospital consists of seven blocks, or pavilions, parallel with the river, and connected by corridors. It has 680 beds, with 1,800 cubic feet of air space for each bed. I noticed nothing very new in the arrangements. The ventilation and drainage were very good. The wards were all alike, and had two open fire-places in the middle of each, with a ventilating shaft around the flue of each one. The windows were plenty and large, going well up to the ceiling. I noticed a want of hard-finish on the wall of the wards, and of such close joints in the floor and in the angles of the wainscots as is now considered a *sine qua non* with us in hospital construction. I have no doubt trouble will result from vermin and from infection very probably by-and-by. This seems remarkable in a building were money was no object, comparatively speaking. The main bath-rooms are in the basement, and very complete, but I should suppose that a greater proximity to the wards would render them more useful. The beds and bedding appeared to me as not up to the standard of similar institutions in our country. In the walls, over each bed, were irons and sockets for curtains or testers, but I saw none actually in use. Much useful room is taken up by the unnecessarily massive architecture of the building, as was admitted and regretted by the officer who showed me around. There is the theater or lecture-room for the medical school of the hospital, entirely distinct and at some distance from the hospital proper. Near it is the dead-house, and connecting the latter with the basement of the hospital is an ample subterranean passage. This hospital has an immense out-patient business, and the rooms for this purpose, as well as the dispensary, are very large. The latter seemed very well arranged indeed. The business offices of the hospital are ample and handsome. One thing struck me here as well as elsewhere, viz, that they received all contagious diseases, including small-pox, into one of the pavilions, about 60 feet removed from the next one, and of course connected by corridors. Some of the non-medical officers of the hospital and their families had their quarters in the adjoining pavilion. I was informed that the governors of the institution prided themselves upon receiving all classes of cases, as a part of the traditional policy of the hospital, and thence resulted the reception of small-pox cases. It is quite a good illustration of the traditional policy and conservatism for which England is so remarkable. Indeed, I found out afterward that the naval hospitals had no better arrangements. In our country, and in most others, municipal or general laws would interfere in such cases.

Although any one must be impressed by the imposing size and massive build of St. Thomas Hospital, I must confess that, in regard to its administration, cleanliness, etc., it did not seem to me to compare very favorably with similar institutions in our own country..

19 H

THE ROYAL VICTORIA HOSPITAL AT NETLEY.

On the 2d May, 1872, I visited the "Royal Victoria Hospital at Netley," the principal hospital of the British army. I was most kindly and hospitably received by Inspector-General Francis Wm. Innes, M. D., C. B., who is the senior medical officer and who ranks with a brigadier-general.

Netley hospital is by this time so well known that any description of it would seem almost superfluous. It may be as well, however, to make a few general remarks in regard to it, premising that my principal object in visiting here was to see the medical school Its situation is a very fine one, upon a slope of loamy and gravelly soil, and looking upon Southampton water, with a climate as fine as any in the south of England. It is a little below the ruins of the celebrated Netley Abbey, and upon land formerly belonging to it. It is only a confirmation of the sagacity of the Netley abbot and his chapter to say that a fairer exposure, or more pleasant situation could hardly be found, whether for an abbey or a hospital. The natural drainage is exceedingly good.

Vessels of large draught anchor in Southampton water, and go above the hospital. A long and handsome pier or jettee was built when the hospital was founded, with the intention of having the troop-ships with invalids to come alongside it and land the men there. But that side of the river shoals so gradually, and the rise and fall of the tide is so great, that the landing there from vessels of great size is practically abandoned. The invalids arriving from abroad are sent around from Portsmouth, either by smaller steamer or by rail. This must be considered a drawback to the thoroughly successful working of this really great institution.

The buildings contained within the government grounds (which are most ample for any contingency) consist of the hospital proper, laundries, kitchens, stores, and other offices back of it, and also the laboratory of the army medical school. There is a row of buildings for the temporary accommodation of the women and children of the married invalids sent from abroad, the mess hall and quarters for the medical officers, the house of the military commandant, and that of the principal medical officer; and finally, at some distance to the rear, an insane hospital, quite recently built.

The hospital proper is an immense building, said (commonly) to be a quarter of a mile long. It is necessarily an imposing building, although there is not much in its architecture *per se* to make it so. It appears to be well and substantially built, and is not unfrequently visited by the Queen, who laid the corner-stone, and after whom it is named. I found a little jealousy existing in other quarters on this account. On two stories wards, having a capacity of about twelve beds each, open upon the general corridor, which is closed in with glass, and runs along the front of the building. In the main or central building a few wards are in the front, with the chapel, etc., in the rear, and all opening upon the same general corridor. The ground floor is occupied by the numerous offices, dining rooms, orderly rooms and quarters, required by such an establishment. Great distances have to be traversed in the ordinary service of the hospital, which is a very great defect.

The arrangement of the wards and corridors is such that, to insure ventilation and to carry on the duties, it would be impossible to cut off any ward, or number of wards, entirely. In case, therefore, of contagious or infectious diseases occurring, or in case of the hospital being crowded with wounded, the corridors would be nothing more than conductors of disease from one ward to another. Some form of pavilion would be infinitely preferable. This was freely admitted in the course of conversation by one of the principal medical officers. Under the present use to which the hospital is put, as will be explained further on, these considerations do not weigh as they would in time of war or epidemic disease.

In the center building of the hospital proper are a very large chapel, an amphitheater for the lectures of the medical class, and a museum and library; attached to the wards are rooms for opthalmoscopie, microscopic, and other examinations connected with the practical service of the wards. But the medical class have also rooms for chemistry, microscopy, etc., in another building, to which I shall refer when I come to speak of the medical school.

In the hospital the service of the wards was well done, and the wards themselves in good order. The water-closets, lined with enameled slate, were as good as any I ever saw. The neatness of the beds, bedding, and floors, however, was not equal to that of most naval hospitals, and I could not divest myself, when in the wards, of the idea of being in a field or camp hospital. One reason may have been the want of white bed-spreads, and that the beds not in use had the mattresses and bedding rolled, as in barrack-rooms, and also that they are now crowded by the unusual number of invalids, just arrived from abroad, principally from India. Netley may, after all, be termed a great receiving and distributing rendezvous for military invalids from all parts of the world. Large numbers only remain here long enough to verify their cases, when they are transferred elsewhere, discharged the service, or pensioned.

The capacity of Netley may be stated at 1,000 beds. On the day I was there there were nine hundred and ninety-seven patients. This large number was due to recent arrivals from India, the plan having lately been adopted of sending invalids from India in the winter for the most part, passing through the Suez Canal, and arriving in England in the spring. This is better, of course, than an arrival in winter, and it was found that the cases of pneumonia, etc., so common in debilitated men, coming from warm climates, were much diminished in number from former years. Indeed, there was but one very serious case of pneumonia in all this crowd of sick men, who had been so suddenly transported from a tropical climate to an English spring. I may mention that there seemed to be an unusual number of cases of well-defined aortic aneurism among the Indian invalids. Some two or three of the most remarkable of these I was shown I also saw two cases of hepatic abscess, which had opened through the diaphragm, of which one was apparently doing well, while the other seemed likely to prove speedily fatal. Dr. Maclean, the professor of military medicine, who has had great Indian experience, stated that recovery in such cases was not so rare. The only cases I ever saw (two in number, in China) were both fatal. The greater number of the Indian invalids at Netley appeared to be the subjects of malarial poison, chronic dysentery, debility, etc.

I will now pass from the main building to the stores, laundries, kitchens, and other offices, which seemed ample for their purpose. They are entirely plain and unpretending; situated immediately in the rear of the main building, in a well-paved court. They are of brick; mostly in two low stories, so as not to impede too much the circulation of air. The laboratory, etc., for the medical candidates, is a part of the same range, which forms three sides of a quadrangle; the main building forming the fourth side.

About a quarter of a mile from these buildings, higher up the slope, and directly in the rear, is the insane hospital, quite recently built, or finished. It is in grounds surrounded by a high and substantial brick wall. A house is about being built, within the walls, for the medical officer in charge of this department, which is now permanently established. This insane hospital is comparatively small; and the building does not seem particularly well suited, either in plan or details, to its purpose, having been built by the royal engineers, apparently without consultation with those who are skilled in such matters. Extensive alterations and improvements are, consequently, already in progress, rendered necessary for the comfort and safe-keeping of the unfortunate inmates. The whole system of heating was also undergoing alteration, at great trouble and expense, after being in use just a sufficient time to prove that it did not fulfill its purpose.

It was explained to me that a large insane asylum was not so necessary for the army, owing to what I must characterize as the very peculiar system adopted in the English army, in dealing with the insane of that branch of the service—indeed, that this insane hospital was, at present, like Netley itself, more a place for verifying and classifying cases than for their permanent retention and treatment. Insane soldiers who become comparatively well are often discharged, especially if they have friends or home to go to. Or, they are sent to certain civil establishments for the insane, where they are paid for at the rate of about £40 per annum. Or, finally, they are discharged, and returned to the parishes to which they belonged before enlisting, and it appears that these parishes are bound to receive and take care of them. This explanation was quite sufficient to show why a small insane establishment was necessary.

On a lawn, back of the main hospital, was pitched a lot of tents, which had been made ready in case the accession of invalids should exceed the capacity of the building, which was nearly full. I learned afterward that these tents had been put to an unexpected use (very soon after my visit) in sheltering some eighteen cases of small-pox landed from one of the troop ships. Fortunately the disease did not spread. These tents were of ordinary bell shape, of large size, but, I should think, not so well suited to the purpose as our hospital wall-tent.

The buildings for the reception of the regimental women and children, who are here awaiting the convalescence or discharge of their husbands and fathers, are well removed from the other buildings, and in a fine airy situation.

The house of the military commandant, near the entrance of the grounds, is a very neat cottage, of ample size, and the same may be said of that of the principal medical officer near it.

Among the buildings there only remains to be noticed the mess-hall and quarters for the medical officers and candidates. This is a handsome building, of ample size, with the mess-hall, ante-room or drawing-room, kitchens, and other offices on the ground floor, and the quarters on two floors above. The candidates are obliged to give a receipt to the barrack-master for their rooms and the contents, and to make good any willful injury. This gives them, at once, in a practical way, a sense of responsibility for government property. The mess seems to be kept up in good style, and the mess regulations to be good. The whole thing cannot fail to have an excellent effect in introducing the medical candidates to this quite important part of military life and customs; while it conduces very much to their present comfort. The regular medical staff are members of the mess.

THE MEDICAL SCHOOL AT NETLEY.

As my principal concern, at Netley, was to see the army and navy medical school, I may now proceed to that. The organization is as follows, viz:

The governing body, called the *senate*, consisting of Director General Sir J. Galbraith Logan, M. D., K. C. B., army medical department, president; Sir James Ranald Martin, C. B., physician to the council of India; the professors of the army medical school; and the principal medical officer at Netley, (*ex officio*,) members of the senate.

This school has a distinct and independent existence, under the secretary of state for war. It is governed by its senate, which holds a meeting for the dispatch of business once a month, or oftener if necessary. Every function pertaining to a senate, or governing body, is exercised by it, but no act of the senate is binding until it has received the approval of the secretary of state for war.

The professorships in the school are as follows: Military Surgery, Deputy Inspector-General T. Longmore, C. B.; Military Medicine, Deputy Inspector-General W. C. Maclean, M. D., C. B.; Military Hygiene, E. A. Parkes, esq., M. D., F. R. S.;

Pathology, W. Aitken, esq., M. D. These gentlemen are well known as authors, as well as teachers, and none stand higher in their respective departments. To them had recently been added from the royal navy, (on account of the reception of naval candidates for instruction,) for the chair of Naval Hygiene, Staff Surgeon John Denis Macdonald, M. D., a fellow of the Royal Society.

There are also four assistant professors who are taken from the army; two being staff surgeons-major, one a staff surgeon, and one a staff assistant surgeon. There is also a secretary, who is a gentleman of extensive scientific acquirements.

I do not see how I can better illustrate the working of this excellent institution than by taking the case of a candidate who is entered there.

In the first place he goes through the competitive examination (in London or Chelsea) for his position, whether in the army or navy, just as with us. If found qualified, he is sent to Netley, instead of going raw into the service, as he would have done a few years ago—indeed, as they did in the English navy until this year, when seventeen naval candidates have been received, on precisely the same footing as the others. Next year the number will be increased. Arrived at Netley, the candidate assumes his uniform and goes upon duty. He is still considered on probation. He has quarters furnished him, and receives five shillings a day, about enough to defray his necessary expenses, as their mess, while handsome, is large and well managed. He remains at Netley four months. Two months are passed in the wards, and two under special instruction.

Let us take the service in the wards first. Here, under the supervision and instruction of the staff surgeon in charge of his division, the candidate has a clinical course, including various methods of diagnosis, and especially the mode of investigating the history of diseases, in relation to the previous life and service of the enlisted man. "The candidate is required to call in the aid of auscultation, the microscope, etc., and to apply the various chemical tests for the purposes of exhaustive diagnosis." For this purpose rooms convenient to the wards are provided, and fitted with appropriate fixtures, and the walls have diagrams, etc., bearing upon the subject to which the room is devoted.

The regulations in regard to recruiting, sick certificates, etc., are explained, and the candidates made to examine men for these purposes.

The candidates are put in charge of wards under the supervision of the staff surgeon of the division. They are held responsible for the ventilation and general neatness and cleanliness of the ward, as well as for the keeping of the different books and papers. The regulations in regard to prescriptions, diet, etc., are very stringent. The candidate is also required to keep a case-book, in addition to the regular hospital books. This case-book is examined at the termination of the course of instruction, and marks are awarded for the manner in which it is kept. The points to which the examination of the candidate's case-book is particularly directed are as follows, viz: professional merit, literary merit, attention to detail of regulations, and general neatness. The regulations for the conduct of the candidates are very voluminous, but appear complete and satisfactory. Candidates on duty in the wards "are to remain in their wards until 11.30 a. m., daily. They may then go to the library, where they must be found until 1 p. m., so as to be within call for any casual duty, unless required in the laboratory, microscope-room, or opthalmoscopic-room, or for examination of recruits, or in the lecture theater." In addition to this they have to perform, in rotation, the duty of orderly officer.

The candidate commences this duty at 9 a. m., and finishes it the next day at the same hour. While on duty he must be in uniform, and must remain in the room appointed for him, unless called away on duty, when he is to leave a memorandum of where he is to be found. He visits the wards and dining-rooms with the orderly-sergeant at each meal-hour; and at 9 p. m., to see that all orderlies are present, and all patients in bed. At meal times he sees that the diet and extra diet are properly cooked and served.   He asks if there are any complaints, and if there are any, is to investigate the matter; if the complaint appears just, he is to see justice done, taking care to state the facts in his report. At 4.30 p. m. he inspects the meat and bread prepared for issue for the following day.

During his tour of duty the orderly medical officer is responsible for the sanitary condition of the wards, and that the patients are personally clean; that those allowed to be up are properly washed and dressed; that the wards are well aired; the water-closets, etc., clean and without smell; that excreta, poultices, dressings, etc., are at once removed; that no undue noise or irregularities exist; also that the nurses are attentive, and carry out instructions. The orderly officer has charge of instruments and appliances for any emergency or accident, for which instruments he is held responsible.   He does not leave the hospital for his meals, but is supplied with them by the mess-man without extra charge.   At the end of his tour of duty the orderly medical officer has to make a report in a prescribed form, which is really a certificate, over his signature, that he has performed all his duties.   This report is made to the principal medical officer.

All candidates are required to be present at all *post-mortem* examinations, and not to leave before the inspection is over. One or more of the most remarkable *post-mortems* form a subject for examination at the end of the course.   The candidate who had charge of the case in the wards is required to furnish a complete abstract of it, to be read aloud before the *post-mortem* is commenced.   He has then to take notes of the *post-mortem*, and insert them in his case-book, as well as in the necrological register of the hospital.

It is thus to be seen by this partial sketch of their duties, that the candidates while serving in the wards have not much leisure time.

Having spent two months in the duties of the wards, the candidate passes to the laboratory, etc., while those who have been at work in the latter relieve those who have been in the wards, but both still attend the same general lectures.

I believe it was the intention, when the school was first established, to have the candidates there for six months; but at present, as I have previously stated, they only remain four months.

No excuse is received for absence from a lecture excepting duty elsewhere, or leave from competent authority. In all other cases a certain number of marks are lost, and are deducted at the close of the session from the total number gained.

LABORATORY.

" The practical work in the laboratory is intended to familiarize the candidate with the processes he may be called upon to perform, in the analysis of drinking-water, air, food, and soils." Candidates are obliged to pass a certain time at work in the laboratory; but they are permitted to work at other hours, and as late as 10 p. m., if they please. They are only required to see that there is no waste of material or gas.

In the microscope-room is carried on, at regular hours, the study of morbid anatomy and the microscopic examination of tissues. The number of candidates is so small that in addition to demonstrating the work for the day by description, plates, the black-board, or by typical specimens from the museum, the professor has the opportunity of passing round and of observing the progress of each candidate. In this way the advantages of public instruction and private teaching are combined ; and it was quite pleasant to observe the industry of the pupils and the apparent good relations between them and their preceptor, the well-known Doctor Aitken. Each candidate has a space to himself at a long table, under a good light. He is provided with a microscope, and other necessary instruments for his exclusive use. He has a closet, with lock and key, for keeping these instruments, for which he is responsible, and is required to give a receipt. Candidates are here, as in the laboratory, required to pass a certain time at work; a portion of which time is allowed for cleaning up and putting away the instruments. But they are allowed and encouraged to return to their work at spare hours. Absence is only permitted when actually on the sick-list or with leave from com-petent authority.

In obtaining leave of absence the application must be made to the principal medical officer.   But the professor in whose division the candidate is serving, or (if he is serving in the wards) the staff surgeon of the division, is first to countersign the application. The approval of the lecturer for the day (if there is a lec-ture) is also to be obtained.   In fact, practically hardly any leave is had.   When given it is generally on Saturday and Sun-day, and then the candidate, if he has duty, must procure a sub-stitute.   Leave is only granted at other times in cases of the most urgent necessity.

LIBRARIES.

There are two libraries at Netley, to which the candidates have access, under proper restrictions.   The first is the " medical staff library," which is the property of the officers of the medical depart-ment of the army, and which is sustained by their entrance fees and donations.   For the use of this library candidates have to subscribe two shillings a month, beside an entrance fee of ten shillings.   The other library is called the " medical-school library," which is the property of the government, and for the use of which no fee is paid.   It is not worth while to enter into the rules and restrictions applicable to those using the libraries.

MUSEUM.

There is a museum, consisting of a collection of specimens in natural history and in geology; a large number of specimens of pathological anatomy, having special reference to the more prev-alent diseases of military life; a collection of materia medica and alimentaria, with specimens in their natural and prepared states.   Here, among the alimentaria, are to be found the princi-pal seeds, grains, and dried and prepared articles of food, from all parts of the world.   There is also a collection of plans and models of whatever is used in the army for the conveyance, sup-port, or protection of wounded men, with models of tents, hospitals, etc. Indeed the museum is outgrowing its room very fast, and a large and interesting collection of heads is necessarily excluded, and is placed in cases in the passages, an obviously unfit place in a hospital. Some of these heads are rare, and have been procured by medical officers serving abroad, at the risk of their lives. The collection of venomous insects, serpents, etc., is large, and derived from the same source.

The professor of pathology, in his course, not only gives practical instruction in the preparation for preservation of morbid tissues, but instruction is also given as to the mode of preserving and sending home from abroad specimens of comparative anatomy and of natural history.

It would serve no particular purpose to detail the various subjects, and sub-divisions thereof, which are treated of by the lecturers on military medicine, military surgery, and military hygiene. Suffice it to say that the course seems to be a thoroughly exhaustive one.

It would seem impossible for any young man who has passed the preliminary examination, and who then goes through the course at Netley, to be otherwise than well prepared for his duties in whatever part of the world his lot may be cast.

The names of candidates who pass the preliminary examination are sent to the director-general, and to the professors of the school, arranged in the following classes:

1st. Those who have passed a pre-eminently distinguished examination, the characters which distinguish the excellence of each, and their capacity for special service. These are arranged in order of merit.

2d. Names of those who have passed creditably, arranged in alphabetical order, giving the topics on which each one has excelled, or fallen short.

3d. Names of candidates who have passed the minimum examination arranged in alphabetical order, with a statement of the particular branches in which each has been found deficient. This is to enable the professors to carry out their instruction with a definite aim as regards each class.

As the examination at the end of the Netley course settles the final position of the candidate in the service, it becomes doubly his interest to be industrious and well-behaved.

A plan has been initiated of placing upon a marble tablet, in the hall of the hospital, the name of the candidate of his year who, in the judgment of the medical board, and of the senate, has most distinguished himself.

I asked whether any candidates were thrown out, and was told that it did not occur, as the examination before coming there secured the very best of the applicants. Then the excellent mess arrangements, and the being thrown at once into an official position and atmosphere, together with constant employment, are excellent restraints, as well as the best preparation for their general duties in the service. Should any candidate render himself liable in any way, however, either through misbehavior, or idleness or incompetency, he would be permitted quietly to retire or would be dropped by the senate.

There were several Indians among the candidates. They wore the same uniform, enjoyed the same privileges, lived at the same mess, and had the same charge of wards as the others. They were likely to be placed with native regiments in India, as I understood, and it was conceded that they deserved great credit for having successfully competed in a foreign tongue for their position, and that their acquirements were good. But I fancy that while all official courtesies would be observed, and no petty jealousy of their position or success existed, the old prejudice of race would still hold its sway, and that social intercourse between these persons and white officers and families would not be very cordial. This was not stated in so many words, but it was easy to see that it was so. I state the fact as I found it, because the time, some think, may come when we may have the same experiment to try, although with a very different race.

As I have before stated there have been this year for the first time, seventeen naval candidates admitted to this school, and a naval professor appointed. Their course is precisely the same as the others, except as to the peculiarities of naval hygiene. The whole number of candidates was between fifty and sixty, but it is intended to increase the number of naval candidates next year. The naval candidates wear the naval uniform. It was considered highly desirable that they should have the advantage of this admirable course, and they are accordingly received here by the consent of the war office, the navy bearing the proportionate share of expense. This is a most advantageous arrangement for the navy, as so much was already provided and in working order at immense benefit is derived at a very moderate expense.

Having hastily sketched the main points observed in my most gratifying visit to Netley, and having omitted much for fear of greater prolixity, I have respectfully to suggest how easily a somewhat similar institution could be formed for our naval and military candidates in connection with that unique establishment the Army Medical Museum at Washington. It would form a splendid nucleus for such a school, and all would be interested in adding to its collections. Washington is now a city of sufficient size to afford a plentiful supply of subjects for dissection and for operations on the *cadaver*, while there should be but little difficulty in arranging for hospital service and clinical instruction. The expense would be trifling for the numbers would be small. Plenty of capable men could be found both in the Army and Navy who would be happy to take the position of instructors at their ordinary pay. At any rate it would be perfectly easy to try an experiment in this connection, which I feel confident would turn out a successful one, and a lasting credit to the administration which has the liberality and foresight to inaugurate it.

Without doubt there are many older medical officers who, from the want of a earlier practical teaching and experience caused by the demands of immediate service following upon their entrance, would be glad to avail themselves of the privileges of instruction such an establishment would afford.

Haslar is the largest and most important of the naval hospitals of England, not only on account of its capacity and proximity to the greatest dock-yard, but because it also supplies bedding, medical necessaries, and medicines to the service afloat. In addition to this its laundry washes for the large Indian troop-ships regularly. It is situated in Gosport, in full view of Spithead, the Isle of Wight, Portsmouth, and its great naval yard, and is in as airy a position as can be found in such a flat locality, and very accessible for boats at high water as well as by an excellent road. The grounds are extensive, now comprising more than eighty acres, while the hospital itself (founded in the reign of George II) is an immense establishment. It consists of a range of substantial double brick buildings, for the most part three stories high, and extending around three sides of a quadrangle. Upon the ground floor, within the quadrangle, is an arched cloister, or corridor, extending completely around the buildings, forming a sheltered walk and means of communication. On the fourth side of the quadrangle, in the center, is a chapel facing the main entrance. In the rear of this is the cemetery, with a substantial wall and iron fence.

Although this hospital was built so long ago, it was designed by an architect who was evidently a far-seeing man, of enlarged views, for the wards are to-day quite comfortable and well ventilated, although perhaps rather wider in proportion to their length, etc., than modern ideas favor. The ceilings of course are not so high as they would be in a recently constructed hospital. The wards are so arranged that modern conveniences and improvements have been introduced without very great trouble or expense. The air of comfort and cleanliness, throughout the whole establishment, was very pleasant, and the good care and kind treatment received by the patients was manifested by their bearing toward the medical officers. The beds and bedding of the men's wards were very neat and nice. In most of the wards a cheerful open fire was burning in a grate, giving an air of homelike comfort, and at the same time proving an efficient means of ventilation.

On the day I was there there were four hundred and eighty-three patients in the hospital, of whom twenty-five were officers of all ranks. The capacity of Haslar, each ward and room being filled, is about one thousand. This includes accommodation for seventy-five officers, many of whom have two rooms and a few three. The average of cubic feet of air for each bed in the hospital is upwards of 1,100 feet. This varies considerably, for in one large ward it is nearly 1,800 feet, and in some it is only 1,000 feet, The greater number of the wards in ordinary use have over 1,200 cubic feet to the bed.

Haslar has been much relieved of late years, by the removal to Great Yarmouth of the naval insane, who were formerly kept here. Lately the population has been slightly increased by the reception of some of the very aged and infirm Greenwich pensioners. Greenwich hospital itself has lately been diverted for the use of the naval college, and the pensioners are now allowed to live where they please, but they can be received into Haslar as patients. In such case their pensions are stopped and their expenses charged to the "Greenwich Hospital Fund," which is a very large one.

At the end of one wing of the hospital, and forming a part of the building itself, is the small-pox ward. This is capable of partial isolation, and has a separate airing ground for convalescents, but I must confess my surprise at finding such a ward in the hospital at all. There were several inmates, too, and I managed to gather that small-pox then existed to some extent in Portsmouth and its vicinity, and that people employed in the dock-yard there had recently been obliged to leave work on that account. The

20 H

cases in Haslar, however, came from vessels in commission, and principally from those at Spithead.

There is a museum and library in the hospital, both deserving of more attention than I was able to devote to them. One hundred pounds per annum is devoted to the preservation of the museum, its increase being principally due to the zeal of the naval medical officers.

In a very convenient situation, and so arranged as not to occupy too prominent a position, are a new and extensive laundry, a large and convenient store-house near it, and other offices. Over the general store-house is the dispensary and laboratory. From these supplies are issued, not only to Haslar but also to the navy afloat. They were at work re-arranging the dispensary, in consequence of an order lately issued, of which the following is an abstract: "The lords of the admiralty have issued a stringent code of regulations for precautions against accidental poisoning on board Her Majesty's ships and at naval medical establishments. In future all medicines of a poisonous nature are to be put up in bottles or jars of a dark blue color only, and to bear labels of a yellow color having the word *poison* printed in bold letters over the name of the medicine. All medicines of a harmless nature are to be put up in bottles of white or a pale green glass, or in jars of white ware, and to be distinguished by labels of a green color. All medicines labeled *poison* are always to be kept under lock and key and apart from others. No white labels or labels of any other colors than yellow or green are to be used for medicine bottles or for dispensing."

Dr. Salmon expressed complete satisfaction with all the offices of the hospital except the general kitchen, which is in the basement of the main building, and considered defective. There are, however, a number of diet-kitchens connected with the wards, which would relieve the general kitchen.

Extensive airing grounds are provided for the convalescent patients, both officers and men. These grounds are walled, but have terraces and walks sufficiently elevated to afford an uninterrupted view. The grass and shrubbery are kept in nice order, and seats and summer-houses provided. There are also extensive grounds in front of the officers' residences, which are quite commodious. The kitchen gardens of these houses are so arranged that they do not obtrude upon the view over the lawn, and are rendered more productive by being placed close under the shelter of these walls.

The alterations, repairs, etc., are carried on at this institution by an officer who is called the clerk and agent, and who is borne on the navy list. In case of any construction, repairs, or alterations being considered necessary, the medical officer in charge makes out a request for it, the medical director-general receives and approves it, his recommendation carrying great weight. The matter is then decided upon at the admiralty, under whose orders the clerk and agent carries them out. This officer occupies an excellent house in the grounds.

About three years ago a radical change was made in the government and police of this and other naval hospitals. Previous to that time they had a military governor, who was charged with the discipline, police, and guarding of the hospital and its grounds This is now dispensed with, and the entire charge in every respect is vested in the principal medical officer, who attends to all the details of the government, police, and working of the hospital, subject only to the admiral in command at Portsmouth.

The principal medical officer consults with the deputy medical inspectors and staff surgeons in charge of divisions when called upon to do so, but his duties are for the most part executive and supervisory. He appears to have no sinecure in conducting so large an establishment.

I was informed here, and also at the office of the medical director-general at Somerset House, that no trouble in discipline or in any other way had resulted from the change alluded to above, Indeed, that the practical working was acknowledged to be good even by those who had originally opposed the change.

The police force of the establishment consists of details from the metropolitan police, who wear the regular police uniform. The strict and intelligent manner in which they performed their duties was spoken of in the highest terms. The men are selected by the police inspectors in London from those who have distinguished themselves by good behavior. They are generally young or middle aged men. This is considered a very desirable place, and the men are very careful so to conduct themselves as to be retained here. They have proved so efficient that no change is desired. The nurses allowed by the admiralty are one to every seven patients. At present they have about one to nine.

I presume it will be unnecessary to be more prolix concerning Haslar; I will therefore close with some account of the medical staff, etc., to enable the Department and the Bureau to see the organization in this respect. I should state that the number of medical officers for duty is obviously too small, which entails more constant labor, both professional and clerical, than seems right and proper. This, however, is only my opinion, as I heard no complaints on that point. The medical officer in charge is Inspector-General James Salmon, esq., M. D., who has Sir Gilbert Blane's medal, and is honorary physician to the Queen.

There are two deputy inspectors-general, who divided the professional supervision in the hospital, one staff-surgeon, and three assistant surgeons who have all passed for surgeons. There are also a chaplain and the clerk and agent.

There is a very large number of servants and laborers, amounting to between sixty and seventy, including foreman of laborers cooks, butler, carpenter, gas-fitter, barber, postman, washerman, washerwomen, laborers, scrubbers, and seamstresses.

THE ROYAL HOSPITAL, YARMOUTH, FOR THE INSANE OF THE NAVY.

Before leaving England I made a visit to Great Yarmouth to see the naval insane hospital, of which the medical director-general was evidently very proud, and not without reason, as I found on going through it.

Yarmouth is in a very bleak and raw situation, and about as far removed from the great centers as it is possible in England for a place to be. This is to be regretted on several accounts, the principal of which is that the climate necessitates extra vigilance in regard to pneumonia, etc., with which the insane are so liable to be affected.

The history of the occupation of the building as an insane hospital is as follows :

Built early in the present century, when general naval actions were common, it was in use but a few years when the general peace took place. The navy, having no present or prospective use for the buildings, turned them over to the army, by which they were for a long time occupied as barracks. Finally the army ceasing to occupy them they reverted to the navy, and, as the care and treatment of the naval insane in some more systematic and special way was then attracting the attention of the authorities, it was determined to fit up the buildings in question for this purpose. This was in 1863.

Deputy Inspector-General William McLeod, esq., M. D., royal navy, was ordered to take charge of the establishment in July, 1866, and he has remained in charge since that time. Dr. McLeod is so thoroughly capable, so interested in his work, and now so experienced, that his tenure of office is probably permanent, as it is manifest that any change must be undesirable. Associated with him on duty is Staff Surgeon Whicher, who has also been there for several years. There is also a clerk in charge of stores, etc., attached to the hospital. These officers occupy very comfortable residences outside of, but close to, the hospital. Dr. McLeod has entire charge, and is responsible only to the medical director-general of the navy and the admiralty, and corresponds directly with them.

It may be as appropriate a place as any to state that every patient received here for treatment has to be received upon the same medical certificates which the act of Parliament requires for other insane establishments. These certificates are forwarded to the medical director-general, who judges from them whether the person is a fit subject to be received at Yarmouth, and who orders accordingly.

The buildings comprising the Yarmouth establishment are constructed of brick, two stories in height, and built in the form of a quadrangle. Attached to them are a store-house, kitchen and buttery, laundry, and other offices, which are surrounded by walls, as are also the airing grounds for the officers and men. Terraces, however, are so raised from the grounds away from the fences and walls, that the sense of confinement created by walls is in a measure done away with. Covered seats and walks are arranged in these grounds looking south, to allow patients to take the air with comfort either in very sunny or rainy weather. There are also convenient drinking-fountains arranged for the use of the patients.

The quarters of the officers under treatment are in the front of the quadrangle, mostly on the second floor, and are exceedingly comfortable and well furnished. There is a dining-room for convalescents attached. On the floor below is a handsome parlor, as well as a room in which, out of hearing, but still in full sight, the patients may see their friends.

Extreme attention is paid to cleanliness, especially in the bedding. Dr. McLeod had the bedding and bed-clothing turned up for me frequently in both the officers' and men's rooms, and I have never seen any more admirably clean.

My visit was entirely unannounced, and I saw everything at an early hour, and without preparation. There seems to be no limit to the amount of clothing used—every article of wearing-apparel or bed-linen being changed whenever soiled. There were some paralytic cases which had been in bed for five years, and Dr. McLeod assured me he never had bed-sores among them. This he attributed to complete change of clothing whenever wet or soiled.

Curtains were provided for the windows, and engravings are plentifully hung in the passages and day-rooms, both of the officers and men, and other means of ornament are resorted to to take off any bare or prison-like air. There were, in many parts of the establishment, flowers in pots in the window seats, and jars and other ornaments for the mantles to make things cheerful.

Dr. McLeod assured me that he never had had assaults committed with these apparently handy missiles, and no more broken than would occur in any ordinary establishment. In speaking of these matters he said that the government was extremely liberal in carrying out all his suggestions except in regard to matters of ornament, which he himself regarded as an important feature in the treatment of the inmates. He began to obtain these things from the bone and slush sold; and it is wonderful to see how much he has accomplished.

Large day-wards are provided for the men, where they have different occupations and amusements, as well as separate dining-rooms. No patient who is able to be up and dressed is permitted to be in his dormitory in the day time. This enables them to thoroughly ventilate and police the rooms and beds.

There are now there about three hundred men and between thirty and forty officers, and yet there are a number of spare rooms for officers, and two complete sets of men's wards vacant. In the portion of the quadrangle opposite to the entrance and on the ground-floor are the rooms for patients (other than officers) who, from disposition to quarrel, etc., require a separate room at night.　Great care is taken in this respect; one man who is noisy or quarrelsome, either by day or night, being sometimes sufficient to set off a whole ward, as one hysterical woman will set off every other one within hearing.　These separate rooms open upon a corridor, and are visited every hour during the night. The contents of the close-stools provided for each of these rooms are emptied as soon as used, no matter how often or at what hour.　The sheets are changed each time they are wet, no matter how often that accident may occur.　There are strong rooms, but Dr. McLeod said he rarely had occasion to use them.　They were padded in the usual way, and the padding covered with painted canvas, which was found to be much better than the "kamptulicon" or any other cloth prepared from caoutchouc, as when excreta were rubbed upon it it could be washed without damage, while the prepared cloths easily rotted.　The same testimony was borne at Netley.　In cases where men were destructive in their tendencies at night, a bed was made on the floor for them in a single room, the bedstead and other furniture taken away, and a nurse put on duty.　When an officer became noisy or outrageous he was sent during the day to a handsome room large and nicely furnished, and warmed by hot water pipes.　There he was kept in charge by as many nurses as his condition required.　The effect of these surroundings and of this simple and humane treatment was described as marvelous in most cases.　All the rooms have inside shutters opening half way up, to prevent damage and to modify the light in certain cases.　The epileptics are in a ward communicating with one in which are the bed-ridden paralytics, so that one nurse can watch both rooms at night.　The nurse has a small room in the center, between the two, with a light so arranged that both large rooms are illuminated sufficiently.　The light is high up, behind glass, and can be controlled only from the nurses' room.　There is a window on each side of the nurses' room, from which every bed in both rooms can be seen.　I may mention that in addition to the watch within doors at night the grounds and offices are regularly patroled. I will explain elsewhere how vigilance is secured on the part of these men.

The water-closets had just been rebuilt, and are now detached from the buildings sufficiently to allow a space for ventilation by lattices. They connect with the wards, and are quite as easy of access as the old ones, which were within the line of wall of the building itself. There is no possibility of a patient disarranging anything, or of doing himself any harm in these water-closets, and they were as entirely free from odor as any I have ever seen.

The bath-rooms had just been re-arranged, and were ample. A Russian bath was in process of building. Bathing once a week at least, for both officers and men, is compulsory, and the patients are at those time more particularly examined for the detection of vermin, or of any contusions or injuries, or the effects of any injurious practices.

Dr. McLeod has just finished, at an expense of five or six hundred pounds, a set of rooms with a small diet-kitchen attached to the day-wards for the idiotic and more helpless patients. These rooms are for two experienced middle-aged female nurses. He is anxious to try whether these will not be better fitted to take charge of this unfortunate class of patients. The admiralty cheerfully consents to supply the means to try the experiment.

To proceed with the buildings: There is a very convenient and very excellent dispensary with a thoroughly competent apothecary. I found the expenditure in this department was about the same as for five hundred men afloat; at least the cost of drugs is about that. The proportionate expenditure of cod-liver oil, tonics, etc., to that of other classes of medicines is very great.

The buttery, kitchen, etc., were in perfect order. The laundry was unusually large and complete in consequence of the immense amount of bed-linen, blankets, and clothing constantly in use. In fact, the quantity seemed to me to be perfectly enormous.

There is a large store-house in which everything is to be found which can possibly be needed in such an establishment. It is under the charge of a disbursing officer, and everthing is issued on requisition.   There is also a tailor-shop with a hired foreman, in which all the outer clothing of the patients is made, and rooms in which repairs are made by females employed for the purpose. I may mention that almost all the work in the laundry and tailor-shop is done by patients, and there is a loom at which one of the patients makes all the cocoa matting used in the establishment. These people are rewarded by a small portion of tobacco and sometimes by a little extra bread and cheese and beer.   Tobacco is served out gratis, but in small quantities, to those who are allowed to use it, and is found to be a most valuable incentive to industry and good conduct.

I should have mentioned that if an officer's friends choose to clothe him they are permitted to do so, but otherwise they wear a sack-coat, trousers, and waistcoat of stout blue navy cloth. The men wear the same, but of coarser material.

Unless officers have families dependent upon them, the most of their half-pay goes to contribute toward their support, and the same is the case with men who have pensions.

In regard to the building generally, I may say it is wonderful how well, by judicious arrangements and alterations, they have been adapted to their purpose.   The forlorn air of a public asylum is avoided, while the safety of the inmates is entirely provided for.   Indeed, there have been but two elopements during the last five years, and in both cases the men were found in the town the next day.

I have several times already alluded to the kind and judicious treatment received by the patients here.   I was told that the cures were quite up to the average, and that the deaths were about ten per cent., mostly among the paralytic.

I may mention that Dr. M. dissents from the opinion commonly held in naval circles that insanity is frequently caused by masturbation.   On the contrary, he considers it a symptom, and that it is almost invariably the result of spinal irritation.   It is not, however, either my business or purpose to enter into any purely medical question in this connection.

The system pursued here in regard to the nurses differs entirely from that of other naval hospitals, and is so important and full of instruction that I may be excused for dwelling upon it.

Of course it is of the utmost importance to have experienced men of health, sobriety, strength, and temper. They carry their lives in their hands almost, and there is scarcely a position in life requiring more watchfulness and firmness combined with good temper. These qualities are sufficiently rare, and it requires greater inducements than the pay offered to ordinary nurses to secure such men. Dr. McLeod has therefore in his hands the power of instant discharge of any nurse found *in delictu*. He told me he had discharged nineteen nurses the first year he was here— most of them, as I understood, for rough treatment of patients.

The advantages these nurses have are as follows : Unlike those in other naval hospitals, they acquire a claim for pension (either for injury in the line of duty, or for length of service) just as if they served at sea. They have certain fixed hours of duty and of leave, and can have their families in the town close by. They are allowed to draw and take home a portion of their ration ; for instance, they may draw their week's ration of beef in one piece. Of course for every additional year the attendant remains there he has a greater interest in retaining his position. In some cases where men had been discharged for cause, they had made appeals through friends to the admiralty ; but Dr. M. had always been thoroughly sustained, and his influence thus preserved.

There is one attendant for every eight patients ; but, as I have stated already, much work is done by harmless patients, much to their benefit and generally at their own request. For professional attendance, supervision of attendants, as well as the working of the institution generally, there are, as I have said before, but two medical officers employed, which seems too few. Dr. McLeod told me that he generally went through the wards four times a day, and he seemed to know the name and the peculiarities of the case of each individual. It is easily seen that it requires peculiar interest in and fitness for the work to enable him to carry it on so successfully.

The diet of the patients of an insane hospital must, from the nature of the case, be much more varied in quality and quantity than in an ordinary hospital. I was shown one man, who, from disability or unwillingness to perform the act of deglutition, had been fed by a stomach-tube for weeks. Yet he was up and dressed, and looked in pretty good condition. Of course such a case would require great tact and a great variety of liquid aliment to keep him in tolerable health. Great care is necessary in mincing meat and vegetables to meet other cases. This is done by simple machinery, and the whole of the culinary arrangements evinced unusual care. The meats are of the best quality, and nicely prepared and appetizing. The allowance of meat is only three-fourths of a pound per man, with three fourths of a pint of excellent mild beer. A great deal of barley and rice is used.

The officers who are patients have, generally, a daily allowance of sound wine, (where it is not contra indicated,) not as a ration, but as a sort of standing prescription.

Indeed there seems to be no difficulty in obtaining anything that is thought necessary for health and comfort upon simple recommendation, the admiralty and medical director-general seeming to have this institution so much and so justly at heart.

The following schedules of the examinations of assistant surgeons on probation, held at the close of the sessions of 1869 and 1871, of the army medical school at Netley, evidence the high professional character of the course of instruction at this institution.

ARMY MEDICAL SCHOOL, NETLEY.

Eighteenth session, 1869.

WRITTEN EXAMINATION.   *(3 hours allowed for each subject.)*

I. PATHOLOGY.   *(Professor William Aitken, M. D.)*

Monday, 2d August, 1869.

1. The hydatid echinococcus cysts, the tape-worm (medio-canellata,) and the guinea-worm, being the most frequent of parasitic diseases among soldiers, give an account of the natural history of each and all the forms of these parasites, stating the sources of each, showing how they gain access to the human body as well as to the bodies of animals, and how they reach the sites in which they are severally found.

2. Give an account of the lesions in the aorta which seem to precede and to favor the development of thoracic aneurism.

3. Private Andrew Ballantine, one hundred and fourth regiment, aged 36, had completed $15\frac{10}{12}$ years of service, and was admitted to Netley from ship-board from India. He had been 100 days on the voyage. He was admitted on the 19th May, and died on the 12th of June, 1869. His service is as fol-

lows: July, 1854, to November, 1854, in England; from November, 1854, to June, 1856, at Gibraltar and in the Crimea; from June, 1856, to Feburary, 1858, in England; afterward in India. During his service in India he suffered from continued fever, from gonorrhœa and from diarrhœa. He was finally attacked by dysentery in January, 1868, and became so debilitated he was sent home as an invalid to Netley. He improved during the first part of the voyage home, but after passing the Cape he relapsed, and was landed in a condition of great exhaustion and emaciation. The discharges from the bowels, during his treatment at Netley, varied from five to ten motions daily. The pulse was weak, sometimes intermittent, and during the last fortnight of his life, ranged from 90 to 110. The motions, always loose, increased to eight or ten daily, of a brown color, emitting the characteristic dysenteric odor. They were passed without tenesmus. He died greatly emaciated and exhausted, the body-weight being only 76 pounds in a man of 69 inches height.

Describe the condition of the following parts:

1. Glands at base of tongue, and the tonsils.

2. Color and consistence of the mucous membrane of the small gut.

3. Color and condition of the several regions of the great gut, as to thickness, thinness, or ulceration.

4. Condition of solitary glands.

5. Condition of liver, especially as to capsule and substance.

Write a commentary on the case in relation, especially—

1st. To the post-mortem evidences of malaria.

2d. To the results of the dysenteric attack.

3d. As to the post-mortem appearances in the liver.

II. MILITARY HYGIENE. *(Dr. E. A. Parkes, F. R. S.)*
Tuesday, 3d August, 1869.

1. What are the points of importance in judging of the purity of water for drinking? What diseases are believed to arise from impure water, and what are the best methods of purification?

2. What is the standard of purity of air? What are the reasons for such a standard, and for expressing it in terms of carbonic acid?

3. What are the conditions of soil which have been supposed to be favorable to the development or prevalence of phthisis, typhoid fever and cholera? What are the conditions of soil supposed to have been instrumental in causing the late outbreak of fever at the Mauritius?

4. What are the chief physiological effects of exercise? What amount of exercise is demanded from the infantry soldier? What is the length of an ordinary march? What weight does the soldier carry in heavy marching order, and in what manner should the weight be disposed? What effects may result from ill-arranged accouterments and dress?

III. MILITARY SURGERY. *(Deputy Inspector-General T. Longmore.)* *4th August,* 1869.

Gunshot Wounds of Joints.

1. Describe the features which distinguish a gunshot wound of a joint from an incised or punctured wound of a joint.

2. Describe the surgical steps to be taken in field practice for the treatment of gunshot wounds, both uncomplicated and complicated wounds of the several joints named in the margin. Explain the motives which determine your decision in each case in which you consider the best treatment to be amputation, excision, or the adoption of conservative measures.

a. Shoulder-joint.
b. Elbow-joint.
c. Wrist-joint.
d. Hip-joint.
e. Knee-joint.
f. Ankle-joint.

(NOTE.—"Frame your replies respecting the several joints included in the question under distinct headings, and in the same order in which they have been placed in the annexed list.")

Optical examination of the eye.

1. Explain the principles on which the diagnosis of emmetropic, myopic, and hypermetropic vision by means of a convex lens is founded.

2. Describe the process by which the degree of myopia and hypermetropia may be determined by a convex lens. (NOTE.—"Write an example in illustration.")

3. What conditions determine the nearest, and what the most distant, points of distinct vision of an eye?

IV. MILITARY MEDICINE. *(Deputy Inspector-General W. C. Maclean.)   Wednesday, 5th August,* 1869.

1. Private A. B., —— regiment, ætat 35. Home service, 5 years; foreign service, 8 years; family history, good.

Present state: Is emaciated and has a listless and dispirited appearance; complexion muddy; eyes discolored and expressionless; lips bloodless.

Muscular system: Wasted, soft, flabby.

Respiratory system: Normal.

Circulating system: Heart's action feeble; a soft systolic murmur audible in cardiac region in the recumbent position, which cannot be heard when the patient stands.

Digestive system: Appetite impaired; digestion imperfect; prone to diarrhœa from slight causes; spleen and liver are enlarged; the former can be felt and seen to extend into the pelvis.

Urinary system: Urine contains albumen, but no tube casts.

The blood, when examined under the microscope, is deficient in red corpuscles. The patient, unless warmly clothed, finds it difficult to maintain his natural temperature, and is liable to attacks of ague, particularly in wet and cold weather.

Diagnose this case. Give an intelligent commentary on the symptoms and appearances, adding your prognosis, with reasons annexed, and lay down a rational plan of treatment.

2. Your attention having been called to pulmonary phthisis as a disease of armies, you are required to give—

    a. The causes which appear to operate in exciting this disease in military life, including the observed effects of climate, if any.

    b. The form of the disease usually met with in the army.

    c. The means of early diagnosis.

    d. General principles of rational treatment.

3. Describe, *a*, the different forms of insolation; *b*, the sequels of this affection; *c*, the treatment, including that of the most common of its sequels.

21 H

ARMY MEDICAL SCHOOL, ROYAL VICTORIA HOSPITAL, NETLEY.

Friday and Saturday, August 6 and 7, 1869.

PRACTICAL EXAMINATION.

1. MEDICINE, *(1 hour allowed.)*
2. SURGERY, *(1 hour allowed.)*

Division ———, *Ward No.* ———.

Make an examination of the case of ——— ———.

Twenty minutes allowed for the examination.   Written notes may be taken.

You are required to write concisely a history of the case, your diagnosis, prognosis, the probable effects of treatment, and the influence of the disease (or injury) on the man's fitness for service as a soldier.

Thirty minutes allowed for this description.

3. HYGIENE, *(3 hours allowed.)*
    1. Examination of the sample of water (1) before you.
        a.) Physical examination.
        b.) Qualitative examination.
        c.) Quantitative examination for chlorine, oxygen, total hardness.
        d.) Determine in sample (II) the total, permanent, and removable hardness.

c.) Determine in sample (III) (the distillate of ½ litre of water) the amount of free ammonia in grains per gallon.

2. Reading of barometer, with corrections.
Determination of dew point, amount of vapor, elastic force, etc., by Glaisher's tables.

3. Microscope : state the contents of packet.

4. PATHOLOGY.

1. Examine the portions of tissue placed in the dishes. State of what organ each is a part and describe its morbid condition,

2. Describe the lesions shown in the preparations numbered 1, 2. 3, 4.
State what parts are shown in the preparations.
Describe the lesion or lesions which are illustrated, and the probable stage of the disease to which it corresponds.

3. Determine the magnifying power of any one of the microscopes, and append the scale used.

4. Describe and name generally what you see in the fluid contained in the test-tubes, examined under the highest power.

5. Name each of the preparations placed under the microscopes on the table.

ARMY MEDICAL SCHOOL, NETLEY.

Examination held at the close of the twenty-second session.

I. MILITARY HYGIENE. *(Doctor E. A. Parkes, F. R. S.)*

Monday, July 31, 1871. (3 hours allowed.)

1. What is the usual length of marches; how much ground is got over per hour; what weight will the infantry soldier carry on active service; and what are the chief conditions during marches which may affect his health?

2. What are the chief diseases arising in camps, and what precautions would you take to keep camps healthy? What should be the amount and kind of food on active service?

3. Give a general statement of the sickness and mortality of the soldier in India, and state especially what steps you would take in anticipation of or during an attack of cholera.

4. Give a brief statement of the best known facts on the effect of a hot climate on natives of a temperate region.

II. MILITARY MEDICINE. *(Deputy Inspector-General W. C. Maclean, C. B.) Tuesday, August 1, 1871. (3 hours allowed.)*

1. Under what conditions are typhus and typhoid fever generated in camps? Give the symptoms of typhus under the following heads, and in the following order:

(*a*) Character of the chill.

(*b*) When prostration appears.

(*c*) Describe the exanthem; when it usually appears; the one which it most resembles; and the diagnostic signs.

(*d*) The head symptoms and usual condition of mental faculties throughout the disease.

(*e*) Chest symptoms.

(*f*) Abdominal symptoms.

(*g*) Urine.

(*h*) Temperature from first, and as usually observed throughout the disease.

(*i*) If case terminates favorably, when does the change usually appear, and in what manner?

(*k*) Describe the anatomical lesions, contrasting them with those of typhoid fever.

(*l*) The most common sequels of the disease.

(*m*) Give a summary of the most rational treatment.

2. 1. What is the probable source of danger from encamping on ground lately occupied by a body of men, among whom cholera has prevailed?

   2. What is the standing order to be observed when cholera appears in an epidemic form in barracks in India, and what is the object of this order?

   3. What is the object of frequent inspections of men when cholera prevails?

   4. Define exactly what you mean by the term "premonitory diarrhœa" in cholera.

   5. At what hour does cholera most usually attack?

   6. What is the difference between the temperature of the surface, and that in the rectum in the stage of collapse?

   7. What is the period of suppression of urine in very severe cases?

   8. What is the condition of the respiratory functions during collapse, and what the prognostic value of very rapid respiration?

   9. Describe the evacuations from the first setting in of the disease up to the time of convalescence.

  10. What is the prognostic value of bloody evacuations in this disease?

11. In what condition are the lungs usually found after death, as regards blood contents and weight? How does Doctor George Johnson explain this condition? State any reasonable objections that have been brought against the theory.

12. How should you treat premonitory diarrhœa?

13. What should be done with the evacuations of cholera patients?

14. What are the objections to the use of opium when the disease is established?

15. If urine is long suppressed after re-action appears, what would you do to aid nature in restoring the secretion?

III. MILITARY SURGERY. *(Deputy Inspector-General T. Longmore, C. B.) Wednesday, August 2, 1871. (3 hours allowed.)*

Question 1. Give an account of pyæmia as a complication of gunshot wounds in military hospitals, mentioning in your reply—

 a. The classes of wounds which appear to be most liable to the supervention of pyæmia and the probable explanation of this special liability;

 b. The train of symptoms by which it is usually ushered in, and accompanied to its termination;

 c. The circumstances in campaigning which favor its development;

 d. The means of prevention; and lastly,

 e. The treatment.

Question 2. A patient comes before you who is hypermetropic and presbyopic.

 A. Explain the nature of these visual conditions.

 B. Describe the steps by which you ascertain the amount of hypermetropia and presbyopia of the patient.

 C. Assume any degrees of hypermetropia and presbyopia you please and then calculate the focal powers of the lenses that will correct them.

Question 3. Describe the treatment of gunshot wounds of the head, dividing your reply under the treatment of—

    a. Contusions and wounds of the scalp.

    b. The same, together with contusion or fracture of the cranium, but without depression of bone.

    c. The same, but with depression of bone.

    d. Wounds with penetration of the cranium.

IV. PATHOLOGY. (*Professor William Aitken, M. D.*) *Thursday, August* 3, 1871. (3 *hours allowed.*)

Question 1. What is lardaceous disease? Describe the character of the lesion, anatomical and chemical. In what textures and organs, and in what parts of these organs, is the lesion found? How is the lesion to be recognized after death with and without the iodine test-solution? Give the composition of the iodine test-solution, and describe the conditions under which lardaceous disease is brought about.

Question 2. What do you understand by "hæmatoma?" In what form and in what part of the body has the lesion been shown to you? What is the nature, its usual site, and the circumstances under which it is to be developed?

Question 3. Sergeant Thomas Eyles, aged 33, after thirteen and a half years' service was admitted into Netley hospital from India, after a voyage of forty-six days. He had served in India five years, and two and a half years in Malta. He is reported to have suffered from gonorrhœa, 40 days; splenitis, 32 days; bronchitis, 20 days; orchitis, 12 days; diarrhœa, rheumatism, and hepatitis. The duration of illness before admission was 234 days, and was diagnosed as "ulceration of the stomach."

The points of striking character in the history of the case are-emaciation excessive; he could only lie on his back inclined to the left side, relieved by sitting up in bed and leaning forward. Breath of very fetid odor. Respiration easy, 20 per minute; lancinating pain in right side on deep inspiration; intense bad taste in the mouth; appetite gone; frequent inclination to vomit;

fixed pain immediately below ensiform cartilage, extending to the right side over hepatic region; abdomen sunken and tympanitic, and exquisitely tender on pressure. Symptoms were believed to indicate the stomach as the seat of disease; others pointed to the liver; and the detailed medical history sheet referred to,attacks of dysentery at Nusserabad.

Describe the morbid conditions of the liver, including its dimensions, and the relation of the lesions to the stomach, and also to the state of the intestines, the conditions of which are required to be described.

REPORTS

UPON THE

HOSPITALS, CHARITABLE INSTITUTIONS,

AND

PECULIAR DISEASES OF PERU.

BY

JOHN M. BROWNE, M. D.,

MEDICAL INSPECTOR, U. S. NAVY, FLEET-SURGEON PACIFIC STATION.

PERUVIAN HOSPITALS AND CHARITABLE INSTITUTIONS.

By the courtesy of Señor Don de la Barrera, director of the Sociedad de Beneficencia Publica, and under the immediate guidance of C. S. Rand, esq., whose attention cannot be too gratefully acknowledged, Passed-Assistant Surgeons Ver Meulen, Culbreth, Ayres, and myself, were permitted to inspect the hospitals and charitable institutions at Lima.

The Society of Beneficence has the administration of the hospitals, asylums, cemeteries, "caja de ahorros," or savings-bank, and the gratuitous schools at Lima; also, the administration of the various societies of cofradias or confraternities, the management of the land and house property of the institution, deriving its resources from the rents of said property and that of the confraternities, together with a percentage from the national lottery, government subsidies, private donations, inheritance, and intestate estates. The works actually perfected by the Beneficencia during the past year amounted to a sum exceeding $165,000,

Our inspection commenced at the *Hospital de San Andres*, the only civil hospital for men and boys in the city. Situated in a densely populated district, without architectural pretension, of one and two storied adobe buildings, inclosing a front and rear court, this hospital contains six hundred and fifteen beds, constantly occupied, and yet is insufficient for the requirement, yearly

increasing.   Wards of various sizes, insufficiently lighted and badly
ventilated; each dedicated to its patron saint, a large altar with
ornate appointments and surroundings being placed in a semi-
rotunda, from which diverge a few of the principal wards.   Floors
of asphaltum; roof of wood; painted high walls; windows small
and far removed from the floor; unsupplied with baths or water-
closets.   Bedsteads of iron; mattresses of wool; colored blankets;
cotton sheeting.   Every ward had too many. beds, and, in a few,
a greater defect was noticed in the presence of galleries filled with
beds; fortunately three wards have had their galleries removed,
refashioned, and have gained a better salubrity by increasing the
light and ventilation, but others yet remain.   One ward, say 130
feet long by 26 feet wide, deprived of lateral ventilation by its
construction between two others, had upon the floor and in the
galleries one hundred beds, an agglomeration that has too unhappily assisted in exposing a population in the time of its period-
ical infection.   Originally the hospital was constructed for three
hundred and fifty beds, but the continual increase in application
for admission caused other wards to be built whose sites en-
croached upon the garden, and to preserve it these galleries were
erected, and although the number treated at one time amounted
to over seven hundred, the demand continues and probably the
galleries will remain until the new hospital is completed.   The
hospital is in the immediate care of Sisters of Charity, certain of
them having the management of the kitchen, laundry, and linen-
room, and, as in Chili, the pharmaceutists of the establishment.   The dispensary and laboratory, kitchen, and laundry were
well equipped and in good order; general cleanness fair.   Drainage ought to be good, the city sewerage consisting of acequias
or streams of water, covered and uncovered, running through the
streets.   A large and tolerably well worked garden, supplied with
fruit and flowers, is in pleasant contrast to other surroundings,
and affords a purity of atmosphere not otherwise attainable.   The
interior court-yard contains the chapel; baptism, profession of
faith, and marriage being of frequent occurrence.   Among the
variety of diseases encountered the most common were phthisis,

dysentery, pneumonia, malarial and typhoid fever, hepatic disease, rheumatism, scrofula, and syphilis, with the effects of
accidents in the surgical department.

During the year 1871 there were subsisted 12,544 sick, at a
cost of nearly $85,000. Of these patients 11,049 were charity,
1,353 paying, and 142 prisoners, of whom 10,646 were discharged,
1,348 died, and 550 remained.

Next the *Hospital de Santa Ana*, devoted to the treatment
of women and girls, plain adobe buildings, of one and two stories
in height, originally of cruciform construction, now irregular by
additions from time to time, affording courts, and with a luxuriant
garden, comprises quite a tract, suitably inclosed. Four spacious
lofty walled wards, with fair ventilation and light, and several
smaller wards less high, poorly lighted, and deficient in ventilation. In the center, facing the entrance, the transepts being to
the right and left, is a large and elaborately decorated altar, bearing the statue of the holy patroness, whose rich vestments are
plentifully hung with silver, votive offerings, the grateful acknowl-
edgment of the faithful for benefits received. Asphaltum floors;
painted walls; wooden roof; windows near to and also in the
roof, and in some of the lesser wards skylights alone ventilate and
light. Bedsteads, cots, and cradles of iron, with frame supporting
and inclosed by white curtains, wool mattresses, white blankets
and bedspreads, cotton sheeting. Principal wards occupied by
women, others by children, and women who have given birth
while under treatment, the only condition upon which infants are
received. No water-closets seen; baths few and indifferent and
removed from the wards; five hundred beds. General appearance of the main wards attractive; cleanliness good. Chief diseases noted, phthisis, pneumonia, fevers, dysentery, chronic diarrhœa, cardiac disease, brain softening, and diseases peculiar to
women and children. The kitchen, laundry, and linen departments
were spacious and excellent, presided over by Sisters of Charity,
as also the dispensary and laboratory, large apartments thoroughly
and elegantly equipped.

To this hospital, under the charge of the sisters, is attached an asylum-school for orphaned girls. A new saloon, recently added, increases the number of girls from fifty, the original maximum number, to seventy. Instruction in the catechism, common branches, French language, sewing, embroidery, artificial flowers, washing, ironing, and cooking, constitute the moral, intellectual, and domestic education of these orphans, in a manner not to lose sight of their humble condition and the modest position they must assume in the world. In this hospital the administrative and economical service intrusted to the sisters is evidently performed with fidelity; alike the afflicted and the orphan receive their consoling and useful services.

There were subsisted in the Hospital de Santa Ana during the year 1771, 8,711 sick, at a cost of nearly $60,000, including the expenses of the internal school and maintenance of the girls. Of the patients 7,390 were women, 1,316 children, and 5 prisoners, of whom 7,637 were discharged, 739 died, and 335 remained.

In close vicinity is the *Hospital de San Bartolomé*, (military;) built of adobe, with a two-storied frontage of pleasing architecture; other buildings plain, of one or two stories, all arranged to inclose two quadrangles. Front and sides of first quadrangle afford apartments, simply furnished, for the officers of the institution and sick officers, there being for the latter twenty-six beds. Wards large and small, crowded with beds, five hundred and eighteen in number, badly lighted and worse ventilated, with roof of wood, painted walls, and floors of asphaltum, save in a new addition where wood is substituted. Usual altar and representation of the patron saint. Bedsteads of iron, mattresses of wool, colored blankets, cotton sheeting. Uncleanliness, vitiated air, gloominess—an unhappy and unattractive combination. The majority of the patients were suffering from phthisis, pneumonia, dysentery, diarrhœa, fevers, typhoid and malarious, syphilis, scrofula, rheumatism, and injuries. Kitchen, laundry, and linen-room, well supplied, well kept, spacious; dispensary and laboratory beautifully fitted, attractive and worthy of praise. The Sisters of Charity have immediate management.

For the year 1871 the cost of subsisting 10,329 sick amounted to $90,000. Of the patients 455 were officers, 9,874 soldiers, of whom 9,745 were discharged cured, (434 officers, 9,311 soldiers,) 156 died, (5 officers, 151 soldiers,) 8 soldiers deserted, and 420 remained, (16 officers, 404 soldiers.) The difference in favor of this hospital, respecting the mortality over the others, has explanation from the fact that in the latter the largest number of cases possess the greatest severity, while in the military hospital cases are admitted, however slight may be the indisposition, and frequently the applicant seeks only a rest from the hardships which enter into the life of the Peruvian soldiery, either real or assumed.

As the other active hospitals and asylums are of less importance than those described, and have neither in architecture or equipment a superiority, a brief mention of each will suffice.

Hospicio de Insanos, (insane asylum.)—During the year 1871, 363 insane were maintained at a cost of $29,000. Of these 195 were men, and 168 women; 90 were discharged, 28 died, and 245 remained.

Hospicio de Huérfanos Lactantes.—Orphan asylum for both sexes not exceeding seven years of age. Five hundred and five supported in 1871 at a cost of $32,000. Of these 219 were male, and 286 female, of whom 163 were discharged, 135 died, and 207 remained.

Hospicio de·Huérfanos de la Recoleta.—Orphan asylum for boys of all ages. One hundred and sixty-eight supported in 1871 at a cost exceeding $27,000, including expense of education in college; of these 19 were discharged, 11 died, and 138 remained.

Hospicio de Huérfanos de Santa Cruz.—Orphan asylum for girls over seven years of age. One hundred supported in 1871 at a cost of more than $15,000; of these 7 were discharged, 1 died, and 92 remained. A charity school is attached to this institution for poor girls of over seven years of age, and an asylum for children of both sexes from two and a half to seven years; also a dispensary. The school during 1871 had 250 girls who were taught the catechism, sacred history, grammar, reading, writing, arithmetic, politeness, sewing, weaving, embroidery, and other manual and domestic labors. To these girls a dinner is given every Saturday with alms that may be donated by the charitable. Gratuitous consultations are held three times a week in the dispensary, and visits made by three physicians, two paid by the Beneficencia, and one by the sisters, who assist with food, clothes, and bedding, the cost of which is defrayed by a monthly subscription, or other extraordinary resources.

Lazareto de la Inmaculada Concepcion.—This and other lazar houses were constructed on account of yellow fever. In 1871 1,105 sick were subsisted at a cost of $11,000; of these patients there were 1,017 men and 88 women, of whom 868 were discharged, 150 died, and 87 remained.

Asilo de Mendigos.—This asylum provided for 259 beggars during 1871, at an expense of $20,000, 148 men and 111 women, of whom 45 were discharged, 73 died, and 141 remained.

Hospicio y Colegio de Maternidad.—This lying in-asylum assisted 358 parturients in 1871, all being gratuitous, except one; 347 were discharged, 2 died, and 9 remained.

Hospicio de Santa Rosa ó Asilo Candamo.—This asylum, founded under the protection of the patroness of Lima, honored by the possession of the picture that adorned the old chapel of the university, was opened in December, 1871, having been erected by the Beneficencia, agreeably to the provisions of the bequest of Mr. Candamo. It furnishes a home to 50 girls, orphans, or the unfortunates, under the direction of the sisters, and is said to be a true school of domestic arts for the girls of the people.

General cemetery.—Number of burials in niches 3,115 males, 1,820 females, exposed 759, giving a total of 5,694 for the year 1871.

Civil cemetery.—The necessity of a cemetery for depositing the remains of persons not professing the Catholic religion was generally recognized as a consequence of the epidemics from which, of late years, Lima has suffered. The Beneficencia made the government aware of this public necessity, and from it received authority in 1869 to construct and administer a civil cemetery. Purchasing a piece of ground, the preparatory works, at an expenditure of $8,000, are already terminated. Estimates for the future works, including a chapel, amount to $20,000, and the plans and designs indicate beauty of architecture and solidity. It is to be desired that the same may have completion at an early day, thus satisfying one of the most indispensable requirements of a population that already numbers so many foreigners.

Hospital "Dos de Mayo," (*2d of May.*)—The urgent necessity of a large hospital, constructed after the most approved modern plans, has long been acknowledged by the Beneficencia, not alone from the fact that the existing hospital accommodation is entirely too inadequate for the requirements of an increasing city, but that in a square, a little more than 300 yards long by 200 broad, are situated the principal market of the city, and three hospitals that in the autumn and spring contain ordinarily, in ill-ventilated wards, 1,600 to 1,700 sick. With such incentives the Beneficencia authorized the first preparatory expenditure for the erection of a superior and extensive hospital, in July, 1868, and to November, 1871, had expended thereon the sum of $300,000. The solidity of the work accomplished corresponds to the importance of the establishment. This extensive edifice is of one story, save at the corners of the *façade*, which are to be ornamented by domes, and the chapel rising from the center, which is two stories in elevation, with superimposed dome, supported by pillars and surmounted by a second dome bearing a cross, the entire architecture being elaborate and effective. Lower foundations of stone, upper of brick, and walls of adobes. As the walls are ready for the roof, an examination, assisted by the architect's plans, enabled a nearly correct idea to be formed as to its future appearance—a square, walled by a building that has 600 feet frontage on either side, within which are separate buildings for wards, etc. This building-inclosure is divided into a large number of apartments of different

22 H

lengths, but of the invariable width of 23 feet, (except the corner circular rooms,) and are to be used for the dead-room, anatomical amphitheater, operating, convalescents', dining, servants', sleeping, and dining rooms, general kitchen and dependency, laundry, ironing and drying rooms, coal, provision, and other store rooms, and cisterns. The principal and two carriage entrances give admission to the first *patio*, which will be beautified by floral gardens. Around the *patio* are rooms of the porter and guard, sleeping and drawing rooms of paying patients, reception-room, office and book-keeper's room. A covered corridor connects the first with the principal *patio*, and gives communication to five rooms for the medical officers, four for chaplains, four for the superintendent, and three for depositing-rooms, (clothes of patients on admission.) The principal *patio* in center of the inclosure is quite large, octagonal in shape, and has the chapel in its center, surrounded by gardens and walks. Radiating from this *patio*, and connected with it by roofed corridors, are six buildings, the future wards. Two of these buildings are 198 feet long by 72 feet wide, (wards 192 by 27,) two 185 feet by 72, (wards 180 by 27,) and two 142 by 72, (wards 137 by 27.) Each building is divided longitudinally into two wards, of which six are for surgical and six for medical purposes. Each ward at the end farthest removed from the *patio* has two nurses' rooms, (sisters,) and communicates by roofed corridors with two rooms for ward service, and water-closets, urinals, and discharge-receptacles, which have outlet in the *acequias* or drains of running water. At the extremity of two buildings only are bath-rooms, eleven baths in each. Between these divergent buildings, indeed in every part of the inclosure not built upon, will be flower-gardens, arbors, and walks, and a side door from every ward opens directly upon one of these gardens. To the rear of the chapel, and connected by the covered corridor to the octagonal *patio*, is the dispensary, laboratory, library, and parlor, and to the rear of these a square with center garden, surrounded by the dormitories, parlor, chapel, dining-room, washing-room, kitchen, laundry, infirmary, linen-room, baths, and water-closets appertaining to the department of the Sisters of Charity. A plaza in front will contribute to the salubrity and beauty of the establishment. The chief objection to be raised is in the arrangement of the wards; having adopted only in part the pavilion plan, the division by a partition lessens the light and ventilation otherwise afforded. Again, the ventilation will be somewhat interfered with by the inclosure-building, which, however, appears essential in view of the site and surroundings. A greater number of baths, supplying each ward and private apartment, would be an improvement; yet in general plan and arrangement it is so vastly superior to the hospitals described, that it seems entitled to a liberal approbation. According to the estimate of the architect the sum of $272,000 will be required for its completion, which might occur at the end of the present year if the necessary funds are available.

The only public hospital at Callao is called the *Guadalúpe*, being under the administration of the Beneficencia of this city. Located at the northern extreme of Callao, and at the corresponding terminus of the Alameda, about three-quarters of a mile from the landing at the *múelle*, its general plan is quadrangular, being divided into two unequal parts by a transverse building, thereby forming two *patios*, the anterior incomplete on the side facing the street, inclosed partly by a wall and fine iron fence which occupies the center of the barrier, and is handsome in design and workmanship. Entering the gate one is admitted into a paved court about 100 feet square, two-thirds of which, inclosed by a neat iron fence, is cultivated as a garden, bearing a choice variety of plants, arranged in beds regular and fanciful in figure, and having in the center a fountain playing over iron-work of appropriate design. The court is surrounded on three sides by a corridor wide and spacious, with a wooden floor raised two feet above the ground, from which convenient communication is had to the several offices of the institution; appearance pleasing and satisfactory. Passing through a wide door in the center of the transverse building the inner *patio* is reached, around which

the wards are arranged. Largest wards 100 feet long by 50 wide;
high ceilings; asphaltum floors; lighted by side windows and skylights; deficient in ventilation. Through the middle of each ward
runs an incomplete partition, ten feet high, continuous with the
length of the apartment, except where openings exist, to facilitate
the passing from one division to the other. Each ward contains
about fifty beds closely approximated. Bedsteads of iron, with
frames to support curtains or netting; wool mattresses, *scarlet*
blankets, cotton sheeting. A small, badly-located room contains
a few ordinary bath-tubs, inadequate for the establishment. No
water-closets or discharge-receptacles noticed; general want of
cleanness. One ward is appropriated to females, and was half
filled at the time of inspection. The diseases observed were
usually the result of mal-nutrition, asthenic and pectoral diseases
predominating. There was no apparent classification or arrangement of the patients according to disease, save the surgical cases,
which were in a separate ward. The kitchen is an adjacent and
spacious building, adjoining a butchers' department, and has a
common range and abundance of copper utensils; laundry, of
good size, and efficient; dispensary, rather small, but handsomely
and generously equipped; laboratory, small, clean, neat, and well
furnished with vessels of metal and porcelain. The medicines
are compounded, dispensed, and many of them made by one of
the most intelligent of the sisters, who daily makes up an average
of one hundred prescriptions. The pharmaceutical department
is the most satisfactory of the entire establishment. An operating-
room, lighted from the roof, had a good, adjustable table of modern pattern; instruments not examined.

At a short distance to the rear of the main edifice are two one-
story buildings, each about 100 feet along by 30 wide, reserved
for contagious and infectious diseases, at present unoccupied.
These quarantine-houses present nothing of import, either in construction or arrangement.

The Guadalúpe Hospital has been in operation six years; has
four medical officers; serves alike for civil and military purposes;

can accommodate 450 sick, average number being 300; is immediately directed by twelve Sisters of Charity, principally French. In plan and general arrangement the hospital is efficient, and is susceptible of being well ventilated. Considering the actual closeness, and in some of the wards the existence of offensive odors, it is singular that so emphatic a defect should not have a prompt removal. As before remarked there is a want of proper cleanness, chiefly observable in the condition of the floors, bedding, and curtains, reminding one of the military hospital at Lima. Another defect, partaken of by the other hospitals, is that too many patients are bedded in the same ward, and in the present instance this overcrowding would seem to have no explanation, unless it be for the convenience of the attendants. Again, the partitions through the wards are objectionable, and their presumed utility is not manifest. These views are sustained in a letter received from Passed Assistant Surgeon Ver Meulen, stationed at Callao, who has made a thorough inspection of the hospital, and to whom I am indebted for detailed information.

Attached to, but independent of the hospital, respecting access, is a girls' school under the care and tuition of two of the sisters. Two large school-rooms, airy, clean, and well furnished. The school-books have inscribed the names of 400 scholars, of age ranging from four to fifteen years. They are taught the essential elements for a common education, domestic and manual labor. Daily attendance very irregular, not averaging more than one hundred.

In the cemetery at Callao there were buried during the year 1871—

In nitches, perpetually 82
In nitches, temporarily 366
In graves 1,122

Total.. 1,570

Men 755
Women... 264
Children, male... 303
Children, female 248

Total.. 1, 570

Deaths resulted in the majority of cases from fevers, phthisis, pneumonia, dysentery, dropsy, variola, dentition, wounds, scorbutus, bronchitis, and apoplexy.

During the visit of the flag-ship at Callao, Passed-Assistant Surgeons Culbreth, Ayres, and myself passed over the built portion of the Callao, Lima, and Oroya railroad as the guests of Mr. Cilley, its superintendent. This road, being constructed by Mr. Henry Meiggs for the Peruvian government, will cross the Andes at an elevation of 16,200 feet, with a summit tunnel 3,000 feet in length, and will terminate at Oroya, the head-waters of one of tributaries of the Amazon, distant about one hundred and thirty miles from Callao.

Proceeding by rail for a distance of forty-seven miles along the left bank of the Rimac River, we reached San Bartolomé, the present terminus, and from thence by horse a few miles farther on, we witnessed the wonderful engineering that builds a railway along heights heretofore considered inaccessible. This visit enabled an inspection of one of the hospitals of the company, and gave introduction to two remarkable diseases peculiar to the district and comparatively unknown to the profession, an account of which is the purpose of this communication.

Verrugas, meaning warts, is a disease strictly limited in its locality, and unobserved until the present, except in Peru. Its district extends from latitude 6° south to 15° south, at an altitude of from 4,000 to 7,000 feet in the Andean valleys situated on the sea-side, while goiter appertains to the valleys of the eastern declivity, on the side of the Amazon, as at Huánuco. In the valley of the Rimac River the disease prevails for a distance of twenty-two miles, including the beautiful but unhappy *quebrada* or ravine of Verrugas, sparse in vegetation, picturesque in scenery, rich in cascades, whose pure and deliciously cool waters have ever had the popular reputation of being the cause of the singular and and extraordinary disease that gave its name to the *quebrada*.

The verrugas existed in the time of the Incas, and is probably the disorder that attacked certain of the Spanish invaders as mentioned by Prescott in the "Conquest of Peru." Tschudi mentions it in his memoir of travels, and is said to have furnished a monograph for a German medical journal. It is alluded to by Dunglison. Dr. Fasset, a physician at Lima, gave an account of the disease in a newspaper of that city. Excepting the above, I am not advised that any description has appeared in medical literature.

The verrugas attacks the native and stranger alike, respects neither age, sex, nor condition, is uninfluenced by season, and occurs but once. It would be interesting to know if it would be susceptible to return again to the person who may have lost the benefit of acclimation. Mr. Cilley thinks he has found this disease in the mule and dog.

The Indians attribute the malady to the drinking of the water of certain springs in the infected localities, some of which are supposed to be more powerful for its production than others. This belief is entertained by a majority of the natives, but is discarded by the foreigner, since an analysis of the water shows its remarkable purity, and many who have not drank the water have had the disease in its worst form, while others who have partaken of it freely and for a long period, remain unaffected. The supposition that it may be occasioned by the action of certain metals, especially antimony, is equally untenable. Is it due simply to the miasms that produce the simple intermittent and typho-malarial fevers of these valleys? Dr. Fasset regards the affection as a particular form of scurvy, which replaces the petechial spots of the fevers of the Oroya, and considers the circumstance to be not indifferent for the reason that it appears to weaken the gravity of the latter disease. As the malignant fevers of the Oroya seem to have had origin by the breaking of the ground for railroad purposes, their connection with the verrugas, a disease as old as the history of the country, is not apparent. It seems to be independent of the local fevers, for it is manifested without them. It is inexplicable why it exists only in Peru, and is confined to the declivity of the Andes directed toward the sea, while goiter is limited to the declivity situated on the side of the Amazon.

The period of incubation is from three weeks to one year; duration, from a few weeks to one or two years. I saw a little girl three years old who remained two days only in Verrugas quebrada, then returned to Lima, when the disease made its appearance three weeks after, and though mild in its progress was emphatic in type. A gentleman in Callao informed me that his brother passed one day in Verrugas quebrada, leaving the place at sunset, and the disease developed itself five months subsequently. All cases that have appeared in Lima or Callao, were persons who exposed themselves in the habitat of the disease. It is not contagious, is very dangerous, and requires the greatest precautions. The disease commences with a decided febrile attack, often mistaken for the access of the local intermittent, and in every case the paroxysm is accompanied by osteocope, or rheumatic pains. This fever may be present every day for weeks, but disappears at the period of eruption; until then the pains and swellings of the bones, and fibrous and muscular systems exist with greater or less persistency in any part of the body, shifting in character, and worse at night. When the eruption does not immediately follow the disappearance of the fever, the pains, often attended with spasmodic contractions of the fingers and toes, may continue for months, with, in other respects, ordinary health, suffering at night, with a sense of stiffness and soreness in the muscles during the day, when comparative comfort is present. The advent of the eruption is watched for with great interest, as there is an impression, by no means confined to the illiterate, that the life of the individual may depend on its appearance ; its arrival, therefore, is a subject of social congratulation. It is thought it the growths do not appear on the surface they may develop in any of the internal organs, preferably the lungs, in which case suffocation is induced by the hemorrhage occasioned.

Succeeding this indefinite period of fever, or its absence, follows the eruptive stage. The eruption consists of little isolated points, purplish red, usually acuminated, which delay not in becoming red vesicles or tubercular fungoid growths of all dimensions, from the size of a pea to that of a medium-sized orange. They invade any portion of the surface, having preference for the head, face, and extremities, especially the palms and soles, also the eye, nose, and ear, and apparently affect the entire thickness of the skin. These growths are soft, vascular, and at first have a uniform surface, but ultimately a scab forms here and there, the covering becomes attenuated, and the slightest friction excoriates, and veritable hemorrhages occur. If vesicular, the ordinary hand-shaking ruptures the vesicles, and bleeding ensues. They are not painful, may remain for months, and frequently shrink and slough off, leaving a very slight scar, save in persons of a strumous or depraved habit, when ulcers are left. Removed by the knife or scissors the bleeding may be excessive or moderate. Invading the lungs, intestines, or other internal organs, equivocal symptoms result, which prognosticate a fatal termination. It sometimes manifests itself under the skin, in which case the touch reveals small flattened tumors. At other times are observed little, roundish, oblong bodies having the appearance of hypertrophied sebaceous glands, which can be detached from the skin, and then have resemblance to grains of boiled pearl barley.

I was informed that an examination of the blood and eruptive growth of a verrugas patient with the microscope revealed nothing special or original.

Ordinarily the treatment is purely empirical, consisting of a tonic and stimulating regimen, as concentrated decoctions of roasted maize, wine, beer, coffee, and tea. The Indians, reputed as very successful in the treatment, promote perspiration for fifteen days by means of vapor-baths in the intent to bring out the eruption, and, when established, danger ceases and recovery ensues. During these fifteen days the patients are supported by copious draughts of roasted corn coffee and sweet wine. With the profession the fever is treated by diaphoretics, warm baths, and quinine, in the constant endeavor to hasten the eruption. In the absence of fever, the iodide of potassium, with the infusion of gentian, is employed for the mitigation of pain and to induce eruption; tonics and stimulants in the eruptive stage. The growths are removed by ligature, the application of caustics, or with better result by the knife or scissors. The hemorrhage is always controlled by the liquid persulphate of iron.

By present mail I forward a package containing a verrugas growth taken from the temple of a boy nine years of age. The specimen was presented by Doctor Arias, surgeon in charge of Esperanza Hospital.

In my communication No. 20 I noticed a disease, popularly termed the "*Verrugas*," limited to certain districts and altitudes of Peru, and which, though existing in the period of the Incas, had only been made prominent by the construction of the Callao, Lima, and Oroya Railroad through one of said districts.

The building of this railway, in a portion of its course, has most unhappily been attended by the prevalence of a pestilential fever, direful in effect, which seems to have had creation by some act incident to the construction of the road, as it has been confined to the line of grading, and had no previous existence, and, as an indication of its origin, is commonly called the "Oroya fever." Commencing at La Chosica, 33 miles from Callao, at an elevation of 2,800 feet, its locality extends along the course of the road through the valley of the Rimac River, for about 22 miles, to the elevation of 6,500 feet. In the same locality prevail the verrugas and simple intermittent fevers, diseases sufficiently distinctive in symptoms and type from the one under notice to discredit the theory of a common origin.

Dr. Fasset, of Lima, in an article written for one of the newspapers of that city, is of the opinion that the so-called "Oroya fever" is but an aggravated form of the pernicious paludal intermittent fever that is common to marshy localities, or where rice is cultivated, and particularly in the deep, hot, and humid valleys of the Sierra. He considers this paludal fever to result equally from an alliance with what he terms the "atmospheric intermittent element" with the "toxical miasmatic principle" of the marshes, and that in the localities where it reigns yellow and typhus fevers never have existed, and cannot. He says: "This principle (the cause of pernicious paludal intermittent fever) not being contagious, they are forcibly banished to their marshy localities, and exclude entirely from their latitudes yellow fever and typhus, and do not undergo any other metamorphosis than that of masked fevers." Certain it is that the atmosphere circulates badly in the humid gorges of the Sierra, impregnating itself easily with the marshy miasms proceeding from the decomposition of a scanty vegetation, under the influence of solar heat during the day, while the cold commences as soon as the sun disappears behind the mountains and permits vapors to condense in these valleys, a circumstance which cannot make otherwise than a perceptible impression upon their inhabitants, and predisposes to fever. The work upon the road in many places, by the ground being broken up, has occasioned the emanation of a fetid odor, more offensive than that of sulphureted hydrogen. It may be that this telluric miasm, acting upon a system previously impressed with the miasma of the ordinary intermittent, may develop a highly malignant fever.

This fever attacks by preference the whites, the mongrel, and especially foreigners. Acclimated persons offer a moderate resistance, but negroes, Chinese, and Indians are most exempt, although the latter are peculiarly liable to yellow fever. It subjects to a second attack, does not preserve from yellow fever, nor does the latter grant immunity from it. Happily it is limited to its region, for its toxical principle, being non-contagious, is not ambulant. It is sufficient only to remove to a short distance to be withdrawn from its influence. Departing from Lima, the railroad follows the left bank of the Rimac, and until it reaches La Chosica the workmen are only subject to the simple intermittent; from thence, where the verrugas waters commence, they are exposed to this pestilential fever up to the point where begins the cold climate of the Sierra.

The "Oroya fever" is inconsistent in symptoms, no single case, or even a majority of cases, being typical. As it differently presents itself it assumes the character of typhus, pernicious remittent, and yellow fevers. It intermits, or may be continuous. In a conversation with Doctors Crow and Ward, in the service of the railroad company, I learned that each case was peculiar, being no guide for that which might follow. They very frankly confessed that the disease so readily assumed a variety of form, was so varied in its attack, intensity, duration, and so uninfluenced, or but slightly benefited, by any treatment thus far employed, that it was a mystery, save its lamentable frequence and fearful destruction. These gentlemen regard the disease as a typho-malarial fever, which opinion appears correct, judging from the cases presented for observation.

Death may occur in 24 hours from the attack, though the duration of the disease usually is several days, and in some cases prolonged into weeks. Doctor Rush, an American physician in the company's service, died in thirty-six hours from the first invasion, apparently in ordinary health until the moment of the attack. In certain cases a slight attack is followed by a seeming convalescence, the patient goes out, a relapse ensues, and he dies suddenly. It is the rival of yellow fever, equally formidable, and, though differing in many of the symptoms, the result is nearly the same. It has been observed that, if the access belongs to the quotidian type, it is favorable if it delays, and, on the contrary, it is unfavorable if it anticipates when of the tertian variety.

In the commencement the symptoms are usually the same. Intense cold, accompanied by severe pain in the head, loins, and limbs, succeeded by febrile movement, varying in intensity, with continuance of headache, pain in loins, etc. This stage is followed by an intermission, remission, or the severity of the fever may subside into a feverish condition which has continuance, or the paroxysm may be succeeded by copious sweats, affording no exemption from other paroxysms. The intermissions and remissions are exceedingly regular, or after a single one the fever may become continuous. Prostration, relaxation of the muscles, and anæmia are often sudden, and followed by aphony.

Early in the fever nausea and vomiting usually occur, the matter at first being yellowish and greenish in color, then brown, then resembling coffee-grounds, and finally melanic. There are severe pains in the region of the spleen, liver, and stomach; no tympanites when unattended with peritonitis, but contraction of the abdominal walls toward dorsal spine, in some cases iliac tenderness, with absence of gurgling sound. The bowels are generally constipated, therein differing from the grave cases of the pernicious paludal intermittent of the country, when diarrhœa, often bloody, supervenes. Intelligence may be good or a maniacal delirium at the outset. Petechial spots occasionally found, urine brown, as in yellow fever, but not often suppressed, except with peritoneal complication. Tongue presents a gray coating or greenish yellow at first, but becomes red and raspatory. Sordes not frequent, gums bloody, breath tainted. The blood seems deprived of hematosin and globules. The patients take an icteric tint like that of yellow fever.

As the disease progresses the ataxic symptoms denoting the typhoid state are more evident, viz, low delirium, sordes, subsultus tendinum, etc. The comatose or convulsive state frequently happens, and the last condition appears to be less dreaded, however violent it may be, than the first, except a nervous trembling of the limbs and tongue, a bad augury.

I was unable to obtain any satisfactory information as to the morbid appearance after death, post-mortem examinations having been very rarely performed. Doctor Fasset asserts, however, that the pathological alterations produced by yellow fever are perhaps surpassed by the pernicious paludal intermittent fever, of which he regards the "Oroya fever" as a variety. He states that these alterations are constant in the spleen; that the liver experiences as often alterations in its mass as in its consistence, and even in its adherences to the peritoneum; that the lungs are frequently altered; that the muscular system is very relaxed, and that the heart presents the aspect of a soft or flabby mass.   It would certainly be interesting to know if the abdominal lesions are essentially those characteristic of typhoid fever, or approach them in any degree.

The obscurity attending this fever has naturally occasioned the employment of nearly every remedial measure in its treatment; unfortunately, with few exceptions, no marked benefit has been derived.   In the incipiency the hot bath and a mercurial cathartic are often resorted to, and subsequently the greatest reliance is placed on quinine, turpentine, and the mineral acids with spirits.

I regret that my visit to the infected district was, of necessity, very brief, and as a consequence the observations on the verrugas and Oroya fevers are imperfect and unsatisfactory.   I trust that one or more of the medical officers attached to the south squadron of this fleet may have the opportunity and inclination to thoroughly investigate these extraordinary diseases, and that they may be pleased to communicate the result of such inquiry to the Bureau.

EXPERIMENTS AND OBSERVATIONS IN NAVAL HYGIENE.

BY

E. D. PAYNE, M. D.,

SURGEON, U. S. NAVY.

23 H

While at sea, with a clear sky and gentle breeze, the thermometer marking 73° F. in the shade and 81° F. in the sun, I made the following experiments :

I had one of the men put on an ordinary blue cloth mustering-cap, beneath which, on his head, I placed a small thermometer and had him walk up and down the deck in the sun for ten minutes. At the end of that time, the thermometer marked 104° F. I then had him put a white linen cover over the cap and again walk for ten minutes in the sun. The thermometer again marked 104 F. Previous to this, I asked one of the most intelligent men on board if he thought such covers afforded any protection from the heat or added in any way to comfort. He said he thought the cap much more comfortable with the cover on than off, for use in hot weather, and it kept the head cooler.

From the above experiment it would appear that the white linen cover over the cap in reality affords no protection, and the comfort derived from it is simply one of imagination. If the cap was made of white duck, and no cloth interposed between it and the head, the difference in the temperature would be great and the comfort real, as I will show below.

On the same day and under the same conditions, I made the following experiment: I took a Navy cap for officers which had eyelet-holes pierced through the top, put the glazed cover over it, and walked for ten minutes in the sun. At the end of that time the thermometer under the cap marked 104° F. I then tried it for ten minutes without the cover, and the temperature was 93°

F.   Finally I put on a white-duck cap of about the same pattern as the cloth one, and again walked for ten minutes in the sun. At the end of that time the temperature was 83° F.

From this experiment it would appear, first, that the glazed cover should not be worn except for protection against storms; second, in comparing a cap with an air-chamber and having holes for ventilation with one (as the ordinary cap for sailors) which sits close to the head and has no ventilation, the difference in temperature is in favor of the former by 11° F.   Third, in comparing a cap made of white duck and having an air-chamber, with a cloth one which sits close on the head (as the sailors) and is covered with white linen, the difference is in favor of the former by 21° F.   From which it would appear that caps should be made of white duck for warm weather, and that blue caps with white covers, as a substitute, should be discarded.

I regard the cap at present worn by sailors in the Navy as altogether objectionable.   A rim, about one and a half inches wide, fits the top of the head, immediately surmounting which is a disk of cloth, about ten inches across.   There is no air-chamber to keep the head cool, and the cap is heavy.   It does not extend far enough over the forehead to afford protection, and no peak protects the eyes; neither does it extend far enough down the head behind to give any protection.   In fact, it gives no protection to the head, except to a small circular space on top.   As a matter of comfort, it has none; and as one of convenience, it is so easily blown off by the wind, and so often knocked off to go overboard when aloft, that it might almost be pronounced a nuisance.   A much better cap was some time ago served out, made of felt.   It clasped the head better, came farther down on the brow and behind, and had quite a large air-chamber.   But it was disliked by the men, because, they said, it irritated the skin and wore the hair off the top of the head.   This objection might hold as against the material of which it was made, but would not affect its shape.

If a cap could be made somewhat on the plan of what is

known as the Scotch traveling-cap, pointing down over the fore-head and over the back of the head, and large enough in the top to afford a good air-chamber, with holes pierced through the top, and made of good material, I think it would be a great improvement on the one now in use. One of white duck should be made for hot weather. I think the duck, if of good quality, would have sufficient stiffness to retain its shape, and would not allow the transmission of the sun's rays—qualities not obtained if the cap be made of linen. Or a frame could be made of heavy duck or very light canvas, and over this could be worn a linen cover as at present over the blue cap, which would permit a change, and give an opportunity for always having a clean, white cap.

I suppose it would be a difficult matter to reform even the present opinion of the men on the general style of their caps, and the introduction of a peak to the cap would be scouted both by officers and men; yet it is none the less true that men, who are exposed to all kinds of weather as much as sailors are, should have their heads protected from both sun and storm, and their eyes properly guarded, and that a ventilated chamber to the cap would be a great comfort.

I have also objections to the cap now in use for officers. The peak is not large enough nor of the right shape to protect the eyes; the air-chamber is not large enough for comfort, (especially when made, as many are, smaller than the regulation pattern;) and it does not come far enough down on the back of the head to protect it from the wind and rains. If an officer wears a cap which sits just on the top of the head, and deprives that portion of his head of its natural covering by having the hair cut short, (which is frequently done,) the result in cold and wet weather must be rheumatism of the scalp, or general catarrh from this exposure, for I think there is no part of the body more sensitive to undue exposure, nor one with which the general system more readily sympathizes, than the back part of the head and neck. A cap so stiff and cumbersome as the regulation one, having for its recommendation neither elegance of form nor comfort to the wearer, is hardly the one for the Navy.

Believing that the Government intends that the shoes furnished to enlisted men in the Navy shall be of good quality, and also believing that the regulation shoe does not fulfill that intention, on the 30th day of March, 1871, I drew from the paymaster's stores of the United States ship Jamestown a pair of what are called calf-skin shoes, of the style known as Oxford ties. The fronts were made of calf-skin; the quarters of split-leather; the quarters and the sides of the fronts were lined with deacon-skin; the soles were one-fourth of an inch in thickness, including the welt, and fastened by stitches five and a half to the inch, rising above the sole of the shoe.

I put on the shoes and wore them on the open, wet deck after a rain, trying to avoid places where the water of the deck would rise above the upper edge of the soles, that I might ascertain how long it would require to wet my feet by absorption of moisture through the soles and stitches. In half an hour my feet were wet.

I then ripped the sole from the shoe and cut it open in several places, that I might see to what extent it had become affected by the water. It was soaked through, and I could wring water out of it by twisting it between my fingers. The filling between the inner and outer sole was also saturated, and the insole was wet for some distance beside the seams.

The inner surface of the piece of leather which formed the outer sole had not been shaved or scraped, but presented the original roughness of the leather, and the leather had been neither pounded nor rolled, aside from what it originally received to convert it into sole leather, to give it hardness and durability. Between the inner and outer sole was filling, representing a little more than a quarter of an inch in thickness, a trifle more than that of the outer sole and welt combined. Its first appearance was that of leather, but on closer inspection it tore up like pasteboard, and had a large quantity of fine straw mixed with it. I soaked it in water, and reduced it to a pulp. It then appeared to be a mixture of leather chips ground fine, with straw-paper pulp, and glue, mucilage, or other adhesive material. I suppose a mixture of this kind is first prepared, and before it hardens is rolled into boards, from which is cut the insoles for these shoes.

In the above description I believe I have given one of a fair sample of shoes of that description known as calf-skin shoes served out in the Navy. The facts stated were witnessed by Commander B. Gherardi, Lieutenant-Commander C. S. Huntington, Lieutenant Asa Walker, and Paymaster G. R. Watkins.

I believe that such shoes answer neither the ends of comfort, durability, nor economy, and that a shoe which, in its construction, would cost a trifle more to the man, would be found much cheaper for him.

In the construction of such a shoe the uppers, fronts, and quarters should be made of calf-skin, and lined with deacon-skin. Before the outer sole is put on, the leather for it should be first pounded or rolled, after the rough surface is first shaved off, in order to harden it, thereby rendering it less easily soaked by water, and making it much more durable, and the stitches by which it is attached to the uppers should be counter-sunk, to prevent being worn off and allowing the sole to spring from its place, and should not be less than six and a half to the inch. The filling, which in reality acts as an inner sole, should be made of leather instead of chips or paste-board.

The supply of under-clothing for enlisted men in the Navy, as regards suitableness and quality, is a subject which I believe worthy of consideration. I also believe that some change from the universal issue of the quality now in use would be of benefit.

During the late cruise of the Jamestown, in the Pacific, I had good opportunities for testing the value of such considerations, and my frequent observation was that a large percentage of the men who applied for admission to the sick-list were either without proper under-clothing or neglected to wear it. Their neglect was usually the result of dislike to the heavy articles served out during such periods of our cruise as were passed in the tropics. To such an extent was this dislike put in practice, by neglecting to wear such garments, that I made requests to have the men examined at morning quarters, thereby trying to detect the neglectful and force them to their use. This measure had the desired effect; and a good opportunity for comparing it with the one of allowing the men to follow their own inclinations was found at Panama, in March, 1871. At that time we were in company with a ship whose crew was but a little more in numbers than our own, and, while our sick-list was only from six to ten, hers was soon above thirty. The explanation was simple: our men wore under-clothing, and no special care was exercised to compel the men of the other ship to do so. And it is not surprising that when men are worked during the day, in such a climate as exists at that place, that they perspire profusely, and on every opportunity throw themselves down for rest in the coolest spot they can find; neither is it surprising that when men are allowed to lie down on the deck, with no under-shirt on, and the outer one freely thrown open, with a smart breeze coming under the awning-apron, (as I have witnessed,) that thirty men, out of a crew of about two hundred, should soon be down with fever.

So nearly as I could ascertain, the men do not make so much objection to wearing under-garments as they do wearing, in warm climates, that which is issued. Men frequently made application for permission to buy lighter articles on shore, and often took the responsibility of so doing, and run the risk of punishment, rather than be forced to wear the heavy articles they would otherwise be compelled to.

Those which are served out are, I believe, all of one quality, and made of heavy, dark-blue material, and there is no change provided for or contemplated in passing from cold to hot climates. The texture is entirely too heavy for hot weather, and it is rendered still warmer by the dark-blue color. The color is further objectionable from the fact that it allows the garment to be worn to the condition of filthiness before washing, without being specially noticed. I think the color is objectionable for this reason alone, if no other. The very fact that a lighter color readily shows dirt is a reason in favor of its adoption rather than against it, because it would then be washed when it became dirty.

The quality which is now in use seems all that could be desired for cold climates, but I believe it would be a great advantage to have its place supplied, for use in warm climates, by a quality which would be both lighter in texture and lighter in color. Then the men would be found to wear it more regularly, and would at all times be protected from sudden changes of temperature.

It is objected that uniformity could not be preserved, and that the men would be careless in their changes, and really suffer more than they do at present, and that it would be excessively inconvenient to supply two different articles of clothing for the same purpose. But I do not think these objections tenable. There could scarcely be less uniformity than at present exists, when some wear the regulation shirt, some white ones bought on shore, and some none at all; and the same care which would be requisite to keep under-clothing on the men who receive what is now served out, would be sufficient to keep them at their proper changes, and not greater than that which directs changes from blue over-shirts and pants to white. As for the question of convenience and economy, it could scarcely be compared with the consideration of the inconvenience and expense of having thirty men out of a ship's company of about two hundred down with fever, as in the case mentioned above.

ON SOME OF THE DISEASES AND PECULIARITIES OF THE PACIFIC ISLANDS.

While on an extended cruise through the Pacific Islands in the United States Ship Jamestown, during the years 1869–'70, I was enabled to observe some of the diseases peculiar to them, the habits of life of the natives, and note the effect of these on the population.

The Hawaiian Islands are now recognized as among the civilized countries of the world. A well-organized government and strict administration of laws insure safety to the resident, and an apparently delightful climate invites immigration of those who see in these islands an important future. Being a connecting point between the California coast and New Zealand, Australia, and Fiji, with a monthly line of steamers crowded with freight, and its importance as a sugar, cotton, and coffee growing country, the question of climate is one for consideration. The temperature varies between 75° F. and 85° F., as a general rule, but sometimes falls below the former and rises above the latter; and the influence of the atmosphere is so soothing, so soft and mild, that it induces persons subject to pulmonary complaints and those needing soothing influences on account of nervous debility to seek it as a place of either temporary or permanent residence. Especially is it regarded as a favorable place to visit by those suffering on account of the fogs and harsh winds of the California coast. Spoken of as the garden spot of the Pacific, it has much to attract the eye, in the beauty of some and wildness of other parts of its scenery; and the bracing influence of sea air is added to these scenes, as completing the requisites for recuperation and attractions for a residence. These combinations are spoken of with much apparent satisfaction; and to accept the statement with its full meaning would be to accord all that is claimed on this account. But while this soothing influence in the atmosphere may exist, and the beauty of scene and sea-air be added, there is to my observation quite a different interpretation to be put on the desirability of residence for some cases of disease. Instead of a place to be sought, I think it one to be avoided. Those who have lived there for three or four years will admit that the system becomes gradually undermined and enervated by the continuance of these gentle influences, and that they find it necessary to go, once in a year or two, to the California coast for recuperation, or change from one part of the islands to another. If they go to California, they get change of scene and air, and come back re-invigorated; if to one of the other islands, or to a different part of the same one, they are benefited, but not in the same degree. They will also admit that after becoming acclimated, that is, when the system has become enervated, they find themselves able to perform only a given amount of work each day; that, by properly regulating it, they can get through this amount and keep it up; but that every extra amount of labor gained and time saved, must be paid for by a corresponding amount of lassitude and depression and time lost. Under such influences as these, persons of debilitated systems, from whatever cause, would hardly recuperate. And while I knew of two cases of pulmonary consumption go steadily on to a fatal termination, I cannot name a person permanently benefited, in any disease, which could be referred to the climatic influences. Indeed, it seems surprising that people of California should seek the islands for benefit of health, when their own climate affords all that could be desired. The coast line of fogs and winds extends but about twenty-five or thirty miles inland, beyond which is an atmosphere at once dry, bracing, and so mild that flowers bloom the year round. I hardly think that any one who has examined and compared the two climates would hesitate to recommend that of California. So strongly was I impressed with this opinion, that being consulted by a man suffering from nervous prostration, whom I believe many would have sent from California to the islands, I recommended him to go from there to California.

In the Pacific islands the native population differ so much in complexion and smoothness of skin, that they may almost be said to be divided into three different classes, those of the southern, middle, and the northern islands. In the south, represented by Fiji, New Zealand, and Navigator Islands, (called Papuans, and generally believed to have gone from Papua,) they are very dark and have very rough skins. This roughness of the skin is believed by many to be typical; and I would believe from my own experience that what is said may be true, a blind man might distinguish them by this peculiarity alone. In the middle islands, including the Society, Marquesas, Gilbert, and Marshall groups, they approach the lightest shades of complexion and smoothness of skin; and of these, the Marquesans are the lightest, smoothest, and fairest. The Hawaiians appear to occupy an intermediate position between the two extremes. They are neither so dark and rough as those of the southern islands, nor so light and fair as the middle ones. Why those of the higher latitudes should attain to the highest color and those of the lower the lightest color, contrary to the general law of races as applied to climatic influences, I am not prepared to state, and will offer no explanation. That the Hawaiians were originally North American Indians, the middle groups peopled from the Malay Islands, and the southern islands from Papua, does not answer the question; they have too many forms, ceremonies, and habits in common. One of the first questions to be asked in such a statement would be, where did the Papuans come from?

So many different people have been found as the representatives of the lost tribes of Israel, from the North American Indians to the copper-colored races of the Old World, and so many evidences are brought forward to show that each individual people has the right to represent them as claimed, that the evidences in favor of these people may be considered with the rest. It is not a new question as applied to them; it has been talked of for years by those familiar with them.   I have mentioned that they have forms and ceremonies in common.   These are also claimed as evidences in favor of the Indians.   Here is a connecting link between the two.   I have seen a fine representative of the North American Indian, what might be termed a typical specimen, in the person of a Fiji chief, and an equally typical Papuan native of the Gilbert Islands.

The circumstances of common forms and ceremonies and common peculiarities of race, would indicate a division and wide diffusion of what was once one people or an intermixture of what were originally different peoples to form what is now the population of Polynesia.   These people all have their prophets and traditionists, who are selected from the young and carefully instructed, generation by generation, in the traditions of the tribes.   A man who has lived in the Marquesas for more than twenty years has carefully collected a large number of these traditions and songs, and very kindly allowed me to make copies of such as I wished. They comprise accounts of the creation of the world, the deluge, and many more, so wonderfully in accordance with the biblical record as to be surprising.   And these, he says, he has traced to come down through one hundred and forty generations.   Would it be likely that a people so closely adhering to traditions would have none which gave an account of a mixture of races, if such had taken place? or would the traditions of separate people, who each preserved theirs with tenacity, be found to blend harmoniously in a few generations to represent one race?   I think not.   I should rather think that the fact of common customs, traditions, and peculiarities of race, widely diffused, would indicate an emanation from a common source.   If for one of these peoples it is claimed these forms and ceremonies entitle them to represent the lost tribes of Israel, then all are entitled to the same consideration. These forms and ceremonies are, circumcision, which is practiced rigidly all through Polynesia; the shaving of the head in many different ways and patterns, though not always for vows; cannibalism, the old sacrificial feast in a state of degeneracy; and *hulus* and *luous* which, though now indulged on every occasion which can find excuse for unusual gluttony and lust, was the old gathering of family tribes.

Some of these have been much modified by the influence of missionaries and the establishment of laws, but the natives cling to them nevertheless. Even in the Hawaiian Islands, which have for many years been civilized, the *hulus* and *luous* are given in a bearable manner from distinguished natives to distinguished visitors, and indulged, as occasion offers, in the coarsest manner, in quiet places, by the lower orders.

Cannibalism is not now thought of in the Hawaiian, Society, or Navigator Islands, but in the Marquesas, Fiji, and other groups it is by no means extinct. It is a sacred institution with them. They believe that when their gods put an enemy in their hands it would be an insult to deity not to offer him as a sacrifice. And for this purpose all the instruments and places used in the horrible rites are held sacred. A gentleman in Marquesas informed me of two instances in those islands within a few years, and though at the time of our visit to Fiji the islands appeared to be under good rule, and crime was in less percentage than in large cities of the civilized world, recent events have shown how readily the natives return to their primitive customs when they believe the hand of foreign power no longer represses them.

The influence of white men has steadily progressed in the Southern and Hawaiian Islands; but through Micronesia those who have sought evidence have been of such low character that they are not only despised by the natives, but treated little better than slaves.

The population of the Hawaiian Islands now numbers about 60,000, and is said to be rapidly decreasing. Their natural inclination to idleness and filth, their ready adoption of all the vices of the whites, added to their own licentious habits, the large amount of venereal disease and leprosy are spoken of as the chief causes. Drunkenness can hardly be said to be a very efficient cause at present, however much so it may have been formerly; for though the natives are very fond of intoxicating drinks, and, when they can, indulge in them to the greatest extent, yet the evils arising from such sources are so well recognized by the government that selling or even giving a native intoxicating drinks is punished by such heavy fines as to keep the evil in check. Were it not for these laws, steadily executed, it is believed that drunkenness might be recognized as one of the principal causes.

The licentiousness of the people is considered one of the causes, as indeed it would be the curse of any people. So abhorrent to the sense of civilization is the licentiousness of the whole of Polynesia, that we are ready to lay untold evils at its door, beside charging to its account a large proportion of the diseases which afflict the people. While it may be responsible for a large amount of disease, I am doubtful if it be the cause of a rapid decrease among the people of these islands. Among other people it may act as efficiently or more efficiently than other causes. Let us apply a test, as far as possible. In the Hawaiian Islands there are so many causes operating to the same effect that we will leave them out of the question, or rather try to solve the question with regard to other groups, and then apply it to Hawaii. Fiji may also be counted out, for though the natural lasciviousness of the people is recognized, it cannot be indulged to the extent it might were it not for the law, for in Fiji adultery is punished by death, and the girls marry young. But in the Society, Marquesas, Gilbert, Marshall, and Caroline Islands the natives indulge their passions to the fullest extent, and retain their numbers of population, and this, too, when not more than three children to a marriage are the rule. Not only that, but so large an amount of disease exists among them—as syphilis, leprosy, elephantiasis, and ichthyosis, singly or combined—as to give the impression that the whole population is diseased. The American consul at Tahiti (a gentleman resident for many years) told me that 95 per cent. of the population were afflicted with venereal disease; that a great deal of it was hereditary, and that there was scarcely a native-born child which did not in a few years show evidences of transmitted syphilis. He also said they generally attained to old age, and instances of extreme old age were not rare, and that the population of the islands remained stationary at about eight or nine thousand.

In the Marquesas Islands we have a people scarcely, if any, behind the Society Islands in point of licentiousness. The women have as many husbands as their fancies dictate, and their husbands think it no discredit to recommend their qualities and hire them out to strangers. I was told by the overseer of a plantation that he had seen one woman, on the occasion of a *hulu*, receive the embraces of forty-two men, and had been told by an eye-witness of another who received one hundred! Such conduct could not be termed beastly, for beasts would not indulge in it; it seems reserved for brutes that are worse than beasts. It can hardly be credited, yet my informer was a man of responsibility, and did not otherwise appear given to telling large stories. Yet this people, so licentious and depraved, was a thriving people in population up to 1864. In that year small-pox was introduced to a people up to that time free from it, and in a few years reduced their numbers from twenty to eight or nine thousand; accomplishing in a short time what all their lust, and the evils growing out of it, had previously failed to do. It is not likely they are more licentious now than they were previous to 1864, yet up to that time it had not reduced them in point of numbers.

It is the same with the Gilbert, Marshall, and Caroline Islands. If their increase by birth was rapid there might be a sufficient number constantly added to the population to compensate for large losses by deaths from disease and wars; but numerous children are a rare exception, and from one to three is the rule. If we apply these facts, can we say that licentiousness is to them a cause of diminishing the population? And if in them we recognize the most licentious people on the face of the globe, (a proposition I hardly think can be doubted,) living under influences generally regarded as tending to shorten life, will it not have an influence on our opinions as applied to other races?

24 H

The barrenness of the women is recognized as another cause which tends to reduce the population, by checking the natural increase. Abortion is also mentioned; indeed, barrenness and abortion are said to go hand in hand; the one producing the other in many instances, when the former is not the result of natural defects. It is asserted, even by medical men, that the native doctresses, who keep their remedies a secret, are in the habit of giving a drug which produces not only abortion but barrenness. Whether this be true or not I am unable to say, but it is generally believed. It is said that women resort to it from motives of spite or jealousy toward their husbands. Another method is by mechanical means; the subject of it lying flat upon the back while the doctress kneads the abdomen with her hands or treads it with her feet, having first thoroughly rubbed it with oil.

The venereal disease is very common through all the Pacific Islands, though not as much so in Fiji as in others. In the Hawaiian, Society, Marshall, Gilbert, and Caroline Islands it is very common. It is so intimately mixed with leprosy and ichthyosis that it is sometimes difficult at first sight to determine which is the disease presented. Indeed, there are those who regard the leprosy as an aggravated form of syphilis; and I heard of one man in Honolulu who offered to take any of the government patients, called lepers, and cure them on the principles of treatment as applied to syphilis. Whether any such were put in his hands or not I am unable to say, but presume they were not, for the minister of the interior, who has general supervision of all hospitals, is a physician of good abilities, and the staff surgeon of the king has immediate charge of the leper-hospitals.

So wide-spread was the syphilitic disease supposed to be in the Pacific Islands, and our men had such ready access to it, that I expected to have a great deal of it under treatment. In this I was disappointed. The journal of the Jamestown shows comparatively few cases.

I was informed by the American consul at Tahiti that the native doctors are very successful in the treatment of syphilis, and he mentioned instances of the constitutional disease which had resisted the skill of educated men being cured by them. Their medicines are said to be very powerful, but are kept secret.

Leprosy has been recognized as a disease of Polynesia, and it presents both forms, the tubercular and anæsthetic. As I have before stated, there are those who claim that it is an aggravated form of syphilis, and in some instances they might almost be pardoned for so doing, where the two are combined. But so accurate are most of the well-pronounced cases to the descriptions of leprosy, that I think no doubt need be entertained on the subject.

In the Hawaiian Islands the disease is believed by the best men to be contagious, and the well-pronounced cases are removed to the leper hospitals. One source of its transmission from person to person is believed to be by smoking. It is a common practice for one out of any number gathered together to light a pipe, take a few puffs himself, and then pass it around. It is believed that poisonous matter is thus conveyed from a leprous ulcer in the mouth of one person to a healthy membrane in another, and the disease propagated. There is also something supposed to exist in their manner of life which induces it, and their filthy habits, love of intoxication, sleeping in damp places, may, perhaps, all combined, give some reason for the opinion. Or there may be something in the nature of the soil or exhalations, as Wilson shows, calculated to induce the disease.

It would be unnecessary to go over a typical case and present it ; the disease is too well described by Wilson to need it. There is one evidence of it, however, which he does not mention. In the anæsthetic variety, there is a symptom which precedes anæsthesia. It is an irresistible and fixed turning inward and upward of the little fingers. After this comes anæsthesia, then ulceration. The ulceration generally commences at the extremities of the fingers or toes, taking one joint after another until the hand or foot will look as cleanly amputated as if done by the knife of the surgeon. It generally commences at the extremities. but not always. I have seen sores which could not be mistaken. occupy-

ing the insides of the ankles and wrists, deforming the member
before it dropped off, by turning the hand or foot inward and
upward.

It is also believed there is no hope of cure. The disease may
be stationary or latent, but never disappears entirely. The end
may be in two or three years, or it may be much longer. The
surgeon in charge of the leper hospitals told me he had many
times fair hopes of a cure, but in every instance had been disappointed.

Through Micronesia I saw many cases of this disease, but I saw
many more in which there appeared to be a mixed form, in which
the first noticeable feature was a thickened, fissured, rough skin,
which might almost be called alligator-hide, easily recognized
as ichthyosis. How this is acquired, they do not know. It comes
on young children, youths, and adults; but it usually commences
on the belly of a child, and gradually spreads until the whole
body is covered. When affected by it alone, they are never sick,
and it interferes in no way with their occupations. It is not contagious, but is thought transmissible from parent to child. This
form of disease seemed the lot or inheritance of nearly all the
natives of the Gilbert, Marshall, and Caroline groups. A person
once affected by it is never free from it. In the skin of a person
thus affected I believe I have seen the white patch and tubercle
of leprosy, and have seen the ulceration which could not be
doubted. In the Society Islands and the Pomoto group, elephantiasis arabum is common. It attacks not only the legs, but the
breast and scrotum, and is supposed to be contracted by sleeping
on the moist ground. In these islands acute diseases are rare,
and fevers and pulmonary consumption almost unknown.

In the Fiji Islands, the two diseases most feared are dysentery
and *theea*. The dysentery is generally of a dangerous form, and
frequently fatal. *Theea* is a muco-purulent ophthalmia, causing
great pain and frequently destroying the sight of the eye affected.
It is thought to result from the sting of an insect or the lodgment
of a flower pollen. I had a case presented to my notice. The

whole conjunctiva of the affected eye was highly inflamed, and there was considerable discharge, though it had not progressed to the stage when it becomes muco-purulent. At the point of highest inflammation there was a minute white spot slightly raised above the surrounding surface. I saw it early in the attack, and treated it with a mild solution of acetate of zinc and wine of opium in water, with the result of its being much better in three days and well in a week. So dangerous and destructive had this disease been considered, that the result in this instance was regarded with astonishment.

Dropsies—general anasarca—the result of diseased livers from kava drinking, though not common, are not rare. I tapped Tui Sevuka, while at Fiji, and drew off about four gallons of fluid, much to his astonishment and much to the gratification of the Rev. Mr. N——, who pronounced it a good missionary work, as enhancing the value of the white men in the eyes of the natives. And this man, who was considered a great warrior, and one of the greatest enemies of Thakambau, said he would think white men gods if they did not die.

Kava is prepared from the kava-root, by a process of maceration, and drank in a state of semi-fermentation. Its effect passes through that of excitement and intoxication to temporary paralysis, which may last two or three days. It is the native drink through the whole of Polynesia. The *Eva* plant grows in the Marquesas Islands; whether elsewhere in Polynesia I do not know. My attention was called to it by the governor. I at first confounded it with kava, but he made a distinct difference. The stems are about one-fourth of an inch in thickness, corrugated, or rather annulated, pea-green, and grow three or four feet high. The leaves are oval, a little more than two inches in length, pea-green on the upper surface, and white and downy beneath. The fruit is about the size of a small lime, pea-green on the surface, has a dull white pulp containing two seeds. The seeds are soft and spongy when fresh, but become shriveled when dry, nearly round, about half an inch in diameter, and a sixth in thickness.

They are used as a poison, and produce symptoms similar to strychnia.   The castor-oil plant grows on the banks of the streams in Fiji.

In habits of dress the natives of the Hawaiian Islands may be said to be civilized.   That of the men is after the European style, as is also that of the women of the higher orders.   The lower order of women wear a loose dress, which falls from the shoulders to the feet.   This dress for the women is also adopted through the whole of Polynesia where the missionary influence is felt; and in some islands of the Marshall and Caroline groups, where the missionary influence is not felt, it has been adopted at the suggestion of the traders for cocoa-nut oil, who supply not only plain calico, but fine silk dresses.   Beside this robe they adhere to the native *malo* (*maro*) or waist-cloth.

In the southern islands the men wear the *tapa*, in large folds about the body, and hanging to the knees.   In the Marquesas they simply wear the *malo*.   In the Gilbert Islands the men wear a mat tied about the waist, which reaches nearly to the knees, and the women a petticoat made of fringed bark from the pandanus.   In the Marshall and Caroline Islands this is reversed.

Tattooing is common through all the groups.   It is prohibited, but not prevented, in the Marquesas.   All that one has to do who wishes to be tattooed is to go from Nukahiva to one of the other islands or to the mountain, and it is done by one of a profession.

In food they have great variety, except in meats; and even where they can be procured they are not sought, as row-fish and *pöi* are preferred.   Baked dog is said to be a favorite dish, and is indulged in at *luous*.   Beside these, bread-fruit, bananas, plantains, and cocoa-nuts are the articles of subsistence.

The question of caste is carried to the nicest points of distinction among them, and is adhered to scrupulously, or its neglect punished with great severity.

For reasons which are obvious, when their habits of life are considered, family names are transmitted from the mother's side.

She, being a chiefess, may select whom she pleases for a husband, without in any way prejudicing her caste, and her offspring will be of her caste. But if a chief should choose a common woman for a wife, the children would be plebeian.